SHADOWS
OVER CASTLE RISING

FANNY CRADOCK

SHADOWS OVER CASTLE RISING

E. P. DUTTON & CO., INC. | NEW YORK

Library of Congress Catalog Card Number: 76-11893

ISBN: 0-525-20128-9

10 9 8 7 6 5 4 3 2 1

First American Edition 1977

To Dear Vi (Lort-Philips)
who understands, remembers and echoes with regret
'*où sont les neiges d'antan*'.

Acknowledgement

The author wishes to express her very great gratitude to Mr Matthews, librarian, London Library, for his infinite patience in researching information for this book during a period of over three years, and also to her colleagues in the *Daily Telegraph* Information Offices.

Contents

The Family from 1907 descending

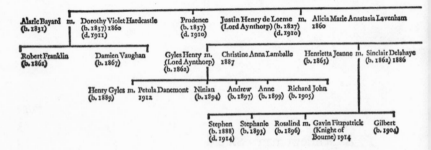

Alaric Bayard (b. 1831) m. Dorothy Violet Hardcastle (b. 1837) 1860 (d. 1911)

Prudence (b. 1837) (d. 1910) — Justin Henry de Lorme (Lord Aynthorp) (b. 1827) (d. 1910) m. Alicia Marie Anastasia Lavenham 1860

Robert Franklin (b. 1861)

Damien Vaughan (b. 1867)

Gyles Henry (Lord Aynthorp) (b. 1862) m. Christine Anna Lamballe 1887

Henrietta Jeanne (b. 1865) m. Sinclair Delahaye (b. 1862) 1886

Henry Gyles (b. 1889) m. Petula Danemont 1912

Ninian (b. 1894) Andrew (b. 1897) Anne (b. 1899) Richard John (b. 1905)

Stephen (b. 1888) (d. 1914) Stephanie (b. 1893) Rosalind (b. 1896) m. Gavin Fitzpatrick (Knight of Bourne) 1914 Gilbert (b. 1904)

from Justin, Lord Aynthorp

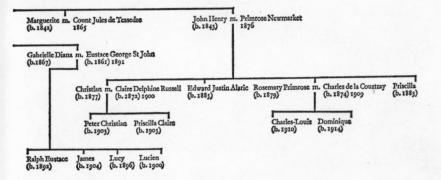

Marguerite m. Count Jules de Tessedre
(b. 1842)   1865

John Henry m. Primrose Newmarket
(b. 1843)   1876

Gabrielle Diana m. Eustace George St John
(b. 1867)   (b. 1861) 1891

Christian m. Claire Delphine Russell   Edward Justin Alaric   Rosemary Primrose m. Charles de la Courtray   Priscilla
(b. 1877)   (b. 1872) 1900   (b. 1885)   (b. 1879)   (b. 1874) 1909   (b. 1883)

Peter Christian   Priscilla Claire
(b. 1903)   (b. 1905)

Charles-Louis   Dominique
(b. 1910)   (b. 1914)

Ralph Eustace   James   Lucy   Lucien
(b. 1892)   (b. 1904) (b. 1896) (b. 1900)

Author's Foreword

Dear Reader,

As in Book 1 *The Lormes of Castle Rising*, this second book and all which follow are based upon my own family; but with characters which I have created. The great majority bear absolutely no resemblance to any persons alive or dead. The sole exceptions are Justin Aynthorp's wife Lady Aynthorp who, at Justin's death became The Dowager; Stephen Delahaye, 'Plum' and Nanny. I drew to some extent upon the 'Gran' who appears in my first memoirs *Something's Burning*, for the Dowager. She was my maternal grandmother with whom I lived from the age of one to ten. Stephen was a close relative; but because of the character I prefer not to disclose which, if my readers will permit me this somewhat natural reticence.

'Plum' was drawn from Gran's coachman/chauffeur and 'Nanny' from my own Nanny.

In deference to you I feel I should explain that the whole idea for this Saga stemmed from a discovery I made when researching in my antecedents. I discovered in Morant's History of Essex, I quote; '*Gilbert de Pêche, Bart. sometimes called peccatum for he was a very wicked fellow*'. For me the penny dropped as I read this entry for, since Norman times, when my family came to Britain we have had in almost every generation, 'a very wicked fellow'. So I decided to weave my long story around these 'runts', at the same time endeavouring to show the gradual disintegration of a once-powerful family partly through the deprivations made by these 'wicked' fellows but chiefly through the increasing taxes and death duties which as everyone knows have reduced many such families to poverty.

The name Castle Rising came into my mind when some years ago I wrote a first draft of the first twenty-five thousand words of Book 1. Later a dear friend pointed out that the real Castle Rising is a ruin in Norfolk. By this time the name had become inseparable from my thinking. So, I sited my Castle Rising in Essex, whence came my own family, and have studiously avoided any possible implications that there could be even the slightest link with the real Castle Rising or its owners either past or present.

Fanny Cradock

1910–1914, Below Stairs

In the Castle

The Housekeeper	Mrs Peace
The Butler	Albert Sawby
The Dowager Lady Aynthorp's Personal Maid	Palliser
Lady Aynthorp's Personal Maid	Pearson
Lord Aynthorp's Valet	Daniel Groom (Sawby's cousin)
The Chef	M. André
The Cook	Mrs Parsons
Head Footman	Edward
2nd Footman	George
3rd Footman	Richard
4th Footman	William
House parlourmaids	Mason and Appelby
Kitchen maids	Joan and Eliza
Scullery maids	Agnes and Mabel
Boots	Sam
Yardboy	Alfred

In The Laundry

Mrs Sawbridge (head gardener's wife)
Sally Sawbridge (their daughter)
Mrs Tomkins (2nd gardener's wife)
Mrs Dick (3rd gardener's wife)

In The Nursery

Nanny Pringle
Nursemaid Rose
Nurserymaid Rose

The Schoolroom Staff

Mademoiselle Blanc
Fraülein Schmidt
Mr Sissingham, Tutor
Mr Wickham, Tutor
Mr Prewitt, Music Master

In The Stables and New Garages

Head Groom	Plumstead ('Plum')
Grooms	Pike and Perry
Stable Lads	Will and Ted
Chauffeur	Simpkins
Van Driver	Wootton
Mechanic and Maintenance	Tom Singe

In The Gardens

Head Gardener	Sawbridge
2nd Gardener	Tompkins
3rd and 4th Gardeners	Dick and Flead
Gardeners' Boys	Billy, Joe and Willy (sons of Sawbridge, Tompkins and Dick)
New Stovehouse Gardeners	Sidley and Redding

On The Estate

Land Agent	Philip Brandon
Thatcher	Gillings
Head Gamekeeper	Switch
2nd Gamekeeper	Wittle
3rd Gamekeeper	Postle

4th Gamekeeper	Lucey
Carpenter	Peak
Assistant Carpenter	Paradine
Chief Kennelman	Joe Crocket
Assistant Kennelmen, Nos 1 and 2	Andy and Bob
Stoker	James ('Jimmy-the-Coke')
Pigman	Abel
Hedger and Ditcher	Tibbins

Replacements After Declaration of War, 1914

Land Agent	Mrs Henry de Lorme
Footwomen, Nos 1, 2 and 3	Wilkins, Spurling and Raikes
Lady Gardeners	Jean and Joan (Stove-houses), Alice and Mary (under-gardeners)
Groomswomen	Gay and Nancy
Stable Girls	Poppy and Daisy
Chauffeuse	Elizabeth Brown
Estate Driver	Stella Lemming
3rd and 4th Gamekeepers	Ruth Parker and Doris Haines
Assistant Kennelmaids, Nos 1 and 2	Phyllis and Lily
Assistant Carpenter	'Old Joe'
Stoker	Luke (Tompkins' 2nd son)
Governess	Miss Poole (Ex-social secretary), replacing Fraülein Schmidt

CHAPTER I

A Gentlewoman's Shield

Eighty-three-year-old Justin Aynthorp had been dead one week. His son Gyles thus assumed the title and his late father's place at the foot of the family dining table. Facing him, in her equally new position at the table head, sat his wife Christine, now Lady Aynthorp, while Gyles' Mama, the Dowager, had quietly but resolutely moved to the seat on her son's right hand when she first reappeared for dinner after her bereavement. Now she sat with the closest members of her family around her. She had asked Christine to see that everyone stayed for port. Tiny, straight-backed, with a few more fine lines etched into the corners of her mouth she looked them over while Sawby, their inestimable butler, placed the port decanter to Gyles' right and held watching brief as the footmen placed the various tazzas of fruit and nuts upon the table. Then, by some esoteric sign to indicate that he was satisfied – just – he nodded to signify they might withdraw and followed them out of the double doors closing them softly behind him.

'Well Gyles?' the Dowager made a question of the two words.

'Not very, Mama,' Gyles said ruefully, stroking his long chin with one elegant hand.

'Indeed?' his Mama watched him fill his glass, pass the decanter and lean back with a faint sigh against the carvings of the big gilt chair. With maddening deliberation he then removed his monocle, polished it with a silk handkerchief, replaced both in eye and sleeve and surveyed his relations in their deep mourning garments. He observed his mother's dress, unrelieved black save for a thread of white at throat and wrists ... his wife in black gauze, her beauty emphasized by it, though he saw with a slight shock how thin she had become and remarked how this had sharpened the lovely line of chin and throat, while the faint blue shadows beneath her eyes only served to make them seem even larger. He transferred his gaze reluctantly to his Aunt Dorothy, the Bishop Alaric's wife, or as he thought of her inwardly, 'his living relict'. Her jet embroidered gown offended him, the shiny satin jarred, so he looked away hastily . . . to the Bishop himself who seemed as if someone had let most of the air out of him like a deflated balloon . . . on to the unfortunate Delahayes, tearful Henrietta, whose otherwise distinguished countenance was marred by an almost permanent expression of anxiety . . . to her silent, pre-occupied spouse, the mild, all too mild Sinclair, now almost completely turned in upon himself by constant buffetings from his distressing offspring . . . on once more to the St Johns, Primrose in black velvet and pearls, her long fingers playing about the stem of her glass and her husband John, 'honest John', ran Gyles' silent designation for this man whom visible emotions never seemed to touch – unless, of course, they were concerned with a prime piece of horseflesh.

This roving assessment swung to undisguised admiration as his eyes rested upon his favourite aunt . . . old she might be, indeed certainly, lined she was, inevitably, and deeply sorrow-ful, but still a beauty with that rare vintage beauty of good bones, fine nostrils, great eyes and inextinguishable sparkle – even now – which made her, his Aunt Marguerite the little Countess the darling of them all.

And now the tempo changed once more as Gyles examined the John de Lorme offspring, Claire, the eldest, looking absurdly young in cobwebby black lace . . . then her con-ventional, always diplomatic husband Christian, the born soldier, the perfect *aide-de-camp* . . . then Claire's now startlingly chic sister Rosemary, wed only one year to Charles de la Coutray and come from their French *château* for the funeral despite being manifestly pregnant. 'It suits her,' Gyles decided. 'French life suits her too,' and his thoughts marvelled, 'how unchanging we all are. How fundamentally French, especially our women folk.'

Lastly he looked at John's Priscilla, now twenty-seven, technically on the shelf but factually far from it and generally acknowledged to be a 'Distinct Handful'. She sat now, supremely graceful in a swirl of black faille and wearing an expression of lovely serenity which Gyles acknowledged was generally the external manifestation of some naughtiness in train. He brooded for a moment on how that dangerous expression told nothing of her wayward character and he smiled to himself at the 'naughty puss'.

His 'tour' was almost completed. In a swift swing to distaste he examined Bishop Alaric's two middle-aged, unmarried sons, Damien and Robert, both of whom did such delightful *petit point*! This came in for *tremendous* admiration from their unalluring cronies. Even so they represented to the new head of the family little more than 'a demned effeminate pair of old pussies in trousers'. Once more Gyles glanced away, on and past his eldest son on whom his eyes rested for just an instant of warm approval.

During this appraisal the Family had made quiet small talk with great resolution, but so acute was their instinct to their new '*seigneur*', that the instant Gyles opened his lips to speak they became silent.

He began, 'What I have to tell you is I hope a succinct précis of what I learned this afternoon from the Trusloves.' He paused again; but certainly not because he thought there was anyone present who did not know the Trusloves and understand what his words meant. The family of Trusloves had been solicitors extraordinary to the Lormes for so long now that they seemed to have become part of the Lorme inheritance.

Gyles resumed.

'As you will recall, the matter of our means and property under entail was raised as little as three years ago at m'father's eightieth birthday party. Therefore you do not need me to tell you that when the dear old octogenarian died I inherited in money and property somethin' in the region of four and a half millions, give or take a thousand or two and, additionally the assessed value of our paintin's which represents somethin' above five hundred thousand pound.' Gyles broke off to drain his glass, observed that the decanter had completed its first tour and was with him again, so refilled his glass in a leisurely manner and relaunched the decanter. During all this Henry watched him, listening intently with a slightly grim expression round his young mouth. At his father's last words, however, his expression lightened as 'Good for us,' thought he contendedly, 'I in my turn will be able to give my Petula a good life and freedom to stretch her wings without financial strictures.'

Gyles glanced at his son as he continued, seeming to read his offspring's thoughts.

'Well, now, I have to inform you that since 1907 there has been a further iniquitous increase in these confounded death duties. If this kind of thing is not checked, an Englishman's Castle will cease to remain his home for he will no longer be enabled to maintain it in a fit and proper manner. It presents itself to me as an unscrupulous form of blackmail. I do not for the life of me comprehend on what possible grounds this Government has any right to assume a stand and deliver attitude to old families like our own, to whom they owe so much in service, loyalty and the employment of many thousands of underprivileged people. Why, I would wish to know should we keep 'em and still provide from our private purses the wherewithal for the financin' of half a hundred wild cat schemes?'

Christine sparkled at this outburst. She lowered her eyelids discreetly. The Dowager actually permitted a tiny chuckle to slip through her parted lips then speedily camouflaged it into a slight cough; but could not restrain herself thereafter from commenting, 'Very right and proper sentiments. Spoken, I may say, just as your dear Papa would have done.'

'Well Mama,' Gyles expostulated, 'wait until you hear what I have to tell you! Do you realize? Can you possibly credit that our death duties now stand at a scandalous eight per cent!' and he fell silent to allow the fact to seep in. A subdued but horrified murmur rippled around them.

'Oh yes,' Gyles repeated grimly, '*eight per cent on any estate over one million pounds*. This, in plain language, and as the Trusloves confirmed this afternoon, means that we,' he corrected himself, 'I, on behalf of you all am *compelled* to hand over close on four hundred thousand pounds of *our money* to these highwaymen in office just because m'father has been killed in the huntin' field.'

This so roused Sinclair that he actually spoke.

'Income tax is up too,' he contributed in deepest gloom, staring into his port, 'what with one thing and another I tell you all that IF these taxes are not Very Firmly Checked we shall reach the point where we shall not know where our next penny is comin' from.' After which, colouring at his own eloquence, he withdrew again into his normal passivity.

'Four hundred thousand pounds,' said John, likewise galvanized into speech, 'what will you sell, dear feller?'

'Nothin',' said Gyles sombrely.

'Then what . . .?'

'Do I propose in order to offset such banditry?'

'Yes.'

Before Gyles could make further answer John de Lorme became the magnet for attention.

'In my view, my dear feller, this will not be the last of such malpractises,' he said sombrely. 'Indeed I would go further, and say that it is only a beginnin'. If one takes into consideration the rumblin's which are disturbin' Europe it is far more on the cards that they will multiply.'

Gyles nodded.

'Exactly, therefore before raisin' this matter with you I worked out what could and in my view should be done. I admit to takin' the long-term view. Let me disabuse your minds concernin' makin' good such deprivations overnight; but let us not cloud our perceptions by assumin' – however enragin', in fact downright impertinent these levies are – that we cannot weather the storm at this juncture.' He looked up, met his mother's eyes and raised eyebrows above them.

'Timber dear?' she inquired. Gyles shot her an approving glance.

'Timber, Mama, and highly perceptive of you as usual. Can you conjecture what the other proposals concern?' he managed a slight smile.

'I think so,' she rejoined calmly, 'your father's project for a *Musée* or am I incorrect?'

Gyles twinkled. 'You are not. No wonder the servants say you have a finger in every pie – you miss nothin' do you?'

'But surely,' Henrietta protested, 'such things will increase expenditure not help us to retrench?'

'I said long term, dear sister,' Gyles answered a trifle tartly. 'In my view we must plant trees and more trees, for there will always be money in timber, of that at least I am absolutely certain.'

Bishop Alaric was by this time nodding sententiously so Gyles continued.

'Of course, we must accept that there will be no revenue therefrom for many years; but it is nevertheless an obvious move. We must likewise spend money in building m'father's museum.' He suddenly warmed to his theme, joined his long fingers tip to tip above his dessert plate and indulged in a little prophesy.

'I have a theory' – he appeared to his watchers to be musing aloud – 'that there will come a time when many people will be curious to see the treasures we possess. That they will pay their sixpences and shillings to examine them and to learn of the history of Castle Rising's acquisitions through to the tenth successive century. Y'see IF Sinclair is right we *shall* eventually be decimated. Not as a family but as a breed. Perhaps the best way to signify this is to call us landowners. Few would deny that there are many among us who are not scrupulous in their care of their inheritances. Though we know how rewardin' it is to servants, tenants and owners alike when an estate pattern is carefully achieved and honourably maintained. Yet despite this self-evident fact, there are the explorers who are never on their estates – leavin' everythin' to agents; there are high-spenders gettin' themselves into the hands of the Jews; and fellers who under-invest in the future, or fail to honour their commitments in the present and can look back over their pasts, where they can see but chose to ignore clear evidence that these tactics have brought 'em close to ruin before and will only do so again – given ample opportunity, which is precisely what they are takin'; treatin' inheritance as though it were a bottomless crock of gold! *They* will be the first to go to the wall! It is a short step onwards to the point where the old law which governs supply and demand will work in our favour – by which I mean we who have always taken our estate responsibilities very seriously. The less there are of us the stronger the appeal will become and the more sheer curiosity will grow concernin' our way of life and our possessions. Part of THEIR pleasure could well be in raisin' their hands in horror at our past extravagances and mutterin' about Marie Antoinette and cake!'

Consternation in varying degrees spread over the faces of Gyles' listeners.

'My deah feller,' Bishop Alaric remonstrated, 'surely you're not proposin' to have a horde of the proletariat swarmin' all over our home, makin' a litter all over our grounds and draggin' squallin' brats all over our flower beds?'

'Spoken like a true Christian, my dear Uncle,' murmured Gyles his eyes glinting dangerously.

Sinclair added his unwelcome mite with, 'not to speak of thoroughly upsettin' the pheasants!'

Gyles permitted these somewhat revealing remonstrations to wear themselves into silence. Then, speaking very quietly, 'I envisage nothin' so abhorrent as you are suggestin',' he replied evenly, 'for it would be equally abhorrent to me and to Christine – though in a somewhat different context! However, let us now treat with facts. IF we can find – and I think I have done so already – a suitable area, both remote from the Castle yet situated so as to be readily accessible from one of our gateways, then I think we may build our museum. I also envisage building an adjacent tea house of some kind which can be staffed and maintained by those of our employees who have technically "retired". They would, I believe, welcome such a fresh interest for their waning days. Then the younger wives, when not occupied in their cottages with their offspring, can assist with the service of teas and such like during the summer months.'

This conveniently put a damper on their initial protests, but it was Henry, playing with a slender, gold handled dessert fork who said softly, almost as if to himself, 'It takes an awful lot of sixpences to make four hundred thousand pounds . . . sir.'

'I know it does,' Gyles nodded, 'but this is only the beginnin'. Let me tell you somethin' else I have in mind.' This worked so powerfully on the men of the family that the port made a faster circuit than it had ever done before at a Lorme dining table and thereafter they all sipped assiduously, as though by doing so they hoped to find Dutch courage with which to meet more of the new Lord Aynthorp's awful revelations.

The offender himself was perfectly at ease as he resumed, 'You all know that feller called Escoffier who is cookin' so superbly at the Carlton? André almost genuflects when his name is mentioned! Well, I got chattin' to Escoffier after that stag dinner given by old Bobby Danvers to celebrate his "National" win the other night. Escoffier was brought up to take a glass of old Madeira and our congratulations. After a bit the man asked me if I ever allowed anythin' to be sold off the estate – y'know, surplus from our game bags. I told him no, because in m'father's day I knew the idea would cause a monumental volcanic eruption. Anyway, ultimately I gave him permission to approach Philip. I said, "Take the matter to my agent my dear chap by all means." So to sum up, I want your assent to the creation of big new plantations in D'Hauteville's Spinney and in the risin' ground beyond on old Parker's field. I told the chap the other day if he let his land lie fallow I would appropriate it and he was perfectly willin' to part with a parcel of about forty acres all told to which I shall add a further hundred. Likewise I want you to approve the buildin' of a modest Museum; one so planned as to allow for expansion in later years. I also wish to increase our stock of pheasant and partridges so that we can build, very quietly and gradually, a promisin' little traffic in surplus game. Now all this need not impinge upon us in any way whatever, save for the invitin' a few more guns to a few more shoots. The rest can be in Philip's charge. He can order the whole boilin' under my supervision and Henry's. Philip can see the game is bagged, dispatched, entrained, invoiced and the dues collected and entered against the charges involved in stockin' up.'

Gyles was by now well launched upon his schemes. The same instinct was quickening in him as had prompted him to profit by the advice of those men whose financial genius had helped him to make a killing in 1907.[1]

Henry chuckled, 'It's ingenious, sir,' he smiled 'anyway, count me in, please, I'll be more than happy to back you and to help in any way I can.'

[1] See Book I, *The Lormes of Castle Rising.*

'Oh, it's ingenious,' Alaric admitted reluctantly, 'and it is certainly less distasteful when represented to us as you have done. IF we can be sure that absolutely nothin' will be done which might destroy our old and hallowed pattern then I must confess I am seriously tempted to offer my support.'

'I would point out,' the Dowager's quiet voice quelled the lot of them as her head went up and she looked coldly down the table, 'that my son, *my eldest son*, currently Head of the Family, is in no wise called upon to consult any of you. Had it been my late husband who had put forward these proposals they would have been launched as a *fait accompli* and none of you would have been given the chance to air your several views. I suggest that it is extremely handsome of Gyles to take a less arbitary line,' she paused, looked about her and added two words, 'don't you?'

There was never anyone like her for launching a *coup de foudre*.[2] First there was a stricken silence rapidly followed by several hasty murmurings and disclaimers. During these the Dowager and Christine put down their table napkins almost simultaneously and the rest of the women followed suit. The Dowager had decided that there must be a limit imposed in respect of her eldest son, even as her late husband had merely imposed his own – Absolute Monarchy at all times within the Castle boundaries – and as she smilingly acknowledged to Christine, as they proceeded towards the dining room, 'It had worked very well, my dear, so do NOT let any of them undermine Gyles' or your authority.'

Alone with the men Gyles was pursuing his outlines assiduously. 'I would like to go further,' he resumed, 'by proposing an economy as opposed to an investment. I ask you in all seriousness whether or not it is a shade erring on the side of the improvident for us to allow stovehouse peaches, apricots and nectarines to rot, simply because at certain times of the year we are overstocked to the point where, even after generous contributions to the Cottage Hospital and to the many of our friends who are not so lavishly endowed, we are left with tremendous surplus? Would you consider it *infra dig* for Philip to dispose of them for filthy lucre?'

[2] Thunder bolt.

'To whom?' inquired Sinclair interestedly.

Gyles grinned, 'That feller Caesar Ritz at his new hotel. By the by, I heard the other day that he is installin' a *bidet* in every bathroom and would you believe it, Royal Doulton were instructed to make 'em all, the chamber pots, washbasins, jugs and even soap dishes. The feller's makin' the money fly all right; but then that's my point, that's what I have in mind! Ritz is makin' the money fly but he's pullin' it in too. I was told, oh with the utmost deference and courtesy, that if I wanted a table durin' Ascot week I should have to let him know by the end of the month!'

'But we shan't be goin' to Ascot this year shall we, I mean we shall be in mournin'!' Henry exclaimed.

'It will all depend upon Mama,' Gyles replied firmly, 'if she decides to copy Royalty, wear black at Ascot and go just the same, then most certainly we shall be there. Anyway,' he put down his empty glass, 'enough of this for tonight, we've held the servants up an unconscionable time already. Let us join the ladies.' And Henry, as usual sped to do 'door duty' as he irreverently named it.

Below stairs was in a ferment of irritation, frustration, unrest and speculation. A quorum of gloom presided over the table in the Steward's room where Chef André was pouring his employer's brandy into his steaming mug of coffee and Miss Palliser, the Dowager's personal maid, known to the footmen as 'old vinegarpuss' was sipping her tea in an aura of exquisite 'refainment', her little finger cocked in the air like a dog's leg at a lamp post, while the other three fingers and thumb clasped the cup handle in what appeared to be a grip of acute discomfort. Facing André, the inestimable Sawby was opening and closing his gunmetal half-hunter every few minutes, diving into his pocket for the watch, adjusting his steel-rimmed spectacles, removing them, cradling his balloon of Uptairs cognac, sipping it, diving again for watch and spectacles and repeating the performance. Finally, the fourth present, Mrs Parsons, that scourge of the kitchen and scullery maids, snapped out, 'For pity's sake Mr Sawby stop them fidgets, you're making my corns throb!'

Sawby paid no heed, 'An hour gone since I withdrew my footmen for the dessert,' he muttered, 'and not a lady withdrawn! Coffee not even served! Therefore my footmen is restless to get their work finished, I tell you I DON'T LIKE IT AT ALL. It's troublesome, that's the long and the short of it. Something's UP, you just mark my words!'

Mrs Parsons set down her cup and held her over-pale-cook's hands to the coal flames in the small grate. 'When ain't something UP I should like to know?' she inquired sepulchrally. 'No sooner is 'is dear late lordship gorne and all *that* 'orrible to-do than it's locked in the library they are with Mr Gyles . . . er 'is new Lordship,' she corrected herself hastily at the look of awful reproach from Palliser, 'and there's 'is lordship tearing about with summink 'uge and 'orrible 'idden under a Very Funny Clorth.' As usual when agitated Mrs Parson's aspirations flew in all directions.

'Not a word she has been said in my 'earing,' appended Miss Palliser, 'eet ees mos' strange I theenk!'

' 'Orrible suspicious of more trouble I'll dare swear,' agreed Mrs Parsons sucking her teeth portentously. At that moment the bell from the drawing room rang through the servant's hall. It sent Sawby shooting out of his old alpaca and into his black in seconds. Wrenching open the door he issued his orders, 'Look slippy there, George, Richard, Robert, pick up your feet young feller-me-lads and let me know whether or not the gentlemen has also left the dining room.'

They found the room empty. They conveyed the information hurriedly to Sawby as his head appeared remarkably soon afterwards in herald to his entire presentation complete with the brandy and liqueurs tray while the footmen dashed down behind him to retrieve the coffee tray and M. André's exquisite, tiered Sèvres dish with its equally exquisite burden of *petit fours*. These were in due course processed towards and into the White Drawing Room. The moment soon came when Sawby inquired from the door, 'Will there be anything else my lady?' and Christine replied, 'Nothing thank you, Sawby.'

Then the door closed and the Family was alone again.

They were likewise 'off' again. The family temperament, buffeted by the awful events of the preceding week, ravaged by their grief, left them despite it all still capable in their astounding resilience, not only of rallying round the new Head of the Family but also of conjuring up from somewhere in the depths of their highly volatile temperaments a few not inconsiderable bubbles of enthusiasm for what the little Countess hereinafter referred to as Gyles' 'New Project'.

Now, as she poured her inevitable *tisane* Countess Marguerite inquired interestedly, 'From where do you intend drawing your Musée material, my dear Gyles?'

Gyles reflected. 'Well, first of all my enchanting aunt,' he told her, 'I intend havin' display cabinets made for swords and other martial implements. You will doubtless recall that at Henry's comin' of age the insurance feller's comments to m'father were transformed into the tinder box upon which the first sparks were struck.'

'And fans,' supplemented Christine, 'with little carefully hand-written descriptive notes like, "This fan was made and the stems jewelled in Florence by *Benvenuto Cellini* at the commission of one Rupert de Lorme."' She added as an aside, 'No need to disclose how he came by it. It is no one's business that Rupert was a brigand, but the romantic connection of it being dropped at the feet of another Lorme by Gloriana and given to him for his lady as a mark of favour could be told and thus explain how it came to be in our possession today.'

'I suppose,' observed John drily, 'we do not point out that he actually filched the fan while bedding his monarch's mistress either?'

'Children,' reproved the Dowager half-heartedly, 'let us not rake at the coals even in so small a matter. Runts are a solely Lorme affair, as always. So,' she continued, 'we could do patch boxes and snuff boxes too could we not?'

'Not mine I can assure you,' said Marguerite sharply rustling her skirts in disapproval, 'but Gyles I do have one sensible suggestion. You must undoubtedly have a *coin d'honneur* for our great beam[3] with its unique inscription.'

'Of course Aunt,' Gyles agreed smilingly, 'and according to its current restorers it will need to be enclosed in a special glass case which must be maintained at a certain temperature if

[3] See Book 1, *The Lormes of Castle Rising*.

the whole thing is not to disintegrate.'

'Pray how will that be done?' Primrose inquired interestedly.

'Some modest form of stove house heating I think,' Gyles replied, 'which, I am assured, may be laid in such a manner that it becomes extremely neat but can be reached at all times from the outside of the casing so that the interior remains totally undisturbed. As far as I can gather the casing will be encircled by low-laid hot water piping to which the glass is resistant. I will show you the design tomorrow if you are interested.'

Regrettably, by the next morning there was no time for such ploys as yet another even more dreadful bombshell was timed to explode among them at the breakfast table, by the head of no less a person than Gyles Aynthorp himself.

In one short week he had established beyond any possible dispute that he was as capable of irascibility as his late father. His first show of temper had followed swiftly upon the interment of his father in the Lorme private chapel. Memorial services were to come – inevitably – but privacy in the first awful impact of their bereavement was taken as implicit and all who knew them were well aware that such would be the case. By the time Justin Aynthorp had been laid to rest under yet another stone slab in the Chapel, the Truslaves *Père et Fils*, the family's tried and trusted solicitors were indulging in a little preliminary throat clearing preparatory to the reading of the will.

This contained no surprises except that the late peer's private estate was so surprisingly solvent! This permitted him to leave one hundred thousand pounds to Petula Danement and still have a considerable sum to pass on to his widow for her private use and enjoyment. His comment upon Petula's bequest was typical, 'for her pleasure and with deep affection from her ever loving Grumpy,' which nearly proved the undoing of the family's self control. But they managed and they managed dinner too, and then they went into the library and they opened the Casket which contained what they had regarded as their Heirloom or Talisman for over nine hundred years.

They had no inkling as to the contents of that Casket, and

the shock of discovering it to be the Lady Mathilde's chastity
belt was very great.

In the meantime poor Plumstead, or Plum as he was known
to everyone – the Head of the Lorme Stables in whose arms the
dying Justin had been gathered after his fatal fall – had
attempted to communicate with his new master. Finally the
two met as Gyles slipped out for an early ride. Plum made a
sorry mess of the encounter, for he was not only so incoherent
as to make no sense whatever; but also so obviously distraught
that Gyles, with an inward sigh, surrendered his ride and
followed him into Plum's private loose-box sanctum where he
endeavoured to sort the old man out. Even more incoherently
Plum tried again, beginning, 'First when I took 'is Lordship's
'ead in my lap 'ee said "don't", and again more weakly – like
"don't" and then 'ee moved 'is 'ead an' I thort 'ee 'ad gorne.'

Gyles nodded. 'Now let me see if I have got it right so far,
m'father fell, you reached him first, you took his head in your
lap and you thought you were too late?'

'That's right,' nodded Plum, tears unashamedly coursing
down his withered-apple cheeks, 'but then 'ee moved restless
like and 'ee said them two don'ts. All by themselves like and I
thought as 'ow 'ee didn't like me 'olding 'im.'

'What absolute rubbish!' exclaimed Gyles briskly, 'whatever
he meant it was most certainly not that, you darned fool.
M'father held you in the greatest possible esteem, so please do
not be foolish. Try to go on there's a good chap.'

'Well then, like I said, 'ee seemed to go orf, and then quite
sudden 'ee said "open the Box" quite loud and clear it wos and
them wos the larst words as 'ee ever spoke.' Plum's tears were
dripping on to the bit of harness he was gripping. Gyles
cleared his throat and tried again. 'Well what is it that worries
you? Not knowing what he meant?'

'No sir, I mean your lordship, it ain't that. It's wot I tole
Sawby who tole me I couldn't see you becorse you wos locked
in the library with the rest of the family.'

'And what did you tell Sawby?'

'That I couldn't nowise pass on 'is Lordship's last words
proper to *your* lordship.'

'But why old chap?'

'Becorse,' said Plum, sensing the import behind the words in some curious instinct born of his passionate devotion to 'the Family', 'I shall never know 'ow to pass it on. Did 'is lordship say *"don't open the box"* or did 'ee say *"don't"* for summink else, and then quite separate, like one of the sharp orders of 'is *"open the box!"* '

By a superhuman effort, Gyles pulled himself together and spoke gently to the old man, using all the assurance he could muster, 'But if I told you that it was only a family joke and that it did not and couid not matter which way m'father meant it, it was of absolutely no importance whatever to the Family, WOULD YOU BELIEVE ME?'

Plum stared back at his master and Gyles held his gaze.

Then, 'No sir, not no how,' he admitted sadly, 'and there's a fac'. But thank you, sir, for trying. At least sir I feel better at 'aving told you what my fears are.'

Gyles opened his lips once more but the words he wished to say simply would not be uttered. After a moment he began to curse instead and even to blaspheme, with such aptitude, such fluency that Plum looked up in blank amazement, the tears drying on his old cheeks until at length a slight, horse chuckle escaped him.

When Gyles ceased: 'Well now my Lord I trus' you feel better, for I can tell you as I do and no mistake. I never knew you could cuss that wunnerful. Better nor wot 'is late Lordship could do I will be bound. Wunnerful fluent that was and there is no denying it.' Gyles gazed at him, speechless at last and then he too grinned.

'All right Plum,' he said resignedly, 'I'll explain in so far as I can; but this is a Family matter and I can only go so far. First I might have known you could not be deceived and I apologize for trying. But this I can tell you with absolute confidence and assurance. It makes no difference whatsoever to what we have already done. There *was* a Box and we have opened it; but no matter what m'father had said, we had reached a point in our history when we were predestined to open the Box. Having done so, everything will go exactly as before and you can have my sworn word upon that.' Saying which he held out his hand to the percipient old man.

'Wot does predestined mean, sir?' Plum asked.

'It had to be, nothing could stop it for it was so ordained, long, long ago.'

Plum examined the outstretched hand. 'That I will believe, sir, my lord, and thank you; but all the same there are worries tied up with that there box and the opening of it which I don't pretend to understand nor don't want to, but I know it and I don't like it one bit.'

And with this Gyles Aynthorp had to be content.

He told Henry. He told all the men of the Family and there was much discussion after dinner, once again in the library.

When he had done, 'It must be the oldest practical joke on record,' said Henry ruefully.

Without warning Gyles erupted and the startled expression in everyone's eyes gradually gave way to recognition as, 'Never let me hear you make such a heinous comment again,' he said with cold fury, 'such a remark, at such a time, and in such circumstances can only be dismissed as worse than wicked – *it is vulgar!*' So saying he removed his monocle, replaced it and glared, incensed at his eldest son. His words galvanized them all.

Damien protested, 'Well Uncle Gyles . . . really, I mean it's a pretty disgustin' object, isn't it?'

The Bishop contributed his mite, 'Indubitably it cannot be returned to the Chapel,' he intoned turning extremely red and then whitening again.

'And why not?' Gyles inquired dangerously, a small muscle beginning to twitch in his left cheek, 'is that not a matter of viewpoint? Pray let me present mine now.' Without a second's pause into which any comment could be inserted he went on, 'A gentlewoman's cloister to her chastity and the custodian of her purity, while her lawful husband was at the wars . . .'

Robert giggled. Gyles quelled him with a glance. The Bishop appeared to have sunk into apathy. Henry chose this moment to apologize. 'I am sorry, sir,' he stammered. 'I understand, I did indeed speak out of turn. I can only admit that I had not seen it, er, in exactly the light you now present.'

Gyles would not be appeased. 'In what other light,' he asked dangerously, 'may such a thing be considered by such a family as we represent I would desire you to tell me?' Happily he did not wait for elucidation but ran on, 'a gentlewoman, on her deathbed has forward vision. Now according to the church such things are either a gift from God or a visitation from the Devil. Which, therefore would you consider the Lady Mathilde's prophesies to be?'

The Bishop was plainly remanoeuvring himself. Gyles, receiving no reply resumed, 'I think,' and now his voice was quivering with rage, 'we may safely assume it was the former, since accordin' to our history the vision came upon her *uninvited* and wholly without deliberate invocation.'

'Quite,' said Alaric lamely, but he was not to be allowed to escape either. Gyles pounced upon him. 'I am glad you agree,' he snapped. 'If there are no other dissenting voices from any of you I will submit my proposition to you all.'

Henry checked back an exclamation with some difficulty. His father, in present mood was giving a very good imitation of his own late parent in a temper and for any Lorme in such humour to submit anything to anyone was totally out of character.

No one spoke. Gyles waited a few seconds then stated what he intended should be done.

'We shall return the heirloom to its casket. We shall simply replace the cloths which enfolded it with others which are not falling away with age. We shall then take all back whence they came – to the Chapel – now that we have Alaric's consent so to do,' his voice had a faint ironic timbre for this, 'and there replace it in its niche.'

'Hey, rein in a bit old chap,' protested John, 'after all . . . I mean . . . well, it IS a Chastity Belt ain't it?'

Gyles swung round. His eyes narrowed, 'Are you by any chance thinkin' SEX?' he asked his uncle scornfully, 'concernin' a gentlewoman who bore the ancestor to whom we owe everythin' . . . one, moreover, no' – as John attempted to reply – 'pray let me finish; one whose carnal body as I believe you might wish to call it, Uncle Alaric, has been dust for over eight hundred years. You will be remindin' me that love laughs at locksmiths next I dare suppose?'

'Not at all,' said John hurriedly.

This did draw a stifled sound from Henry, but he repressed it. The great, gilt clock on the mantelshelf ticked into the silence. A log crunched and fell. Somewhere beyond the windows owls were hooting mournfully.

Gyles stood up. 'There is just one more thing I should say,' he stated and to Henry his voice held a distinct note of challenge. 'I will say it now. Then I will leave you to consider it while I perform the office I have proposed. When I return from the Chapel I will ask for your acceptances or rebuttals. *Uncle Alaric, do you accompany me?*'

Alaric boggled. He hesitated, managed to stammer, 'Oh yes, my dear boy ... so like your father ... yes ... yes ... certainly ... only right and proper that I should.' But he did not move. He was clearly floundering, and resembled nothing more than a pathetically de-flated spectre of the man that he had been before.

'Then shall we go?' It was a command and sounded relent-less although in perfect courtesy.

As Alaric rose very slowly, Gyles glanced once more around the table.

'I further suggest,' he flung at them, 'that from this moment onwards we treat the opening of the Casket *as if it had never happened.* Above all, we should undertake never to disclose anything of what *has* occurred in here this evening to the women of our family other than Mama, who was with us when the Casket was opened.' After which he turned to leave them, saying to his Uncle, 'After you, sir,' and going out as if he were the old man's gaoler.

CHAPTER 2

For Seven Days

The secret held by the Family concerning the opening of the Casket[1] lay heavily upon them. It seemed as though the old, serene, unassailable security and tenor of Castle life – which had been marred heretofore only by the recurring 'runts'[2] – was now totally imperilled.

In the past, when these family traits had recurred, power, influence and the careful manipulation of vast sums of money had ensured their concealment. Thus no breath of scandal had ever remained to taint the Lorme name. The combined, equally constant Family talents for secrecy had secured them a seemingly unblemished record for what, when this century had passed would be coming to close upon a thousand years.

The Family was at breakfast when the new bombshell was exploded among them; at least, all of the Family at present living in the Castle. Alaric and his unalluring Dorothy had betaken themselves to their episcopal palace. The younger ones were off upon their equally lawful occasions and the Dowager was, of course, breakfasting in her rooms, attended upon with her customary waspish solicitude by her maid Palliser. The rest

[1] *Casket.* See Book I, *The Lormes of Castle Rising.* The Casket was regarded by the family as an 'Heirloom'. It had been handed by the Lady Mathilde, on her deathbed, with instructions to give it to her fourth son Henri de Lorme whom she prophesied would establish the English line of this Norman family. Down the centuries it had lain hidden in a niche in the family Chapel. It had never been opened, although no implicit embargo had been made by Mathilde against so doing.

[2] *Runts.* From Norman times to the present day records extant proved that there had been a recurring strain of wickedness in the Family, who had spent fortunes and themselves in concealing these major peccadilloes so that the name remained unsullied to the world at large.

sat around working their way through the many and various stages of an Edwardian breakfast. Behind them Henry, in riding breeches, was debating the competitive appeals of kedgeree made by Mrs Parsons – for chef would have none of such barbaric hodge-podges – and *truite au bleu*. These latter were set out in readiness with the *courtbouillon* shivering on a hot plate. Finally, making his decision for his breakfast fish course, Henry lowered a trout gently into the bubbling liquor, glanced at his wrist watch and returned to table. 'Four minutes for my trout,' he announced to the table at large.

Gyles looked up over the top of the 'Hatched, Matched and Dispatched' column of his *Times*. 'You'll be takin' them under statutory weight any minute then,' he commented.

'What do you mean, sir? Four minutes is plenty for a six ounce trout and y'know André sends them up duly marked anyway.'

'I think a six-ounce trout requires five minutes, and a four minuter should be regarded as perilous close to fishin' under weight in my water.'

'I see,' Henry rose again, crossed to the main hot plate, lifted a silver cover and helped himself to a muffin. 'Dashed good these muffins,' he observed, returning to put his on his side plate. Then he went back for his trout. First he sought a cut lemon and some thin brown bread and butter – the muffin would come later – then another glance at his watch to confirm that he had dissipated the requisite four minutes and he removed the lid, withdrew the two handles inside and so lifted the fish on its inner, perforated base. After a moment's draining he slid it on to his plate.

'Want my pearls, darling?' he queried of his most favourite aunt, the little Countess.

'Only one, thank you, my love, on a tiny scrap of brown bread and butter, but pray no lemon juice, my dear.'

Henry picked up his two forks [3] and carefully excavated under the trout's gills for the 'pearls' which lay cached behind. Intent upon this minuscule ploy – there was never a Lorme

---

[3] At this period two forks were always used for fish and those Victorian *nouveau riche* innovations – fish knives and forks ~ were and still are in certain circles regarded as unacceptable.

who would not subscribe infinite trouble to any pleasure at the table – indeed even as Henry sought Marguerite de Lorme's 'pearl', that elegant old creature was carefully folding a triangular slice of paper-thin, brown bread and butter, *butter side outwards* in preparation for the arrival of her tit-bit. When challenged upon this score she pointed out with sweet reason, 'If the butter side is folded inwards the tongue does not convey the direct flavour of it to the taste buds, therefore to eat it any other way than this is *imbecile!*'

While the small change of Lorme family life was thus being disseminated over the breakfast table, Gyles remained concealed behind his *Times*, only permitting one hand to emerge around it to grasp his coffee cup and draw it back behind the same screen. Having read the entire front page with some care, and in so doing failed to find any of his acquaintance therein, for his wife either to congratulate or condole with, Gyles turned inwards for more general information and *en passant* a headline caught his disinterested glance. '*Peer's niece arrested – suffragette raid smashes windows of No. 10.*' He almost dismissed the all too familiar heading, then, curiosity as to *which unfortunate peer* arrested him from turning the page and he read on ...

'God in Heaven!' he ejaculated.

'Really Gyles!' the little Countess looked up. '*Must* you blaspheme at the breakfast table? This is becomin' a trifle in excess of even yer father's tantrums,' she protested. For answer Gyles strode round the table to where his wife and aunt sat side by side. Stretching over them he held the paper between them and thundered, '*Just read that!*'

They did so. There was a quick movement as Christine clasped his wrist, 'Oh my darling I am so sorry!' she rose to stand beside him and on the instant, and with a fiendishness of timing, the door was opened by Sinclair, and Henrietta walked in.

'Oh no!' Gyles exclaimed in consternation, then, 'I suppose you two must know?'

'Know? Know what?' Sinclair inquired, closing the doors, 'I say, Gyles, you do look put out, is anything toward?'

'Toward is it!' Gyles exclaimed.

During these exchanges Henry was skimming down the

page. Now he cut in abruptly. 'I am about to pull the bell, sir,'
he said loudly, 'by your leave, what you need now is the Royce
at the door immediately. Stephanie appears in court sometime
after ten this morning. You must be there. When we have
despatched you sir, I propose to follow just as soon as I have
alerted the Trusloves on your behalf . . .' and he suited action
to words so that by the time Sawby appeared in the doorway,
Henrietta had only had time to moan quietly, 'Stephanie!' after
which she obligingly slid unconscious to the floor.

Sawby side-stepped her neatly, as Christine lifted her head;
then, 'Do you require any assistance my lady?' Receiving a
quick, 'No thank you, Sawby,' he then addressed himself to his
new employer.

'You rang, my lord?'

'No I rang,' said Henry, 'Is it nine twenty or nine thirty for
the fast train to London?'

'Nine fifty, sir,' said Sawby.

'Too late, I'll drive.' Gyles put down the paper once again.
'Christine, my love, be good enough to find me some money,
plenty of it and Sawby.'

'My Lord?'

'Keep the papers from the servants until after luncheon at
any rate.'

Sawby coughed. 'My lord the newspapers are all warmed
and ironed by the footmen before being brought to your
Lordship's bedrooms. The, er, entire domestic staff have thus
become acquainted with the bad news, your Lordship.' He
added rather helplessly, 'It was inevitable, my lord, as I had no
pre-knowledge of what the newspapers contained.'

Gyles nodded. 'Well oblige me by telling them that *I*,' he
made some emphasis upon the pronoun and then repeated it,
'*I* would regard it as a personal favour if they would be good
enough not to bruit this affair abroad, at least until I have got
hold of it in some measure.'

Henry had gone and now reappeared in the doorway carrying
a coat, hat and pair of gloves and a small monogrammed
Gladstone bag. 'There's a thousand in here, sir,' he announced,
'two clean handkerchiefs and a note pad and pencil. The
Royce is comin' round now, I'll drive up too and do my best,

sir, not to break my neck in so doin'.'

Gyles nodded, assumed the garments one by one from his son, and with a quick, 'Well done,' and 'Tell your mother I will be in touch with her as soon as possible,' he was running down the steps to the waiting car.

As he settled himself in the driving seat he remembered something, sounded the horn, brought Henry and Sawby to the top step. 'Henry, I forgot something.'

Henry ran down and draped himself over the horn to listen.

'Tell old Truslove to go round to Bow Street immediately but to act cautiously; then he may take such steps as he deems necessary before my arrival. Tell him to wait for me at all cost. How much money have I in here?'

Henry repeated, 'A thousand, sir.'

'Well, bring more, oh, and bring young Ninian with yer. He's got a good head on his shoulders and will keep you company without bein' a dam nuisance.' So saying he let out the clutch and the Royce gathered speed down the drive.

In the breakfast room Sawby, standing at Christine's side, was inquiring, 'Would you like me to leave you my lady or shall I just send my footmen away?'

Christine, who had left her sister-in-law to hysterics and the worthy Pearson, shook her head and rallied her composure.

'Please stay Sawby. We all have complete confidence in your discretion. Furthermore there is absolutely nothing that we can do now except wait. I think perhaps it would be a very good idea if you sent for some fresh coffee.'

Sinclair came into the room at this juncture.

'Precisely what do the papers say?' he inquired wearily, slumping into the nearest chair.

'That Stephanie has been arrested for throwing a brick through a window at No 10 Downing Street. That she has spent the night in Cannon Row[4] police station and that she, together with a number of other militant suffragettes will appear at Bow Street Police Court this morning.'

[4] Among the 'weapons and irons' still held at Cannon Row Police Station are a set of bolt-cutters, lest, ever again, anyone should contemporaneously chain themselves to railings as did the militant suffragettes during the pre-1914 period.

Sinclair nodded several times, then in an equally weary voice he speculated, 'I wonder just how long it takes to become a "militant suffragette"? Would you imagine my dear sister-in-law that the matter could be accomplished overnight?'

Christine shook her head, and looked at him with profound pity. 'No, dear Sinclair, I would not be so foolish as to suggest any such thing. Anyway, it is not a subject to which I have given much thought. I have of course regretted that women should so demean their sex as to do the monstrous things of which one reads; especially so in the case of gels and women of gentle birth; but you must accept and we must *all* accept that the spirit of martyrdom causes people to act in the most extraordinary ways. Did I not read of some peeress in her own right who had actually gone to prison for such offences and there gone on hunger strike to the permanent damage of her own health? There must be I fear two ways in which this "suffragism" can be regarded. Ours is the way of women who see no need for equalities between the sexes.'

'Well, thank God for that anyway,' said John heavily, as he walked in and poured himself fresh coffee. 'If it were not in the very worst possible taste, and speakin' as a ridin' man, I could very easily prove to any of those silly sensation seekers that equality between men and women is a terminological inexactitude. You cannot equalize the sexes.'

Sinclair coughed in warning, and a bright sparkle, instantly quenched, shone in the little Countess's eyes.

'Why do you not go on John?' she invited him, 'Our French blood makes us less prudish than our English counterparts.'

He looked shocked at this and muttered, 'Oh but I could not, the idea is quite untenable. Really, dear sister, you transgress beyond what men can say in the presence of the fair sex . . . ever!'

'Then I maintain,' she insisted, 'that you were in error in raising the matter at all.'

Henry, in an ulster with a bowler hat in his hand was standing in the doorway, an interested listener to the latter part of this exchange.

'I'll be away and catch m'father if I may,' he said hurriedly, 'Ninian's fetchin' the *Bouton* for me, but I would like to hear from you before I go, Mother, what you consider is the "other point of view" concernin' suffrage and women's rights.'

'Why?' Christine inquired. She gazed at him directly and saw nothing of which she disapproved.

'Because I respect your judgement and I think that essentially you are the most fair minded among us.'

'Very well then.' Christine propped her chin upon her hands and gazed out through the windows at the parklands beyond. 'In the first place my son,' she began, 'without experience one can never pass fair judgement. Within our experience there are no valid reasons for wishing to embrace this cause. I do not wish to have the vote, because, brought up as I have been, with wealth and privilege for which I am truly thankful, I know that if I so wished I could sway men's opinions politically at the dinner table far more effectively than ever I could at the bar of the House. There is nothing original in this, all our political hostesses are engaged upon similar ploys all the time. You have only to think of Lady Londonderry. Such women's husbands make the political bullets. *They* are speeded to their objectives when their gowned and bejewelled wives entertain their victims to country house Friday to Tuesday or in London at the great receptions. These are not really social occasions at all; but merely elegant vehicles for the swaying of men to other men's, er, "causes" by women of vast political experience who are wise enough to wield their power under the rose.' She paused for thought and then resumed.

'Examine the case of women of another kind, women without wealth and privilege. In their case I can believe without, as I said, the requisite experience – that *if* I were such a one I might very well embrace the self-same cause as Stephanie.'

Henry strode across and kissed her, 'That's my darling,' he said approvingly, 'I'd like to hear more but I must go. As it is I am glad you do not have to chain yourself to railings; but I wholly agree that we must try and help poor Stephanie if that is what she feels she must do for other women's causes, since her own could so very easily remain the same as yours.' He kissed her, received a loving, somewhat absentminded pat and was gone while Christine sat on.

Below stairs Sawby was saying in tones which brooked no

argument whatever, 'When the bell rings, *then* you can clear and not before, so let me hear no more about it. Richard to the silver, George to the glass and Robert clean them trays until I can see my face in them and while about these duties pray be silent for I wish to think.'

The women of the family sat on at the breakfast table for a very long time. Eventually Christine sighed, rose and murmured, 'I must go to Mama and break the news to her. After that there is absolutely nothing that we can do except wait in patience until we hear from Gyles,' and, gathering up her unopened letters, she prepared to leave.

The little Countess looked up. 'My dear,' she warned, very softly, as Christine pulled the bell, 'Have you not forgotten something?' Christine, pulled, then replied looking puzzled, 'No, I think not, but what has occurred to you dear Aunt?'

'That every newspaper man in London will be hammering at our doors any minute now', said Marguerite drily. 'Oh, it is alright, for I can take care of all that for you. If you will go to Alicia now I will undertake to instruct everyone so that we may remain, as it were, in a state of siege, at least until we have all had time to know what has happened and what Gyles wishes us to do.'

Christine whitened.

'Press,' she repeated distastefully. 'Oh, how absolutely horrible!'

'None the less inevitable,' reiterated the indomitable little Countess.

'Then please, darling, do what you will,' Christine rallied with a fleeting smile of gratitude. 'Pull up the drawbridge, man the battlements, or whatever is our modern equivalent. I am not very skilled in such matters, but oh how I wish we were back in the days when we could rain boiling oil upon them from a great height!'

With which un-Christian, but devoutly sincere wish, the new Lady Aynthorp went to commiserate with the old one.

In later years Gyles Aynthorp confessed that the drive to London on that clear spring morning was among the longest and most nerve-racking experiences of his life; by comparison to which Bloomfontein was as nothing and Mafeking a mere incident.

At first there was little traffic on the roads and Simkins sat rigidly beside his master as the latter gave the Royce her head. They made very good time; but when they touched the fringes of the City, through which they must pass to reach their objective, their troubles began and grew until it seemed as if every horse-drawn vehicle conspired to slow them down. It was not enough that brewers' drays lumbered across their path; that rag and bone men in their decrepit carts jig-jogged directly ahead of them and would not give way by a single inch, while hansoms and horse-drawn buses formed a tangled press through which the Royce could not be thrust. In addition, crossing sweepers ducked beneath the horses' hooves and came up with their heads agonisingly close to the gleaming mud-guards. Time and again a clear space through was closed and tangled once again before the car could shoot across it, until, practically demented, Gyles at last pulled up before Bow Street Police Station and dismounted stiffly. Simkins immediately slid into the driving seat and sat there staring ahead of him – the acme of impassivity.

Mr Truslove senior, more pelican-like than ever, pecked his way across the pavement hurriedly, raised his top hat as if nothing untoward had occurred and greeted his client.

'Good morning to your lordship. I trust your lordship has had a good journey. Mr Henry spoke to me on the speaking tube and I am fully prepared for your very welcome arrival.'

'I had a damnable journey thank you Truslove. Where can we talk in privacy? and Truslove *where is she*? And where is my thrice foolish aunt Miss Prudence?'

Mr Truslove dropped his voice, 'Miss Stephanie has been taken to Holloway with the rest of the prisoners in a black Maria to spend a week in custody, on remand.'

Gyles stared down at the attentuated little man increduously.

'In prison . . . on remand . . . God save us!'

'Yes indeed my lord. I received your message just as I was leaving chambers. I came straight here by hansom. I discovered on arrival that Miss Stephanie had not yet appeared so I set about obtaining the necessary permission to see her in the, er, cells.'

Gyles mouthed the one word, 'Cells!'

'I obtained this permission, not being entirely unknown here as you might say and down I went. I am bound to tell your lordship that the young lady was just leetleest bit un-co-operative. Not to mince matters my lord she shouted at me to go away, quickly. She said she had – believe me I am truly sorry my lord to pass on such deplorable information – but she did say that she had found her chosen way of life and would brook no interference from the Family in the ordering of it. She said her soul was free at last and a great deal more in the same vein. Had I not made some special and very discreet approaches in the Right Quarter it is my considered belief that Miss Stephanie would have pleaded guilty. As it was, her tirade was interrupted by her being summoned to appear in court and she was led away by a woman warder. BUT I had paved the way, though I am forced to admit that the next time she appears, unless she undergoes a considerable change of heart, though nothing she has done so far can lead us to expect such a transformation, then she *will* plead guilty.

'I must also confess that I failed completely in the matter of obtaining bail for her. When the magistrate said, "remanded for one week in custody pending the discovery of further relevant information', she stood up and shouted 'no bail, no bail, no bail,' over and over until ultimately she was . . . er carried from court struggling and still screaming "no bail".'

As the old lawyer, somewhat reluctantly unburdened himself of this sorry tale, he was watched intently by a stout, seedy looking individual in a brown Derby, a half-chewed cigar between his teeth, nicotine stained fingers folded around a small notebook. This person now approached them, shouldering his way through the crowd upon the pavement.

''Ave I the pleasure of addressing Lord Aynthorp?' he inquired ingratiatingly, loosing a noxious smell of stale liquor and tobacco over Gyles.

Gyles glared through his monocle, 'And what the devil is it to you, sir,' he demanded, 'whether or not I am the person you so name? I may tell you your addresses are most unwelcome. Pray leave us, sir.'

'Nah, nah that's no way for a peer to carry on,' the beery one chided. 'I might get difficult, mightn't I?'

Gyles' temper flared on the instant. 'In which case,' he said, 'I should bloody well knock you down.'

'Oh, I shouldn't do that if I was you, my lord. We 'ave 'ad enough violence in your family for twenty-four hours,' the man countered cheerfully.

Gyles gripped the old lawyer's arm. 'Come into the Royce,' he urged, 'Simkins can drive us round and we can talk in peace without the dubious benefit of this drunken rabble.'

Caught off his guard as he hurried with Truslove towards the waiting car he heard a totally different voice call out 'Lord Aynthorp' and involuntarily turned. The press photographer was ready. He caught Gyles full face as he turned and saw both man and camera. Click went the l⋅ter. Gyles made a quick movement towards him but Truslove had his arm and managed to pull him away.

'For God's sake don't antagonise the press at a time like this, my lord, pray get into the car. Do you not see you are in the thick of it now and must on no account become involved in any scrimmage?' All the while he spoke he pulled and pushed like a small pinnace attempting to nudge a destroyer, until he almost shovelled Gyles into the waiting vehicle and immediately shot in himself like an agitated rabbit into the mouth of its burrow. Simkins moved off at once.

The photograph appeared in all the London evening papers. The following morning the daily newspapers featured it once again. With only the slightest variations, the sub-title read *'Lord Aynthorp arrives too late to see militant suffragette niece Stephanie Delahaye.'* Next to it was a picture of a black Maria with Stephanie among the girls and women being bundled into it in considerable disarray. In a third picture Sinclair was seen standing alone on the pavement outside Bow Street. *'Father mourns foolishness of militant suffragette daughter'*, this one explained and added as supporting text a long and partially false paragraph concerning the parents themselves.

*   *   *

By the time Henry and Ninian, in the former's de Dion-Bouton, had caught up with them, Gyles and Mr Truslove were standing in the hallway of Prudence de Lorme's 'chambers' being given the dubious benefit of an almost incoherent explanation by a very tearful Primrose Sprout, Prudence's companion and Stephanie's alleged chaperone.

Gyles struck the wrapped knocker very gently, the door was opened on the instant and by the time Henry and Ninian turned into the straw-spread *cul-de-sac*, Primrose had closed it again.

As soon as Henry observed the straw – laid down to deaden the sound of horses' hooves whenever there was serious illness in the vicinity – he realized how his errant cousin Stephanie must have escaped from supervision. At least he thought he did. He halted his car a few yards behind the Royce.

'Well here's a pretty kettle of fish,' Ninian grunted, removing his goggles and wiping some of the dust from his eyes with a not-too-clean pocket handkerchief. 'I say Hen, she must be pretty ill.'

'Well yes,' admitted Henry cautiously, 'provided it's her that *is* ill! Lor what shockin' grammar!' He climbed out rather stiffly and began unbuttoning his long motoring coat. 'I suggest we chuck these in the back so as to make a fairly presentable appearance, what?' and he began rolling up the dust garment as if it were a ground sheet and he back at School Corp manoeuvres. Then as he turned to mount the white steps, 'Oh it's her all right,' he acknowledged gloomily, lifting up the flannel-bagged brass door knocker. 'Oh I say, what a jamboree this is goin' to be!'

Primrose took some time to answer this second summons. She had banished the maids to their quarters and was, even now, escorting her first callers down the wide, turkey-carpeted general corridor which led to a mahogany door inset leftwards and with a small brass 'No 2' affixed upon it. There was a key in the door which was propped open. Silently, she slipped in, awaited the two men and gestured them into a sitting room upon the right.

'I will summon the Doctor immediately,' she told them, 'he only lives around the corner and comes very frequently.

He fears the worst I think,' and so saying the ready tears coursed once more down her swollen face, from which Gyles looked away distastefully, while Mr Truslove, standing back a pace, examined his small button boots with great attention.

They had not long to wait. Gyles, his head throbbing at the speed at which these events had come about, stood drumming his long fingers on the window pane. Dimly through the net-veiled glass he saw his son's car, realized the two boys must be waiting on the doorstep and asked Mr Truslove diffidently, 'Truslove, I fancy Mr Henry and Mr Ninian are upon the doorstep, would you perform the good office of admitting them if you please?' Thus he was alone and so remained as Primrose returned ushering in the doctor, a frock-coated individual of obvious integrity and distinction, who bowed low at the introduction and then requested Primrose to leave them alone awhile.

'Miss Sprout,' Gyles addressed her as she turned obediently to leave the room, 'I do believe my two eldest sons are at your front door. Mr Truslove has gone to admit them. Would you I wonder put them into some other room for a few moments while I talk to your good doctor?'

The somewhat sodden creature nodded and hurried off. Gyles seated himself and invited the doctor to do likewise.

'My Aunt,' he began, 'has in the past taxed her strength greatly with her manifold activities and I merely wish to know how serious is her condition now.'

'Very,' replied the doctor.

'You fear the worst?'

'One always hopes that the worst will not eventualize my dear sir, but Miss de Lorme is elderly, distraught beyond description concerning your niece – I may say in this context, to ease you of explanations – that I have read the papers this morning.'

'Just so,' said Gyles shortly, 'then may I take it that my aunt is dying?'

'I fear that may well prove to be the case. Pneumonia, you know . . . her heart . . . she is being most excellently well taken care of . . . a very good and reliable nurse, IF one with unfortunate, er, political interests.'

'Eh?' Gyles looked somewhat startled. 'Good God, not another of 'em!'

The doctor inclined his head, 'A good woman and a fine nurse but indisputably another of this misguided movement . . .'

'Oh, really,' exclaimed Gyles with some impatience, 'have women lost their heads entirely?'

'I fear . . . some . . . have,' the doctor admitted with a fine show of reluctance. Before more could be said, the door reopened and a woman in nurse's uniform revealed herself, 'I'm sorry, doctor, but could you come?' she asked quickly, then turning to Gyles, 'I apologize for the interruption, sir.'

Gyles realized with an abrupt sense of shock that this nurse was gently born. Having risen at her entrance he now reseated himself and began pondering upon the ramifications of this 'women's suffrage nonsense' as he had been wont to call it in the past, dismissing it as one dismisses the buzzing of a few irritating mosquitoes. He recalled that he had gone so far as to declare roundly to the assembled breakfast table, 'These women should be given a good whipping and a thoroughly rummagin' dose,' which merely won him a reproving 'Gyles pray do not be coarse' from his Christine.

Now, waiting to hear if his eldest aunt was alive or dead Gyles began to question the rightness of his sweeping statement. Had some a cause sufficient to justify such degrading and extremely vulgar public exhibitions as they were currently making of themselves? Having demanded of himself, in the quietness of the extremely Victorian sitting room, he had no time to reply to his own rhetorical question, for once again the door opened and the doctor returned, closing it carefully behind him.

'I regret to tell you, Lord Aynthorp,' he said formally, 'that your Aunt has passed away. She died very peacefully,' he added, 'her heart simply stopped beating.'

'I see,' said Gyles levelly, not seeing anything at all very clearly for the moment. Then he asked for and obtained some telegraph forms, sent for his sons, acquainted them with the news of their great-aunt's demise and rapidly filled in several forms for them to despatch.

'And when you have so done, Henry, go back to Mr Truslove if you please and I will join you with as much speed as possible.'

Henry sped about his errands.

'We shall of course take my Aunt home,' Gyles informed the waiting doctor's frock-coated back. The man stood by the window until Gyles spoke and then he turned.

'I can have all in readiness by tomorrow morning,' he said reassuringly. 'If I am not mistaken this is the second bereavement on which I must condole with you, and both in such a very short space of time! May I offer my sincere sympathies.' He held out his hand and Gyles took it.

'That is so,' he said curtly, 'and I thank you; but now I am sure you do not wish to be unduly delayed. That very worthy nurse will permit me to see my Aunt and will make all the necessary arrangements I am confident, so I need not delay you longer, sir.' Thus did he dismiss the doctor and having so done he went in search of the Pelican and his sons.

CHAPTER 3

The Lady Constance

They took rooms at Browns' Hotel and engaged a private sitting room. Before they went thence, and before Groom, Gyles Aynthorp's new manservant and a cousin of Sawby's had been taken to the station by Plum in the dog-cart with fresh clothing for all the three Lormes, Gyles went into his aunt's bedroom with the nurse, whom he was startled to learn was a peeress in her own right and the sister of a man with whom he had been at Harrow. Having learned her rank he thus addressed her only to be *reproved*, once the bedroom door was closed behind them once again.

' "Nurse", if you please, Lord Aynthorp, will suffice in our exchanges. I have no need of my title for the work that I have elected to do.'

Gyles nodded, 'Well then will you please inform me Nurse who is that pathetic and somewhat sodden individual Miss er, Sprout?'

The vestige of a twinkle lit the steady grey eyes which met his. 'She is a clergyman's daughter. She is also, er, one of US. She will, I think, return to her father, though her ever present fears are at war with her convictions. She is afraid that if he ever discovered what she was really engaged in doing, the shock would kill the good old man.'

'I see,' Gyles looked down at the slight figure. 'Will you tell me something else?'

The eyes never wavered. 'Certainly, if it is within my power.'

'Then,' said Gyles, '*why* do you do these things?'

She shook her head, 'Lord Aynthorp, this is neither the time nor the place. If you really wish to know you may call upon me at this address either this evening or tomorrow morning.' She slipped one hand inside the bib of her apron, brought out a purse and from it took a card which read The Lady Constance Comyns, 17, Stanhope Gate. 'Is there anything else you wish to know?' she then inquired.

'Yes,' Gyles replied, 'but I will abstain from asking you now though I will gladly avail myself of your very courteous invitation. I am in, er, something of a quandary.'

Now there was definite sympathy in those unwavering eyes.

'You have been undone have you not, in the family sense, by the unavoidable publicity?'

'Exactly so,' Gyles looked away and as he did so the training of a lifetime deserted him in the presence of what he inwardly accepted as 'one of m' own kind'. He burst into speech.

'Nine hundred odd years of unblemished record, by sufferin' and concealment and now a silly flibbertygibbet of a girl – a born hysteric, not a dedicated person at all – has undone all that my family have done to preserve our good name untarnished by scandal.'

A feather-light hand was laid upon his dark sleeve, 'Lord Aynthorp, I believe you are in desperate need of someone in whom you can confide.'

Then as Gyles stiffened, she added, 'Oh I know it would be entirely alien to your nature to admit that this was so, but although we are strangers to one another I believe a word or two from me, IF you will consent to listen, might serve to bring this unhappy series of events into a slightly less terrible perspective.' Gyles' mouth tightened, but good manners controlled him, he made a slight inclination of his head, as if in hommage to her daring. Then his own thought corrected itself, 'her *courage* would be a better word' – it decided.

'Shall we,' he asked in a flat voice, 'return to that small withdrawing room that I may listen.'

She crossed to the sitting room, sat down and folded her hands together. Gyles closed the door and seated himself in an unsuitable, buttoned, nursing chair.

Then she began.

'You are perfectly correct in what you say about your niece. She *is* a born embracer of lost causes. She is not a person dedicated to a single, lusty one and therefore you may have no hope for her. IF she had been as I am and as so many of we women are for the cause of Suffrage, then you might have looked forward one day to her being looked up to, respected, admired, even venerated for what she had helped to do.'

'By throwing bricks through prime ministers' windows, by chaining herself to railings . . .?' he could not repress the words.

'Yes indeed. Have you ever thought what courage it demands to summon up the necessary impetus to perform such public acts? Have you ever considered what it must mean to gently nurtured women to endure the horrors of forced feeding?' The soft voice halted, then resumed, 'I speak as one who has already experienced this torture . . .'

Gyles had been contemplating his hands. He now looked up, startled, 'You?'

'I and many others like me. Lord Aynthorp, this is not the moment for us to make exchanges of any real import to either of us, with one exception. It is that I honestly and sincerely believe that in six months' time your niece, Stephanie, will have forgotten all about women's suffrage. If I am right, you can then lay in her path another sacrificial interest which does not invoke publicity. You have only two alternatives in any case. You either leave her with us, let the notoriety continue, indeed accelerate and with it your shame and discomfort; then rein in until one day in the possibly far distant future you may find that your niece is spoken of with respect and admiration . . . or . . .'

Gyles' eyes were blank with astonishment. 'And gentle-women in England now abed will think themselves accursed they were not here and . . .' he broke off.

'Exactly,' said Lady Constance, smiling her acknowledge-ment of the apposite Shakespearean misquotation. 'You have a surprisingly flexible mind. Now will you reflect? Will you decide? And when you have decided I think I may be able, should you agree with my assessment of Stephanie's character, to help you, in the matter of that other interest. No,' she cor-rected herself, 'it would be better described as a counter-irritant without harmful side effects. I might also be able to suggest how you may extricate the girl from her present predicament and contrive to make her look just a silly chit, which for her sake would be the better part.'

Gyles leapt to his feet, 'Lady Constance, I will wait upon you tonight. In the meantime my two sons and my lawyer sit waitin' impatiently in some other room, I know not which. Pray conduct me to them and let me say now that, while I cannot possibly be expected to understand or sympathise with your point of view I stand deeply in your debt for your great kindness in my very difficult situation.' So saying, Gyles picked up one of the slim hands and lifted it to his lips. 'Whatever else you are, Lady Constance, Nurse, you are a very gallant woman,' and so saying he opened the door for her to pass.

When Gyles Aynthorp stood by the side of his dead Aunt and looked down upon the peaceful face, his first thought was that she had been in essence a very handsome woman whose character had compelled her to suppress such looks as she undoubtedly possessed. Then he thought about her life and what an empty one it had been. 'Substitutes,' he acknowledged should have been her epitaph, '*Causes* for people, *crusades* for a spouse and *pamphlets* for children.' Sadness at such waste, rather than maliciousness added the mental rider to his epitaph, 'Whenever Aunt Prue was offered the choice of two evils she always took them both.'

He had noticed a small bowl of jonquils upon the table in the sitting room. Something by which he was embarrassed sent him back into that room, where he picked the jonquils from the bowl, shook off the water upon the rug and took them back to this barren, dead, ever-anxious gentlewoman. He laid them between her crossed hands, that she might take something of beauty with her to her grave. Then with a long slow look about the equally barren room he turned away and left her.

Safely within the protective custody of Browns' they held a council of war; but first Gyles insisted that they ate. He ordered luncheon to be brought, at three p.m., into their private room. He chose cold pheasant, a magnum of *Mouton Rothschild* '78 and some Stilton. They were waited upon by two

old men whose faces and names were both familiar and who
knew to perfection what was required of them. Thus, when the
birds had been carved and laid before them, the salads of
Romaine and *lames de truffes* tossed in cream and grape juice
and set to one side of each cover, the roomy glasses hand-
warmed for each man and then quaveringly poured to two-
thirds precisely, the old men withdrew; able to calculate to a
nicety just when it would be required of them to return and
replenish at least the younger mens' plates.

When they were ready for their Stilton, cut unquestioningly
'high, low and middle' as was right and proper so to do, Gyles
opened the council with the words, 'I had a very remarkable
interview with the, er, nurse, Truslove, during the unconscionable time I kept you and my sons waiting this morning.'

'The Lady Constance is, I presume to whom your lordship is
referring?' remarked the Pelican, popping a titbit of Dorset
Knob and Stilton into his beak.

Gyles looked slightly taken aback. 'Really, Truslove, you still
surprise me. How the devil did you know . . .?'

'Because, my dear sir, I was engaged by her papa when she
first entered upon the same course as Miss Stephanie. I have
followed her progress closely ever since.'

'With any success?'

'None whatsoever,' the beak closed with a snap and Mr
Truslove began choosing a piece of celery from the silver
banded crystal jug.

'Who is she, sir?' inquired Henry looking from one grave
face to the other.

'Your late aunt's nurse, a militant suffragette.'

'Oh lor!' said Henry, 'Nin and I thought she looked
perfectly topping in her uniform.'

'I am inclined to agree with you,' said Gyles surprisingly,
'but that alters nothing.'

He then explained what had passed between them and went
on to discuss his invitation to visit the Lady Constance that
evening.

'I should go if I were you,' said Mr Truslove, nodding his
head up and down. 'Oh yes, nothing but benefit could arise
from such an encounter. She is a very intelligent young woman

you know, and one who will not be turned from any purpose.'

'I could see that,' Gyles acknowledged drily, 'but in what way might I benefit? Yours is a curious choice of words.'

Old Truslove permitted himself the mere ghost of a chuckle. 'She is a very formidable young lady, my lord,' he pronounced at length, 'very for-mid-a-ble in-deed. If she has invited you, and she has done so, then she has something to say. Do not overlook the fact, sir, that she had had more opportunity than any member of the family to observe Miss Stephanie's behaviour.'

Gyles erupted, 'What *has* been goin' on Truslove? I have the feeling that we are gropin' in the dark and I dislike it. How have we been deceived in this affair? Really these Delahayes are passin' devious.' He paused and looked at them as the thought struck him suddenly, 'Where the devil is Sinclair? after all she is *his* daughter. He said he was following us to London.'

Once more, with startling timing the door opened and Sinclair walked in. 'I am sorry to be so late,' he apologized. Then, despairingly, 'I have heard about Prue,' and, looking very grey and rather bent, he deposited his hat and cane upon a nearby chair.

'Never mind that, old boy, have you had luncheon?' Gyles sounded faintly embarrassed. Sinclair nodded and drew up a chair.

'André sent up a tiffin basket for me to munch on the train; but I could not at first leave Hetty. She was distraught.' He passed a slightly trembling hand across his head, 'Oh really, absolutely distraught! Gyles what are we to do? Have you any news?'

During this inevitable preamble Gyles merely busied himself with the tantalus on the sideboard. Now he passed a brandy balloon across to his brother-in-law and commanded him, 'Drink that and you will feel much better. Rest assured we have matters in hand; but there is nothin' we can do at present. We are just embarkin' upon a council of war.' He caught his sons' eyes in turn and gave each a tiny shake of the head, as much as to say, 'Let the poor devil sink some brandy first and then we'll tell him,' and they fell silent until a scrap of colour began to creep back into Sinclair's prematurely sunken cheeks.

Then surprisingly he spoke first. 'Y' know,' he said wearily, looking down into the amber liquid in his glass, 'this all dates back to a letter Hetty received when I caught that chill in the huntin' field.'

They stared at him incredulously, 'My dear chap,' remonstrated Gyles, 'are you feelin' alright?'

Sinclair essayed a wraith of a smile, 'I'm not ravin' I do assure you.' He broke off and looked about him, 'Might we have some cigars, dear boy? I came out in such a turmoil I found my case was empty. Ah, thankee.'

Gyles had passed his case without speaking and there was the old familiar twitch which his father had so often manifested lurking at the corners of his mouth denoting rising impatience and the imminence of an explosion. However, he held himself in check until Sinclair had unbanded, pierced and finally lit his cigar, watched somewhat cautiously by the other three to whom the condition of Gyles' personal barometer was all too obvious.

Then, with one hand holding the cigar and the other clasping a lean ankle Sinclair recounted the whole incident. It had occurred he told them when he was forced to trot back ten miles in the pouring rain after taking a toss in the hunting field and landing in a small stream. This in turn developed into a streaming cold and kept him indoors and fretting for more than a week. During this time Henrietta had received and passed to him, a long, carefully crossed and re-crossed letter from Prudence who was taking a sabbatical from her suffragette activities and actually staying with the French family who were chaperoning Stephanie while the girl attempted to improve her French – a deplorable necessity for any Lorme connection.

In the same letter, very casually and carefully as Sinclair recounted, Prudence had suggested that there was little or no purpose in the girl staying on any longer as she showed no aptitude whatever for the French tongue – in itself a remarkable lack in a member of the Family – and moreover, was both frustrated and unhappy. Prudence disclosed how the girl herself had approached her and asked if she could return to England with the express purpose of advancing her potentials as a debutante by developing both her singing voice, which was quite sweet, and her ability upon the pianoforte.

'It was Prue who suggested the solution to us,' Sinclair told his audience. 'She said she was moving into the centre of London, takin' some rooms, and had engaged the services of a clergyman's daughter as her companion. It was Prue who proposed that this person, Primrose something as I recall, should conduct Stephanie to and from the Royal Academy of Music thus ensuring her protection at all times and Prue who begged us to lend our support to the scheme as she was so fond of the girl and the girl of her.' At this point Sinclair leapt to his feet and began pacing up and down.

'It was a deep-laid plot I tell you. I am beginning to get inside the minds of my deplorable children. Prue was up to her hocks in the Suffragette movement even then and did not care who knew of it. Prue must have gone out to the *Château* and talked Suffrage to that credulous fool of a gel of mine. You know what a lunatic the child has always been over strange causes! Well as I see it they made their plans, we fell in with them, they got together and these chambers of Prue's were no more than a convenient meeting ground for those damnable suffragettes. Of course Stephanie became involved. Now Prue had an enormous conscience and this must have weighed on it very heavily. What I think then came about was that between the worry of her guilty secret, the strain of her suffragette carry-on and her already weakened state of health the whole sorry boiling conspired to make her ill. Then something – I doubt we shall now discover exactly what it was – stopped Stephanie from coming with Prue for Henry's Ball,' Sinclair went on. 'I believe it was firstly because she did not want to, but secondly because she was not able. I cannot put my finger on the precise explanation but you will surely recall how ill and worried Aunt Prue was and how anxious she was to get away as soon as possible?'

Again that slightly shaking hand was passed across his head. Then he went on, 'I do not think there was a word of truth in what Prue said about my daughter having contacted this Spanish influenza and having almost recovered; but not sufficiently to justify taking the risk of a journey in February. It all hangs together. Stephanie was very probably in prison on some trumpery charge, not in London I think, but somewhere in the provinces and very possibly under a false name, which is why we never heard of it. Then Prue tore back to town and got the girl, how we may never know exactly; but it was all futile and to no avail. Give a girl of Prue or Stephanie's character one taste of martyrdom and you are lost because they have the burning brands of the fire around them they will never be dissuaded from their course of immolation in the flames.' Sinclair stopped abruptly, and sat down again.

In all the years that Gyles had known him, his brother-in-law had only once made such a lengthy peroration before; when his son Stephen had committed his last act of treachery and folly.

Mr Truslove cleared his throat. 'I think, sir, Mr Delahaye,' he said, 'that I am inclined to agree with almost every word which you have spoken. I think you have given us a pretty accurate summary of what has happened and while I sympathize with you most profoundly, I do believe that unless a solution may be found along the lines of a counter irritant or attraction with which to bait Miss Stephanie out of this trap we shall fail to make any impression whatsoever and the scandal will, in consequence, escalate.'

'What solution can there be?' Sinclair groaned, 'except to kidnap the girl and imprison her? This is not the Middle Ages, my dear chap.'

Henry started in his chair, looked around him expectantly and asked, 'But isn't Steph under age?'

'Of course she is,' snapped Sinclair.

'Then surely,' Henry almost shouted the words, 'you have the solution to the first part in your own hands.'

Gyles intervened. 'Now, Henry,' he said grimly, 'you were a splendid help to all of us over the Stephen affair but don't chance your arm too far my dear feller, what difference does it . . .' before he could complete his own sentence Gyles broke off. Mr Truslove, with his pelican head to first one side and then the other, watched the four men arrive at the same conclusion simultaneously as he swivelled his small, pouch-enclosed bird-bright eyes.

Gyles swung round on the old lawyer. 'Will it hold, Truslove?' he demanded brusquely. The old man nodded several times. 'Oh yes, my lord, it will hold, it only remains for Mr Sinclair here to decide whether or not he wishes to intervene.'

'Can I?' Sinclair asked.

'Of that there is no doubt, sir. Your daughter is a minor, escaped through a childish prank from her guardian. It all holds. We have the evidence in plenty. Miss Prudence's illness, the lack of adequate chaperonage, Miss Primrose's influence, and that of the Lady Constance . . . Oh yes, we have all we require to get the girl returned to your custody Mr Sinclair, as a first offender and a minor under undue influence from older persons who sought to undermine her duty and suborn her character . . .'

Henry just had time to whisper to Ninian, 'Batten down yer hatches Nin, here comes the hurricane . . .'

The air was suddenly very cold.

Quite softly, in the pause which followed, the new Lord Aynthorp inquired, 'Always supposin' that none of us minds defaming the dead, makin' an innocent clergyman suffer; blackenin' the name of a very courageous gentlewoman all, if you will forgive me Sinclair, to save one worthless chit from the penalty she so very rightly deserves.'

Sinclair looked at him sadly.

'No comment, Gyles,' he agreed with a deep sigh, 'my daughter is not worth such a sacrifice and I for one would never be able to lift my head again if I were to subscribe to any of it. Hell and damnation, what a tangle!'

The council of war continued. The waiters cleared away, replenished the coal fire, drew the curtains and obtained permission to switch on the new electricity.

Outside a newsboy was crying, 'Late extra, read all abart it, late extra.'

'That will be us,' said Gyles, 'Ninian, run down, dear chap, and get us some evening papers.'

When at length Gyles had seen the photograph of himself, and that of his niece he went out and walked along Piccadilly, into St James's Park. As night came down he found himself standing under Big Ben. The great clock struck the hour of six. Then he hailed a hansom and was conveyed to Stanhope Gate.

Meanwhile, for a sheltered girl, the experience of being conveyed by Black Maria to Holloway Women's Prison was horrifying enough. Each prisoner was forced none too gently into what appeared to be an upright coffin in which there was only one small hole, large enough for the face to be thrust against, in order to breathe the stale air as the vehicle rattled and swayed, banging and bruising the experienced and the inexperienced alike; for some of these 'prisoners'' compartments were so small that they did not enable the inhabitants to raise their hands and arms sufficiently to steady themselves against the sides. So bang, rattle, jerk, the interminable-seeming journey continued until they were released and thrust out on arrival into the entrance of Holloway. The great gates clanged behind them and the doors were secured once more, with a great rattling of bolts and clinking of keys.

The smells assailed her as Stephanie tumbled out, cringing and blinking in the sudden glare of naked gas light. They were recognizably the smells of pungently strong carbolic, and a curious, composite odour which gradually identified itself to the girl's sensitive nostrils as an amalgam of used, stale air, rotting cabbage, cheap cocoa, wet tea leaves and old sweat.

She choked upon it and leaned against the wall coughing. The tears had dried in streaks upon her muddied face for she had fallen after throwing her brick and as the policeman rushed upon her. In falling she had been spattered with mud and it was in this fall, as she went down, arms splayed frantically, clutching at anything, that her hand had slid flat into the path of an oncoming policeman's boot. Now the fingers were half crushed and crusted with blood. She had lost her hat altogether. There was mud too upon her matted hair which had escaped the net into which she had pinned it that morning. It hung in draggled rat ends about her face. In truth, there was nothing of the well-born young lady about her now, for the plain gown and cloak she had assumed were all torn and muddied too and her skin was stained beyond recognition.

This was then followed by a night in the cells at Bow Street

upon hard benches. Then came her appearance in court and
now this terrible journey . . .

Cowed by her experience, far indeed removed from the
defiant girl who had embarked so hopefully upon her chosen
course, Stephanie sank into apathy and submitted to the rough
handling all remand prisoners had inflicted upon them by the
women warders. They seemed to direct all the force of their
accumulated spleen upon such victims. Finally, sobbing helplessly, the girl was pushed into a tiny cell which was furnished
with only a plank bed and a mattress stuffed with coconut
fibre – for which the container was, as usual, filthy. Two coarse
sheets, two hairy blankets and some kind of plaited matting
rug completed the tally of bedding. In this place Stephanie
passed twenty-three hours out of every twenty-four of the next
seven days. For the remaining hour of each day she was
walked, in her own clothes, around and around a bleak yard
wearing only the thin cloak in which she had set forth so
bravely upon her mission. The wind in the yard whipped at her
shoulders. She shivered unceasingly. Back in her cell she had
only one foul wooden spoon with which to eat the equally foul
food. Being young and experiencing the gnawing pangs of real
hunger for the first time, Stephanie attempted to eat; but the
coarseness and unwholesomeness of the food and the disgusting
slop served with it were rejected by her pampered stomach and
she merely threw up, whereupon she was given a rag and
bucket and made to clear her own mess with a blow to the head
and a mouthful of abuse to encourage her. When she had been
brought to the stage where she could only suppress her screams
by pressing her bent wrist into her mouth and driving her teeth
into it to create a counter-irritant, Stephanie began to pray.
She prayed as she had never done before. She prayed for fortitude and threw herself down thereafter sobbing upon the pain-
ful palliasse. She prayed for courage, and crouched shivering
behind the door whenever one of the wardresses so much as
rattled her keys in the lock. She prayed for defiance and
cringed back when the woman shouted through the grille at her.
Then on the second day, a woman strode past flanked on each
side by a warder. One of her eyes was closed from some blow.
Her upper lip was bleeding; but as she went by she managed a

distorted grin and shouted, 'Cheer up chicken, God save the suffragettes!' before another blow silenced her.

That gave Stephanie something to sustain her. Her lip was not cut she reminded herself and her crushed fingers only throbbed, so what was that to a blow in the eye such as she had just seen? From that moment she began to dredge up some remnants of the endurance she had thought was automatically hers because of her love of the Cause and Jesus Christ, all unknowing that such fortitude is hardly won, such endurance painfully achieved and that nothing comes to those who seek to sacrifice themselves, save pain, suffering and degradation. It is only when these things have been accepted willingly that the first steps towards the road to martyrdom are taken cheerfully.

Staring, red-eyed, over her inthrust wrist, from which she had bitten so deeply that a thin trickle of blood ran down; whimpering like a bruised animal, icily cold after her exposure at 'exercise' Stephanie began to change. For the first time, she experienced an inkling of what was really involved in obtaining what she had maintained for so long was the end of all her desires.

She slid slowly down against the wall into a crumpled heap in the corner. Against the facing cell wall, scratched with innumerable names and obscene messages which said nothing to her innocence, Stephanie began to see pictures. She saw Nanny rocking, her carpet-slippered feet and released from the servitude of those little buttoned boots, resting on the rim of the fender from which rose the fireguard with little Richard's 'smalls' airing upon them before the cheerful fire. She saw Rose laying the table for tea, spreading the stiffly-starched white tablecloth, setting out the cups with the rabbits and chickens on them, the plates of bread and butter, the sponge fingers and the little Fairy cakes with the pink and white sugar on the top.

A rivulet of saliva ran from one corner of her mouth onto her shaking hands. She saw herself in unbecoming yellow merino banded with navy blue braid seated at tea in the Music Room, listening to little Lucien playing the pianoforte and hearing her own voice saying scornfully, 'All that work for a few silly little cakes,' as George carried in the tea stand with André's special

iced *gateaux* in miniature – the weekly treat for all of them . . .
save Stephanie.

A wail escaped her as her stomach cramped with hunger.
There was a bang on the door almost immediately. 'Enough of
that,' came the shout. 'Silence in there or I'll give yer something to complain about!' But Stephanie thought on about
those little cakes for a very long time and with a dreadful
craving.

'I'll tell you summink,' confided one woman warder to
another as she picked her teeth reflectively and watched the
militants march round on the next day's dreary exercise.
'There's one 'ere as will not be coming back. She's not the stuff
what martyrs is made of. I fink she's 'ad enough already.'

'That long, thin one with the fancy name? The one from cell
52?'

'That's 'er. You'd noticed too? . . . no talking there No. 6,
stand back a pace.'

In the solitude of her cell Stephanie sobbed herself to sleep
once more and this was the end of the third day of her remand.

The three days following Stephanie's disastrous appearance in
court were, as the bulk of their English acquaintance would
have summarized them, 'tarsome' to the family, this being the
accepted definition of any almost unendurable situation of
crisis as summarized by the English upper classes.

The Dowager coped in tight-lipped silence, her small face
seeming to become smaller still until the moment when she
stood at the windows of her Castle suite to watch the hearse
bearing away the mortal remains of her eldest sister-in-law for
interment – by stipulation – in the village churchyard. She
watched the slow progress of the black-plumed and caparisoned horses. She watched as the pall bearers fell in behind.
She saw how a sudden gust of wind tugged at the crêpe about
their hats drawing the lengths upwards so that they gave the
uncanny impression of many black-sleeved arms waving a final
goodbye. Only then did she allow a long-drawn sigh to escape
her and in the solitude of her room sat down in a high-backed
chair, rested her immaculately-coiffed head against it, closed
her eyes and surrendered herself to pain.

Her granddaughter was in gaol like a common felon. Her daughter Henrietta was in a state of total collapse. Her son-in-law Sinclair was becoming embittered, prematurely aged – a stoop-shouldered epitome of defeat on two legs. Man might well be, according to Mr Carlyle, 'a forked radish' she reflected, but it was of the utmost importance to everyone's moral fibre that each radish could maintain itself upon its fork and not buckle under the weight of inevitable troubles. Thus thought the tiny creature to whom any recognition of defeat was as impossible as it would have been to the late Queen Victoria.

Alicia Lady Aynthorp rose at length and crossed to her *escritoire* on which reposed an opened letter which she now read for the second time.

'Not only dearest Mama,' it ran, 'do we await Stephanie's release with the greatest trepidation but, as if this were not enough – and all London whispering behind its hands at the scandal which has smirched our good name – there are also some most disquieting rumours concerning the King's health. At my club the talk is of little else and speculation is rife as to whether we are being allowed to know the true seriousness of His Majesty's condition. As you are aware, I have known Sysonby since childhood. When I found a suitable opening and made comment upon our mutual anxieties at my club he just closed his mouth tightly and turned away. I fear things are very bad, as indeed they seem to be for us; but I am hoping against reason that Lady Constance's opinion will be borne out by Stephanie's attitude after seven days of what must be a horrible experience. It cannot be otherwise for any girl who has been gently nurtured, even though we all know that she has resented her background as much as poor Aunt Prue did. However we can only wait, and pray that all will come about so that we may again reach calm waters. What the strain must be upon you my dear is past imagining. I reproach myself now for having allowed Christine to tell you. On the other hand you are so astute that I do not believe any of us could have been clever enough to conceal it from you. Mama please, for our sakes, for I know that you cannot care for your own any more, *please rest* and let this storm break over your head in so far as you can possibly do so. I know this is asking far too much; but then your whole life has shown that you have ever been able to achieve the seemingly impossible.

Your ever devoted, anxious and loving son,

Gyles.'

She stood a very long time with the letter between her ringed fingers. The flounced sleeves of her filmy black tea gown had fallen back disclosing not only how painfully thin she had become but how the flesh of old age showed crimped and swung a little because her fingers shook.

She laid the letter down at last. She looked up to where above the burning coals and the brass and steel fender the other half of her life looked down at her in oils – her husband Justin. She had chosen the Lavery of him. Lavery had painted him coming round the topiary into the knot garden, a gun beneath his arm, his blue eyes in their craggy countenance alight with the fire at which she had warmed herself for over fifty years. 'He wants me,' she told the portrait, 'so I must stay awhile, my love.'

CHAPTER 4

The Verdict

It seemed as though some curious fog enclosed the Castle. The occupants moved about as if groping slightly. The pace of servants and employers alike was noticeably slowed. It affected them all in different ways. Nanny of course could scarcely ever be found doing anything but rocking. In consequence Rose, her nursemaid, was run off her feet and tearful with it. Sawby stalked about in slow motion with a countenance so grim that in his presence the other servants spoke in whispers. Mrs Parsons was alternately hysterical and viperish, Chef André surrendered to petulance and evinced little interest in the food he cooked, even that which was destined for 'above stairs'. He muttered at intervals about going back to France and *'il n'y a rien à faire ici . . .'*

'Wot's 'ee say?' Mrs Parsons demanded fretfully; but no one understood and André would not explain.

Pearson reported to Christine, during the routine hundred brush strokes which she gave her mistress's hair each evening, 'We're proper flattened my lady and that's the truth.'

Christine nodded wearily.

'As we are ourselves Pearson. Whom do you think is the most disturbed among the staff?'

Pearson did not even allow herself time for reflection. 'Chef is, my lady,' she replied promptly. 'He keeps muttering to himself, something about re-tour of France.'

'Retour en France?' Christine asked quickly.

'Yes, my lady, and something else "ran affair see" it sounds like but I'm sure that isn't right.'

Christine pondered. At last light dawned; *'Rien à faire ici?'* she queried.

'Yes, m'lady,' said Pearson.

'Do you know what it means?'

'No, m'lady.'

'It means there is nothing for me here, nothing to do here
. . . and that he wishes to return to France.'

'He never will,' said Pearson confidently. 'It will pass.'

'I think so too,' Christine agreed. 'Even so I think I shall
send him home for a week or two.' She stared at her own reflection in the looking glass. 'Yes, I think that would be a good
idea.' Then her thoughts continued; but these she did not
share with her maid. 'Mrs Parsons will then have too much to
do and we shall all suffer from her resultant bad temper; but it
will bring her about and I will go upstairs and deal with Nanny
myself.' And so thinking she surrendered to Parson's attentions aware that if she did not she would be late for dinner
which was of course unthinkable, even in such circumstances
as now existed.

The one person who had expressed no views, vouchsafed no
opinions was, surprisingly enough, the little Countess. All she
had contributed was a pursing of the lips, a hardening of the
jaw line and the one un-helpful comment, 'We can only wait
and see.' Clearly there was a great deal more going on in *her*
head than she was prepared to disclose to any one. It was only
when she and her sister-in-law were closeted together in the
latter's private sitting room that she gave slight indications as
to the direction in which her mind was turning.

The pair of them had elected to make a brief withdrawal.

They excused themselves from dinner in favour of a quiet
supper together beside the fire at a small round table. To the
spectator, had there been one, they might have been sitting for
a conversation piece by the late Lord Aynthorp's favourite
contemporary painter – Lavery.

The firelight shone upon the polished hearth furniture. It
danced upon the lace tablecloth which fell in graceful folds to
the *gros point* carpet. When Palliser lit the candles in the small
porcelain candelabra the little plumes of light began to posture
in the silver and the glass. Palliser had then received from Sawby
a bowl of spring flowers, arranged as a Victorian posy, by
himself; circles of white freesias offsetting circles of violets.

Now these filled the room with their fragrance as the fire warmed them on the centre of the small table. Both ladies were in loose *peignoirs* of lace and embroideries and their beringed fingers curved around the stems of two wine glasses. They sipped and Marguerite smiled at her sister-in-law.

'You know, this may have been sent as a lesson to us,' she observed surprisingly, 'I have a theory about it. I think the time has come for us to be less protected and more aware and this may serve as a means of achieving that now necessary state.'

The Dowager gazed at her thoughtfully. In response she began quoting the poet laureate:

'The old order changeth yielding place to new and God fulfils Himself in many ways, lest one good custom should corrupt the earth'? She made a query of the quotation and Marguerite nodded.

'It may be so indeed. We have always had our instincts, although for the most part we have brushed them aside; too fastidious perhaps to meddle in what our religion has taught us it is better not to probe too deeply.'

Their old eyes met. 'Black hounds,[1] and prophecies and such like,' murmured the Dowager softly.

'Exactly so.'

'Before you develop your theme I would raise a single query, no not a query, a statement. No hound ran when Justin died, Marguerite.'

Marguerite frowned at the winking liquid in her glass.

'He never did my love . . . *for the women of the Family*,' she reminded her sister-in-law dryly. 'He may well have run for one or other of our menfolk whom I am confident would say nothing unless directly tackled. They are, I would add, busily engaged upon being highly secretive about several other matters at this moment.'

'Such as?' there were curious undercurrents in the old voice now.

'Such as,' Marguerite paused, deliberated, decided to speak and then said, softly but with great conviction, 'why, whatever Plum told Gyles about the matter of opening the Box. It was dropped, you will recall, like the proverbial hot potato.'

[1] See Book I, *The Lormes of Castle Rising*.

'Ahhhhh,' it was the merest whisper of sound.

'Ahhhhh, indeed,' echoed Marguerite, 'you only confirm MY theories.'

The door opened and Palliser came in pushing a large silver trolley hooded by a great silver cover.

'May I serve you with the supper miladies?'

The Dowager sighed again, shook out her napkin and replied evenly.

'Yes please, Palliser, and then you may leave us and we will attend to ourselves, thank you.'

The corners of Palliser's mouth went down; but even she knew well enough that such a fiat was beyond questioning. After a while they were thankfully alone again. They both sipped their consommé, put their cups down and like two frailly beautiful old conspirators their eyes met over their raised table napkins.

'What, I wonder, would it have to do with that Box?' It was not so much a question as a reflection.

'Well, what would it? You tell me dear Alicia.'

'I think it would be better not to conjecture,' said Lady Alicia. 'Yes I think so too; but if we are correct in our assumptions, and they decide to keep secret whatever it was, it will work powerfully upon the minds of those who made the decision.'

They allowed the remainder of their soup to become quite cold. They were at the bare bones of the matter and the subject must by its very nature dominate all else.

'You mean,' now Marguerite's eyes were down and she played, quite unconsciously, with a tiny crumb of bread, rolling it between her small fingers, 'you mean,' she repeated reluctantly, 'in terms of our Family superstitions.'

Marguerite rose and began pacing slowly up and down the room.

At length she turned and faced her sister-in-law.

'Then you pray tell me what in your innermost thoughts you believe concerning the potency of such things.'

The silence hung between them. Into it a coal cracked apart. A small piece fell on to the hearth to flame away unnoticed. They were fully enmeshed now.

Lady Alicia spoke hesitantly, she who never hesitated.

'You mean, do I believe that we have brought trouble upon us as a Family by opening that Box if indeed such has been done?'

'Yes.'

'I do not know, Meg, that is the truth. I do not know, but,' she turned almost fiercely, 'I do know that it is our bounden duty to do nothing about it.' As her companion did not reply she went on after another pause, 'I think we are two old women whose times have nearly run their courses. I think that to-morrow and tomorrow are not for us. We shall have no part in them and therefore it behoves us to keep our own counsel, to bow to the inevitable and to accept that the younger ones, who will carry on when we are gone, *must* be allowed to make their own decisions without interference from us. We shall never know *in this state of being* what lies ahead. Therefore, if we are not to be participants we must not hinder our young by any form of influence or expression of opinion. In short we must be silent and leave it all to them.'

Marguerite's eyes filled with tears. She came over to her sister-in-law bent above her and put her lips to her cheek for an instant.

'You were ever wiser than I, Alicia. Therefore I need only add, *so be it*. If that is your decision I will abide by it and stand aside. It is not easy, for we have steered a long course under these roofs, but it is right, of that you do convince me.'

Lady Alicia had not yet done. She moved a trifle restlessly. She put up one hand to touch the face against her own, with a movement which was almost protective.

'Before we leave this,' she pressed, 'I would like to know what you will do if Christine raises the matter. She is as sensitive as we to family matters. She is also both wise and terribly observant. If we two have come to identical shared conclusions do you not suppose she will do likewise, even if she has not done so already? This, after all, is the real crux of the affair. Christine *has* her place in her house of tomorrow. What should we do to ensure we do not imperil her confidence concerning the future?'

Marguerite was recovering her poise rapidly. With the old

familiar gesture she put her hands to her hair, patted it lightly, as if to do so gave her reassurance, and then spoke in quite a different tone, one which was almost brisk.

'I think we should, if cornered, make light of the whole affair. Refuse to countenance any suggestion that any of it is of vital import. We cannot deny ourselves, but we must not deny her any reassurance we can furnish. Lightness must be the key. Do you not agree?'

Lady Alicia was in shadow now, her head propped on one hand as she stared into the dancing fire. Slowly she nodded. 'Yes I think so, an attitude of "and oh my dear I shouldn't bother your head one way or another". After all, it was never recorded that the Box should not be opened.[2] As my memory runs it was the King who was superstitious and this only because he had a guilty conscience over his foreswearing the oath he took upon those old saint's bones! And he was not a member of the family. Am I not right?'

Marguerite did not answer her directly, but continued to be brisk.

'Perfectly right,' she side-stepped, 'that we take exactly that line. I am in complete agreement.' Then their eyes met again and this time the truth flamed between them and would not be denied.

Marguerite stammered out the words. 'But, even so . . . one has . . . one's moments of being . . . afraid . . . does one not?'

'And fear,' Lady Alicia reminded her, 'is man's only enemy. You know, my dear, I think we have said enough. If we do not attempt to make some semblance of a meal Chef André will probably make good his threat to leave us. Come now, let me give you a morsel of quail. André does them so beautifully . . .'

While an unappreciated supper was being served to the two old ladies of Castle Rising, on the adjacent estate Charles Danement and his daughter were sitting together in the Stuart dining room of their home, against a background of linenfold panelling and family portraits. They dined in amity, removed from the necessity of making small talk to Sir Charles' perpetually ailing elder sister whose duties as 'chaperone' to Petula and *châtelaine*

[2] See Book I, *The Lormes of Castle Rising*.

of the old Manor House were gradually becoming less and less onerous as Petula gathered the reins of domestic government more and more firmly between her young fingers.

'What is it?' Charles inquired drily of his daughter, 'which denies us the, er, pleasure of your aunt's company on *this* occasion?'

'Migraine,' said Petula briefly, 'you know father, one is tempted to observe that Aunt Eustasia enjoys the worst possible health!'

Charles chuckled appreciatively, 'Unmarried women do, unquestionably. They have to divert their energies and interests into some peculiar channels as they advance in years.' His voice became very bored as he heaped Stilton on to bread. 'Maiden ladies are a fascinating subject for analysis. Your dear aunt had occasion once to inquire with great earnestness of your cousin Stella why she had to love men when there was God to love?'

Petula looked up amusedly. 'What reply did Stella make?'

Charles fed himself a further morsel, took an appreciative sip of his port and told her, 'With what I have always regarded as the acme of self-restraint dear, naughty Stella refrained from telling her, for which I do believe the Almighty will grant her exceptional dispensation.'

'If she does not try you too far, Daddy, I believe she causes little irritation to me these days. Rather is the boot somewhat upon the other foot! I am sure she spends much time in prayer for my regeneration as she considers me "altogether far too free in my ways, and upon occasion my dear positively dominating which is shocking in a young female of gentle birth".'

The imitation was deadly in its accuracy and Charles shouted his approval. Then becoming graver he asked, in a diminished voice,

'What *is* your attitude to all this, Pet? For you must know whatever it is I will go along with your decisions.'

She nodded. 'Of course I do, and thank you; but you need have no cause to worry. I am not proposing to "do" anything, one way or the other.'

Charles looked at her questioningly.

'Meanin' I suppose that you have decided to go along with

your future husband's motto?'

'Meaning just that Daddy. I have loved Henry for a long time now and I am engaged to marry him. If every other member of the family were to find themselves in H.M.'s prisons I would still be of exactly the same mind. I will marry Henry and do my best to tend both him and Castle Rising. If you like, "*Mon parti est pris . . . aussi*",' and she gave him back the Lorme motto with her own appendix.

'But how much do you mind?' her father pressed her.

'Not at all,' the reply came without hesitation, 'if a silly girl, obsessed with a desire for martyrdom elects to embrace a cause which is supported by a great many wonderful women, women both of the people and of birth and breeding; and if in the execution of her wishes she brings down scandal upon the House of Lorme that is unfortunate; but clearly unavoidable.' She set her elbows, outrageously, upon the table and propped her chin on her interlaced fingers. 'Henry and I will cope. Anyway, if you want my opinion the whole thing will blow over.'

'Blow over!' exclaimed Charles, astonished.

'Yes, father. Listen carefully, my darling, because this is a generation subject. You cannot be expected to sympathize. I will put it this way: were I a different girl from the one I am, and not in love and longing to get married I would probably be a suffragette myself.'

'Good Gad,' exclaimed her startled parent, 'I trust you will become nothing of the sort!'

Petula shook her head.

'My interests lie elsewhere Daddy, but I must say my sympathies are to a large extent with these women. What is more, it is my belief that in a few years time, when they gain their objective they will be heroines not hounded criminals.'

'To think,' Charles mocked, 'that all unknowing I have been nurturing a viper to my bosom!'

'Daddy, you have been doing nothing of the sort. I told you you would not understand; but I think I can make you see that this will not, in the long term do the slightest damage to the Lorme name or to Lorme integrity – rather the reverse,' she added cryptically, '*if* Stephanie can stay the course. Aunt

Henrietta is such a *weak* woman and that in a Lorme is surprising. I can fully imagine Stephanie cracking. As a matter of
fact I have been trying in the past two days to imagine what
impact prison would have on me if I found myself in her circumstance. I think I'd crack *unless my convictions were strong
enough to sustain me.*'

Her now speechless parent gazed at her in consternation.

'So,' she continued, speaking slowly and very carefully,
'Stephanie's may be, but I doubt it. The core of all her opposi-
tion since she was a little girl has been an inner consciousness of
her inadequacies as a Lorme, so she has turned another way.
She found religion too hard, remember? She turned from that
to women's suffrage, because she was in close proximity to an
older woman who already burned for what was *her* umpteenth
"cause" – a woman moreover who was in exactly like case, an
ugly duckling! The root of all this lies in the fact that Stephanie
is unable to compete with Lorme beauty, grace and
talent.'

'Omigod! I beg your pardon,' Charles exclaimed, by now
quite bewildered. 'You do not talk at all like a young girl.
Where do you get such notions from I would like to know?
Certainly not from me.'

She twinkled at him, 'Don't be naughty, Daddy, you know
well enough you were a bit of a rebel and a free thinker in your
day. I *do* get it from you. Remember I have also had the most
wonderful privilege while growing up. Besides you and my
brother I had Grumpy.'[3] She said this as if she had possessed
the Elixir of life in him.

'And what in the world a rakeshell of an old self-indulgent
had in common with a slip of a chit like you beats all imagining!' Charles exclaimed.

'We understood each other,' she told him equably. 'We
always did. I saw in him that extra something which inspires
men. Well women *can* be inspired too! Grumpy was *enormous*.
He was larger than life, bigger than anyone I have ever met,
wise too, under that naughty, exhibitionist exterior. We talked,
Daddy, and from as far back as I can remember, I asked him
difficult things. He always explained. He never put me off with

[3] The late Lord Aynthorp; see *The Lormes of Castle Rising*.

nonsense. I can remember even when I was tiny, Grumpy and I went riding and I asked him this and that and he always gave me answers with such wisdom and patience and humour that he was my lesson in life, my life class if you like, better than anything all those stupid governesses tried to pump into me with their silly blackboards and their rotten Mrs Markham's *History of England*. When I told Grumpy what I had learned he took hold of the dull old facts and gave them life for me. He roamed down the corridors of history for my instruction in such a way that I never knew I was being instructed. You need not be jealous! How I loved him was quite apart from how I love you and you have your own place. It, too, is "special". Grumpy just turned me inside-out and made me feel frightful if I had ever done anything "cheap" or "below the salt" as he used to call it.'

The unusual tears were glistening now, 'I miss him. He would have seen what I see in this Stephanie problem. As things are none of us knows, and we can only wait and see.' Thus did she unknowingly reiterate the words of the two old Lorme ladies.

While Gyles was sitting in her first floor drawing room with Lady Constance, Henry was staring somewhat abstractedly into the fire. Eventually Mr Truslove terminated his subdued conversation with Ninian and got to his feet.

'Well, gentlemen,' he announced, 'I will be getting along if you have nothing further for this evening.' He hesitated, then addressed himself to Sinclair.

'I would respectfully submit, Mr Delahaye, that there is much to be said for leaving the matter until the morning and attempting in the interim to obtain a good night's sleep. Also I will bid you good night.' So saying he gathered up his shabby Gladstone bag and his gloves, and addressed himself to no one in particular, 'I fancy a brisk walk before dinner so I shall cross the Park on foot.'

Ninian jumped up, 'Capital thought, sir,' he said eagerly. 'I will come with you. Coming, Hen? We need a breath of air in our lungs, even if its only London air . . . It'll be a positive relief to stretch our legs . . .' he paused, hesitated and looked at Sinclair, 'will you mind, sir, if we cut along for half an hour?'

Sinclair shook his head, 'Go on with you, I'll stay here quietly until your father returns,' he added with a pathetic attempt at a smile – 'I am somewhat anxious to hear what he has to say as you may imagine.'

'I think it's a rotten shame,' Ninian confided to his older brother as they ran down the stairs, 'poor old Uncle Sinclair seems absolutely done in . . .'

'Yes,' Henry answered him abstractedly his mind clearly upon other matters. 'I say Mr Truslove,' as the little man drew level with them, 'would it have to be such a personalized appeal as you outlined up there to my father? I mean, couldn't you, with your influence, do it all before we got back into court? I dunno what you do do, sir, but it always seems a flamin' miracle; if you could get at the old beak about Steph' being under age isn't there a way Sinclair could take the load . . .?'

They came out into Dover Street as the last of the lamp-lighters cycled past carrying his long pole. The street lamps shone on the wet pavement, for it had rained in the afternoon and there had been insufficient wind to dry them. Now everything seemed curiously burnished by it. It made the windows sparkle; it shone on the silk hats of the men coming in and out of chambers; it lit on the flanks of the steaming horses and reflected the lamplight in the turning wheels of cabs and carriages and broughams.

'Let's cut down here Hen,' suggested Ninian turning left-wards, 'then we can get clear across into St James' and stretch ourselves.'

'Well now,' Mr Truslove admitted a trifle breathlessly, beginning to trot in order to keep abreast of his young clients, 'I will admit my own mind has been running along some such lines. If we were to proceed a little more slowly for a while, Mr Henry, it is possible I might be able to cast a little light upon the matter; but young sirs, it must be under the seal of confidence you understand. I would not like to mislead such anxious men as your father and your uncle before I have given myself time to reflect and indeed act upon my reflections,' with customary caution he added, 'if any.'

Typically, when he had explained himself, pacing sedately

between the two tall boys, he looked up at the younger with his acute bird-like glance and inquired in masterly exemplification of the *non sequitur*, 'Mr Ninian, if I may be so bold young sir, to what fortunate circumstance do we owe your presence in term time I would be very relieved to know?'

'Oh that's alright,' Ninian reassured him, 'I got leave of absence, sir, for Hen's twenty-first. Then m' father let me stay for the, er, meet and it's more or less dragged on . . . m' father's talked to the beak sir, it's all accordin' to Hoyle – I swear it is!'

Which was a little more than the *modus operandi* was which Mr Truslove had worked out for himself. When he left the two boys and returned to his family he was in abstracted mood throughout their 'domestic' dinner. He carved, as usual; but his mind was not on his work. He rose as usual when his wife, two daughters and younger son left the heavy, mahogany-furnished dining room with its scarlet merino curtains and its silver-laden sideboard.

Once alone with his port, unable on this occasion to confer with his son and junior partner, the old Pelican allowed his mind to peck away at the problem undisturbed. When at length he pushed back his chair, returned the port decanter to its cupboard and extinguished the lights, he was not unduly surprised that his family had retired for the night. They were accustomed to noting signs and portents. In their own fashion they were as sensitive to them as the Lormes were to the human barometer who headed their house. 'Your father is thinking,' was a familiar phrase upon the lips of the astonishingly large female whom little Mr Truslove had taken to wife. With the beginning of autumn encroaching upon her years, Mrs Truslove had developed dewlaps. These were the seismograph to which her small brood responded. When her dewlaps quivered, she resembled nothing more than an agitated turkey hen clucking her brood around her because she took a whiff of fox upon the wind.

Tip-toeing, the little family lit its candles and trod aloft. When young Truslove put his key in the door Mama was leaning over the banister rail. She put a warning finger to her lips, inclined her head downwards and towards the dining room and mouthed 'shussh' and 'thinking' to her attenuated son who was harmlessly returning from the somewhat protracted courtship of the lady of his choice.

Mr Truslove encountered him as he lit his candle. He stepped into the hallway, said 'Ahah', inquired, 'How is Miss Amelia? Flourishing I trust?' To which his son nodded sparingly.

'Then perhaps you would be so good as to step this way, yes?' Then together they returned to the dining room and relit one small candle.

The ensuing days hung heavily. Gyles decided there was little purpose in his staying in London for the remainder of Stephanie's seven days' remand. So he returned to Essex following the hearse upon its dismal journey. He attended the simple ceremony in the village church, noting with appreciation the presence of every available man of his family. Bishop Alaric knelt as a mere member of the congregation. His Dorothy sat within the Castle as did all the women of the Family and presently the dreary words of Christian interment were being spoken over the open grave. Gyles thought rebelliously, as he stood, head bent,

'I will *not* submit to this when my time comes! The body is a vessel which is vacated once its purpose is fulfilled. It is no more than an unwanted garment! I think it a discourtesy to our creator to leave it for worms to feed upon. Mine shall be disposed of tidily, and with speed, for by that time I will be fully housed elsewhere,' and so thinking, obediently, if only by reason of long habit, he made the sign of the cross with his black gloved hand and turned away from the graveside.

In the late afternoon, as the spring sunshine was fading, Henry and Petula went down to the stables, stealthily and very conscious of the wrong that they were doing. 'If Grandmama should see us,' Henry thought guiltily, creeping along by the topiary, holding Petula's hand.

Grandmama was in fact at the windows once again. She saw them very clearly. She saw Plum amble from his den, and very gently she eased open a casement in order to hear the faint clatter of the cobbles which bespoke the horses being led out. Then she was rewarded by a final glimpse of the two young things as they walked their mounts cautiously towards the home park and the hills beyond. Her sad, old face was lit by a gentle little smile as she turned away and closed the casement up again.

'I had better order some crumpets for their tea,' she decided, pulling the bell.

It was too damp for them to lie across the rim of the saddleback and look down upon the farms and fields which would one day belong to them and be dominated by their rule. So they walked the mares very slowly instead, speaking little, content just to be together again. Even with their resilience they were still slightly dazed by the speed with which all these grim events had come upon them.

After a while speech began to flow between them more freely. Petula told him what she had said to her father, and he in turn gave her his report on what had occurred in London. In conclusion he said, rumpling his copper head with that familiar gesture,

'Pet, we're too close and it's all too soon. But y'know things do tend to go in threes. After,' he paused, rallied and went on, 'after the perfection of my twenty-first we had three thunderin' wallops. The old octogenarian, this thing with Steph' and now Aunt Prue's dead too. There I think it will rest and we shall get a bit of respite for a while. Old Truslove's got something up his sleeve and you have good reason to know, as I have, what a wily old bird he is. I think we shall come about. And when we do,' he half turned in the saddle and looked down at her, 'then my darling, we will be wed.'

Her face clouded.

'You cannot marry me,' she said firmly, 'for a year after your grandfather's death. It would be . . . revolutionary. And besides, I couldn't. I loved Grumpy far too much to set convention aside for my own ends concerning him. We will wait, and it will be all the sweeter for it. It will be next spring Henry, no, not next spring, June! I have always wanted to be a June bride. And I want to be married here, in the chapel, where Grumpy will be with us . . . can we do that?'

Her voice went on dreamily, 'I want to walk to church on my father's arm. I want to wear white. I want all my friends and family about me. I do not want a big London wedding, of course, it would not be at all the same; but I do want a big reception here, and André to make my cake. André is very down in the dumps at the moment. No one can even taste his food, poor lamb. How would it be if we went down to see him after tea and asked him if he could begin to make a few designs for us and for the buffet and everything? It would give him an interest, don't you think?'

Henry nodded, groping for the right words.

'And then I shall take you away from everyone and we will go to Italy together, and then to Greece. After that we will visit the lakes of Sirinaga and pick water-lilies from among the golden carp and sleep on a houseboat, on waters which are blue at dawning, blue with the lilies of those fabulous lakes.' Thus they dreamed together.

In Holloway it was the fourth day of Stephanie's remand.

On the fifth day Nanny took a hand in affairs and went bumbling resolutely on her little buttoned boots to the door of Christine's sanctum. Nanny scratched upon it, waited with some impatience and eventually receiving no reply she just thrust her head around the aperture and inquired somewhat hoarsely, 'Madam, may I please come in?'

Christine admitted her, gave her a high-backed chair, dismissed Pearson and wondered what on earth this abrupt visitation presaged.

Nanny came straight to the point.

'Madam,' she began. 'My lady I mean, can I have a new room ready for Miss Stephanie in two days? Quite new, madam. Plain but tasty, with 'er religious books but pretty. They tell me that George can hang a pretty piece of wallpaper if called upon and I have found one with little garlands on, all young girls and boys in pretty costume. Please madam, the girl will be ill past our imagining. Miss Henrietta is collapsed. There's only us, and we must see the setting is right for that poor girl's recovery if so be such is possible.'

'But Nanny,' Christine expostulated, 'how do we know that Miss Stephanie will be coming home at all?'

'Me corns,' said Nanny solemnly, 'they never fail me, me corns is throbbing the way they allus do for an unexpected arrival.'

Try as she would Christine choked a little at this but managed to camouflage it with her pocket handkerchief.

'Your corns, you say Nanny?'

'Yes, my lady. Now I'll do everything and Mrs Peace will lend an 'and and if we can just have your permission we can give that ornery lass a new environment to come home to I can promise you.'

Christine reflected. After all it could do no harm! It would give the staff something to think about. It would serve to draw their attention away from all this endless speculation. So why not?

'Of course, Nanny, anything you wish,' she then agreed. 'Will you use the same room or another?'

Nanny cast a glance at her employer out of one beady eye. She was manifestly nervous as the plaiting and unplaiting of her knotted fingers now disclosed. 'Well now, my lady,' she said hesitantly, 'I thought as how Miss Prudence's room would suit us best for the purpose we have in mind.'

'Oh,' exclaimed Christine, 'Oh Nanny!'

Nanny sat quite still.

'You mean because Miss Stephanie cared for her?'

'That's right, my lady!'

Christine sighed deeply. 'She will probably be very ill, if she does come back at all. But go ahead Nanny, it cannot do any harm, and just concentrate on the fact that the rooms may have to be used by a professional nurse too, if they are used at all.'

On the sixth day, Ninian, to his flaming indignation, was sent back to Harrow. He calmed down somewhat after a thirty minute session with his father; but was still angry and frustrated as he flung cricket boots and books and clothing about in shocking disarray, informing Henry during the creation of an appalling mess that he was to go to London with them in the Royce and then be driven to School, not by Gyles but by

Simkins. 'And the only consolation in *that*,' he wound up dolorously, 'is that Simkins lets me smoke. Admittedly the chap only has gaspers but he'll probably let me stop and buy some Turks,' after which he touched his brother for a 'fiver' and to his own undying astonishment received a further 'tenner' from his papa by what must have been, as he confided to Simkins 'a demmed fortuitous oversight', as they sipped an amicable pint together, well outside 'bounds' but well on the way towards Harrow and what Ninian spoke of bitterly as his forth-coming immolation in his 'male Holloway'.

Henry and his father returned to Browns'.

At her own request an extremely elegant note, folded into the fashionable 'wafer' and sealed with her own crest, was brought by Lady Constance's footman to Brown's'. It asked that Lord Aynthorp permit her to call upon him with her Aunt on the way to a 'committee meeting'.

'In the hope of which my aunt and I will send word to your rooms when we arrive.'

The message came. Gyles descended immediately, and found the Countess and her niece standing contemplating the Nottingham lace drapes and the veiled traffic beyond the shrouded windows. The aunt, after inclining her head in acknowledgement of their introduction withdrew a few paces to a further window and Lady Constance, somewhat flushed at the older woman's chilly acknowledgement explained ruefully, 'She insisted upon chaperoning me. She knows of your predicament, and while she is in sympathy with you, having me to contend with in her own family, she resents being seen with me, lest by inference she were included in my – er activities.'

Gyles smiled back reassuringly.

'I do not imagine anyone would so construe her being in your company, Lady Constance,' he assured her with some amusement, turning a moment to study the uncompromising side-view, the frigid profile and the general emanation of utter disapproval which surrounded the Countess like an aura. He hesitated.

'Could I not suggest we seat ourselves?'

Lady Constance glanced again at her aunt.

'We are on our way to a meeting for the rehabilitation of Fallen Women,' she explained hurriedly. 'I would not wish to delay my aunt longer than is necessary, so let us remain standing if you please. I only have this to say to you. I have already, through the good offices of Mr Truslove, obtained permission to see your neice in the cells tomorrow morning after she has been returned to Bow Street. I have reason to believe that what I have to say to her may, after her experiences in the past week, persuade her to remain silent when she is brought into the dock. That is all. But I would, with the greatest respect suggest, Lord Aynthorp, that thereafter you leave the child to her parents if so be you are given the opportunity.' So saying she gave him a formal little bow, tucked her gloved hands back into the muff which dangled from one wrist and said quietly, 'I am ready Aunt. Lord Aynthorp and I have said all that needs to be said.'

In another moment Gyles found himself alone. He stood in his formal clothing on the bright red turkey carpet framed by the heavy red and gold swagged drapes which looped and convoluted across those flounces of Nottingham lace veiling the windows. He was on his way out of the Hotel to dine at his club. His hat, cane, gloves and evening newspaper lay neatly across one plush upholstered chair. Potted palms in great profusion sprouted from marble pedestals. From the stairway two large Negroes stood in perpetual poise for flight, wearing a crown of gas brackets and globes upon their black curly heads. Portraits in oils of bewhiskered Victorian gentlemen and bustled Victorian ladies looked down from their huge and heavy frames. Into this epitome of restraint, this Mecca of discretion, Gyles said loudly, 'I said precisely nothing . . . however . . . !' and turning with a shrug, picked up his impedimenta and walked swiftly from the room.

Henry dined with young Danement. His future brother-in-law had proposed himself, saying,

'Why not take a chop with me, Hen? I happen to be in Town. I am supposed to be goin' on to the Cavendish Ball, but that's as maybe. I could dress later. Supposin' I was to pick yer up around seven thirty we could go to some quiet little place in Soho and then perhaps look in for an hour at the Empire.'

After the past few days the prospect was very tempting. Henry realized there was nothing more which could be done until the morning. A casual glance at the evening papers settled the matter. Marie Lloyd and Albert Chevalier were both on the Empire bill and such earthy temptations were irresistible! So at seven thirty, in black tie he presented himself at a crony's rooms where young Charles was staying, and in due course the pair strolled off together into Piccadilly.

Outside the Ritz a few cars and carriages were debouching residents who swept across the covered pavement still wearing their day apparel and prior to dressing for their various evening's entertainments. The horsedrawn buses rumbled by declaring their devotion to *Cadbury's Cocoa, Allen's Malvern Ales* and *C. J. Eveson's Coals*, on the hoardings across the sides and down their stair heads. The spring air was not yet mild and March showed every promise – having come in like a lamb – of reversing itself and going out like a roaring lion; so the two young men hailed a Hansom cab and 'Where to, guv'nor?' wheezed the cab driver.

'Rules, cabby and make it sharp,' Henry replied closing the cab front upon himself and his companion. 'I fancy a dozen or so of best Whitstables,' he confided in young Charles as they bowled towards Eros where the old women were still at their baskets – straw hats tipped rakishly over their beery old faces, shawls drawn tightly across their shoulders against the rising wind. This came in gusts down Shaftesbury Avenue and whipped errant strands of paper against the bare feet and ankles of the crossing sweepers. Over their heads a banner fluttered proclaiming '*Creme Simon Is Best, to Ladies*': – *all the most beautiful women use Creme Simon* . . . Charles reached up and prodded the cabby with the silver top of his black cane.

'Hold hard, cabby, we need buttonholes,' he shouted. The cabby eased up, none too gently, Charles leaped out and was soon back with his two penny carnations, one of which he passed to Henry. The other he already sported in his button hole, having submitted to the flower 'gal's' lusty badinage as she pinned it in position.

'Bawdy old beldames, ain't they?' he observed cheerfully as the cab swayed back into motion.

'Rules is it now, young gentlemen?' inquired the resigned cabby.

'Yes, Rules. Sharp as you like cabby I fancy a glass or two of the Widow, don't you, Hen?'

CHAPTER 5

Another New Cause

It was a perfect spring day. The daffodils bloomed in great golden companies over the greensward behind Rotten Row. Small armies of sentinel hyacinths marshalled them closely together behind their bordered regimentation. A chorus of bird song rose from the branches overhead where the trees unfurled their small, tightly-rolled flags of green in greeting to the sun. In the distance the waters of the Serpentine, glimpsed between the massed shrubs and trees, showed a disturbed and ruffled surface as cotillions of excited fowl skimmed fandangoes and shot to flight with an abrupt scuffling of the waters. They flew a little, sank back again, intoxicated by their own energies, and Henry reining in with his father watched them amusedly. The ride had cleared his head. He and his father, knowing what lay before them, in some degree at least, had ordered hacks to be brought round to them from the stables in Bruton Mews and thus at eight a.m. were taking a brief respite by the Serpentine before their return gallop back along the way that they had come.

It served its purpose. They passed few of their acquaintances and those few only acknowledged them with a brief lift of their crops. They returned to the Hotel and did justice to the admirable breakfast provided. Not so Sinclair. He had declined their invitation to join them. He complained of a headache, nibbled at a piece of dry toast, sipped in a desultory way at his coffee and withdrew behind his copy of *The Times*.

'There is something in here about Aunt Prudence,' he announced suddenly, 'I will read it to you!' He cleared his throat. 'It is headed "*In Memoriam*". It says "*The members of the Holloway Branch of Women's Suffrage deeply regret the*

passing of a loyal and selfless member of their Organization. The
Honble Prudence de Lorme was a tireless worker for the Cause
who, despite increasing ill-health gave of her utmost both in time
and money to that which she held to be a cause of unassailable
rightness. She will long be remembered by all her fellow workers.
Now her name joins the growing tally of martyrs to our Cause.
Signed, Members of the Holloway Branch etc.," and at the
bottom there was another signature, that of *Christabel*
Pankhurst.'

'Thank you, Sinclair,' said Gyles expressionlessly, 'Henry
pass the toast if you please.' If Sinclair had read that her
Majesty Queen Alexandra had suddenly embraced the cause of
women's suffrage, it is unlikely that Gyles would have made
any more colourful comment. The new Lord Aynthorp had
decided upon his chosen course of action. Come what might
upon this awful day he was determined to hold himself in
check as he had done so successfully throughout his father's
lifetime.

As ever, the irrepressible twinkle crept to the corners of
Henry's mouth; but he kept his eyes down and breakfast ran its
course uneventfully. Then Mr Truslove joined them and it
was time to go.

As they debouched from their cars, they encountered Lady
Constance on the steps. She was descending. To their surprise
she merely bowed, passed on and entered a waiting carriage.
Mr Truslove did an abrupt about turn and trotted after her.
He spoke with her a moment over the door of the carriage and
then stood hat in hand as it drew away from the kerbstone.

'Has her ladyship been rebuffed?' inquired Gyles as Mr
Truslove rejoined them.

'On the contrary,' said Mr Truslove. 'Her words to me were
"Mission accomplished, Mr Truslove, now you have no
further need of my presence". Then she drove away.'

After all the waiting, all the anticipation and all the frustration, the end came in so very brief a space of time as to leave
them bewildered as a flurry of geese after crossing a road
between an onrush of thundering hooves.

The name was called. Sinclair gripped his hands together.

Gyles sat with his hat tipped low over his Norman nose. Henry put up one hand to his head to rumple it and was quelled by a Truslove glance. *Stephanie Delahaye!* The bedraggled object, white as the linen bands worn by Counsel was propelled forward. The magistrate ruffled some papers. There was the proverbial silence in court, unbroken by even a cough. Then Sir Willoughby Passmore began to speak.

'It has been brought to my notice that you are a young person of some social status in this world of ours. It has also been indicated to me that you are not old enough to plead, being, according to my information, three days short of your seventeenth birthday. You will therefore now tell the court that this is so by saying either "yes", or "no", and nothing more.'

He waited. The whispered "Yes", was barely audible, but he seemed content.

'Therefore,' he resumed in his dry, old voice, as his fine hands folded themselves together and his hooded face fixed its hooded gaze upon her. 'Therefore,' he repeated, 'it does not come within the compass of my office to inquire of you whether you plead guilty or not guilty to the charge which has been incompetently brought against you.'

At this last Stephanie's head came up in incredulous astonishment. Sir Willoughby resumed, 'I am not empowered to ask and you are not permitted to reply, for you are still a minor. As such you are not responsible for such acts as you now stand accused of – quite erroneously.'

The voice paused to allow time for the full import of his words to impress themselves upon all present. Then came a rustle around the press table, and a scuffle as several journalists bolted towards the door. Down came the gavel with a resounding thwang and . . .

'Any unseemly interruptions and I will have this court cleared instantly,' scolded Sir Willoughby. 'Gentlemen of the Press will remain seated until I have completed my findings. Those who have chosen to scamper unseemly away will be debarred from this court for seven days and furthermore will surrender themselves in contempt after this hearing.'

He then took a pause of some twenty seconds during which no one present even dared cross or uncross a leg. Then, to a frozen court the old voice began once more in quite a different tone.

'Is Mr Sinclair Clarendon de Courcy Delahaye in court this morning?' the voice asked conversationally.

Sinclair rose instantly.

'I am here your worship,' he said clearly.

'Then pray have the goodness to step into the witness box.' Before Sir Willoughby could complete his sentence Sinclair moved, very erect and brisk. So to the witness box the eminent judiciary now directed his hooded scrutiny. Then . . .

'You are the male parent of the prisoner?'

'I am, your worship.'

'Are you willing to concur with my decisions in the matter of this alleged offence?'

'Unquestioningly, your worship.'

'Then,' the tone was quite as brisk now as Sinclair's movements had been. 'I so direct that *you* shall be bound over in your own recognizances of one thousand pounds to undertake that your daughter Stephanie Marie' – he glanced an instant at the paper under one fine hand – 'de Courcy Delahaye shall abide in your house, adhere to your rulings, keep the peace in all manners and directions and on her behalf pledge that she will nevermore engage upon any such activities or associations *until she is of age*, when she shall be entitled to make her own decisions.'

Sinclair bent his head in silent acquiescence.

'I therefore further remind you that should you fail to so control and exert your restrictions upon your child it is you who will be held responsible in law. Should the court's attention be drawn to any misdemeanour by Stephanie Delahaye for the ensuing period of four years and three days it is you who will come before this court to furnish reasons why, as her male parent, you should not go to prison in the second division for a period of not less than six months. Case dismissed.'

Once the Court had officially pronounced its relinquishment of Stephanie, everyone from women warders to the policemen on the doors evinced their willingness to help.

The limp rag which was Sinclair's daughter was handed over

and helped into an anonymous, waiting cab. This had pre-viously been drawn up at the nearest point to the side entrance through which they were all led in order to avoid the waiting Press. With Henry and Sinclair supporting the girl and the rest of the men encircling them they progressed towards the cab unmolested. Then Stephanie was borne away, not to Browns', but to her late aunt's home where, to their combined astonish-ment the Lady Constance awaited them – in her nursing uniform. Here she assumed instant and total command saying only, 'Please give the child to me and I will see what can be done with her at this juncture.'

Instead of showing a proper reluctance the helpless men were only too thankful. They obediently 'handed over'. Henry and Sinclair carried the girl through to her room laid her upon the bed and were promptly dismissed with a hurried 'Please wait for me for a few moments. I will come to you as soon as possible.'

Helplessly, Sinclair paced the small withdrawing room, now at windows, playing with the dangling cord of a blind which Lady Constance had urged them to keep closed – 'Lest the Press happen to come this way and catch a glimpse of you!' and now perambulating between a table covered with braid and bobbles and the small fire in the hearth.

The rest of them, Gyles, Henry and the faithful Truslove sat about in attitudes of total discomfort, doing as they had been asked by a woman who, according to their dearest principles, was totally unacceptable.

Eventually, after a long silence, broken only by the sound of doors opening and closing and the soft flurry of fast-moving footsteps, Mr Truslove cleared his throat, preparatory to embarking upon a proposal which he indicated by his attitude was one which he did not relish.

'Ahem,' said he, stroking his beak as if to derive some solace from this action. 'Ahem! It is incumbent upon me,' he man-aged eventually to extract from himself, 'to endeavour, your lordship and gentlemen, to put forward a proposal which on the face of it is, er, monstrous.'

Gyles looked up expressionless.

'Monstrous?' he inquired.

'Yes, your lordship.'

'And in what particular would that vary from the tenor of the past few days?' Gyles asked with a certain irony.

'Er, very little, your lordship, I agree. Oh, believe me, I do so entirely agree! but it is my duty, indeed my sole use to your family for me to advise, and, er, counsel, not to say attempt to persuade, if such a thing were possible.'

'What now?' Sinclair paused in his pacing, 'are there more shocks to come Truslove? for I am bound to tell you I do not think I can endure much more at this juncture.'

Mr Truslove tidied his feet into two little parallel lines, examined them intently and then spoke to them. 'Might I with all deference ask of you all one initial question?'

'Yes,' said Gyles shortly.

'Then it is this. Do you not consider that the Lady Constance has been the one person who has brought about a situation which is at least somewhat more tenable than any we could have encompassed?'

'Yes,' said Gyles again.

'Then, another question, IF you please.' He waited; but as no one spoke he asked it. 'Do you not think that Miss Stephanie is in a very sorry state?'

'Yes,' the monosyllable came a third time.

'And is it not *likely*, I put it no higher than that, that Lady Constance is the most suitable person to nurse Miss Stephanie back to some semblance of both physical and mental health?'

Somewhat remarkably, for Gyles showed by every muscle in his face that he had grasped the gist of Mr Truslove's diplomatic peckings, the head of the family did not erupt. Instead he said in a voice quite devoid of expression,

'I must presume Mr Truslove, to interrupt you at this point. I am not a fool. It is manifest to me what you are trying to elucidate. So may I put it into words for you?'

'Pray do, your lordship,' said Truslove miserably.

'You wish to propose that Lady Constance, in her capacity as nurse, is invited to the Castle to nurse Stephanie, as you said both physically and mentally, back to some semblance of health and sanity?'

'Exactly so,' Mr Truslove, eyes firmly fixed upon his little boots dredged the words up somehow.

'Then let us examine the facts.' Still Gyles spoke without heat. Henry, by now thoroughly alarmed at his parent's unexpected reaction eyed him with the greatest suspicion and unease.

'You are proposing that a notorious suffragette, nay, militant suffragette, albeit a gentlewoman, and therefore one who should know better, should be invited to *our home*, as she appears to be the one person who can exert any influence upon my niece?'

'Exactly so,' said Mr Truslove again, sounding as if someone were strangling him.

Gyles let the ensuing silence lie among them as if it were a corpse. He looked away into the middle distance, which gave him the somewhat unattractive wallpaper to study. Sinclair looked at Gyles. Henry looked at him. Mr Truslove seemed inexhaustibly fascinated by his boots.

'That Lady Constance is both intelligent and perceptive,' said Gyles at length, 'is indisputable. I therefore give you back a question. Do you regard it as within the bounds of possibility that she would agree to such a proposal?'

'I have no doubt of it.'

'And consent to so disguise herself in order that we could not be brought to total ruin –' Gyles paused, said again very coldly and dispassionately, 'total ruin,' he repeated thoughtfully and then went on, 'by being associated, *in our own Castle* with Women's Suffrage and all that it implies?'

Mr Truslove squirmed with misery. 'I do not believe she would consent otherwise.'

'And to whom goes the delightful responsibility of so inviting her? *without* benefit of my wife or the Dowager Lady Aynthorp's consent, nor come to it, that of the Countess, all of whom must be dragged down into this quagmire if it ever got about.'

Mr Truslove so pulled his beak that it seemed as if in his distress he was endeavouring to wrench it from the centre of his attenuated countenance. Seemingly this gave him courage, for sharply, he looked up now, met Gyles' chilly gaze and said with tremendous bravery, 'You, my lord.'

Henry sucked in breath as if someone had thumped him in his solar plexus.

Sinclair stopped short in his pacing and stared incredulously. Gyles nodded slowly.

'I . . . thought . . . as . . . much,' he said and it was all he said. He was on his feet immediately and the door opened and closed again behind him so abruptly that Sinclair had not even time to close his astonished mouth when they were without the dubious benefit of Gyles', in this case, quite terrifying presence.

If he had erupted they would have felt easier. If he had poured invective upon Mr Truslove's bent head, or if he had turned and rent Sinclair for getting such a cocatrice . . . *anything* would have been less intimidating than this icy calm and the total refusal to communicate his thoughts.

'God's Boots!' said Henry sepulchrally. Sinclair clicked his tongue and resumed his pacing. Mr Truslove looked at the young man with pained reproach. Then they waited, and waited . . .

They waited so long that Henry's stomach began sending him appealing messages concerning the urgency of food. Finally Gyles reappeared in the doorway for just long enough to hand Henry a telegraph form, together with a sovereign and the request that he go round to the nearest post office and despatch the telegram immediately. 'Take the car and don't dawdle.' Then he was gone again and the door once more closed behind him.

Of course Henry read the telegram. He was confident his father would have expected him so to do. It said *Prepare isolated suite for Stephanie and nurse. Arrange for all meals to be served in situ. Child's condition demands absolute privacy and quiet. Expect us before dinner. Coup de foudre ended in damp squib. Could make legal history but child really ill. Keep Henrietta away. Love Gyles.* It was in French otherwise the contents would have been known to all adjacent villages in a very short time.

Henry stood not upon the order of his going, but delayed his coming back sufficiently to buy a small churn of milk from an astonished milkman on his afternoon rounds and a bag of buns

from an adjacent A.B.C. The buns were very new and exces-
sively full of currants. He ate two on the return journey, drank
all the milk and walked up the steps with the little churn and
his father's change in one hand, the remaining nine buns in a
paper bag and one between his teeth.

He had not expected Gyles to open the front door. His
father's expression made Henry choke on the last mouthful of
bun.

When he had spluttered his way into the withdrawing room
all he could manage weakly was, 'Sorry sir, here's your change.
I was starving and I owe you sevenpence for buns.'

A sudden flash of laughter lit Gyles eyes, the corners of his
mouth quivered.

'Can I have one?' he asked holding out one elegant hand,
'I'm starving too. Let us see if Mr Truslove will welcome a
bun.'

Thus the other two men saw them. Sinclair took out a
pocket handkerchief and wiped his forehead.

'Incomprehensible!' he exclaimed regarding them as if they
were an affront.

'Not at all,' Gyles replied blandly, 'have a bun, old boy, you
will feel better!' Sinclair shook his head shudderingly.

Mr Truslove took one observing, 'Very fortuitous, thank you
very much.'

Henry excavated his fourth bun from the bag, set it upon a
needlepoint chair, covered it with a handkerchief and sat
on it.

'Wh- wh- what's that you're doing?' demanded Sinclair so
overwrought now his eyes were almost starting from his head.

'Like the elephant,' said Henry, 'makes 'em go further.' He
turned to his father, now perfectly at his ease again. 'You see,
sir, it was a book, in the nursery. About Edward a red teddy
bear and his friend the elephant. They ran away. They only
had sixpence. So they spent it on thirteen currant buns like
these. When they had got a little way down the road they felt
hungry, like me,' he sat on another bun. 'So,' he returned to his
tale, 'they stopped and ate buns, then they went on and got
hungry again; but when they looked in the bag there was only
one left so the elephant had a spiffing idea. He said, "Put it

under my behind which will squash it very flat and make it go further". Well it does you know, sir, and it squashes all the currants which makes 'em taste better.'

It was too much for Mr Truslove. He began to laugh, a little shrill tee-hee-ing sound which he was totally unable to control. He went on laughing. The tears began to run down his face, and still he laughed. This was so unexpected and so contagious that Henry began laughing too, until at length Gyles joined in and the three of them were still laughing, and wiping their streaming eyes, watched in total bewilderment by the distraught Sinclair, when the door opened and Lady Constance appeared.

As the men rose to their feet, 'Forgive me for interrupting your luncheon,' she said coolly, 'but the patient is now ready, so we can leave whenever it is convenient to you, Lord Aynthorp.' She had drawn her hair back tightly under her white cap. She had also acquired a pair of steel-rimmed spectacles.

CHAPTER 6

Sinclair's Hair Shirt

The weeks now slipped by in comparative quiet, for which the Family was profoundly thankful. Being doubly in mourning it was implicit that no-one would call, nor expect any calls from the Lormes. For a year from the death of Justin Lord Aynthorp the Family would automatically opt out of Society. It was normal procedure.

At first Stephanie remained immolated in her remote quarters. For a while she was critically ill. Not only had shock and exhaustion levied a heavy toll, but her hand, through neglect during her week on remand, had become poisoned. Septicaemia had resulted and for a while the girl's life hung in the balance.

The family doctor, who had learned better than to evince even a grunt of surprise at any Lorme happenings, was at the Castle two and even three times a day. At one point he remained the whole night; during which Sinclair, with Gyles and Henry in support, punished brandy in the gun room and sat waiting restlessly for The Worst – as the occupants of the servants' hall described the crisis. The only comment Doctor Jamieson made was when he came wearily into the gun room as the spring sunshine touched the rim of the gardens; sank into a shabby leather armchair and vouchsafed, stretching a grateful hand for a glass of brandy which Gyles held out to him, 'She's turned the corner, now youth will do the rest; but that Nurse is really a most remarkable woman!' He sipped the brandy, then looked up in surprise as Sinclair turned tail and bolted.

'That's all right, old chap,' Gyles reassured him, 'he's gone to tell the gel's mother.'

Declining Gyles' offer of bed and bath the doctor took himself off, promising to return later.

March gave place to April. On the last day of the month, when the grounds were still bright with the swaying heads of late daffodils, the home park flooded with great swathes of their gold and the china white of narcissi, Gyles tucked his wife's arm resolutely inside his own and led her down the drive. In the meantime he had managed to indulge in a protracted session with their head gardener Sawbridge. During this, Gyles had outlined his intentions concerning the super-abundance of hot house fruits and his determination to add a further stove-house to the present assembly. Then he made a direct request, that Sawbridge bring all his well-known skills to bear upon increasing the production of out-of-season strawberries for sale to the great hotels and restaurants of London. At first Sawbridge was horrified, then Christine joined them, and, perceiving which way the wind blew, took a hand. She pointed out gently.

'You see, his lordship's chief concern is for the future, Sawbridge. With the excessive and ruinous death duties which he has to meet since the death of his dear, late lordship, we are both absolutely determined to anticipate any further encroachments in the matter of taxes and similar governmental impositions so that we may ensure we shall never have to dismiss any members of our outdoor, or indoor staff, even supposing that matters become graver than they are at present. The more the estate can be made to pay its way in these extremely difficult times, the greater the safety of employment for everyone concerned.'

This little display of arch-diplomacy not only turned the tide completely in Lorme favour but also served as a talking point throughout the villages. ' 'Is lordship is allus thinking of 'is staff,' became a theme amongst them, which, as Gyles remarked thankfully, 'Strengthens my arm as nothing else could have done.'

Then came the opportunity for their first real foray into the grounds. Stephanie was by now convalescing. There was even talk of moving her to her new quarters – the now completely redecorated rooms previously occupied by her late Aunt Prudence which had not proved suitable while she was critically ill.

In this felicitous serenity Gyles and his Christine crossed the main drive, skirted the paddock and stabling and thus came, via the Urn Garden and the Pleasaunce, to the back of their Castle.

At length they reached the bridge which spanned the river at the point where the grounds had been transformed – in the days of Capability Brown – into a vast upward sweep of sward studded with rare, flowering *prunus* which rolled to a summit on which reposed a stone folly of no excessive beauty but of great value, as Gyles was at some pains to remind his wife.

They performed an unenthusiastic circuit, examining it distressfully.

'The best we can say of this,' he mused as they completed this exercise, 'is that it has been here for some considerable time and has become an integral part of the landscape.' His eyes turned from it and rested upon Christine. She was dressed for walking in the country. A trim brown tweed suit displayed her slim figure to perfect advantage. Under her flowing skirt the wind enabled him to gain an occasional glimpse of well turned ankles in their small brown boots. On her head reposed a most fetching fur beret from which a tiny curl had escaped. The wind had flushed her cheeks in a manner most becoming.

' 'Pon my soul, Christine,' Gyles exclaimed, 'I am bound to say you do not look a day over eighteen. How lovely you are, my love.' They smiled at one another then he took her hand and led her down the long, gradual slope on the farther side of the disparaged ornament.

'What I have in mind,' he explained, 'is now made manifest. See how a quirk of nature – one which had first gained Henri de Lorme's profound approval when he came ridin' through what was then a dense forest nine hundred years ago – has bent the river almost double upon its course just here, and then see how it comes round again to meet us in the second hollow. See, too, my love, how the water encloses us as in a peninsula,'

Gyles indicated by waving his stick at the long protruding tongue of grassland.

'I admit it is enormous for our present requirements, but over there,' again his stick lifted to point the direction, 'across the river's bent elbow lies Lower Aynthorp Lane which as you know becomes in turn the way to Little Aynthorp Station. If we were to cut a road from the lane to the river's edge and bridge the water there I believe it might have great appeal, provided we chose the design wisely. We would then have ample room on the farther side for the tetherin' of horses, and the accommodation of drays, carts, gigs and carriages. Then from here,' he thumped the ground to which they had descended, 'if we levelled off a bit of the risin' ground behind us, we could erect a Palladian structure to house our public "treasures." I also think that on this, the approach side, we should construct a wide, shallow rise of steps with, perhaps, an ornamental balustrade to give it distinction and thus strike awe and admiration among our rustic visitors.'

Christine laughed. 'If we were to widen the shallow steps in their descent,' she twinkled, 'and so construct the balustrade that it curved round to enclose, as it were, a wing of ground on either side we could perhaps erect two fountains in two stone pools. Oh, Gyles, I think this is absolutely right, my darling, but do let me have my pools and fountains! Think how charming they would look with perhaps some golden carp swimming about – we could perfectly well spare some from the Great Lake.'

'Why not,' he agreed, his eyes warm as he watched her vivid little face.

'Well then,' she concurred, 'I shall like it all tremendously. I can see it completed already. You have been so very wise – as you are always – for it will be completely hidden from the Castle unless we fail to level off sufficient of the present height. Yet it will still be manifestly a part of it – the best part in terms of landscaping – for it will come upon people as another element of surprise; yet the road frontage will make it perfectly advantageous for our visitors.' She broke off, and small gloved finger to lip frowned slightly as she looked about her.

'Where will you site the proposed Tea House? and the, er, washing and other facilities? I assume they will be separate ones for men and for women?'

Gyles looked slightly crestfallen. He removed his monocle, as always when caught off-balance, polished it assiduously, replaced it and smiled ruefully.

'There you have me,' he admitted, 'I had quite forgotten ... well now ... let us see ... How would it be if we laid out a zig zag in topiary leading from the side of the Museum? No one *on either side* with the front zig being an entrance and the back zag an exit for both the males and females? Then while we might be able to indicate the twin presences with some very modest sign, neither need to be crudely apparent ...?'

They spent a wholly absorbing afternoon. Within a week Gyles and Henry were closeted in the former's old office, which he had flatly refused to relinquish in his assumption of the title. Here they conferred with their chosen architect, a man who would most certainly have drawn down the maximum of invective upon his luckless, flowing locks from Gyles' irascible papa. Gyles thought as much while watching him. Claude Challoner suffered externally through his internal eagerness to be seen as a man of unquestioned artistic bent – as it were, on sight. In his black velveteens, with loose silk shirt and floppy silk tie he more resembled a student out of *Trilby* than a sound and reputable architect; but Gyles having seen a considerable amount of Challoner's work was able to overlook such irritants. With a slight smile Gyles recalled his intolerant Papa's comment upon the 'artistic temperament'. This, the late peer had defined as 'a disinclination for work and a rooted objection to soap and water'. However, as the designs were right and so was the estimate, Gyles ordered full steam ahead and turned to other matters.

At this juncture the indomitable little Dowager and her sister-in-law Marguerite took a hand in the affair and were to be seen thereafter trotting about the lesser-used rooms and even rooting about in some of the more accessible attics, trailing an escort of clucking Sawby and attendant footmen who began these forays empty-handed and ended up like extraordinary beasts of burden, staggering under the weight of ancient chests and curious boxes. These men were harassed, too, in the matter of 'paintings-which-could-be-spared', a subject upon which Family opinion had to be taken. Ergo, the White Ballroom became the room designate for 'viewing' despite the fact that this had last been used for the famous fancy dress ball at which Henry had finally gained Petula's permission to slip his engagement ring upon her finger.

In this healthy counter-irritant to mourning and now that Stephanie was well on the way to complete recovery and had even been permitted to take a little walk on the arm of her nurse, her reabsorption into Family life was made less awkward as it had been contrived to appear in some degree quite casual. Henry, for an example, encountered the girl leaning upon the nurse's arm as he dashed through the garden door on to the South Terrace. He was tearing towards his father's office and only paused to rumple his copper head and say, 'Oh, hello Steph'. Good to see you about again, hope to see you at tea,' and dashed on, the ice broken – for him.

The Dowager and the little Countess made delicately arranged 'accidental' first encounters too. With complete naturalness, which was in fact exquisitely contrived, they too played a casual hand, as did the rest of them and were received, to their utter astonishment with wan smiles and seeming gratitude from the frail, white-faced young woman. For so she had become. She had also permitted Mrs Pearce – most astonishing feat to all the family – to dress her hair becomingly, though none knew how the austere and skirt-rustling House-keeper had achieved this miracle. Suffice that with *châtelaine* clinking, her own hair dressed as ever in remarkable simulation of a sweet which baby Rupert clamoured for from the village shop and very rarely obtained, one known as a 'whipped cream walnut'; she whisked into Stephanie's rooms and whisked out again without vouchsafing anything. Her mein, as ever, defied the burning desires of all the upper servants to question her.

All this was so felicitous that no one, not even the Dowager had observed that Sinclair was becoming more and more harassed and stooped. He now started, when addressed unexpectedly. He fidgeted with his hands and generally evinced

all the outward signs of extreme nervous tension. Whereas
Henrietta was putting on weight. She had previously become
sadly attenuated. Her hair now shone with health too, while
her expression in repose was only this side of sheer rapture.
She was revelling in the sudden metamorphosis of her awkward
daughter from a cold, unapproachable creature into a doting
daughter, one who was ever willing to perform small duties,
comply and be in all ways a most delightful person. Only
Sinclair suffered and had Lady Prudence been about she at
least would have spotted what was going on.

Stephanie's seeming regeneration was merely reaction in
character. She was unchanged. Certainly she had undergone a,
to her, horrifying experience; but, and here lay the ineradicable
part, *she had experienced the inside of a prison*. Therefore she
knew, or foolishly imagined she knew, all there was to know
about prisons. So, the fact that her own Papa, whom she had
hitherto thought cared not a whit for her – save in the matter of
social compliance and decorum – had secretly, through the
years, so loved his erring Stephanie that when she deliberately
brought disaster, not only upon the family but *primarily* upon
him by what she had done, he had accepted this cross and
deliberately, heroically immolated himself upon it! There was
no end to the sheer hysterical nonsense which ran around inside
her foolish head. Papa was a martyr. Papa had made The
Ultimate Sacrifice for his wicked daughter. Papa had put himself within the grasp of the law, sworn away four years of his
life – in which the slightest wrong-doing by his daughter would
result in his total degradation – and, oh dreadful, unbearable
thought! six months imprisonment if she so much as strayed a
footfall from the straight and narrow as defined by that Awful
Judge Person. That evil, cruel man!

Ergo again; Papa was a Saint, an Early Christian Martyr who
went serenely (did she but know the truth!) about his daily life
with the Sword of Damocles poised above his haloed head.
This inevitably resulted in Stephanie resolving to protect Papa
from every possible danger, real or imaginary. She prayed for
him, as was to be expected and this in itself was harmless
enough; but she also sought, as her health improved, to protect
him from himself, from her, from every possible risk she could

imagine! As she recovered so Sinclair sank into a twitching wreck. Did Papa come down the staircase with a shade of his old briskness, Stephanie would be there exhorting him to 'take care dear Papa, walk more slowly lest you might slip and injure yourself'. Did he propose a canter to stir up his sluggish liver, she was beside him on the instant begging him to be restrained, probing into his nether garments to assure herself that he was 'properly wrapped up' and when, if he did manage to escape, he dismounted thereafter before the house, or in the paddock, or by the stables – no matter where, Stephanie, meanwhile dashing from upper window to upper window to mark his progress, would be there, panting and slightly breathless, some noxious brew in hand, coats and mufflers over her arm, in which to wrap and dose him lest he took harm from becoming over-heated.

At night in one of the drawing rooms he would stroll in from his port with the rest of the men and instantly Stephanie would be there with cushions, a footstool, or bending over him as she urged him to be seated, inquiring gently if he did not desire a rug over his knees . . . driving him quietly insane!

The agonizing part from his standpoint was that the aspect she presented by these fussings to the 'rest of 'em' was of a completely docile, thoughtful daughter. It brought smiles to their eyes and lips, benign little nods from their exquisitely dressed heads, grunts of approval from the men. Indeed everyone including the beatific-looking Henrietta – she who had been the family Niobe for so long now – was beginning to regard the Women's Suffrage Disaster in quite a different light and coming round towards believing it had been 'the making of Stephanie'; pipe-filler, cigar-lighter, hand-holder, and even head-stroker *extraordinary*. The tragedy was that Sinclair himself was a natural introvert. Time and again he tried to say something to his wife. Time and again he stammered, stumbled and what came out sounded precious like adverse criticism which was immediately cried down in no uncertain terms by his wife.

Stephanie had become Sinclair's hair shirt, one which chafed to the point when he thought he would become demented! She was, quite naturally, happier than she had ever dreamed possible, while suffering that bit of worry-spicing which made the whole affair so delicious. Watch Papa, take care of Papa, do not let Papa out of your sight, that was her ordering of herself. The wretched man took to tip-toeing out of his rooms and spending hours contemplating the family portraits in the Picture Gallery, the one place where so far Stephanie had failed to find him.

While this situation was developing inside the castle the deterioration in the King's health became widely known.

CHAPTER 7

Paradise Lost

The sun ...
  In dim eclipse disastrous twilight sheds
  On half the nations, and with fear of change
  Perplexes monarchs ...
                                   John Milton

As they strolled back towards the Castle for the ritual of afternoon tea, Gyles mentioned to Christine that the Court
Circular had reported the King's attendance at Covent Garden
on the previous evening for a performance of *Siegfried*. He
added that a friend to whom he had spoken that morning
remarked that 'the king was very wheezy' – adding almost under
his breath 'alas! poor "Tum-Tum"!'

They learned subsequently that the King had also insisted
upon making his customary journey from London to Sandring-
ham for the Friday to Tuesday; obstinately refusing to cancel
his equally standard Sunday inspection of the home-farm
during which he had been exposed to a biting wind. This had
penetrated his already only half-cleared lungs, impaired by his
recent attack of bronchitis. He had then been forced to truncate
his stay and had returned on the Monday, *a very sick man,*
according to current rumours.

Towards the end of the week Gyles had affairs demanding
his attention in London, so he drove up with Simkins. After
luncheon at his club he sent Christine a telegram announcing
that he would not be returning that night and asking Henry to
join him.

Young Charles Danement, Petula's only brother, met Henry
in London by further appointment, so that when Henry

stepped out of his car outside Whites, Charles was already with him and Gyles was coming down the steps towards them. After greeting his father and explaining the presence of his prospective brother-in-law Henry asked anxiously, 'Is somethin' up sir?' to which Gyles answered shortly, 'Yes – the King. Come along in and I'll explain.'

He led the two young men through and up the great staircase to the Coffee Room. There, in a quiet corner he told them.

'It seems,' he explained, 'that the King dined quietly last night with Agnes Keyser in Grosvenor Crescent. She was seemingly greatly distressed by his Majesty's appearance. So much so that she implored him to take a day's rest at Buckingham Palace. To please her the King agreed. The next thing I heard was that the King had written in that diary of his, which he has kept since he was a boy, "*The King dines alone*".' Gyles paused, examined the ash at his cigar tip with what seemed excessive attention to the watching young men.

At length he continued, 'But this time London and indeed all Europe was stirred up into a state of extreme tension. The the next day, yesterday in fact, the King attempted to give his usual audiences. He even insisted upon assumin' his formal frock coat, although by this time he was breathin' with the greatest difficulty. He simply refused to give in.' Again the cigar came in for some more attention. Then 'Later he managed to eat what was for him a very light luncheon, but he smoked one of his customary cigars.'

Once again Gyles paused while, from outside the windows the unusually faint sounds of St James's Street traffic filtered through, suggesting that the street was peopled with tiptoeing wraiths. It struck Henry as he listened that already the major part of the population had joined the waiting crowds outside Buckingham Palace.

At length Gyles took up his story. 'Then,' he recounted grimly, 'the King struggled from his chair, crossed the room and attempted to play with his pet canaries at the windows. But he collapsed. The Queen, who had only just returned from the Mediterranean, was summonsed immediately by Princess Beatrice. This I can vouch for at first hand for I have only just left the Palace. It was in a turmoil. Outside the crowds are thickening hourly. Despite the caution which has been exerted they have got wind of the fact that their "good old Teddy" is failing. Before I left, his five doctors had been rushed in to him. They examined him and then they pronounced that all hope must be abandoned.'

'The King is dying?' Henry stared incredulously.

Gyles nodded, 'Our grand old gourmand is leavin' us. Y'see he has tried for too long to ignore the appallin' discomfort of that great stomach of his, and the equal misery of those congested lungs. The plain facts are that the doctors have agreed unanimously that no human heart could possibly support the constant strain of all that eatin' and drinkin'.' The lean face was severe, almost hard; but neither of the two listeners had any doubt that Gyles Aynthorp was profoundly distressed.

'I must regretfully admit that the King will die and I shall not leave London – yet.'

Even Gyles Aynthorp could not quite achieve what he meant to say.

'I shall not be leaving London until the King is dead.'

The Coffee Room was both still and empty. After a while Charles stood up.

'I wonder, sir,' he asked hesitatingly, 'if it might be arranged for me to telephone m' father? I would like to obtain his permission to stay too, and, er, he is not quite as *au courant* as y'self sir, but even so he might possibly wish to join us don'tcher think?'

'Of course,' Gyles started and rose. 'How thoughtless of me. Come along and we will both have a word with him.' He glanced at his own son. 'You will of course stay?'

Henry nodded.

'I suppose,' Gyles mused as they moved towards the door, 'we may fairly say we are living through history, though I am bound to confess it is a chapter which I for one would most willingly forego.'

The news filtered through to the nation gradually. Gyles Aynthorp remained at his club awaiting, as he explained, a further telephone call which, when it came, would by its very nature be extremely guarded; but the Duke of Connaught had made it perfectly clear to him that Edward would not be their King for many hours longer and he would advise his friend when the time came albeit rather cryptically.

Later in the day Gyles paid a brief call upon Mrs Keppel. She, Gyles learned, had spoken with Agnes Keyser, so with such contacts Gyles knew as much as anyone in England. He then returned to his club, telephoned Christine and later still received a telephone call from Mrs Keppel, who had again heard the latest news. With a heavy heart Gyles listened to her words.

'Our loved friend,' she told him, 'cannot be moved from his armchair. I have been sent for by the Queen so cannot say more now.' She sounded as if she were crying.

Unable to contain himself any longer Gyles went out. He walked to the Palace where Henry and Charles were already somewhere in the crowds. He eased his way forward until he could see the bulletin affixed to the railings. A cinematographer, his machine mounted upon a modern taxi-cab was inching across the Palace façade taking pictures . . . of the bulletin . . . the crowds . . . the stricken faces.

All that Friday afternoon and evening the crowds multiplied. Scarcely a word was spoken. They simply stood waiting with the blanket of silence thickening as the hours passed. At ten p.m. it began to rain. At ten thirty the announcement was made that – out of consideration for the waiting people – there would be no further bulletins that night. Gyles turned away but Henry and Charles stayed on as did the majority of the people. A little after midnight a rush was made towards the gates as the Prince of Wales' carriage came out with both the Prince and Princess inside.

This was really the first intimation to the watchers that the King was indeed dead; but still they waited, seeming too bewildered and lost to move away, until in dismal, sheeting rain the tolling of the Great Bell of St Paul's confirmed their greatest fears: the King was indeed dead.

Gradually the crowds thinned and dwindled away. Gyles, returned to his club, learned that as yet the one last telephone call had not been made to him. A little after one in the morning it came. By its very nature it was extremely guarded, but the Duke made it perfectly clear that all was over.

'During a lucid moment,' Gyles was told, 'The Prince of Wales had told his dying father that his two-year-old Witch of The Air had won at Kempton that afternoon. The King murmured "I am glad". They were his last words. Later he sank into a coma and died just before midnight.'

The young 'rip', whose escapades had concurrently ruffled the feathers of the high-born dowagers and brought grins to the faces of millions of his humbler subjects, had, through the years been transformed into a portly monarch and a superb diplomatist who came to matter profoundly to English politics. That he was also a *bon vivant*; lover of countless beautiful women; of fast horses; of superb cigars; of gambling and of somewhat tasteless practical jokes, only served to deepen the affections of his people in the period which bore his name. He *was* the first Edwardian and every other Edwardian in the land was numbed by the loss of him.

Indeed it became all-too swiftly apparent that this was so much more than just the end of an Era. Within hours of King Edward's passing, men of consequence in the land were prophesying sombrely that without their 'Peacemaker' at the helm, the Ship of State would be caught up very swiftly in a terrible storm. This they all feared would bear it down faster and faster upon a flood which could only carry it to destruction. These were men, and women too, upon whose keen ears fell the faint but ever-increasing thunder of terrible rapids which might well founder the Ship and lead to an ultimate disaster the like of which the world had never before known or even imagined could be possible.

It was not solely a matter of *we shall never see his like again*; but a terrible, newly-awakened, atavistic instinct that *nothing* would ever be the same again and that some dreadful blight would settle upon the nation in the years to come, destroying all that had been most venerated and held most dear.

The King's appeal had been essentially classless. This the spate of informal tributes made clear within hours. The cause was perhaps that he had been a leader in which other men had

been able to see themselves. He had been the extraordinary
man who was likewise ordinary. He was more representative to
his people than representative government. He was the
'average' enthroned; conscious at all times of his high office,
yet, in his unflagging kindnesses and unwavering courtesies,
more fully aware and thus able to make *them* fully aware with
him that if the Brotherhood of Man were to endure and not
disintegrate into groups which would come alarmingly close to
alien species, then Britain *must* maintain a tenacious hold upon
the community of tastes between the givers and the receivers.

Edward VII, R.I. by the Grace of God, of the United
Kingdom of Great Britain and Ireland and of the British
Dominions beyond the Seas, King, Defender of the Faith,
Emperor of India, had not for all his exalted position been a
true 'aristocrat' in the generally accepted, contemporary
meaning of the term. He had merely maintained the dignity
of his position alongside such a liberality of outlook that he had
won and held an unique position in the heart of every common
man.

And now, dark days lay ahead. Great statesmen, prelates,
politicians, lawyers, writers, poets all had an inescapable
prescience of them. The humble merely shook their heads in
dumb bewilderment – and were afraid.

They likewise wept when he went by and the sound of their
weeping dominated even the muffled drums and the tolling
bells when the dead King was borne to Westminster for his
lying-in-state and again when his body was taken across
London on its last journey to Windsor.

CHAPTER 8

Pelion Upon Ossa

Almost overnight the spinneys which fringed the saddle back of hills became like clusters of village gossips as they unfurled their acid green leaves and shook them in the gentle wind. This wind so ruffled them that it filtered the sunlight through on to the bright young grass in a peerless contradiction of shade without shadows.

The rhythm of nature's pulse beat faster as calves tottered to their feet, wavering urgently towards their mothers' udders while, in the styes, seethes of piglets tumbled the straw as they stratified themselves in their frenetic struggles for the sows' laden teats.

The late Lord Aynthorp's mare had foaled. Across the yard of the Penroth Farm a prideful duck preceded her string of fluffy yellow babies who wobbled diligently after her. Jem Penroth, his farm-cart top-laden with steaming muck, reined in with a 'Whoa there, easy on Bess!' as he drew the old mare to a standstill to let the little family go by. He chuckled as he watched the mother duck waddling serenely, taking her time, secure in the certainty that neither Jem nor Bess would ever decimate her precious nursery.

Henry and Petula, early risen, were leaning over a stye watching the antics of the piglets in a harmony of silence broken only by an occasional chuckle.

They had crept out of the silent Castle, their young blood clamouring for air and freedom despite the tragedies which had beset them. Of these the barely quivering flag at half mast on the Castle tower was eloquent.

Justin Lord Aynthorp was dead. Prudence de Lorme had

joined her brother. King Edward VII lay in state at West-minster.

Henry told Petula what he had seen of that mournful procession. The gun carriage, immediately followed by the new King walking, and with him the Duke of Cornwall, heir to the throne and then Prince Albert. Henry had seen the Crown, the Orb, the Sceptre and the Insignia of the Garter resting upon the draped coffin, followed by the dead King's terrier Caesar. All around him rose the muffled sobs of women weeping.

Now, ruffling his copper head on which the sun glinted as brilliantly as it had done upon the symbols of majesty on that coffin, he confided.

'Y'know it's hard to be suitably gloomy on a mornin' like this. It's dashed hard when everythin' feels and smells so absolutely splendid.'

'Then why bother? Just because we, the piglets, that duck and her family, every young thing on the estate is comin' down with a touch of spring madness, doesn't mean, anyway so far as we two are concerned, that we are unfeelin' about our disasters and tragedies.'

Henry, sharply aware of the pronoun smiled at her.

'Ours,' he repeated contentedly; 'but it seems so unfair! With all the ladies about us lookin' so stricken and Uncle Sinclair a total wreck . . .'

'That's Uncle Sinclair's character.'

Henry grunted.

'Always was an untalkative feller, but now he's like a bloomin' zombie with his personal barometer permanently stuck at wet and windy.'

Petula laughed up at him.

'If we only knew what was goin' on,' her voice sounded wistful, 'I think that would make everythin' easier.'

'I'm sure it would but we don't, and I have a feelin' we won't for a very long time. We're all right for lendin' a hand when the heat's on. Now it's all "keep the children out of it", and I just don't care for that at all.'

She patted his hand consolingly. 'Sure you're not just burstin' with spring and curiosity?'

'Aren't you curious?' he was making a shambles of his hair now. 'I mean after all *there she is*! a flamin' stick of dynamite, cloistered in a suite of rooms from which even Nanny is excluded, while Gran must be perfectly furious. I'll lay a pony to a bent halfpenny both Gran's boudoir and the nursery are like seethin' cauldrons.'

'What is she really like?'

'Absoballylutely charmin', and a good looker too! Dead right as well, out of the topdrawer an' all that. What floors me is a woman like her havin' anythin' to do with that suffragette lark. She must be a screw-loose somewhere.'

'Oh no!' Petula's voice hardened, 'quite the contrary in my opinion! I would rather say she has tightened the screws of conscience because she has seen things for herself! IF you consider it seriously, she has become a symbol of an irresistible force. The Government is thus the immovable object. Result – *impasse*! but one day one side will have to back up and cry *peccavi* and I have a distinct impression it will not be Lady Constance.'

'Stone the crows!' ejaculated Henry.

A slight flush touched her cheeks which as he did not fail to observe made her look 'even more ravishin' than usual'.

'It is my belief,' she continued, 'that women can and will gain their objective and take their rightful place in the world. Of course in a sense women have always ruled men – but only under the rose. We have never been able to come out in the open. The comforts of being a woman have been reserved exclusively for the ruling classes. Neither you nor I have any idea of the apalling tyranny suffered by women in the middle and lower classes. If they do not marry they are doomed. One class becomes governesses. They are neither fish, fowl nor good red herring! Too "superior" to take their meals with the staff. Too "inferior" to dine with the Family and consequently immeasurably lonely, their horizons so narrow they just exist and that on what is a mere pittance. At the end of it they go to the poor house, or some basement bedroom where they wait to die, pensionless and probably close to penniless for they have never saved enough for their retirement and have no means of obtaining any other assistance except for charity. This they have been trained from childhood to regard as quite impossible!

'As to the working class, what is an unmarried woman's life like in that pathetic strata? Domestic service or sewing by inadequate light for sixteen to eighteen hours a day to earn a few pence, always fearing starvation when their eyesight fails. None of them have anything to lose by backing Women's Suffrage; but only *selfless*, heroic women like Lady Constance can lead them towards their ultimate release from bondage; earn them the right to become educated, to become trained for decent jobs, to be considered *people* even though they may not marry. Oh, I burn with shame every time I think of what girls like me have and what those poor wretches endure!'

All through this outburst Henry, head bent, stared at the sow. The sow stared back with insolent indifference. Of course Henry would not admit that Petula's torrent of words had shaken him, yet they had. As if someone had thrown him a life line he heard the sound of the breakfast gong.

'Come on, darling, we must run for it,' he caught her hand, 'I don't want a roastin' from his ruddy lordship on top of everythin' else. We'll talk about all this later. Race you to the terrace, go on, I'll give you a good start.'

She rounded on him. 'Don't you see that's what it's all about. Oh you men! if I can't race you level peggin' then you've a right to beat me; but I don't want any damned concessions – oh, now what have I said!' Hand to mouth she stared at him, appalled by her own eruption.

'A mouthful,' said Henry wryly, 'but go on now or we'll be hock deep in tickin's off from the family.'

Unknown to anyone above or below stairs, Gyles Aynthorp had made a very much earlier departure from the Castle. As soon as Stephanie was able to leave her bed and very early one morning a cloaked, bespectacled figure with a nurse's cap upon her head emerged through the seldom used door which opened upon the path leading directly to the family Chapel. She carried a leather-strapped wicker basket. She moved quickly down the path to where this joined the main walk to the Chapel door, then turned sharply and hurried off down the lane. A carriage was drawn up and waiting for her. At the opened door stood Gyles Aynthorp, hat in hand.

'I trust I have not kept you waiting, Lord Aynthorp,' said Lady Constance softly.

'Indeed no,' Gyles assured her, 'you are punctuality itself. Permit me?' He took the little hamper from her gloved fingers, bestowed it within the carriage, handed her in and closed the door. The carriage moved away immediately.

The Lady Constance was leaving Castle Rising. What was said between them in that carriage as it trotted briskly towards Little Aynthorp Station was not known to any other member of the family for four more years; only to the coachman. He also knew that ' 'is lordship' handed the lady out, escorted her into the station, purchased her ticket and personally ensconced her in a corner seat in a first class railway carriage marked *Ladies Only. No Smoking.* As the coachman was Plum and he had been sworn to secrecy and was consequently puffed like a toad with unChristian pride, there was little possibility of any leakage.

They laid the dead King to rest at Windsor. The new King and Queen became the focus of world attention. Everyone who was anyone wore black, and even that most fashionable of the season's gatherings, Royal Ascot, was to become known in after-years as 'Black Ascot' with pictures of great ladies crossing the turf with their black skirts sweeping the grass, carrying black parasols with which they made great play as they paraded in paddock and enclosure. They saw no need to unfurl these highly decorative articles since their complexions were already shaded by immense black picture hats swathed with laces and ruched tulles and further embellished by black plumes and flowers.

The season ended. Autumn came and with it, a further decimation of the Castle's inmates. All thoughts of marriage between Petula and Henry were postponed until January, nineteen hundred and eleven. Then, as everyone assured them, they could embark upon their wedding preparations in an aura of felicity and the certainty of the family being out of mourning by the spring; but it was not to be so.

After the necessary quiet Christmas and New Year, at which

the chief adult indulgence had been centered upon André's elaborate meals, the Bishop's wife complained of feeling unwell.

This was such a regular occurrence that no one was in the least disturbed by it. Politeness compelled them to express a few insincere regrets, though even these were thought dangerous. Experience had taught them to be extremely wary. It required so very little for Dorothy to launch herself into what Henry called, 'Great Aunt D's Martyrdom Speech.'

Indeed, when left to their port Gyles Aynthorp and Petula's father Charles, would often indulge in wry comparisons between Dorothy de Lorme and Eustasia Danement, both of whom, when not pecking at the flaws in their relations' morals, were occupied with the pleasurable ploy of comparing ailments. When so doing, they both assumed the expressions of red-nosed, early Christian martyrs. In those red noses lay the clue; but it never dawned upon anyone that the real and sole complaint from which both suffered was indigestion.

Medical science had not yet advanced sufficiently for any 'acceptable' member of the profession to warn against the dangerous results of combined tight-lacing and continuous over-eating. Gentlewomen laced themselves into steel-framed corsets. They likewise ate hearty breakfasts, drank Madeira and nibbled plumcake at eleven, partook of a nine or ten course luncheon and dinner, with elaborate afternoon tea in between and frequently sustained themselves through the nights with bedside sandwiches and beverages.

Dorothy took to her bed, expressing the pious hope that she would be sufficiently recovered to endure the journey back to their Episcopal Palace within a few days. She did not improve.

Throughout her incarceration, Petula's Great Aunt Eustasia sat by the bed tatting and swapping complaints with the querulous, flannel-nightgowned sufferer. It was only when Dorothy began rejecting food that Miss Eustasia managed to work herself into a sufficient fluster to demand that Dr Jamieson be sent for.

He came. Within a week Dorothy was dead and in early February there was yet another funeral in the family. The Bishop's now authentic 'relict' was laid to rest with immense and solemn ceremony. Bishop Alaric then assumed the mask of tragedy, one which did not appear to have wreaked the slightest havoc upon his appetite, as naughty old Marguerite confided to the Dowager.

The Dowager responded with an appreciative gleam in her eyes. This of course she extinguished swiftly, confining her reply to, 'Poor Alaric does seem to have become a trifle corpulent recently despite his sorrows!' Later, as they all plunged deeper into Stygian gloom it became apparent to everyone that, 'Alaric is gettin' enormous!'

As some men turn to wine, others to spirits and yet more of the older generation in particular to 'punishin' the port', so bereaved Alaric ate. Aware that the talents of his own cook were far exceeded by those of André he took to spending more and more time at the Castle. On every possible pretext he would walk in; then, later progress in, preceded by his ever-increasing stomach; and finally waddle in to spend the majority of his time in the home of his ancestors. When his feet were not beneath a Lorme table he was to be found sleeping off his latest intake in the largest library chair. By the time Petula and Henry were reconciled to yet another year's postponement, the Bishop actually stuck in his chair. He managed to work himself across to the bell pull which he tugged violently. Sawby came in answer, saw, and immediately pulled the bell again to summons further aid. It took the combined efforts of him and his three footmen to extricate the old man.

When at length the Dowager took it upon herself to make the gentle suggestion that '*un peu de régime*' would undoubtedly improve the clerical health Alaric poo-pooed it, asseverating, 'I can assure you my dear Alicia I never felt in better physical health in all my life, though of course my spiritual and mental sorrows are a heavy burden. This I will not deny.'

Defeated for once, the Dowager returned to her boudoir, her *tisane* and her sister-in-law to whom she announced rather irritably, 'He will not consider dieting. The silly old man is becoming a glutton. We have had gourmets and gourmands in this family, we have had *belle-fourchettes* too; but never before have we had one man who combined the propensities of all three. He is worse than old King Hal!'

In the autumn of nineteen hundred and eleven a bored family began a general exodus.

Sir Charles Danement succeeded in persuading his daughter to spend the autumn and winter in India. He proposed they accept some long-standing invitations from a number of 'Bungoes' and 'Wah-Wahs' with whom he had been at Eton. These, in the intervening years had been translated into Maharajahs with vast fortunes who kept great state, many elephants and more motor cars; were renowned for their jewels and their tiger shoots and were also said to entertain lavishly. They had been urging their old friend for sometime to pay them a long visit.

Resignedly Petula agreed when it was pointed out that it was now impossible for her to have the June wedding on which she had set her heart, until the summer of nineteen hundred and twelve.

Gyles furthered the evacuation, whether or not with deliberate intent no one knew; but he advanced as his reason, his failure to find a pair of fountains worthy of the Castle grounds and suitable for installation inside the final curves of the twin balustrades which were to run down from the Museum. He therefore insisted that the only way to find the fountains was to visit Italy. Here invitations would make them free of a number of magnificent Palazzi and villas, some of whose owners were no longer quite as wealthy as they had been in the past.

'Among them,' Gyles told his son, 'if we are both tactful and diligent we may find precisely what we are seekin'. Indeed we can combine fulfilment of our quest with doin' a good turn for some one among our friends who is feelin' the draught a bit; but it will take time and I really do not want to make a choice without you there to confirm the suitablity of our purchases.'

Henry listened gloomily and acquiesced, thinking inwardly that if Petula were not to be there it did not really matter where he went.

In the event, the thus separated, engaged couple enjoyed themselves. Henry was flirted with very flatteringly. Petula was made much of. She came home with some superb rubies, offers of a couple of small kingdoms and vast fortunes by two of her hosts' sons – one of whom had just left Sandhurst and the other who was just down from Cambridge. To these two turbaned magnificents she gave gentle reminders that she was engaged to be married. When she displayed her beautiful square-cut diamond ring in token of it they merely changed their approach and she was further rewarded by a pair of white stallions which she examined longingly, refused with a big sigh and finally accepted with delight when her Papa ruled that she might keep them as a wedding present. Not to be outdone, her other rejected suitor presented himself to Sir Charles and submitted a small gold coffer brimming with exquisite saris which he begged leave to present to his daughter 'as a small wedding gift'.

'Old Bingo' senior, taking his cue from his sons' initial tactlessness, translated his selected gift – a tray of peerless sapphires – into 'a few baubles for your daughter's amusement' adding 'as a wedding offering of course dear fellow and with your esteemed permission'.

The girl came home laden for, as their 'progress' continued, silken carpets, a vast Mughal cabinet with marquetry of ebony and ivory which Sir Charles accurately dated as 'late seventeenth century', a superb painting of Krishna approaching his love Radha, and an ebony and ivory coffer of exquisite Kashmiri shawls were added to her loot.

In between receiving gifts, father and daughter shot tigers and Petula won the undying admiration of everyone by bagging her own with a distinctly tricky shot. The Indians, servants and princes alike, adored her for she delighted in ceremony and was in herself particularly beautiful to their eyes by reason of her very small bone structure, though she was mortified to discover that the women by whom she was received privately had even smaller feet than she! These women she won over by playing with their jewels absorbedly, permitting them to robe her in ceremonial garments and watching entranced when they danced for her.

She stayed in one palace garden while her father went pig-sticking. She wandered through tessellated arches, past dancing fountains and at length sat down beside a lotus pool to trail her fingers in the warm water and marvel at the tranquility.

India fascinated her, seeing it as she was privileged to do.

She stayed at Government House where she participated in a dazzling display of power and the implicit assurance of the almost-divine rights of the British Raj. She was fêted by her father's school cronies; by such experiences she began to appreciate the immense influence her country exerted upon the world. No King of France with his '*l'état c'est moi*' she thought wryly had ever aspired to quite the blind assurance of its own indestructability which this handful of white men who ruled the teeming millions demonstrated to what they called the 'natives'.

Sitting beside the lotus pool after a round of British Raj gymkhanas, polo matches, balls and picnics, her reflections upon it all raised a tiny query which began to niggle her. What did *they* think about it all? How did *they* feel?

Abruptly the warm air seemed to blow cold upon her shoulders. She shivered as if a spectral hand had touched her, reminding her that immutability in human terms could so swiftly turn to mutability.

Then the 'Wah Wah' who was her current host came out and stood beside her. 'Dreamin'?' he asked in the accents of his English public school.

She looked up swiftly, 'No, thinkin' . . .'

'A penny for your thoughts if you please?'

'They might . . . just be worth more, Maharajah,' she said hesitantly, trying to evade the issue, but he pressed her.

Eventually she shrugged her shoulders, 'I was sitting here in this most beautiful garden,' she told him, 'and I was wondering how *your* people really liked *my* people. Deep in their hearts I mean. I was wondering if all *my* people's display of might and power might not grow to be unwelcome from . . .' she drew back, unwilling to speak the word.

'From what?' he prompted, his eyes inscrutable.

'From "interlopers",' was the word which sprang to my mind,' she said very softly.

'Ahhh.' He clapped his hands, a servant came running, he spoke a word or two in Hindustani and the man vanished, to return almost immediately with a pile of embroidered cushions.

'Let us sit and examine the word,' the Maharajah instinctively sank down cross-legged as she had seen Krishna do in her painting.

'Britain has done much for India,' the Maharajah then reminded her gently. 'One day, who knows, the necessary education and training could bring about a change. But we do very well. After all,' his voice lightened and she could not wholly suppress the thought that this was intentional, 'I am not without pomp and circumstance myself! Why should I grudge you yours?'

And with this she had to be satisfied.

While Petula saw what she would never see again, Henry and his father quartered Italy in quest of fountains. Their search was a protracted one for many friends conspired to make their visits highly entertaining. They were also instructive, at least to Henry, for by their very nature, the descendents of the *Renaissance* never tired of displaying their treasures to the appreciative. Nor could they ever be dull!

At first Henry was sorely handicapped. His Italian was very inadequate; but after a short while Gyles obtained the services of a young Italian who owned an art gallery. Henry and he found they had much in common, and from this moment Henry's Italian came on wonderfully. Without seeming to, the young Count taught and Henry assimilated. He took to studying at night which Gyles encouraged until at length he saw that his heir was able to hold his own sufficiently to appreciate even the rather sub-acid wit which flashed between these highly sophisticated Tuscans.

He and his father became very gay. In between grand balls and very arduous hunting expeditions they travelled to Venice to wander through the gardens of the *Villa Pisani*, studying the colonades of the *Villa Rufolo* at Ravello and standing in the *Piazza Pretoria* before the sixteenth-century fountain of *Camilliani* and *Naccherino*. 'Too big,' said Henry outrageously, 'and only one!'

They witnessed a ceremonial ride of the *Carabinieri* which drew from the young man an awe-struck, 'Gosh! and we thought we could ride!' They stood by the fountains of *Diana*, the *Bernini*, the *Trevi* and 'Havin',' as Gyles put it, 'got our eye in again' they began their search in earnest.

Then in a Cardinal's Garden a few miles south of Bologna they 'found' at last, only to discover that the owner, whom the ancient custodian assured them had offered this very pair of fountains for sale not a year since, was visiting the friends whom Gyles and Henry had left only a week since at Abruzzi. Before re-tracing their steps Gyles wrote a letter asking if he might purchase the pair and for what sum if this were in fact so.

To their joint pleasure the custodian who was both percipient and courteous, begged them to pass the time of waiting in the *Castello*; assuring the English milord and his son that this could bring nothing but honour and delight upon the ancient *Generalissimo* his employer.

The pair whiled away the waiting period by hiring two mules of satanic temper on which they ranged the countryside, steeping themselves in its pastoral magnificence. At night an old woman cooked for them and brought them wines. Then Gyles browsed in the *Generalissimo's* library and Henry wandered through rooms and corridors holding a lit candelabra in order to examine the paintings.

They bought the fountains. They stayed a further week to co-opt local carpenters and direct the construction of the containers in which the fountains would travel. Finally, they set out, having seen their treasures launched upon their journey. They arrived home just before Christmas.

Not long after the wanderers' departure, sheer desperation at his daughter's attentions stiffened Sinclair's resolve to escape. He sowed certain seeds. These he nutured patiently, showing by so doing, an unexpected depth of purpose and certainly one of which no member of the Family had ever been aware. He used throughout, as his sole ally and confidante, the family doctor, Frank Jamieson, who was a practitioner of considerable tact and foresight. Sinclair opened his manoeuvres by promoting his own poor health. In the interim he spent many long hours hiding as usual in the Picture Gallery.

The opening of the hunting season gave him his long-awaited opportunity. He caught another cold. This developed very promisingly for his intentions until, abed, almost choked by anxiety as to the outcome, he nerved himself to say to Dr Jamieson in a weak, grumbling voice, 'I'm comin' round to the damnable conclusion that I would do better to get out of England for a while even if it does mean missin' the best of the huntin'. My health don't seem up to it any more which is sheer damn tomfoolery ain't it?'

'No,' Dr Jamieson shook his head, 'I would be most happy to recommend that you spend the next few months in a warmer climate, IF I thought I could persuade you,' he added this last very warily, 'I would say how about Egypt or India?'

'Not Egypt,' said Sinclair quickly, looking some ten years younger on the instant, 'that other feller Justin Lorme the pederast might get wind of me.'

'Oh, ah, yes,' the doctor stroked his neat Imperial, 'and I do believe young Miss Petula is in India with her father. You do know so many of each other's friends!'

'Precisely,' Sinclair looked hipped once more.

'What would you say to Japan? Would you . . . er . . .?'

'I would,' said Sinclair firmly, 'or China.'

'Mind you,' an admonitory finger wagged at him, 'I do not suggest you go without your wife, Mr Delahaye. You may need a little nursing at the onset . . .'

Sinclair suddenly experienced a twinge of unease. 'Would you care to have a word with my wife . . .?' he asked hopefully.

'Of course.'

Sinclair then attacked the heart of the matter. 'Stephanie would wish to come too!' he made a warning of this bold statement.

'Oh, most unsuitable!' Dr Jamieson sounded very firm, 'your girl is progressing favourably. She has settled down quite a bit. I would regard it as highly injudicious to disturb her in any way at all. Do I have your permission to say as much to Mrs Delahaye?'

'Oh yes,' said Sinclair thankfully, casting all further discretion to the winds. 'Y'know I think this calls for a small celebration.' He reached behind him to the bell-pull and tugged at it with quite unaccustomed vigour.

When the wine came and the glasses had been charged

Sinclair raised his to his saviour, gathering up the courage to meet the other's steady scrutiny. Then with a slight smile he quoted him the *Marquise de Deffand*, '*Le distance n'y fait rien, il n'y a que le premier pas qui coute.*' [1]

Sinclair recovered with almost indecent haste. He and Henrietta conspired to keep the news from Stephanie for as long as possible. In the meantime fortune, which had dealt them all such cruel blows in recent months, suddenly decided to smile upon the Delahayes.

Petula's depressive Aunt Eustasia had called one afternoon for tea. She was accompanied by an extremely voluble friend who was making a short trip 'home'. It transpired that it was Stephanie's turn to perform the small duty of 'pouring out', a chore which all the schoolroom girls did in strict rotation. Thus Stephanie was able to listen with growing enthusiasm to the conversation, or rather semi-monologue which ensued.

The Canadian caller explained how, among her many activities amid the thousands of acres farmed by her husband, she was deeply involved in what she called 'this new movement which is coming to mean so much to the women of Canada, particularly those in the more remote country regions'. She called the movement 'Women's Institutes'. She explained that they had been started in the eighteen nineties by a Canadian farmer's wife; and defined their purpose, 'to improve and develop conditions in rural life and to provide a fuller education for countrywomen through a great number of delightful activities'.

Somewhat exhaustedly Christine dutifully inquired, 'And may we know some of these activities?'

Nothing daunted the lady rattled off, 'Why they form choirs! drama groups; share cookery receipts, and gardening methods; attend lectures on horticulture and the arts and crafts and everything always begins and ends with a prayer which makes it so much nicer do you not agree?'

Surprisingly, Aunt Eustasia waxed extremely enthusiastic.

---

[1] The distance is nothing, it is only the first step which counts. The Marquis, in a letter to d'Alembert, 7 July 1763, was commenting upon the legend that St Denis walked two leagues carrying his head in his hands.

'What a splendid idea it would be for our village women!' she exclaimed, 'If it were not for my poor health I am sure I could delight in your project . . .' she trailed off, 'but alas . . .'

Stephanie, who had been listening all agog, actually ventured to interrupt.

'But surely,' she urged with heightened colour, '*You* could organise, Miss Eustasia, and *I* could do the actual work.'

The 'invalid' looked doubtful. 'Would you be interested my dear?'

'Oh I could think of nothing nicer. There is nothing I would like to do more,' she said earnestly. Thus it all began again. True to her character Stephanie was once more ensnared by a new project. As a result, there ensued a number of meetings between the three.

It was almost nineteen eighteen before the project came to fruition; but the initial, somewhat muddled forays into 'Ladies Institutions' as Miss Eustasia called them in an eruption of gentility, kept Stephanie busily absorbed until the autumn of nineteen fourteen when she experienced a Far Greater Call. The departure of her parents thus became almost in the nature of an anti-climax.

Then the widowed Bishop was sent by his anxious Archbishop to a distant Mission. It enabled Alaric to utter sonorous quasi-sincere bromides about 'sacrifice' and 'servant of Christ' and 'call of duty'; but it eventually got him out of the way, when as the Dowager described it he was excavating his own grave with his somewhat ill-fitting bought teeth. She could never bring herself to use the word 'false' which she regarded as 'deplorably vulgar!'

Left to their own devices the remainder of the family amused themselves as best they might.

CHAPTER 9

'That Young Warmint'

From the first moment that he could creep, baby Richard, Christine and Gyles' youngest son, provided irrefutable evidence that he was accident prone.

The evidence was indisputable and each fresh danger set the nursery wing seething and made material for endless gossip and dispute below stairs.

Richard crawled into the large nursery coal bucket, as all babies will do if given the opportunity. In anticipation of such mischief the brass coal bucket had a strong, flap lid which opened upwards. Not only did Richard manage to force this open but, the bucket was half-empty at the time – inserted his small, erstwhile white-clothed person inside and of course let the lid fall, once his behind had been drawn inwards and the lid thus lost its prop. By a merciful accident little old Tim lumbered up the three upstairs flights plus the basement, hauling a hod of coals with which to replenish the bucket. As Rose's cry went up, 'Nanny, I can't find Master Richard!' Tim lifted the bucket and grumbling, 'He be mortal heavy for a n'empty bucket,' he set it down again and lifted the lid.

'Ee you naughty warmint!' he exclaimed, aghast, as Richard's blackened and enraged countenance stared out at him. Tim literally shook the baby out, coal streaked, thumb sucking, but quite unruffled by his experience. In a flash he was off across the floor crawling like a beetle. Tim caught him by the tail of his petticoats and handed him over dribbling spit and coal. From then onwards a plain hod stood beside the fire-guard, and this was two and a half feet high so was out of Richard's reach; but it remained a standard query thereafter – 'Is it out of Richard's reach?' – and if the answer were dubious the questioner, mainly Nanny, would cry, 'Then hurry girl, put it out of his reach at once.'

Richard developed a quite remarkable turn of speed. Nanny, her button boots flashing in hot pursuit, insisted that he covered the length of the long nursery corridor 'faster'n any of my other babies – ever'. It became somewhat like living at the starting point of a race course. Life was punctuated by shouts of 'he's off!' followed by the sounds of thudding feet. He could round a door on all fours in a split second and on one never-to-be-forgotten occasion actually made the servants' quarters from a standing start, while Rose left him imprudently but only for a second, to fetch a safety-pin. He descended by pudgy hand and dimpled knee, in peril of a broken neck, down the three flights, across the hall marble and through the green baize door – he just butted that with his head – and was finally discovered sitting on the servants' hall floor in the hearth of the great kitchen range with his brilliant curls bent as he scrambled for cinders.

'Ohmigawd!' shrieked Mrs Parsons, snatching him back into safety, 'Wot a very naughty boy! Oh dear me wot ever will Nanny say! Now come 'ere to me sink and let me clean you up,' and grabbing the gurgling monster she shouted, 'Joan . . . Eliza – Agnes . . . Mabel – come 'ere at once; Richard . . . George – Edward . . .' The staff came running. The delinquent smiled angelically. Chef joined them. Tim hovered in the background muttering, 'Born to be 'anged that wot 'ee is. A proper young warmint . . .'

No one took any notice. While Sawby was acquainted with the necessity of informing Nanny, the staff crowded round adoringly. Mrs Parsons gave him, 'One-er my sponge fingers.' The footmen rumpled his curls, threw him high in the air and caught him again. He merely shrieked with laughter and shouted, 'More, more . . .'

Sawby descended again all too soon with a crimson-faced Nanny. The staff melted away with almost Richard-like celerity. Nanny grabbed the boy and positively shook him. The result of this – the staff still peeked around the various doorways – was a mystery. 'Whoever learned him?' they asked one another for weeks afterwards, for Richard closed his mouth mutinously, blew out his cheeks and then blew what had not yet come to acquire its latter-day name of a 'raspberry'.

The staff were convulsed. Even Sawby was forced to smile, though he then pulled down his mouth and ordered, 'Now get along all of you, back to your duties IF you please!'

As Richard was borne indignantly aloft he 'bumbled'. This was the junior family's collective name for what Richard clearly imagined was conversation. Only Lucy among them all was somehow intuitively cognisant with 'bumbling' and so a second cry was added to the first, this time of 'Fetch Miss Lucy, I cannot understand a word he says!'

Lucy became Richard's interpreter. 'Bumble, bumble, bumble,' he would go, for very long, seemingly complicated sentences. Lucy, summoned to help, would listen intently. Then as Richard paused to draw breath, 'What ever does he say?' Nanny would then demand and Lucy would oblige with . . . 'He's cold,' or, 'He wants a toffee apple,' or, 'He says he doesn't want to . . .' do whatever it was he had divined *they* wanted him to do. Altogether the young gentleman brought much colour and stress in to the lives of all who came in contact with him.

When in desperation, Christine purchased a pair of reins with harness and little jingling bells thereon, Nanny, driven almost demented by the child's capers, tethered him momentarily to her rocking chair, left the room and returned to find he had climbed up on to the chair, reins intact, then promptly overbalanced and was hanging upside down, going black in the face.

Nanny had to be restored with *sal volatile*. Richard was merely reversed and slapped on the back by the resourceful Rose. After which he began 'bumbling' furiously. Up went the cry again, 'Send for Miss Lucy!' She came trotting in, listened to his complaints – a very long bumble indeed and translated accurately as, 'He says he hates Nanny.'

On another nightmare occasion, he was left sitting serenely on his potty, singing himself a bumbling song. He was then discovered, after only a moment's absence, firmly wedged between two bars of the nursery window, still bumbling contentedly, but with a crimson bottom. He was in fact poised three floors up and staring death in the face.

Stout protection was fixed to *all* the nursery windows. Meanwhile Rose went about her many chores with the loops of the reins secured to one wrist. For a brief period there was respite from drama.

Then, with the boy still tethered to her as she sat doing the nursery 'mending' she dropped her scissors, failed to notice that they had slipped from her lap and Richard grabbed them. He sawed through his reins. He shot from the room and was this time found sitting in the Park, having negotiated the stairs, the hall and the great entrance steps. Edward had failed to close the great doors properly. Richard of course had cut himself with the scissors. When run to earth, he was seen busily dabbing one bloodied paw with an unbloodied one and bumbling intelligibly for once, 'Blug . . . blug . . . pitty blug!'

Gyles was the one who found him. There was A Scene in the nursery when he returned him. Tears, expostulations, and the disclosed past record of delinquencies firmly convinced Gyles that his small offspring was both a tyrant and an adventurer. He said as much to Christine, adding, 'Anything can happen to that one. I would not dare to speculate.'

As the years progressed dementia increased until, in a more than normally fraught moment Mrs Parsons summed up for all of them, ' 'Ee don't want no baby minder if you arst me, wot 'ee wants is a lion tamer, and one wot finds 'ee can resist Master Richard's smile too.'

Then, in nineteen hundred and eight, providence intervened in the person of old Plum. The head coachman and Master Richard made first contact when Gyles, after listening resignedly to yet another saga of his son's misdeeds asked his wife, 'Precisely how old is this wretch, my love?'

Christine half chuckling, half tearful reminded him, 'Three and a half now. Gyles what in the world are we to do with him?'

'Bleed him,' said Gyles shortly, snatching his treasured meerschaum out of reach and separating a pile of important documents from the boy's tenacious hold.

'No seriously, Gyles, we must do something or we shall have no servants. Funnily enough Mrs Parsons adores him, but as for the rest . . .'

Gyles stood up and grabbed his son. He tucked him under one arm, said, 'I'm takin' him to Plum,' and adding, 'Plum's our only remaining hope. Plum must teach him to ride and at the same time break him in like some demned recalcitrant colt! Anyway it's high time he was in the saddle.' Gyles then marched Richard off towards the stables still tucked under one arm. Richard filled these unforgiving minutes by scrabbling through his Papa's pockets, head down, bumbling contentedly and scattering the excavated contents along the way behind them. He much approved this long thin person who smelled of nice things and held him with such casual firmness.

Gyles halted under the stable clock.

'Plum,' he shouted, 'Plum, where are you?'

Plum poked his old head around the entrance to '*his*' harness room, saw Gyles, so came hurrying on his little bandy legs. 'Good morning, sir,' he touched his scanty forelock, 'brought the little feller with yer 'ave you?'

'Yes,' said Gyles setting the boy down. Richard stood four-square on legs wide apart looking at this new person. Clearly he liked what he saw. Equally clearly the rosy, withered-apple face with the kindly eyes registered something akin to adoration as he looked down upon his scrutineer. He saw the vivid curls, the could-be mutinous mouth, the arrogance and the level gaze directed upwards at him from a pair of blue eyes 'as dark as a pair of sailor's breeks', as he told his wife that night; and he lost his old heart.

Richard had already made his decisions. He flung himself forward. By some further miracle managed to precipitate himself safely against the old man's legs, clasped them and demanded, 'Up, up, I like . . . Pick . . . up.'

Plum bent. 'Come on up then, you young limb of Satan,' he held him close, 'for that's what you are and no mistake.' Then, around the little body he peered and asked, 'Is he to ride sir? I 'ad begun to wonder . . .'

'Yes,' said Gyles shortly, 'but you'll have to break him in first. He's wilful, quick off the mark, up to every damned bit of mischief in the book.'

Plum nodded. 'I 'ave 'eard tell sir, driving the women potty is 'ee?'

'He's a young terror,' Gyles affirmed.

'Oh no, 'ee ain't,' crooned Plum, 'he'm 'is own blood, an' 'ee'm is old, darlin', Lordship all over again, that's what 'ee is an' 'ee's not for wimmen . . . yet.' The bawdy old man gave a great chuckle and all his attention to the boy. 'You do as yer tole,' he said slowly and gravely, 'and you'll 'ave a proper pony of yer own. But no ridin' unless you 'elp to groom 'im from the start. Them as don't groom don't ride. An you'll give an 'and wiv' there muckin' out too young feller me lad.'

'Then do I ride?' Richard had to know the full score.

Plum nodded, 'Then you'm ride like the wind to the rainbow and back again.'

'Wif you?'

'Yers my liddle beauty, wiv me.'

Gyles' eyes creased with amusement and with something more as well as he watched this exchange.

'Can you really spare the time Plum?'

'I allus 'as time fer liddle Lormes, and no imperence intended sir.'

'Then you may save the lot of us,' said Gyles thankfully. 'He's driving Nanny insane. Look here, how would it be if I had him brought to you each morning and had him collected before luncheon? All right? good, then just let me know if he proves too much.'

'Me stay,' said Richard imperiously after glancing from one to the other; and so it was that Gyles left the pair of them, wholly engrossed with one another.

Plum knelt down beside him. 'Now you listen ter me,' he said, very serious, and meeting the boy eye to eye. 'Either you does as I say or back you go to that there nursery. Do you understand that?'

The mouth confirmed its capacity for looking mutinous. Plum shook him. 'Answer me and tell me ef you understand. Stay 'ere and 'ave a pony of yer own ter ride and mebbe a little hanimal or two to call yer own. 'Ow would you like to 'ave a baby rabbit?'

They covenanted together, man and babe and from that moment onwards the nursery found a modicum of peace. Within six months, off the bridle rein, Richard took his first fence, his parents leaning over the paddock rail to watch. They saw more than a little boy astride a very small pony, more than sure little hands upon the reins, more than sturdy little legs held 'proper' as Plum indicated proudly. When the boy dismounted and Plum summoned him he came.

'Tell yer pappy your lesson now or no more rides this week or I'm a Dutchman.' Plum commanded.

'Are you?' Richard inquired interestedly.

'Never mind – tell yer lesson.' The challenge, and lingering defiance flashed between them; but Plum won. Richard straddled his legs, something he would always do when called upon to cope. He lifted his head and in the sunlight he repeated ' 'ands 'eld 'igh,' Christine doubled up with silent laughter.

'Nah Nah Nah.' Plum interrupted him, 'that's 'ow I talk, you dam' well say it proper!'

Gyles passed a shaking hand across his mouth.

A moment, in which the little boy looked like a robin, head tipped to one side then, 'Oh deary me! *H* . . . ands *h* . . . eld low and *h* . . . ead *h* . . . eld *h* . . . igh iseasieryourwayPlum. Knees *h* . . . eld close to the *h* . . . orse's side, yer elbowsclose to yerown.'

The parents were laughter agonized, beyond speech. Christine's eyes were brimming.

'Not bad,' Plum acknowledged, 'but gennelmen don't gabble they don't, and ef you misremember and talk like wot I does 'er ladyship will 'ave you away from me fastern two shakes of a duck's tail.'

The parents turned away, in sheer self-defence and fear of giving themselves away; but a temporary solution had been found. Even so Richard *was* devious. As he grew, so, as soon as his bread and milk and peeled, sliced apple were inside him he was lugged off to Plum. From here he was reluctantly withdrawn at 10 a.m. for pot hooks and A. B. C., with one or other of the petrified governesses. Thankfully he was returned again after his post-luncheon 'nap', usually spent in seeing how far he could round his little room without touching the floor and how fast he could get himself back under the sheets when a rattle at the door bespoke imminent discovery. When arnica had been applied to the resultant bruises, he was duly returned to the coachman from whom on one particular occasion he drew down all the old man's wrath upon his impenitent head by greeting him, once the governess was out of earshot with the cry, 'Wot cheer me old cock robin!'

The bawling bout ended, they went off together to tend Richard's growing menagerie. By the time he was five he had acquired a ferret with ways as evil as his own, whom he adored and who when not in a cage Richard wore beneath his shirt where the vicious little beast dozed peacefully; a family of guineapigs and another of rabbits sired by one Jehosophat, a Belgian hare of wayward disposition whose dam, selected by Plum, was a wild rabbit who had broken her leg in a trap. This Plum taught the child to splint. When the break had healed and the two had been mated, a procedure which Richard watched with considerable interest, he looked up at the old man and inquired gravely, 'Wouldn't you say she'd took?' They were both deliriously happy.

Unfortunately the rabbits multiplied, so by night, Plum hit upon the happy idea of abstracting the surplus for his wife's pot, explaining.

'Young rabbits is wild like young fellers. Him's gone a-rovin'.'

In the meantime Nanny requested and obtained an audience with Christine explaining, 'There's something wrong with the boy's nose my lady. He sits quiet enough these days at his luncheon, but his nose is allus a twitch, twitch, twitch.'

Christine undertook to attend one of these meals where she observed her snall son 'twitching' and realised that he was emulating a rabbit. Once again laughter choked her as she struggled to attain sufficient gravity to assure Nanny, 'It will pass. I expect he has been watching rabbits in the field.' Then she went down to the stables and sought the answer for herself. She discovered the growing menagerie to which by now had been added a small grass snake curled up in a box which she guessed the estate carpenter must have made for it; as also the home in which three tortoises stratified, munching lettuces contentedly. She saw all this while her youngest was 'out ridin'' with 'is Pa'.

She saw father and son trotting back through the Park together. She heard the shrill young voice as they drew closer, inquiring, 'Papa when can I hunt?' and failed to hear her husband's reply for Plum was endeavouring to explain these recent additions to the stabling.

'It's all right, Plum,' she eventually assured him, 'there are just two things you must do for me. Make absolutely sure that none of these, er, pets ever find their way via Master Richard to the Castle and try to stop the boy twitching his nose like a rabbit.'

Plum swore a colourful oath and hurried out to watch his pupil dismount.

' 'Ere, 'ere, 'ere,' he shouted, 'that ain't a bleedin' camel! We don't slide down an 'orse's flank like we wos on a teboggan run. Hup with you now and dismount proper.'

Husband and wife moved away quietly, leaving the boy to his schooling in the important matter of dismounting.

The nursery and the schoolroom thus profited by the new arrangements. Richard admittedly acquired a colourful assortment of oaths! But as time passed he learned to discriminate as to where these might be uttered. His standards for this did not, however, include the footmen, and Edward was struck dumb by being told when he brought up a special plate of scones for Nursery tea and in crossing the nursery floor after relinquishing the plate inadvertently knocked over the brick wall which Richard was busily erecting, 'You lumbering son of a sea cook, mind those girt clod'oppers of yourn. Take yer bliddy feet out of my bricks pronto or I'll 'ave your codpiece off you yet.' Edward reeled out speechless to Tell All below stairs.

Mrs Parsons' comment was typical. ' 'Ee don't rightly know what *is* a codpiece I'll dare swear. Don't make mountains out of mole 'ills!'

When Edward incautiously defended himself, 'Codpieces do though!' he was trounced silly for his 'dirty talk'.

By the time Richard was heading towards his seventh birthday, Plum and he had become inseparable; but the collection of 'pets' had overflowed their original quarters and now occupied a third of the boy's time. This distracted his mentor, but ensured a measure of tranquillity for everyone else.

'It's no use my love,' said Gyles resignedly, when he and Christine discussed the matter, 'We will have to resign ourselves to the fact that we are goin' to have a white hunter in the family.'

CHAPTER 10

Christine Reflects

It was during what the Family called in later years 'The Lull' that Christine inaugurated something which she had long wished to do; but had been reluctant to propose during the Dowager's reign.

This too earned nick-names as do most family events in one which is close-knit. To the older boys it was 'spruce-up day', to Nanny 'Mummy's day' and to the smaller ones 'special eats day'. In short, once every week Gyles and Christine took afternoon tea in the schoolroom with both schoolroom and nursery inmates.

It was after one of these visits that Christine spent the intervening time, between quitting the schoolroom and being dressed for dinner, curled up on a windowseat looking out over the walled walk with its long sweep of lawn framed by those deep herbacious borders. These flowers and shrubs formed the backcloth on which she imposed the family 'brood' in turn reflecting, pondering and looking forward.

It had always been implicit among both staff and family that no matter what storms swept through those ancient walls, no word, no whisper even was ever permitted to reach the nursery wing, yet Christine knew that for some time Nanny had been suffering agonies of frustration through the depletion of her brood. Nanny needed babies. The more she had the less she rocked – always a dreaded portent – and as Christine admitted ruefully to herself, the less too she nagged her nursery and nurse maid.

However, as she reflected thankfully, events had worked in Nanny's favour recently since Rosemary, John and Primrose's daughter was returning to England after the birth of her first child. Then, oh most felicitous of events! Rosemary was to leave the baby in Nanny's care while she accompanied her French husband on a world tour. Nanny really would be fully occupied for some time to come! After all, Christine's own youngest, Richard – her mouth curved upwards in amusement as she thought of the now nearly seven-year old rascal, known below stairs as 'that 'andful' – would also remain in Nanny's overall charge for a year or two yet with Gilbert, Richard's contemporary, even if the pair were now partially under care of their new tutor. The tally mounted in her mind. Gilbert Delahaye, Sinclair and Henrietta's youngest, had a very clear-cut character already – hence *his* nick-name 'little Mr Moneybags!'

Christine then examined the situation of the schoolroom brood on whom Nanny was also exerting a considerable influence these days, doubtless because she had not had enough to do with the babies. Anyway, Nanny ruled the current governesses, poked her nose into their doings and generally Made Herself Felt.

Christine sighed, as she began reviewing the remainder of the brood. There was little Lucy St John, already fifteen and due for dispatch to Switzerland to be 'finished' prior to her 'Come-Out' with her cousin Rosalind Delahaye in nineteen fourteen; *and there was Lucien*; here indeed there was food for thought! She brooded over the inseparability of this brother and sister. Where Lucien went Lucy surely followed or, if called away on any pretext, Lucy's great blue eyes would swim with tears and though biddable as always, she would become listless, vague, seemingly altogether lost until she once again could tack on to Lucien and trot off serenely in his wake like a little dinghy tethered to and bouncing along behind her cruiser – Lucien.

Because of a certain delicacy in the child's lungs and the surprising support of his Grandmother, Lucien had stayed with his stammering tutor, Mr Sissingham, instead of going to the preparatory school on which his father's mind had been set. But now, as Christine realized, the battle would be joined again over the question of his going to public school and what, she wondered ruefully, would be the outcome of *that*? One thing she accepted, as she had always accepted it, with seeming serenity – outwardly at least, she would have to exert her famous tact to the uttermost in order to do whatever eventualized as the best for this unusual and beautiful little boy.

Her worries mounted. There was Rosalind to be considered. Within a few weeks now that bird would have gone from its nest, to her finishing school on the outskirts of Lausanne, from whence she would return for the holidays, admittedly; but until the end of the spring term of nineteen hundred and fourteen she would to all intents and purposes be outside the family circle. She would have to have fittings for some of her clothes during the Christmas holidays, but even so everything would be such a rush from the time she left school for good to the time she made her curtsy to the King and Queen. She fell to reflecting upon the awful suddenness with which schoolgirls, without a vestige of knowledge of the outside world were flung into the maelstrom of Society, as with hair up, skirts down, each one in possession of a maid and a jewel box, they were expected to sparkle at sophisticated dinner tables, succeed at dazzling balls and achieve poise and assurance as best they might in the process.

And all this, Christine acknowledged, would also apply to Lucy too. At least she realized gratefully, both girls could make their come-out simultaneously and thus reduce the very heavy expenditure. Then, if her mother so wished, Christine was perfectly prepared to present Lucy herself.

One decision taken, Christine acknowledged thankfully. She would propose a double launching and if Henrietta felt that it would be unsuitable for her to present her own girl after the Stephanie affair she, Christine, would serve as deputy.

She then began to count heads. She superimposed these upon the colours of those borders. There were still two missing! for she had not included Christian and Claire's pair, Peter and Priscilla, in her deliberations.

Peter would be coming up to twelve in nineteen fourteen and should by rights be going to his preparatory school next year and on to Marlborough in nineteen fifteen when he was thirteen. He was destined for a military career and seemed serenely content that this should be so. Well, it was good for children to follow in their father's footsteps. He was a solid, pleasant, beautifully mannered child and was obviously destined to be well content with his prescribed pattern. Happily, Priscilla seemed to be cast in a very similar mould.

Her thoughts returned to Rosalind. Again she reined in, her instincts warning her that here was no biddable one, but all unpredictable, as devious and uncertain as it was possible for a child to be. Wild, Christine decided, her deadly instinct in such matters warning her.

'Shoals ahead,' she murmured, changing her position on the window seat and re-tucking her feet under her flowing skirts. 'And shoals ahead with my Anne and Richard, possibly Priscilla – Claire even now and certainly Rosalind.' She fell to brooding on the Lorme's tainted strain and found herself instinctively recalling the dramas concerning the exquisite Edward Justin . . . and found herself back with Lucien. She shivered suddenly and Gyles, strolling in to his wife's boudoir, saw the involuntary movement.

'Anything troublin' you my love?' he asked tenderly.

Christine looked up, her eyes still shadowed. 'Gyles,' she replied inconsequently, 'I do like the shape of you! All thin, fine bones and that divil-may-care-bit hidden underneath your rather grand austerity.'

He laughed, 'Well, thank you! After that nursery tea there is little room for either grandeur or austerity I would have said.' He came across and kissed her hair. They stood together in silent content for a moment then Christine pulled him down beside her,

'Gyles?' she asked rather desperately, 'what about Lucien?'

Out came the monocle.

'No don't polish that thing just answer me.'

'Difficult,' he acknowledged.

'I know. Is there something odd about those two?'

He polished, replaced, made a query of the two names, 'Lucien and Lucy?'

'Yes.'

'Well – er – in a sense, but I for one do not see how it is goin' to develop.'

She pondered again, finger to lip and then said rather sharply, 'I think we should force the issue. After all Lucy knows she is goin' to finishing school. That, to her intelligence is the writing on the wall. How will Lucien react?'

'And how will Eustace?' Gyles countered dryly.

Christine moved. 'There is only one way in which we can find out.'

Gyles deliberated. 'Yeees,' he finally acknowledged, 'I think you are right. In your own inimitable fashion, bring the matter up after dinner. We are quite alone tonight and a thing like this which has been lyin' fallow for so long can only be bettered by an airin'.''

Quite unexpectedly, the children's Papa raised the matter himself and Christine was saved from starting up what was to her a highly unwelcome hare.

It came when the men joined the ladies in the Blue Drawing Room after a comparatively brief session over their port.

Eustace St John, stirring his coffee, remarked thoughtfully, 'In my opinion it is high time some decision was taken over that youngster of mine, he worries me,' and bravely lifting his head, for he was by nature a shy man too, gazed round at the assembled family.

The Dowager picked up the gauntlet. She looked up from her careful scrutiny of André's *petit fours*, then with one of the tiny *amuses gueules* held between her old, jewelled fingers she inquired blandly, 'Is the child not very well as he is?'

'Well scarcely, *Belle-Mère*,' Eustace's face wore an unusually stubborn look, 'Nine, rising ten and not even commenced to enjoy the advantages of a really good prepper! It's what he needs. If we let things ride much longer he will never even pass his common entrance to Harrow.'

The Dowager – Christine thought deliberately – assumed an unmistakable expression of bewilderment.

'My dear Eustace, you surprise me greatly. Is he not ably instructed by the good Mr Sissingham?' she popped the *petit four* into her mouth, picked up her frame and resumed work on her embroidery, adding as she did so, 'I should have conjectured that Lucien was receiving a better all round training than ever a boy of his temperament would enjoy at even the finest preparatory school.'

Christine caught her breath. The battle was joined and the poor little bone of contention thrust into the arena. No one dared speak. In all their minds, save only the child's parents, lingered the memories of Edward Justin.[1]

Finally with a fast-beating heart and one little pulse throbbing in her temple, which Gyles, Marguerite and the Dowager did not fail to note, Christine took the plunge.

'Is he not,' she began, 'a somewhat unusual little boy. His constitution is slightly delicate as we all know. There is also his quite unusual talent for drawin' and paintin'?'

'Tcha!' exclaimed Eustace impatiently, 'it only needs the healthy atmosphere of Harrow to stamp out all that nonsense! I tell you I have no fancy for a niminy-piminy, greenery-yallery young exquisite in my stable!' he flushed unbecomingly and stared at them in defiance.

Again the Family silenced. Eustace rose and replenished his brandy ballon from the tantalus, then little Marguerite asked very quietly, 'Must he be greenery-yallery, niminy-piminy because he has a talent for artistic things?'

His mother intervened. She too was flushed; but it became her mightily and Gyles watching decided that she was almost as beautiful as his own Christine. She said, 'You know, dears, that Eustace only has Lucien's best interests at heart. He is leading a very cloistered life here. All the children do. They are interdependent and wholly self-sufficient; but with boys the time comes very early when they need to find their feet in the normal rough and tumble of boarding school life.'

Primrose was busily pursing up her lips during this defence.

'At the risk of offending you my dear Gabrielle,' she intervened, 'I would suggest that nothing has shown in Lucien's development that he is of the type for *any* rough and tumble.'

'But do you not see,' Eustace rounded on her, 'that is exactly why we are so anxious! He must grow up and become a man. He must be properly educated. What in the world will happen to him later, when his friends ask him where he was at school if he has to reply lamely, "I stayed at home and had a tutor"? We know boys who are forced into this situation and they're either mentally deficient or else chronic invalids. Good

[1] Exiled pederast, see Book I, *The Lormes of Castle Rising*.

Gad, the lad would be scarred for life!'

Only Gyles heard Christine's whispered, 'Not for the life he will make.'

Eustace broke in again, 'What's that you're saying Christine?'

'Er,' Christine hesitated now, 'I was only reflectin', that it might just be possible that Lucien's way of life would not be handicapped by having stayed at home and had a tutor. Do not be cross dear Eustace. I see your viewpoint perfectly, but if you would just permit me to make mine, I really do believe you would see it all in an entirely different light.'

She fought well and with a marvellous display of tact. But she lost.

As she said to Gyles, when they were sitting in dressing gowns before the fire which Pearson had replenished carefully before bidding them goodnight, 'We have at least gained some respite. The age of miracles is not past. Maybe something will happen to help us to what I am absolutely certain is right for that boy.'

'At least,' Gyles acknowledged, 'he will have until Lucy is presented and a lot of water will run under the bridge before that, or I know nothing of this family.'

It was at the end of nineteen hundred and eleven, and while the Family was still within its latest prescribed mourning year – this time for fat Alaric's relict – that Lucien and Lucy met in the earwiggy old summerhouse which had been their secret meeting place since they could toddle off without much fear of detection.

After the arrival of the worthy Sissingham, Lucien, who swiftly recognized in him an ally and a confidant, disclosed their secret place to the tutor. He, since it commanded an ever-changing aspect of the lake and swans and trees, adopted it as a further rendezvous for private sketching sessions.

On this occasion while the two children conferred, he obligingly 'took a short stroll' of double purpose, since it enabled him to leave the children alone together and at the same time keep a sharp look out for any intruders.

Lucien sat scrumpled up in a battered wicker chair with an enormously high back. His delicate profile with its small, retroussé nose – a further cause of resentment in Eustace – was turned away from his little sister who sat curled up in a matching wicker couch. Lucien was ostensibly watching the activities of the two black swans. 'They're coming up to nesting,' he said softly, adding, 'Lucy, we shall have to be separated.'

'I know,' she sounded close to tears.

The boy turned from his contemplation of the busy swans, 'It will be all right,' he reassured her, 'you see *they* do not know that *we* have made our plans. It only means we must wait until we are grown up.'

'But it's such a long time,' the tears began to fall.

'It will pass,' he said in a most un-childlike manner. 'Move along Lucy-Lou I want to sit beside you.'

She drew in her small feet and tucked her skirts around them so that the pair could share the couch like two little chaffinches sitting disconsolate on a wire in drenching rain.

'Tell me then,' she sniffed, 'make it come alive for me again.'

Lucien had taken up a fold of her serge skirt. Now he was rubbing his fingers over it distastefully. 'When we have our house in London and I make all your dresses you will never wear anything scratchy again,' he told her firmly. 'They will always be soft, some to fall in soft folds, some to float out; but never scratchy like this,' he let the serge fall from his fingers and brushed them together fastidiously. 'And we will make the same kind of beautiful clothes for other people, from our own house which will belong to *us* and not to anyone else.' He laid his fair curls against her blouse sleeve. 'There will be a room in it for my pianoforte and a whole floor, no, two floors of rooms where people will sit and sew on my clothes under ... under ...'

'My direction,' supplemented Lucy, her eyes shining.

'Yes, and you will bring all the pretty girls from your school and their mamas even if they are fat,' this extraordinary child added shrewdly, 'for then we shall have our own money to spend the way we like. I will bring all the sisters and aunts and mamas of those beastly Harrow boys. *And* I shall be very nice to them so that they will. Remember *they* mean me to go to Cambridge too. There was a row about it. Papa said I must.

Uncle Gyles said all the Lormes go to Oxford. Then Papa said all the St Johns go to Cambridge. He said something too about he would have sent Ralph and James if they hadn't wanted to be soldiers. Ugh,' he added, 'horse soldiers, all that smell of shit!'

'Shit?' repeated Lucy doubtfully.

'Well that's what old Plum called it when he was cross with one of the stableboys. He said, "Shovel up that there shit or I'll tan your bleedin' 'ide for you, you young warmint." I remembered because I thought it was such a lovely fat word,' and he repeated it contentedly looking, somewhat unsuitably like an overgrown Botticelli angel.

Lucy looked at him. 'I think we say manure,' she suggested.

Lucien shrugged. 'It's not important. But going to Cambridge is, because they have acting there and dressing up. I know because cousin Christopher told me. He's like Mr Sissingham,' he turned his little face up to his sister.

'Please don't cry, Lucy-Lou, it does something to my inside when I see you crying. I *shall* be alright because Mr Sissingham tells me everything, so I always know long before any horrids begin. That is why we can plan so easily.'

'But,' she gulped, 'we shall not be together.'

He looked doubtful suddenly. Then he gripped his sister's hands with his own small ones and gave them a terrific squeeze. It seemed as if, inside the child a man's wisdom was struggling to show itself.

Finally, 'Everyone has to do some very serious wanting first,' he explained, rather as if speaking to himself and working it all out as he went along. 'Then they have to put up with a bit of not having what they want. If they can stick it then I think they get whatever it is. You simply have to do an awful lot of wanting and an awful lot of sticking it.'

Clearly this programme was unattractive to Lucy who looked most doleful. 'You'll hate Harrow,' she insisted, 'it *will* be beastly.'

'Not always, what will make it so much easier for me is you not being here anyway. You'll be doing this thing they call the Season. I wouldn't want to be anywhere in particular while you are not wherever it is.' He passed a bewildered hand over his slightly damp curls and Lucy, quick to perceive, put one hand to his hot little forehead.

'It's upsetting you now even to talk about it.'

'Yes,' Lucien admitted, 'but only because you are upset. We shall just have to make do. There'll be the holidays won't there? Then we can tell it all to each other and have some comfort.'

The tears came quickly now. Through them Lucy gulped, 'You are my comfort.'

He nodded sadly, 'And you are mine but still we shall be all right. I have always known. They're not voices that tell me because I never hear *anything*,' he sounded cross and rather frustrated, 'but in a funny way I hear with the inside of my head where it doesn't make any sounds. Like my music. I do that kind of hearing and then I only have to play what I hear without any hearing. I know that you and I will make most beautiful dresses and everyone will want us to make some for them, but of course we won't because we shall be very particular.'

By this time Lucy wore a rainbow face, a little smile developing behind the veil of falling tears.

'You see,' he continued reassuringly, his Botticelli face transfigured by his vision of the future for them both. 'I will never be a tough, or a blood or any of those things; but inside me *I am strong* so I *will* have what I want in the end.' He pulled a faintly grubby handkerchief from his pocket, examined it with distaste and said crossly, 'Andrew borrowed it, sorry darling Lucy,' and mopped her face with the offending scrap of cambric.

For the little Countess Marguerite and her sister-in-law The Lull was 'a really most diverting one', for the Museum was rapidly nearing completion. Two special cabinet makers were already installed in the carpentry sheds where they worked intensely at their planing, sawing, staining, polishing and incidentally crooning as old craftsmen have always done over work which is carried out with care and dedicated interest. They were joined by the Castle carpenter, Peak, who was in seventh heaven of delight as was Tibbins the old hedger and ditcher for whom the two cabinet makers also found chores which inflated their helpers' egoes and ensured an atmosphere of the utmost felicity all round.

Meanwhile Marguerite de Tessedre and Alicia de Lorme redoubled their efforts. They quartered the Castle, caused cupboards to be eviscerated, sent their minions up trap doors, into vast attics and generally spent a delightful time, clotted with recollections and speculations as to the origin of some of their more obscure discoveries. These activities eventually gave birth to some suggestions which enchanted both family and staff.

The Dowager, on perceiving that one attic source of possible discoveries was far too precipitous for her old legs, promptly ordered her method of ascent. Her escort at the time had reached imposing proportions. It included not only Sawby, who had put up so much dust that he sneezed intermittently, but the three footmen as well. The Dowager, Marguerite and the dumbstruck servants congregated at the foot of the almost perpendicular steps.

'Yes,' she nodded, finger to lip, 'very steep as you remarked Sawby.' He sneezed again, eyeing her mistrustfully and with alarm for her next words were, 'No matter, you shall tow me up!'

Their expressions were wonderful. 'Now,' she ordered briskly, 'you Richard, run to Mrs Peace and ask her to lend you one of those enormous holland sheets she uses to cover the White Drawing Room furniture when we are not in residence. Hurry man, pray do not stand there gaping at me!' Perforce Richard obeyed.

'We,' she then informed her remaining audience, 'shall sit upon the centre of that sheet – when it arrives. Two of you will stay down here to take the weight in the event of any slight mishap – which I do not envisage of course. The two strongest, George and Edward shall mount the steps, bend down, receive the gathered ends of the sheet and thus tow us aloft in perfect safety.'

Sawby choked. 'You mean, my lady,' he stammered bulge-eyed, 'that you are to have us tow you up in a sheet!'

'Exactly so, ah, here is Richard. Now spread the sheet out –

come along Marguerite,' and so saying she sat down upon it.

Discipline fought with trepidation. The younger men looked at Sawby. Eventually training won. 'Just as you say my lady,' Sawby murmured unhappily. 'Look sharp now, up you go George, and Edward, now gather up those ends first and *as you value your lives hold on.*'

Two pairs of sparkling eyes looked out over the enveloping sheet. Sawby, clearly accepting that it was neck or nothing now, heard the Dowager say with a chuckle, 'Isn't this fun Marguerite?'

'Are you ready?' he asked, as if inquiring if the guillotine's knife was in position. 'Very well. I shall say one, two, three, GO, and on my GO, you will begin pulling very slowly and steadily.'

The wicked old pair were by now convulsed. Sawby counted, said 'GO' unnecessarily loudly and Operation Holland Sheet began.

Once set down upon the attic floor the sisters-in-law emerged, helped by the two flushed footmen. They patted their hair, shook out their skirts and with a gracious, 'Thank you, that was excellently done,' resumed their poking and prying.

One room led to another. They struck horror into the footmen's hearts as they followed respectfully behind, for the little Countess was heard to comment, 'Really Alicia one needs to spend at least a day up here. Next time we must bring a picnic.'

It was the Dowager who espied a great hump of materials in one particularly dusty corner. She poked at it with her stick, managed to topple off several layers of ancient rags in order to prod even deeper, exclaiming as she did so, 'Ahah! what have we here I wonder? Whatever it proves to be it is positively enshrined in rags.'

Suddenly her ferrule revealed a scrap of oak. She commanded Edward to remove everything. She saw how the rags disintegrated as the footman scrabbled. He put up a cloud of dust and at length revealed what seemed to be the tip of some kind of rocker.

Marguerite had lagged behind, for she had come upon a box containing fans. As she investigated, she heard her sister-in-law calling, 'Meg . . . Meg pray come here and bring George with you.'

As they appeared, 'Look!' exclaimed the Dowager, so far forgetting herself as to point dramatically. 'There is something in there upon whose origin I simply dare not conjecture. Pray remove all those wrappings as carefully and speedily as possible.'

She and Marguerite perched themselves upon two ricketty stools nearby and sat whispering together. Fragments drifted to the worker's ears: 'cradle . . . could it be? . . . . lain up here! . . . so many centuries . . .!' Then the object of such breathless speculation was revealed as a small, wooden cradle upon two rockers – a worn, immeasurably old-looking cradle for a new-born child.

The two old ladies went to it and with some difficulty lowered themselves to their knees beside it.

'The nails!' exclaimed the Dowager, 'All wood, not a scrap of metal anywhere! Now cover it up again. Richard help me to my feet if you please . . .' With great concentration and a gentle heave from Richard, she regained the vertical position.

'Yes,' Marguerite concurred, her eyes unnaturally bright, 'we must not dare move it until . . . now who . . .? Oh! the cabinet makers. Mr Pennyroyal, he will surely know!' So the cry went up, 'Fetch Mr Pennyroyal. Hurry . . .'

They sat together with their dreams of bygone days in the dusty attic until Mr Pennyroyal's head appeared through the wide trap door. It was a Strewelpeter head, bleached, wispy and standing out like the headdress of a Viking on either side of his funny little egg-shaped head.

'My lady!' he gasped when he had produced all of himself and was somewhat confusedly bowing and dusting his knees at the same time. 'My ladies what *do* you do in this chamber? Oh deary me! . . . up those pre-cip-i-tous wooden rungs, oh my ladies!' his tone became deep with reproach, '*Does her other ladyship know?*'

'No,' said the Dowager tartly, 'and you need not speak of it either Mr Pennyroyal. Pray be good enough to give us the inestimable value of your experience and let us have your considered opinion as to the age of that *bergère*' . . . she corrected herself . . . 'cradle.'

Down went Mr Pennyroyal. Over went his gnarled, old hands, made shabby with honest usage. 'Old,' he crooned, 'Oh, very old . . . see these wood nails! They were of a shape used by your Norman ancestors my lady!'

The two 'my ladies' were speechless. They regarded each other over the tops of hands clapped to their mouths and their eyes were as the eyes of very young girls.

The hands came down. 'Could it be, Alicia?' and 'Could it be Marguerite?' they said simultaneously.

The Dowager controlled herself first. 'Pray Mr Pennyroyal, she commanded, 'put an age to that cradle for me if you will be so good.'

The man stroked and patted. He peered underneath. He lifted the cradle with infinite care to scrape one horny finger-nail along the bottom. 'I would say,' he pronounced – and now his eyes, too, were bright as blue boot buttons – 'that that cradle rocked a baby when these lands was forests my ladies. I would say as that is English oak as had Norman hands to shape it. That's a cradle in a million that is! I never thought to see such a thing . . .!' He began stroking and crooning all over again.

Thus it was that the Cradle Room of the Lorme Museum came into being. It was also the cause of the Countess of Marguerite destroying several pieces of pasteboard because her hand shook so much her penmanship suffered as she endeavoured to write, between two '*zut alors!*' and one '*imbecile!*': 'A Norman Cradle made of English oak for the first de Lorme born on English soil in the county of Essex circa 1069. It was in this cradle that the Lady Thyra rocked her children. It was brought by Henri de Lorme, founder of this line, to his newly-erected Castle Rising, which was then made of wood only, the timbers being taken from this land which was then a forest. This cradle has rocked generations of Lorme babies and is regarded by the Family as a Very Precious Treasure.'

She took the final copy of this downstairs in her reticule when the gong sounded for dinner. When all the family were once more seated in the drawing room she and the Dowager recounted the story of their most remarkable discovery.

'The clothes about it were rotted with age, and some

beneath had crumbled to powder,' she said. 'There were two arrow heads and a flint inside the little thing. Oh, how very much I wish Gyles dear, that your father had been alive to see it and to know!'

Gyles nodded, bereft of speech. It was Christine who said at length, her eyes dreamy with remembering, '*Belle Mère*, pray tell us how in the world you ever got up to such a place in order to bring this treasure back into the family?'

The Dowager met the questioning gaze of all surrounding her. The concerted stare sparked up an expression in her eyes which brought back her past beauty most vividly for an instant as, almost demurely, and with lids hastily dropped to conceal the light which danced behind them she stated calmly, 'In a large holland sheet, my dear. And now I think I would like to go to bed, it has been a most eventful day.'

When the door had been closed upon her by her son Gyles, he spun round. '*In a holland sheet!*' he repeated. 'Just like that! Towed up one supposes like a bale of straw! Aunt Marguerite, what do you know of this?'

Marguerite chuckled, 'Oh very little really,' she confessed, 'I can only tell you that it was a most inspiritingly safe mode of being borne aloft. I should know, dear boy, because that was how I travelled too.'

CHAPTER II

Mr Prewitt's Secret

Mr Prewitt was the organist who played whenever the Family used their private Chapel for worship. Therefore he practised there. Passers-by would hear the muted sounds of Mozart and Bach filtering through the old stained glass windows into the churchyard.

On an afternoon in late January, nineteen hundred and twelve, little Lucien, trotting beside his tutor, had chanced to hear Mr Prewitt's playing and had stopped to listen. Mr Sissingham, that most understanding of young men had paused too, not so much to listen, although he appreciated such music, as to watch the expression on the boy's face. They were on their way to sketch at a bend in the river where the swans congregated for warmth at this season.

'Would you like to slip inside for a while?' suggested the tutor. 'I will go on if you wish and set up our easels. Then you can join me when you are ready.'

With a grateful glance Lucien nodded. He tore off along the path, stood on tip-toe to open the heavy, iron-hasped door and trotted in. When Mr Prewitt came down again from the gallery he found the child sitting in a back pew. Now Mr Prewitt adored Lucien and privately considered the boy to be a genius, as he had confided in his little wife when they sat beside a small, neat fire, in the small, neat sitting room of their small neat house in Upper Aynthorp.

'I realize that in the station of life to which it has pleased our Creator to call him, Master Lucien could never become a concert pianist in the professional meaning of the term. Oh dear me no!' he shook his greying head sadly, 'That would never do for a young gentleman in Master Lucien's position,' and he had sighed deeply. Yet this had never stopped him from teaching Lucien as if he were to make music his profession when he grew up.

After sitting chatting in the tranquil Chapel, where in the past men had sought Sanctuary and others had spent their last nights in vigil before quitting the Castle, bound for holy wars, Mr Prewitt led the boy to the small organ loft, and gave him a short explanation of the rudiments of organ playing. Then he invited him to try the instrument for himself. The result startled him. He discussed this matter too, with his little wife, who darned his socks as she listened attentively, interspersing his words every now and then with little bird-like tweeps of 'Good Gracious!' and, 'How re-markable!' and 'You do amaze me!' which Mr Prewitt found infinitely consoling.

The outcome of all this was a departure into a realm which as Mr Prewitt acknowledged, 'Is quite beyond my jurisdiction, really most improper.'

He had asked in his child-like way, 'Can one ever say that the ends justify the means I wonder?' to which Mrs Prewitt had answered, 'Oh, if you say so my dear I am sure it is perfectly possible. Just so long as you can be fortunate enough to disclose what you are doing before you are discovered doing it. Otherwise it could be most unfortunate were the Castle Ladies displeased.'

They both thought about this rather frightening possibility; chiefly concerning the extra sovereign a week which Mr Prewitt received for his weekly music class at the Castle. They thought, too, about the further gold sovereign which was pressed into his hand by Gyles Aynthorp after 'Mr P', as his wife called him, had played the Chapel organ for family services. Gyles always extended his hand, greeted him with grave courtesy and thanked him for 'playing for us so splendidly'. It was during these handshakes that Mr Prewitt's palm felt the unmistakable pressure of an extended sovereign.

They both thought concerning how in the world they would manage to make ends meet if these two tremendous sums were taken from them.

'Oh yes,' Mrs Prewitt pronounced at length in tones which Mrs Siddons could scarcely have bettered in her hey day, 'You must be very, very careful indeed my dear.'

Mr Prewitt was always careful. Now he worked himself up into a state of fluttering agitation at least two days before each weekly lesson and when, on the completion of each one, he rose, rubbed his slightly shaking hands together, expressed his gratitude for the 'truly delicious tea', his voice always shook a little as he then appended, 'Will it be in order for Master Lucien to accompany me for a short distance on my return home?'

The answer was always a smiling affirmative. Mr Sissingham was well 'in the know' and was thoroughly delighted at yet another increasing manifestation of his pupil's remarkable talents.

By the spring of nineteen hundred and twelve, while André was expounding his plans for the wedding buffet to the senior staff Mr Prewitt went through this ritual once again.

Simultaneously, as they strolled through the Castle corridors, Alicia Aynthorp patted her sister-in-law's hand which was tucked beneath her arm and suggested, 'Shall we ring for our wraps and take a little stroll my dear, the weather is so felicitous for January.'

Marguerite expressed herself as, '*Enchantée, ma belle soeur*', so the bell was pulled, the wraps were brought and the pair set off, turning in the direction of the Chapel.

'I thought,' the Dowager confided as they strolled along, 'that I might avail myself of this opportunity to make quite certain – for Christine of course – just how many people we can possibly squeeze into the Chapel if Petula really adheres to her avowed intention.'

Marguerite nodded absently, 'You know it is going to upset a very great number of people if she does!'

'By excludin' everyone except our two immediate families and the senior servants within the Castle and on the estate?'

'Exactly. What a pity we cannot have some form of transmission of sound so that if it chances to be a fine day many more could gather in the churchyard and hear everything!'

The Dowager chuckled, 'What a fancy my dear! Can you imagine Alaric booming out the marriage service through one of those megaphone things?'

Marguerite smiled ruefully. 'No I cannot,' she agreed. 'I merely said it was a pity that it could not be so.'

'I think we shall do very well, even so,' said the Dowager decisively, 'if we include absolutely everyone of the smallest family importance in the reception invitations, then we can give them a very rewarding experience by also askin' such a plethora of, er, great names among our acquaintance that they may not only have the opportunity of meetin' them, but what will be much more significant, be able to talk about them afterwards to their acquaintance.' She broke off abruptly. 'Who is that playin' the organ?' she stopped at the lych gate with her small head tipped sideways. 'I have never before heard Mr Prewitt play quite like that.'

They both stood motionless as the organ sounds flowed out to them.

'It must be Mr Prewitt,' Marguerite decided, 'let us go in and hear him properly. Was not this his day for the children's music lesson, Alicia?'

They hurried up the path. 'Yes I think it was,' the Dowager agreed, 'he must have decided to take some practice after he left the music room.'

At this point they pushed open the door and went in. The music poured out over them exactly as it had done to Lucien. They slipped into the nearest pew and sat down. It was Bach, and as the last notes fell away they turned to each other and spoke simultaneously, 'That man should have been recognized!' they exclaimed.

What they did not know was that he was standing beside them. He had quit the organ loft and come down into the Chapel behind them. When he saw them he shrank back in horror to behind an old screen which acted as a draught-protector for the door and there had stood all the while Lucien played, plaiting and unplaiting his trembling fingers in a positive agony of fear and direful anticipation. As Lucien reached the last chords so the wretched man pushed one hand into his pocket for a handkerchief in order to wipe the tell-tale drops of moisture from his forehead and in doing so he dislodged a pile of prayerbooks. They fell with a resounding clatter to the stone floor. The audience of two turned, startled.

Seeing him, 'Why, Mr Prewitt!' exclaimed the little Countess, 'how you startled us . . . good afternoon to you.'

The Dowager looked from one to the other in sheer amazement.

'Good afternoon indeed, Mr Prewitt, but do pray tell us, who is it to whom we have been listening?'

'Oh dear,' bleated Mr Prewitt, now completely distraught. 'Well you see ladies . . . it is difficult to explain . . .' He could say no more. A clear young voice from the gallery rang through the Chapel.

'Was it all right, Mr Prewitt? Oh, Mr Prewitt was it all right?'

The Dowager reacted instantly, 'Yes, it was superb my dear,' she called back. 'We have been listening to you with immense delight. Pray come down here and speak with us.'

Lucien's face appeared over the gallery rail, 'Oh Grandmama, how perfectly splendid. Did you really like my playing? Are you not cross with me? We wanted to keep it a secret until Mr Prewitt said I was good enough to play to you.'

The Dowager's lips twitched uncontrollably. However, 'I loved your playin' my dear; but I do find this shoutin' somewhat exhaustin', could you not bring yourself to join us here?'

The head bobbed out of sight again. There came a sound of clattering as the small figure threw himself down the stairs and tore towards them shouting excitedly, 'Oh I am so glad and so will Mr Prewitt be as well. We were afraid you would be angry, weren't we, Mr Prewitt?' He stood before them panting slightly. His face was flushed, his eyes shone. The impact of his childish beauty caught at the throats of his onlookers.

The Dowager stretched out her hand and touched his curls.

'Now quieten down,' she soothed him. 'Come and sit here with us. Then you and Mr Prewitt shall tell us exactly how this, er, remarkable achievement came about.'

Marguerite turned to the little man, eyes twinkling. 'Pray do not distress yourself,' she reassured him, 'we are just a little startled that is all.'

Mr Prewitt, despite the reassuring reaction of the two great ladies was still in parlous state, yet, from somewhere he dredged up a few shards of courage and attempted an explanation. His stammering was pitiful. 'My lady,' he managed, 'Your ladyships . . . I must assure you . . . never for a moment imagined . . . confided as much in Mrs Prewitt . . . concert pianist impossible . . . accepted this . . . merely thought little boy so exceptional . . .'

Again the Dowager intervened. 'Would you consider returning with us to the Castle and takin' a small glass of Madeira wine in the somewhat more suitable surroundings of our library, Mr Prewitt? Then I think we might send Master Lucien back to his tutor with whom, if I am not mistaken, he . . . er, should rightly be at this hour?'

'Just so,' Mr Prewitt acknowledged miserably.

'Mr Sissingham is clearly aware of what is happening?'

Lucien, unable to contain himself, and after glancing from Grandmother to music master and so back and forth as if watching one of the Doherty brothers playing tennis at Wimbledon, burst in, 'Sis, I mean Mr Sissingham, only agreed to let me have an extra lesson on the organ with Mr Prewitt because he said it aids art and by my music I helped my drawing and painting Grandmama.'

'Quite so,' said the Dowager, rising composedly. 'So now please run along and join, what did you call him, Sis? And I will conduct Mr Prewitt to the library.'

Lucien hesitated, 'Grandmama,' he said pleadingly.

'Yes my dear.'

'You won't stop me playing the organ will you?' The blue eyes began to swim with unshed tears.

'On the contrary we will help you to study in a more orthodox manner. Now do please say good afternoon to Mr Prewitt and run along.'

As they moved out of the Chapel and Mr Prewitt hurried towards the lych gate to hold it open for them, the little Countess looked at the tutor with a mischievous sparkle.

'What a remarkable circumstance it would be,' she observed, passing through, 'if Lucien were to play for my nephew's wedding.' She paused. 'That was what you had in mind was it not Mr Prewitt?'

'So now,' observed Marguerite studying her sister-in-law

through half-closed eyelids after the library door had closed behind the now totally incoherent but ecstatic tutor, 'we have a new organist for Pet's weddin'.' She toyed with a paper knife on the small table beside her, 'Alicia?'

'Yes my dear?'

'Do you imagine that Stephanie could be persuaded to sing for us "Oh Perfect Love" or some such suitable composition?'

The two old conspirators were by now thoroughly enjoying themselves. Their eyes met. Suddenly, and as Marguerite later realized for the first time since Justin Aynthorp had died, his widow began to laugh until the tears ran down her cheeks. It was infectious. A moment more and they were both laughing and they went on laughing until the Dowager drew a scrap of lacy pocket handkerchief from her reticule and dried the corners of her eyes.

'Oh dear,' she gasped, 'how Justin would have enjoyed it all! That poor little man!'

'That wicked old conniver!' Marguerite gasped. 'Plotting and planning and all the time – such courage Alicia! – going in mortal fear of losing his employment with us. Do you happen to know what he earns?'

This sobered them. The Dowager thought a moment, 'One sovereign a week,' she said slowly, 'and I believe Gyles gives him the same as Justin did, one extra sovereign every time he plays for us in the Chapel. Oh dear, how little we know of other people's anxieties! But, as you very rightly say, what really remarkable courage! Now we shall need the same if we are to handle Gabrielle and Eustace with sufficient tact.'

They plotted their course over a *tisane* in Marguerite's boudoir. Pearson served them and heard much that was not intended for repetition below stairs. But then both knew that Pearson never talked with the other servants concerning 'upstairs' affairs, so they allowed themselves the rare luxury of speaking freely before a member of the staff.

'First,' enumerated the Dowager, 'we must try to persuade Stephanie to sing for us. Remember she *did* attend those singing lessons.'

'Umm, yeees,' mused the little Countess, 'and of course I am right in saying that no matter whom she was, the Royal College of Music would never have accepted her if she were entirely without voice?'

'Precisely. Now, do you think I should ask her, or will you? No,' the Dowager contradicted herself, 'of course not, there is only one person who can achieve almost any objective with that gel – her father! I shall send for him, and then tomorrow I shall tackle Sinclair.'

Marguerite rose. 'Then I shall leave you,' she decided. 'You will do far better without me. In any case I wish to see Sawbridge about my roses.'

She pulled her bell for Pearson, and pausing only to pick up her cloak she moved towards the door, '*Bonne chance*, Alicia,' she said and was rewarded by another chuckle.

The interview with Sinclair, who was much improved after his travels with his wife, was nothing if not devious. The Dowager had long been aware of the burden which Stephanie had imposed upon her father by her incessant and manifestly irritating attentions. Since his return these had in some degree lessened; but she still kept a very watchful eye on all her Papa's doings, so in this affair her grandmother saw a way in which to persuade him without too much preamble.

He bowed over her hand, took the chair which his mother-in-law indicated, refused refreshment and, as was his wont, waited for her to begin.

'I have been thinking Sinclair,' she began, 'that despite the Women's Institute projects in which, as you have no doubt observed, Stephanie is partially engrossed, she really does still have far too much time upon her hands.'

Sinclair nodded. He was obviously watchful at this juncture.

'What can one do, *Belle-Mère*? She cannot be brought out. The, er, scandal totally precludes her being launched upon Society. I for one would be heartily thankful if we could find something else with which she could occupy her time.'

The Dowager studied him thoughtfully. 'May I have permission to speak of the, er, disagreeable episode which brought about this present impasse?' she asked gently.

'Why of course,' said Sinclair quickly. 'Especially if it leads to something, as I suspect you believe it might.'

'That is correct. Well now, during those months when the girl was with Prudence she did attend her singing lessons at the Royal Academy did she not?'

'Oh yes, Prudence saw to that at least. I can vouch for it because I have paid the fees. When I did so I took the precaution of enquiring as to Stephanie's attendance. It was confirmed that this was both regular and very punctual.'

'Did you also inquire if she showed any talent?'

'I did,' Sinclair looked very puzzled, unable to take the drift . . . 'The report,' he told her, 'was that she would never make a concert performer – as if I would ever consider such a thing! – but that she had a sweet, very true soprano with,' he frowned, 'what was the phrase the man used? Oh, I have it, with a somewhat remarkable range. Wait a bit, he said something more to the effect as I recall that now that her breathing had been corrected and she had learned how to stand she need never be ashamed of performing at any private gathering.'

'Ah ha,' Lady Aynthorp looked extremely pleased. 'Then Sinclair may I ask a favour of you?'

He smiled warmly at the naughty old schemer. 'Anything in my power of course,' he said simply.

'Then ask the gel to sing for us tonight in the drawing room. No, not tonight. I will ensure a proper attendance for afternoon tea. Ask her to sing tomorrow. The reason why I prefer you to ask her then is because her little cousin can accompany her.'

Sinclair looked dubious. 'Is he good enough?'

The Dowager nodded, 'I think I may assure you on that point. The boy is a quite remarkable pianist and about this I have a deep laid scheme. Just let me have my way at this juncture – then I will explain everything. I can assure you I have nothing in mind for either of them which is not perfectly *comme il faut*, I just want the invitations to both the children to come from you as is only right and proper *en tout cas*. As to what may possibly eventualize thereafter I ask you to take me on trust, if you will be so generous.'

Sinclair rose and began pacing up and down. 'It puzzles me,' he exclaimed, 'that all my children are so unusual. Stephen an out and out rotter, a swindler and a cheat, besides . . .' his voice trailed off, so on the ghost of a chuckle the Dowager completed for him . . . 'besides doing what my husband called "foulin' his own nest" if my memory serves me.'

'Exactly. Then there's Stephanie messin' up everythin' but seemingly singin' like a lark. None of my lot has ever been the slightest bit musical. Accordin' to Hetty the Lormes have not been any more gifted in this respect either.'

There was a distinct expression of pity in the Dowager's eyes as she listened. Whatever caused it, she said nothing except to murmur as if it were to herself, 'I have always believed that out of evil cometh good. Take heart dear Sinclair, for one day you may have reason to be proud of all your children.' So saying she let him take his leave of her.

When she was once more alone she sat for a long while with her hands folded over her silken skirts. It seemed as though she were listening.

Eustace tackled Gyles before the Dowager could do so. He ran him to earth that evening engrossed with a sea of papers in his old office. The lamplight burned brightly on the maps and plans of the estate with which the walls were covered. It shone softly on the enormous deed boxes which were piled high upon a shelf which ran all round above those plans. It threw a small pool of light upon the man himself as he sat, a pipe between his teeth, his dinner jacket exchanged for an old velvet smoking coat, his feet stretched out beneath the desk, shod in velvet slippers which Christine had embroidered for him. In particular, the lamplight illuminated his famous copper-coloured hair and the few faint streaks of white which already showed at his temples.

'You look the picture of contentment,' said Eustace shyly, accepting the shabby leather chair to which Gyles invited him saying, 'Take a pew, old man.'

Eustace sat down and managed to achieve a halting apology. 'I'm afraid I've been a bit dashed awkward about m'y children, came to apologize. Deuced clumsy feller, rather shy y'know, devilish worried too and that's the truth! All this piano-playing, frankly it foxes me.'

Gyles puffed on, as usual playing for time. Eventually he

laid down the pipe, clasped his hands together over his papers and smiled reassuringly.

'Let's get our lines cleared shall we?' he suggested, not waiting for any reply. 'I need scarcely emphasize that Christine and I are unquestioning as to your fundamental motives,' he made a very slight but perceptible emphasis on the word 'fundamental', then went on. 'As this is fact and incontrovertible, I do feel obliged to say that it might be as well to emulate old Agag a little and walk carefully.'

'But why?' Eustace looked bewildered. 'Is not that in itself an abnormal attitude towards one's children?'

Gyles studied his hands. 'Not entirely,' he said slowly, 'if you reflect that there is always in this extraordinary family a possibility that the situation might become so.'

'Abnormal!'

'Yes, but pray do not exaggerate.'

Eustace paled and then flushed unbecomingly, 'are you suggestin' . . .' he broke off, clearly revolted.

'I am suggestin' nothin', except that in Lucy and Lucien you are dealin' with a couple of charmin', talented children between whom there is an extraordinary close bond. In my view dear boy the severin' of that bond must be accomplished with the utmost delicacy or we may all live to regret it.'

Eustace stared uncomprehendingly. Then, 'Gyles, what would *you* do if they were your children?' he flung his gauntlet down, clearly out of his own depth.

This time Gyles did not hesitate. 'I would let them know, by very easy stages the shape of things to come for both of 'em. I would give 'em ample time to become accustomed to what must occur. In that time I would make a very careful check upon young Sissingham's tuition. For example, I believe it is possible to obtain old Common Entrance examination papers and so let Lucien have an advance shot at them. Thus may we assess both his tuition and his capabilities.'

'And if the boy has neither?'

Gyles opened his hands expressively. 'Then you must bow to the inevitable.'

'No Harrow?'

'Manifestly not, if the results should be, er, unsatisfactory.'

'But what will happen to him?' it was almost a cry of despair.

In that moment Gyles took one of his characteristically quick decisions. He had always made them, though his natural instinct for diplomacy usually let them lie fallow until he was able to insinuate them at appropriate moments. Now, exceptionally, he determined to plunge straight in.

'If,' he bargained, 'you will give me your solemn word of honour that you will never speak of it to anyone, never let on that I have told you, I will make what I regard as the only possible suggestion. But,' the blue-grey eyes were stern, 'there must be no goin' back – the issue in my opinion is too grave.'

Eustace shrugged, 'What have I got to lose?'

'Nothing, but you'll have to give me your solemn word.'

'Oh of course.' Eustace brushed this aside. 'I swear, now for God's sake explain yourself.'

Gyles told him of the Chapel episode; the conspiracy of the two old ladies; of their confidences to Christine and of her transference of knowledge to himself. When he had completed his tale he appended,

'I have told you simply because I do most sincerely believe that Lucy and Lucien *should* be separated for a while; but at the same time,' the words came slowly now and he weighed every one of them, 'I think Lucien would be like a poor little fish out of water at the School and if he were my boy I would give him the chance to develop his talents. I would send him to an Art School and a Conservatoire for his music, preferably in Paris because he speaks our lingo like a native and because he can be looked after, watched and helped by various of my family who are either in Paris or at their estates comparatively nearby.'

Had total knowledge sat upon his shoulder and been his familiar; had all the most unwelcome portents which accompanied the opening of the Casket been known to him at this moment, even then he could not have furthered the causes of Lucy and Lucien more completely. But as is ever the case in matters of foreknowledge, while Gyles had the instinct, he lacked the capacity for any clear interpretation and so as only the ensuing years would show, the die was therefore cast for the two children in the direction which Lucien had predicted to his 'Lucy-Lou'.

There was no one even able to remind Gyles of an ancient Chinese proverb as he strove without heat to persuade his brother-in-law, that having wined and dined superlatively well both 'were illuminated, having wine-taken, lacking the wisdom to choose the other way'.

With a great sigh Eustace rose. He went to the windows. He drew back the heavy curtains. He looked out over the gardens where the moonlight was shafting a ribband of silver down towards the lake where it ended in its own reflection and a widening shimmer of silver upon the calm surface. He turned away.

'May I ask one more question?'

'Of course.'

'Then it is this. Is it your considered opinion that my son will . . . will become a concert pianist?'

Gyles shook his head. 'Certainly not.'

'Then why in God's name . . .?'

For answer Gyles gave him Tolstoy, reminding him, 'art is not a handicraft, it is the transmission of feeling that the artist has experienced.' He added: 'He just might become a painter and that could be nothing of which you might be ashamed. What I do feel is that in an atmosphere where he can develop the two very strong talents we have seen that he possesses he will then find his own direction. It may well be neither that we know; but what is inside the child will come out. That is all. In addition we can most certainly rely upon all my French relations to help impart the social graces to your son while he is so doing.'

Eustace then asked, 'Would you advise that he stayed with them in the holidays?'

'Why? What we are striving towards is a rationalization of the brother and sister relationship plus a development of the boy's natural instincts. I would not run so grave a risk as to keep them apart altogether. Let it just be rationalized.'

'When?'

'Oh, as to that I would hasten slowly. Let us see first what Lucien does with his Common Entrance test papers. Let us watch young Sissingham very carefully and while so doing come to a final decision either one way or the other.

Incidentally, I think that tutor should accompany Lucien . . .
if you decide eventually that he should go.'

'And when should that be?'

'In nineteen fourteen, the year those girls have their come-
out. First tutoring, watching, and not only the three of them,
for Sissingham is clearly involved; but also watching the
development of talents; then France which gives us the best
part of two years in which to make the most detailed arrangements.'

Unlike his wife, Gyles won and lived to reflect upon what he
had done with remarkably mixed feelings; but as this belonged
to the young when they reached maturity he then had neither
right nor reason then to interfere. For some unaccountable
reason, when Eustace had left him he felt immeasurably weary
and did no more work that night.

Eustace had never funked his fences. That was the consensus
of family opinion. Moreover, he had a wife who was beautiful,
clothes conscious and, to put not too fine a point upon it,
secretly rather charmed and flattered by the beauty of her small
son – which like her own was classical as she was also charmed
by the contemporaneously described 'chocolate box' prettiness
of her young daughter. She fanned the flames by her instinctive
bias. She soothed the anxious Eustace whom she adored, for
his elegance pleased and satisfied her and the fact that he was,
with it, a highly conventional man. She on the one hand
admired and on the other, with her philosophical and equally
contemporary French logic, accepted as 'male attributes' the
characteristics which bored her. She was prone to pigeon-hole
such things as was customary to her generation. The men
played games, talked sport, referred to each other as old F.H.
or G.Q. or whatever, always tagging on the date line of when
they were at Harrow, Eton, Sandhurst or the Varsity, which
last could only be construed as signifying either Oxford or
Cambridge.

It was her sound French practicality which had played a
large part in her decision to marry a quiet man. This one was,
after all, in line for a title, a not inconsiderable asset in itself. He
was besides well endowed with the very best expectations. Thus

Gabrielle could contemplate with satisfaction her future nomenclature.

She based her assumptions upon the premise that Eustace's elder brother Timothy was a chronic invalid. Therefore when her father-in-law died she could very easily anticipate becoming a Countess. Indeed she had been known to murmur these future titles softly to herself while her maid dressed her hair. 'The Earl and Countess of Bartonbury,' Ralph thus becoming 'Lord Steyne' and their children *Hon^{bles}*.

When the time came for the necessary disclosures, Gabrielle certainly experienced a *mauvais quart d'heure* over the vexed question of an 'Honourable' becoming a pianist, or a painter, but after a while she reasoned herself into an acceptance of the fact that it might prove 'chic' or possibly even enviable. So Gabrielle put up no obstacles.

In the meantime, of course, Lucien wormed everything out of poor Sissingham, for truth to tell the young man was lonely and needed a confidant.

'Who,' as he apostrophized himself in the solitude of his pleasant room, 'could resist the blandishments of such a little angel as Lucien?' Or fail to part with secrets when two small arms were entwined about his neck at bed-time and the Botticelli face lifted to his own while the unbroken voice wheedled, 'Tell, "Sissy" . . . tell Lucien . . . Lucien wants to know.'

The poor wretch Told All. Once more, as Lucien had so accurately predicted to his sister, he could prepare himself; but this time it was a joyous preparation. He merely set himself to play the part of fool. In this he did not reciprocate in confidences to poor 'Sissy'. He sat before blank papers, scribbled incoherent nonsense and deliberately fouled his own academic nest! Only hanging his head thereafter, turning on the tap at which he was an adept, and murmuring through tears, 'I don't know what happened Sissy, I just couldn't think.'

'But you *knew* Lucien,' the poor man argued. He cajoled. He wheedled. He pointed out with sweet if stammering reason. 'If your parents think I have taught you badly they will send me away.' Lucien was then forced into some very hard thinking indeed. Being nothing if not devious the little wretch plotted a cautious course between the Scilla of total ignorance and Charybdis of knowing all the answers.

The French he responded to with fluent pen, the German likewise; but when it came to mathematics he assumed his Motley once again. In vain did 'Sissy' expound, explain and exhort. Lucien's small mouth merely set mutinously and he refused to learn. His grandmother, extremely anxious as to the outcome, elected to attend his lessons. No one could draw the wool over those wise old eyes for very long, so after a few hours spent assiduously embroidering, or turning the pages of books she never read, she saw exactly what the child was doing and detained him – after dismissing the tutor – for a little private interrogation of her own. The outcome of this gambit was a little surprising to them both. Not that she was fooled by her grandson; but she was side tracked. Lucien's intuitive love of beauty prompted him, while she lectured him gently upon the awful error of his ways, going so far as to remind him, '*tu sais mon enfant que je comprend parfaitement bien*'. . . . as he leaned comfortably against one frail shoulder and contemplated the ceiling in the Music Room.

Sitting thus, he replied, '*Grandmère, je sais que vous est courante . . . mais je vous fais un promis; que je ferai de mon possible . . .*' he broke off to stare at the intricacies of a ceiling which had been painted by Angelica Kauffman. 'Who made those beautiful paintings on the ceiling, please?'

The Dowager turned and took him by the shoulders, 'Now Lucien, pray do not try to draw the wool over my eyes. If you so wish I will make a compact with you.'

'What is a compact, *chère Grandmère?*'

'Never mind about *chère* me! You just listen. You are a naughty, wilful little boy.'

'*Oui, Grandmère.*'

She sighed exasperatedly, deliberately looking away from his beguiling countenance.

'Very well then. As you undoubtedly know already, your great aunt Marguerite and I are examining all the Castle possessions in order to discover some which are suitable for our new Museum.'

'*Oui, Grandmère.*'

She hardened her heart and continued, 'If you will promise to study your mathematics as you should, I will promise to take you with us every day for one hour and tell you all about the lovely treasures which are ours.'

He shot off the seat beside her and stood before her, hands clasped. 'Oh I will, I will, but not enough to make my Papa think I can go to that *sale* Harrow please?'

She choked and sought in her reticule for a pocket handkerchief with which to conceal the twitching muscles around her mouth. Then she took that face and held it between her hands.

'Listen to me now and listen properly,' she commanded, 'if I assure you that it will not mean you have to go on with those mathematics at Harrow will you do enough to at least exonerate Mr Sissingham?'

'What's exonerate?'

She told him, not relinquishing her hold. 'And will you tell me the truth?'

'Must I?' he squirmed a little at this.

'Yes or I will not help you.'

'All right,' he nodded reluctantly.

'You deliberately made mistakes did you not?'

There was an awful pause. Lucien looked down so that she could see the length of those lashes as they lay upon his cheeks.

'He should have been a girl,' she thought exasperatedly. Aloud she said, 'Lucien I . . . am . . . waiting.' All the force of her personality went into the three words.

'Will you tell,' he hedged.

'That is not your affair.'

'Very well then, *Grandmère*, yes I did.' And he added almost to himself, 'I have to fight for myself. You know that.'

He won the round. His Grandmother went away to share the dialogue with her sister-in-law. She confessed, wiping tears of laughter from her eyes.

'He is a little devil, a devious, scheming little devil. I am almost come round to thinkin' he could well take care of himself even at Harrow.'

'Oh, but his talents!'

'Exactly so, now you see, what we shall do is check on him

quite relentlessly. IF he assimilates, at nine years old, remember, the information we shall give him, and IF we can then do a round with Eustace and Gabrielle and invite that small fiend to act as lecturer, and IF he has some of the facts at his finger tips, we can prove to Eustace that in the channels of his own interests, Mr Sissingham has brought him on splendidly. Thus we may well achieve both his purpose and our own.'

Marguerite regarded her co-conspirator with equal guile. 'And that is?' she prompted.

'To ensure that the worthy Sissingham accompanies him to Paris. We must have *someone* whom we can wind round our little fingers and who can Tell All and I promise you I can handle Mr Sissingham without much difficulty!'

Yet even the Dowager, intuitive as she was above all the rest, aware as she was, more than any other member of the family what a perilous future could lie before the boy; even she had no inkling of the fact that in this case she was the puppet of forces unknown. Despite this, both the old persons were startled and given a moment of acute unease when, as he had done before on the occasion when Henry had spoken with his Aunt in her boudoir about the Casket,[1] Boney, the ancient parrot suddenly somersaulted in his cage and croaked loud and clear once again 'Pandora's Box . . . Ha, ha . . . Pandora's Box . . . !'

[1] See Book I, *The Lormes of Castle Rising.*

CHAPTER 12

'What Is To Be Will Be'

In the January of nineteen hundred and twelve an announcement was made to the entire staff, who were assembled for the purpose in the big room off the terrace garden door where generations of Lormes had brought their shooting parties for luncheons if, at the eleventh hour rain made *al fresco* eating impracticable.

Christine addressed them from a little dais which Peak brought in. The chairs, upon which she insisted that the staff sat, were recruited from the second Long Gallery and were the little gold ones used for very large Lorme parties. Peak, however, strongly disapproving of such instructions – 'Staff stand before the gentry' – had steadfastly refused to allow the dark green velvet seats to be put upon them.

Behind Christine on the little dais sat the women of the Family, also Petula and her Aunt. The big room was packed to capacity.

The betting had been running high below stairs concerning the details of what she was to announce. They knew well enough it was The Wedding at last; but whilst the heaviest backing among the younger servants was for a London wedding, the older and more experienced ones put their money on the Castle and its environs.

'What I have to say to you,' Christine began after greeting them all and thanking them for coming, 'Concerns Mr Henry's Wedding. As you are all aware Sir Charles Danement is a widower and his aunt Miss Eustasia who is here now, is in too delicate health for her to undertake a large reception at the Manor. Therefore it has been decided mutually that we shall take the somewhat unorthodox course of holding the wedding reception here. All the work and strain will devolve upon you. Only the planning lies in my hands. Consequently, I feel that it will help you all if I run over my proposals' – she had come a long way since her diffident assumption of authority two years ago – 'and then to ask that you all discuss them among yourselves. Should you then have any points to raise, any suggestions to make, no matter how large or how small, his lordship and I will be in his lordship's old office one week from today and we will receive you there. I suggest that if you have some matter to raise which involves one or more of you in the execution, you appoint a spokesman or spokeswoman so that his lordship and I can see each one of you privately and alone. We will break at twelve forty-five for luncheon. If matters are not fully resolved by then we will resume at three-thirty.' She paused, 'Is that quite clear to everyone?'

Approving murmurs of assent made this apparent, so, looking about her, at first questioningly, then with a faint smile, albeit with a slightly heightened colour she continued.

'Due, in part, to our own personal wishes, in part to the bereavements which we have suffered recently, and in part to Miss Petula's expressed wish, the wedding will be a private one in our Chapel. There will only be sufficient seating for close members of both families; but the Dowager has arranged for additional benches to be installed at the back of the Chapel to accommodate senior members of both indoor and outdoor staff. If the rest of you so wish – but this will be entirely voluntary – as many of you as can spare the time can line the route from the main drive to the Chapel's lychgate. Thus you may see the bride and her retinue very clearly.

'Miss Petula will walk to the Chapel on her father's arm, followed by her retinue of bridesmaids and pages. His lordship and I will then follow with the various members of both families. The order will in due course be put up in the Christmas Room where we pack our parcels annually. This will have to be completely cleared for the unpacking of wedding presents and we thought that if all lists were displayed there upon the walls you could slip in from time to time to study them. Then after the ceremony, at which His Grace Bishop Alaric will officiate, assisted by our Vicar, the bride and groom will come from the Chapel and walk to the reception Marquee.

'So far,' she continued, 'there is little work for any of you in what I have explained; but I have not yet come to the crux of the matter. As you will readily understand, we are in danger of offending a great many people of our acquaintance by the limitations of the chosen wedding ceremony. Therefore,' André now sat forward on his chair, hands on his knees, his eyes rivetted upon the speaker, 'we *must* ensure that they are not offended! We believe that the only solution is for us to give a very large reception in a very large marquee which we propose to set up on the sweep of the lawn before the Castle where, by tradition, hounds meet every Boxing Day. Our present estimate is for a minimum of six hundred guests. In addition to the labours involved, I shall need from each head of department an estimate of how many additional workers will be required. Please bear in mind that there will also be a Family house party.

'The greatest part of the work in this respect will fall upon the shoulders of Chef André and his helpers: Mrs Parsons and her gels, Mrs Peace and her staff, though the gardeners under Mr Sawbridge will also have much to do. We shall give a formal dinner here on the eve of the wedding. Sir Charles hopes to entertain for Mr Henry and his friends at a traditional bachelor dinner party, but that is as yet uncertain. The Wedding Breakfast will be served in the big marquee. We shall obtain the services of a military band, the Royal Artillery – Major de Lorme's regiment – to play upon the lawns. After the bride and groom have left, we shall give a small dance for the bridesmaids, to which many of our friends in this county will bring their young people. This dance will be preceded by a dinner party here.'

To her astonishment there was a spatter of applause when she ended. Excitement had clearly kindled them, despite the tremendous burden which she had laid upon their shoulders. Christine was immensely touched, so much so that she once again held up her hand and stilled them.

'And may I say in conclusion,' her eyes were shining, 'that his lordship will be as touched as I am that despite the awful weight of work which this will lay upon you all, you are so kind as to be pleased.'

This was the spark which kindled Sawby. He rose from his seat and bowed towards the rostrum.

'My lady,' he said, 'I believe I may speak for all when I say that we will endeavour to make the occasion a memorable one and will gladly undertake the duties you have so kindly out-lined for us. There is not one here but that loves and respects the future heir, my lady,' Sawby was by now completely carried away, 'and I say here and now three cheers, for the wedding, Miss Petula and Mr Henry.'

The meeting broke up in confusion and Christine with a quick glance at her mother-in-law stepped down and went quietly away. The rest of the dais assembly followed her.

Above stairs, tea had been sent up to the blue drawing room. Below stairs, staff tea was in progress. For once, the entire staff had assembled in the servants' hall. The opened door of the steward's room showed a fire burning brightly but no one to sit before it sipping tea in privacy.

'Wot I say,' Mrs Parsons raised her voice in order to make herself heard, 'is that it's still a n'orrible lot of work for all of us. I only thank God it 'as come in summer wen me rheumaticks is less troublesome.'

This irritated Sawby. He put down his teacup over-loudly.

'Nothing in-timidates me,' he announced a trifle pompously, 'when it comes to administration. What do you actually think about the arrangements Mrs Parsons?'

That worthy blew forcefully upon her tea.

'More work than wot we 'as ever 'ad before,' she snapped, 'and Gawd alone knows wot trouble's in store for me with that dratted Sawbridge.'

By this she referred her listeners to the ancient feud between herself and the head gardener. 'A 'uge 'ouse party, all them nuptual preparations, all them extra servants for us to put on the pomp for, since none of us will ever be adverse criticized by outside employees. All them 'uge breakfuss, bedside san-wiches, tantalusses . . . Oh Gawd, it makes me 'ead split ter think of it.'

Sawby drew down his mouth in grim disapproval. Before he could reply, the incensed André took the floor.

"Ave you thought about me,' he demanded, striking his white jacketed chest, 'I 'ave the 'ole responsibility. *Deux gâteaux de marriage par example . . . le Déjeuner de Marriage . . . nom d'un nom . . .*'

'Wot does ee say?' demanded Mrs Parsons, now thoroughly incensed, 'I carn't understand a word of it.'

'*Zut!*' snapped André, exasperated, 'two marriage cake, six 'undred for *le Buffet*, skitches to make.'

'Sketches,' supplemented Sawby.

'Les *Menus à faire* – to make; there is one thing sure and certain, I must 'ave Jean-Paul to 'elp. Ee mus' come from France, I would tell you, ee ees the bes' *pâtissier et confisier en France*. Pastry cook and sugar worker.' He added at the snarl, 'So why do *you* complain?'

Mrs Peace took over. 'There will have to be a considerable over-hauling of my linen rooms,' she said in measured tones. 'The Beauvais nuns always require six months' advance notice, *with designs*,' she glanced significantly at André who tugged off his high bonnet and wiped his forehead. 'These should go off immediately. Otherwise the buffet cloths and draperies will have to be made in London, so I must ascertain from her ladyship which she wishes.'

At the thought of any of this slipping out of his control, André rallied.

'I will give them to you within two days,' he promised, 'I 'ave it all 'ere, in my 'ead,' and he tapped it significantly.

Mrs Peace acknowledged this with a slight head bend.

'Then,' she outlined, 'there will have to be the buffet table cloths as well, and all Miss Petula's linen for her trousseau, I likewise assume, according to tradition, that the future Lady Aynthorp will have the Present Lady Aynthorp's old suite as her own here in the Castle. Then there will be the planning and listing of the Bride's lingerie. That I must prepare for,' she paused, looking questioningly around, 'will it be milady or Sir Charles who will encompass that trousseau?'

Sawby said firmly,

'Put it down Mrs Peace as your first query for her ladyship

and be sure to have the lists ready so as to carry the matter through if so required.'

He leaned back and poured himself a third cup of tea. 'For my part, I must provide my list of footmen, you Mrs Peace the required additional maids, and I must work upon the wines very carefully in order to consult his lordship, or rather,' he amended with a touch of grandeur, 'submit them to his lordship for his confirmation.' Richard giggled, was quelled with a glance. Then George ventured,

'Who will make the marquee buff-et table, Mr Sawby, it'll be a big 'un for six 'undred or more I dare swear. Wot about the cloths?'

'Pliz,' screamed André, 'I 'ave it 'ere,' again he tapped his head.

'It seems,' observed Mrs Parsons acidly, ''as you 'ave a mortal lot in that 'ead of yours Mister André.'

The litany was being taken up by Joan the senior kitchenmaid who sat with Eliza and the two scullerymaids, Agnes and Mabel. She whispered to her confrères,

'We should never be ready with the washing up if we didn't 'ave more 'elp. Take that one family dinner. Say there's only twenty, that means wiv as few as ten courses – wash, dry and stack remember, let alone the putting away, two 'undred an fifty plates, well over four hundred pieces of silver and cutlery, not counting dessert, and then all the millions of pots and pans and dishes.'

Agnes took up the chant,

'And coffee cups and saucers. Boots can 'elp, but leaving the glasses to the footmen who'll 'ave the silver and gold plate cleaning to do as well we'll need every one of six more pairs of 'ands in that there scullery.'

Sawby heard them. He again intervened,

'Put it down, Joan, and give it to Mason or Pearson. They will take it up to her ladyship. Are you content with six extra for the washin' up Mrs Parsons?'

Mrs Parsons nodded abstractedly.

'Most of all,' she supplemented, 'we shall need re-liable runners wot can fetch and carry, if we was to do that too we'd never be ready. *I believe in runners.*'

Little wizened Boots, who very rarely spoke above a whisper, and that only to Chef André, had the last word on this occasion. This little creature summed up; he whom The System had used most cruelly before he came to Castle Rising, when as a chimney sweep the acid of the soot-encrusted chimneys so damaged his scarred body that he was deprived of any expectation of normal life as a result.[1] He had been salvaged by the late Lord Aynthorp who, as a young man had seen Tim's ruined, unconscious body on the floor when he had been brought down from the great chimney and given up for dead. Justin Aynthorp had thrown his riding whip aside, knelt by the boy, opened the rag of shirt, torn it back angrily, seen what lay beneath and there and then had commanded that the boy be salvaged as much as might be and given employment for the rest of such life as had been left to him in the Castle. Then he had snatched up the crop again and dealt with the Master chimney sweep.

Now the little creature said,

'It'ull be a lotta work. We'll be tired out maybe and our feet'ull trouble us somethin' crool, but I for one wouldn't miss it for the world 'cos it ull be a Very 'Appy Occasion.'

So saying he eased himself off his stool at the far end of the table and went in search of another hod of coal for his chef's greedy stoves.

That night, after dinner Gyles shrugged himself into a thick Ulster. Taking a stick, he strode out through the garden door and struck out across the home park. Some deeply imbedded instinct was working upon him and he was fraught with unease.

The ground beneath his feet was frost-hard, crisp underfoot. Through the old trees the young moon slanted on to the frost-crystallized grass which crackled as he walked. He took the line his son had taken so often in moments of acute distress, heading for the rise and coming thence to the saddle back from where he could look down, as Henry had done, upon his lands and Castle. The old stone was given added splendour by the moonlight. The towers and the buttresses, even the windows,

[1] In extreme cases of soot-acid erosion even the genitals of small boys were thus destroyed. F.C.

lit as they were by lights within, assumed the magical quality which had so intoxicated Plum when he had led his wife across to see Henry and Petula in all the finery of their Fancy Dress Ball on the night of their engagement.[2] Gyles, looking down, felt a fierce protectiveness surge as he picked out the familiar landmarks. Then, as he looked lovingly at what he owned – in trust for future generations, as he reminded himself – so fear came to him.

His sustained association with the great financiers of his day, had begun with the deliberate intent of strengthening the Castle's finances – for so he thought of them – against the inroads made by extravagant Edwardian Lormes; of whom his father was perhaps the most lavish of his experience. This association with 'trade' had developed in the last two years as these men and he had become more intimate. Now it had achieved a state of guarded friendship, alien in many ways to Gyles' own character, but none the less deliberately sustained, and in part at least enjoyed. From such men, as he reflected now, came knowledge, even foreknowledge for he had long ago come to wry terms with the fact that financiers controlled the world, made wars, turned the paths of destiny and were either aware of it with conscience, or else, discarding awareness merely succumbed to the ultimate intoxication whose other name is power.

Carefully, Gyles traced the pattern of his own and the Family's life since the death of his father. Sorrow had come, and as life decrees, sorrow had eased its pressures. There had been shame too in Stephanie's foolishness; but now he was able to see that, after all, the strength of their name and reputation had stood the Family in remarkably good stead concerning this. It had been, in the final stages, a nine-day-wonder which was being forgotten rapidly. Now with affairs firmly controlled, adjustments made, dues surrendered, the heir to be secured in marriage to a girl who pleased the Family mightily; their own personal barometer seemed swung to set fair. Money was being made, and money would be made, with which to meet the current extravagances. There would be the wedding, and that, as he acknowledged comfortably, would be adequately met.

[2] See Book I, *The Lormes of Castle Rising.*

Then in two brief years there would be a come-out for three girls involving a London Season with all that this entailed. No cause for alarm lay in either event, since meticulously tended books showed the costs would be more than met by increasing revenues. The Museum was finished and would be opened after the wedding was over. The pheasants were increasing encouragingly. Their market was ensured as was the market, newly opened, for their hot-house produce. This would undoubtedly develop since he had at his command a sufficiency of monies to meet any necessary capital expenditures which might become essential later. Why, then, he questioned, did restlessness assail him and give him a feeling akin to the Eve of Waterloo; akin to Drake and his game of Bowls; akin even to Nero with his fiddle? It could only lie in the awful anticipation of a war, which, reluctant as he was to admit it, he began to see as inevitable. There was war in the air. Like a hound scenting fox upon the wind he sniffed war and in this he knew at last lay the cause of all his inward unease.

In later years, he was to ask himself,

'What could I have done to offset any of it?' All he had won back by this mental striving was a terrible sounding through the night of 'what is to be . . . will be'.

He walked for miles. Despite the exercise he failed to shake off the familiar who sat upon his shoulder, ephemeral, indefinable, but *there* haunting him as surely as if some gibbering fiend from the nether regions had materialized to clamp a hold upon him and whisper frightful predictions in his ear.

Gyles saw nothing. He felt nothing, despite which he was a man pursued. 'What is to be will be' . . . until at length the cry was wrung from him '*Oh God. Why did we open that Casket!*'

Yet his intelligence immediately refuted the cry. What could a chastity belt in an old box contain which could release Nemesis upon the house of Lorme! For as he saw it, what lay ahead was Nemesis. Gyles strode on, looking down again and again at sleeping farmsteads, tranquil byres, tilled fields and tended gardens. It seemed all so unutterably secure. It *was* secure. What then, save war, could decimate that sweet security? He found no answer.

As the faint first presage of false dawn lifted the darkness he imagined that he was seeing more than a problem concerning his own line. It came to him, this pacing descendant of many like himself, that he was seeing an undermining, a tunnelling beneath, and a thrusting upwards of unseen forces of implacable hatred for all he loved and held in unswerving loyalty – England! The late King had been England in a way perhaps that had never been represented by the Crown since Elizabeth rode out upon her caparisoned palfrey and spoke to her peoples,

'I have but the body of a weak and feeble woman . . .' It was common talk now between uncommon men that this was so. There were forces at work whose dreadful strength could not be gainsaid. These were actively directed towards destruction. They would tunnel, tunnel, tunnel until the reduced, thin crust of protective covering cracked, fell through and crumbled in to nothingness . . .

It was not Castle Rising now for which Gyles feared, but England, and what, he asked himself, could he do for her? Despite his foreign blood, despite his passionately sustained love for France, Gyles loved England. The very characteristics which constantly irritated and bewildered him were an essential part of his devotion. She had close on a thousand years of history, magnificent history behind her. His mind closed up abruptly, shocked by its own analogy. The Lormes had close on a thousand years of history, too, for their fortunes had marched with England's and, if his prescience were to be confirmed, then Lorme history and England's too were indissolubly linked and the one would go down with the other in to the darkness of prejudice and ignorance.

In some curious sense this night-long striding about his own hills purged him; for when he had unleashed the full force of these terrible, incredible, unbelievable fears and forced himself to look upon them, a sense of fatalism enfolded him. 'What is to be will be.' Gyles came by dawn to an acceptance. That it marched with a grim determination to fight every inch of this envisaged rearguard action was likewise implicit, but he purged it temporarily. When the dawn came fully, he re-traced his steps, went wearily into the silent Castle and so to his dressing

room where he flung his clothes down carelessly and fell on the
bed. He was asleep instantly.

In the morning it had all receded. The wolf had returned to
its lair and its howling could no longer be heard upon the night
winds since they too had dispersed.

CHAPTER 13

A Quiet Country Wedding

This was how the Family described the wedding of Henry de Lorme, eldest son of Gyles Lord Aynthorp to Petula Danement. They were not persuaded otherwise by the incidence of a mere six hundred guests to the reception. Nor were they ever conscious that the Union was celebrated other than 'quietly' despite the events which heralded in the great day; nor by those alarums and excursions which occurred throughout it. These were considered normal by their standards.

In a sense the curtain was rung up by a Watcher. He constituted the only witness to the earliest events which were undoubtedly of some consequence.

He sat, in his nightshirt, three floors above the drive, from which vantage point he saw all and absorbed much which by reason of his already very clearly developed character some might be justified in saying he would have been better without.

On the previous day a tremendous army of workmen had arrived by drays. These were followed by several horse-drawn vans which came to rest before the main entrance in order that they could be stationed at the nearest possible point for the evacuation of their contents. Then men with poles and men with pegs, others with sledge hammers and Brobidnagian cats – cradles of ropes – bore their burdens across the grass and began erecting the vast marquee in which the reception would be held and the buffet set up.

Plans had been made since January so the work was done very smoothly. Now in the tingling cool of what promised to be a splendid June day, the great marquee stood ready as did the round tables and little silvered chairs. Gold had been deemed too garish for the occasion so the chairs had to be repainted. For a while, ant-like processions of staff and hired helpers wound their way to and from the garden door carrying the white satin, the lace from Cluny, the sprays of hand-made white chiffon flowers tinted faintly pink at their centres and the great rolls of pleated satin which, when affixed in their appointed places would complete the coverings of the buffet which ran from end to end of the marquee along the farther side.

André, in his shirt sleeves, directed operations. Gradually the pleating was affixed, the satin laid over it, the swags and sprays of roses attached to the front, the laces laid overall and then it was time for the special band of women to appear with the hand-made tablecloths of palest pink satin under white silk organza with which the tables were to be covered at which the guests would sit.

The Watcher was held absorbed by this until the caterpillar of staff dwindled away and the majority of the work went on inside. Then his gaze wandered leftwards, picking up two figures as they plodded through the home park. He recognized them as Plum and his 'Missus'. He was able to follow their progress to the little Countess's special area – the rose gardens. Once they reached the first bed he saw Plum unsling the sacks from his back, hand one to his wife, take another himself and then the pair of them went between the bushes shaking the dew fresh roses so that the only slightly overblown ones yielded up their petals which tumbled onto the soil like giant confetti.

At each bush Plum used his secateurs to cut away the bared stems and then the pair of them like two old gnomes bent themselves double to gather up their harvest and thrust it into the sacks. After a while the rhythm of their movements became monotonous, so the Watcher's gaze moved on once more, while the old pair were far too engrossed upon their ploy to be aware that they were being surveyed. Neither of them looked up. But the witness, searching for fresh sources of interest looked down and, hearing a slight noise, flattened his face against the iron-trellised nursery windows, rubbing his eyes to free them from the last vestiges of sleep.

Two male figures in dress clothes and extraordinary disarray were inching gingerly along the narrow parapet slightly to his right. As the Watcher gazed, astonished at his brother Henry and his papa, so he saw the former reach out to a flying buttress, take a firm grasp upon it, seemingly defying the laws of gravity by the angle at which he did so and, as Richard held his breath, swung himself to comparative safety and the further, leftwards parapet.

'Are you all right sir?' Richard heard his brother hiss very faintly, though he was not aware that the voice also indicated the speaker was somewhat in his cups. He could however see that his hair was distressingly awry and his face smeared with dust.

The second figure, advancing upon the flying buttress, hissed back irritably, 'Damme of course I am, I'm not an old man . . . blast!'

Thus as Gyles reached for the buttress with the seat of his dress trousers rent, a long strand of the black cloth dangling down but the monocle still remained firmly fixed in his right eye.

'Oh Papa,' murmured Richard, totally riveted. That Voice of Authority came again.

'I did this when I was yer age and I'm bloody well doin' it now.'

'Ohhh,' gurgled Richard, 'Bloody . . . bloody . . . Oh Papa! . . .'

Gyles Aynthorp tried again. He tipped his body forward at a perilous angle, grasped the buttress, embraced it, swinging for one agonizing moment in mid-air before he gained a foothold, then stood flattened against the old stone beside his son. He then made a desperate effort to remain vertical and at the same time dust the now deplorable knees of his ruined trousers.

Both men were panting slightly. Both ran their grubby hands over their tousled heads as the sun elected to make a perfectly timed entrance and flood down upon the unmistakable, flaming copper colouring.

'Now comes the tricky bit,' Richard then heard. 'Watch it boy, I've done it before remember! It's the ledge which gives you access to the long gallery window. I took the precaution of leavin' that open . . . I suspected it might come to this . . .' There was a short pause then Richard heard an unmistakable, muffled chuckle. 'For God's sake hurry cautiously, if the servants see us we really are undone.'

Richard wiggled in unbearable excitement and suspense. Father and son were oblivious to anything save the negotiation of that ledge . . .

The chuckle was followed by a murmured '*pas devant les domestiques eh?*' but as Richard's French was sketchy still he did not understand and only paid attention to the ensuing 'Well here goes', followed by an enormous hiccough. Gyles' face creased with laughter,

'Yer in yer cups my boy,' he stated.

'Yessir . . . hic,' Henry agreed.

'And I'm not far off it either,' added his father, 'come on, last lap comin' and we'll 've done it. Now put yer right hand down and grip that sill. Stretch out yer left leg for the pediment. When yer steady, push the open window gently, it creaks like hell . . . I'll follow . . . and keep the old tradition goin'.'

'Old tradition,' Richard mused, spellbound by the scene. He knew about traditon and instantly his mind latched on to the word. 'Then I can do it too one day,' he thought contentedly.

There followed a slight creak, a stifled laugh after which the prospective bridegroom vanished into the Long Gallery. Seconds later there was a rending sound which caught Plum's ear. He straightened, turned, lifted his head – but all he saw was a long, thin, black strand which a sudden breeze lifted and drew out like a pennant.

'Now wot the 'ell is that?' he muttered scratching his poll.

Richard sighed. It was such a long time still to breakfast and his tummy was rumbling. He was too excited to sleep, eager to be arrayed in his white satin page's suit and totally frustrated by the knowledge that past peccadilloes had ensured that the key to the door which gave access to the rest of the Castle beyond the nursery wing would be under Nanny's pillow and would there remain until she awoke and trotted on slippered feet, in her red flannel dressing gown, to unlock it and thus signal the beginning of yet another nursery day. He turned away, intent on finding some satisfying mischief to bridge the gap so missed the sight of his father and Henry when they re-emerged through the garden door half an hour later in breeches and

boots heading towards the stable. By mutual consent they had
changed, shaved and were now off for a canter, to be followed
by a quick plunge into the lake.

It was of course totally unorthodox for father and son to be
together at all on the night before the wedding; but Henry had
wished it so and had stammered out his wishes with his usual
incoherence when emotionally moved. By tradition he was
expected to spend the night carousing with his best man, young
Charles Danement, his ushers and others of his own generation.
Then Charles, discussing the carousel with him had suggested,
'Won't it be a bore to have to come back from London, why
don't we celebrate at the Manor? I'll ask my pater. He's bound
to be asked to dinner with yer family anyway and old Lucrezia
Borgia (meaning his sister's chaperone, their aunt) will certainly take to her bed.'

Henry, doubtful at first, had promptly sounded Petula who
told him she had been asked to dinner at the Castle, too, so the
way was made clear for the two young men. Sir Charles had
agreed to 'put on a dinner for you all and then leave you to yer
own devices', but Henry would have none of it and having
gained his father's assent sought and obtained Sir Charles' too.
Thus it was that both male parents saw in the dawn with the
eleven young men of Henry's choosing. This, when passed on
to Sir Charles' dyspeptic sister, first brought on an attack of the
vapours but ultimately, due to Petula's offers of assistance she
was won round and agreed to arrange this unorthodox bachelor
party which ended in the heir and his eldest son coming home
with the milk, via the rooftops of Castle Rising.

After this, events moved with smoothness towards the climax.

By ten-thirty André was able to ask Sawby if he would
despatch a footman to 'her ladyship' to invite her inspection of
the completed buffet.

'No,' said Sawby flatly, 'I will go myself and hope to conduct
her ladyship to you Monsieur André.' Thus he was enabled to
warn the chef that in matters of protocol he was the *Ultima
Thule* and at the same time ensure a leisurely inspection of the
man's work for himself.

Christine was coming down the staircase as Sawby put his
foot upon the first tread. She carried a sheaf of papers in her

hand, paused, listened to what Sawby had to say, then with a little nod crossed the hall and permitted him to open the great doors for her.

When she reached the central entrance she clapped her hands like a young girl.

'Oh Monsieur André,' she exclaimed, 'you really have excelled yourself!'

Sawbridge and the little Countess who had made their own separate plans had, with their little brigade of workers, transformed the marquee into a bower of pink and white flowers. These stood about in tall silver stands: cascading ferns, heady with the scent of tuberoses, studded with pale pink and white *Dianthus* and great sprays of delicate pink *Sasa-Yuri* lilies. Christine revolved very slowly taking in every detail.

The pair had also contrived holders which had been made upon wire frames so that they could be fastened easily to the supporting tent poles. Now these rose up in columns of *Lilium candidum* while all round the vast interior swags of white roses swung from the sides.

André had for his part designed two semi-circular tables which he had placed left and right, against his buffet. They appeared to be part of it but were so set that with their laces and satins undisturbed they could be moved forward when the time came for bride and groom to cut the cakes. On the right stood the English wedding cake, a seven-tier example of the art of icing and decoration with minute white birds perched upon lovers' knots all round the rims of the rising tiers and an exquisite white sugar Dove of Peace perched upon the top with a beribboned sugar heart hanging from his beak. Christine went closer so that she could read what was written upon it in pale pink sugar.

'Henry and Petula June 17th 1912.'

Her eyes were brimming as she turned to André.

'Thank you,' was all she managed, her hands outstretched impulsively. André bent over them.

'*C'est de rien*, milady,' he murmured deferentially, inwardly tickled pink and also deeply touched. 'Presently I shall complete my *croquenbouche* and then the two cakes will be ready. There are as you will observe a few *pièces montées* to come still, but these I prefer to leave upon ice until *le dernier moment*.' He hesitated then resumed. 'With your permission miladi I will slip from the Chapel as Miss Petula leaves and thus race through the back way to signal my helpers who will then move very fast so that when the 'appy couple reach the receiving arch all will be in place but perrrfectly fresh,' his roll of r's was positively fierce.

'You could not have a better plan,' she smiled, looking in her simple sprigged muslin morning gown somewhat like a bride herself, as André confided in Sawby later. Then Gyles came in, looking surprisingly fresh, and he praised everything, slipping one arm around his wife's slim waist for a moment when the two men's backs were turned.

They examined the tables together. Each supported a shallow silver bowl filled with water and containing a single water lily. As André hurried back anxiously, almost dancing with excitement but holding himself in check as much as possible.

'Nymphea,' Gyles commented, studying the floating water lilies, 'what a charmin' touch!'

'It was *Madame La Comtesse*, milord,' said André shyly.

'Of course,' Gyles agreed, 'and the buffet M. André?'

'I am responsible milord.'

'Again, of course,' Gyles said urbanely, 'no one else could have achieved such a totally elegant effect. Thank you.'

When he had said a few more tactful words to the delighted chef the pair hurried from the marquee.

'I must go to the hairdresser, Gyles,' Christine explained, 'we all have our allotted times, so as to free the great M. André to dress Pet's hair at twelve o'clock.'

At the Manor, Petula had surrendered herself to the women who fluttered and fussed about her endlessly. She stood for them to dress her in her wedding garments, made for her by no less a person than *Monsieur Paquin* who had sent down both gown and train with her going-away clothes by his own assistant. He would be following to attend the reception.

All the while as they turned and twisted her, slipped on stockings and slippers, fastened the blue garters, spread out the old lace which generations of Danement brides had worn over their faces; pinned the great pearl cluster at her throat which the Dowager had lent, repeating the old saw, 'something old, something new, something borrowed and something blue', Petula stood with a faint smile on her lips and her eyes filled with dreams.

She herself moved as if in a dream while Henry stood in the Castle library mixing two more King's Pegs[1] with a distinctly unsteady hand for himself and young Charles Danement who had tottered in some thirty minutes earlier.

'God my head!' he groaned, sinking into one of the deep leather chairs. Henry laughed, holding out the foaming glass,

'At least yer pater's liquor was sound, I haven't the vestige of a mouth, have you?'

'No,' Charles admitted with an answering grin, 'not like old Pop-Eye's bachelor send off when we drank some frightful stuff! I remember young Danby tellin' us he felt as if thirty dirty little Chinese in fur coats were sittin' on his teeth.'

'How absolutely disgustin',' said a voice behind them. They both wheeled round and at the sudden movement Charles clapped his hand to his head.

'Oh I say sir,' he protested feebly, seeing Gyles standing surveying them. 'Be kind sir, I'm feelin' deuced fragile . . . what a night!' Emboldened by Gyles' bland manner he asked weakly, 'How are you feelin', sir?'

'Fragile,' Gyles admitted, moving towards the table, 'distinctly fragile; but I think I shall last the day . . .' He mixed himself a drink.

'Have you got the ring?' he inquired.

'No sir, m'pater's got it. Said he wouldn't trust it to a, what was it he called me? Oh yes "a tipplin' flibberty gibbet" like me. Said he would give it to me at the Very Last Possible moment.'

Charles sank the contents of his glass – registered astonishment and asked, 'I say, sir, did King Teddy drink this regularly?' His voice held a note of awe. Gyles nodded.

'He did, *and* in addition to all those gargantuan meals he ate a huge lobster salad every day of his life at tea time. He was a

---

[1] *King's Peg*: a mixture of champagne and brandy – so called because King Edward VII invented it.

positive Falstaff of a man.' Gyles selected a cigar from the opened box on the table, pierced it, lit it carefully, then when it burned to his total satisfaction he added, on a vibration of warmest affection, 'but then m' father always used to say "give me lusty eaters, I cannot stomach fiddlin' men at the table!"' He too had the greatest devotion to the late King.' Suddenly his voice changed.

'Henry charge our glasses and let us drink to his rumbustuous memory.' His son obeyed. They drank and three glasses smashed against the wrought iron basket which stood beneath the chimneypiece.

Charles shook his head looking faintly dazed. 'I dunno how you do it sir. You look as fresh as if you had been abed eight hours when . . .' he trailed off doubtfully.

'When neither Henry nor I have seen our beds and two pairs of dress trousers are ruined . . .' Gyles supplemented. He broke off as Sawby appeared in the doorway.

'Yes, Sawby, what is it?'

'I apologize for disturbing you my lord, but Plumstead has just inquired of me if your lordship would wish to have the, er, piece of dress trousers removed from the gargoyle beneath the Long Gallery window before the, er, wedding procession commences.'

Even Gyles Aynthorp looked slightly taken aback. Both boys watched him. Then removing his monocle, polishing it, replacing it, he cleared his throat and said,

'By all means remove it Sawby and convey my thanks to Plumstead for his – er – admirable powers of observation.'

Certainly my lord.'

Gyles confessed afterwards that he suspected he saw the vestige of a twinkle in his butler's eyes.

'And shall I send one of the footmen to clear away the broken glass my lord?'

'Yes Sawby please do that too.'

When the door closed the three of them burst out laughing.

'Can you imagine,' sobbed Henry weakly, 'that old dragon the Duchess of Barton and Sale if she'd spotted yer pants danglin' down . . .'

They stifled their mirth as the door opened once more; but

it was only Ninian followed by Ralph and James. 'More King's Peg all round,' said Gyles resolutely. And so the morning passed.

By noon the Bishop appeared, making a splendid entrance, his great stomach going before him as he came in very slowly for by now he was perpetually short of breath. Behind him trailed his sons, Damien and Robert. Presently the library was filled with 'Family' males and remained so until Sawby announced from the doorway that it was 'time to join the ladies my lord; they are assembling now in the White Drawing Room'.

As they streamed in the great room seemed filled with wide picture hats, nodding with plumes, weighted down with flowers. Only the Dowager and the little Countess were yet to make their appearance. All three footmen, supervised by Sawby, were carrying round trays of champagne.

The little Countess then made her entrance and was engulfed by nieces and great-nieces, nephews and great-nephews. Finally there was a soft swish of skirts and the Dowager came in dressed in palest lavender grey, her hair piled high, and on it perched a coquettish tricorne of lavender panne-velvet with a single aigrette at one side.

As usual, she was the best-dressed woman in the room, a tiny fragile figure with a waist as narrow as a girl, the high collar of her dress caught with a single diamond brooch.

Christine moved towards her, took both her hands, '*Belle Mère*,' she told her, 'you look wonderful,' and was rewarded with a little pat from a tiny jewelled hand.

'And so do you my dear – and not a day older than when you were married.'

In the Chapel, made glorious by Marguerite de Lorme's all-white flower arrangements, a small altar boy was fitting the last of the candles into their silver sconces while above, in the organ loft, Lucien and Stephanie got in each other's way while a flustered and over-awed Mr Prewitt endeavoured to sort out their music.

It had been decided and at last agreed even by the shattered Eustace St John, that Lucien would play during the service. Mr Prewitt would play first, Lucien would take over.

This extraordinary child had chosen the Trumpet Voluntary to preface the bride's entry.

Mr Prewitt would then share the honours by bringing the bride in to the traditional 'Here Comes the Bride'. He would also play the hymns which Petula and Henry had chosen: 'Love Divine All Loves Excelling' and 'The Lord is my Shepherd' during which the choir would have its chance and would render the first and last verses of the latter without benefit of the congregation.

Then would come the big moment for Stephanie where, accompanied by Lucien, she would sing Gounod's 'Ave Maria'. Finally, on a signal from Mr Prewitt to indicate that the registry ritual was completed Lucien would transpose and then launch himself into the 'Wedding March' from *Romeo and Juliet*. Finally, and in order to give Lucien time to take up his position once more with the other little pages, Mr Prewitt would play Mendelssohn's 'Wedding March'.

This was the moment to which the two old naughties, Marguerite and the Dowager had been looking forward with such glee. It was to be the vindication of their championship, the peak of their not inconsiderable amounts of deliberate scheming. Meanwhile the whole affair had thrown Mr Prewitt into such a state of nerves that he alternately belched and said 'pardon' behind one hand.

Just before luncheon, Henry managed to slip away to the little Countess' boudoir and there she put her old arms round him as he knelt beside her on her *chaise longue*. Then she gave him her blessing and a small gift.

'It is of little value to anyone else,' she told him, 'but as there was no one in the whole world to whom I could entrust the work of translation I did it for you myself.' She held out the small parcel, wrapped and tied as if it had come from *Fauchon* and contained sweetmeats. 'I have translated – for your eyes only – such of the old diary entries as I have been fortunate enough to obtain.'

Henry stared at her disbelieving. 'You have done that for me?'

'In my own handwriting,' she said with some pride, 'which I have been told is very clear.' She was almost coquetting with him now. 'It may serve to influence you in the years ahead and enable you to take the right decisions if you are sufficiently aware of the long chain of wrong ones which this family's wrong doers have made.'

His young face was very tender as he took the small thing from her. 'Such hours and hours of work,' he marvelled.

'There is even some which was in black letter,' she admitted, 'Justin taught me to read Black Letter.' Suddenly her eyes were full of memories and the words escaped her which she had hoped she would not utter on this day. 'Oh Henry, if only he had been here!'

He put his little parcel on her table. For a moment they were both silent. Then he said very clearly, 'I think he is. I think he has been here ever since I nearly fell off that damned gargoyle comin' home. I thought then that I heard his voice.'

'What did you think he said?'

'Rein in you damn fool and take it easy. Let your head clear first, yer tipsy remember. It was awfully clear y'know.'

'And were you?' she dabbed a wisp of handkerchief against an errant tear.

'Stinkin'?'

'Suddenly the full import of his words penetrated. 'Henry, what were you doin' on one of our gargoyles?'

'Comin' home,' he said, 'm'father was with me,' and then wise beyond his years he told her, to relieve the tension and was rewarded by a bubble of naughty laughter.

'Oh how divine,' she exclaimed. 'Justin must have been there. It is just the sort of thing he would have approved . . . Henry!' she let out a small shriek, 'look at the time, we shall be late! Go boy go, I have my gown and hat to put on yet . . . hurry . . .' She sat forward, reached for her little bell and Henry went, snatching up his parcel and running down the corridor. The tinkling of her bell summonsing Pearson followed him as he ran.

In the nursery, things were getting out of hand. Richard was missing again. Nursery luncheon was upon the table, Nanny was finding it difficult to fasten the waistbelt of her best dress and Rose had forgotten to lay out the black silk Pelisse and jet-trimmed bonnet with which her wedding toilette was to be completed.

Contradictory cries emerged from her room, 'Find that dratted boy and tie him down Rose when you get him . . . George give Violet that tray and run down for some bismuth powders I've got the most shocking indigestion . . . Sit down children and get on with your luncheon . . . no, wait for me . . .'

Andrew, bored by all this female palaver stuck his head round the door of Nanny's room. 'Stephanie's not here either,' he vouchsafed, adding fuel to the fire, 'What's more Lucien isn't either.'

Nanny came bustling out with her waistbelt still unfastened. A large tassel of stay laces protruded from the gap.

Thoroughly worked up by now, Andrew seized the laces like reins, shouted, 'Gee up, c'mon me beauty,' and was turned round upon and given a sound box on his ears for his pains. This caused baby William to loose a tremendous roar, then he burst into tears and began drumming his heels on the floor – being on the flat of his back at the time on the rug in front of the nursery fire. Nanny snatched him up and marched off again.

Into the bedlam walked Richard, saintly of countenance, clearly hock deep in some iniquity. The only evidence of it was a slight tremor inside his shirt front which was quickly stilled by one hand as he seated himself at the table and slopped a large portion of *Pish Pash*[2] on to his plate.

'Gosh I'm hungry,' he exclaimed. 'C'mon everybody.'

Nanny reappeared, fastened amidships at last and panting slightly.

'Where have you been you naughty boy?' she demanded, 'No, don't tell me, get on with your lunch, I don't want a word out of you till you show me a nice clean plate.'

'Yes, Nanny,' smiled Richard and the grass snake inside his shirt did another little heave, then went to sleep.

He had become bored waiting for luncheon so he had sought his chance and while Nanny was dressing had taken off, bound for the stables for just a quick look at his menagerie. Plum was

[2] An Anglo-Indian dish of chicken, rice, milk and onions, standard fare in the Lorme nursery.

not there, he was busy distributing pillow slips of rose petals to the village girls. So Richard just wandered round, talking to his pets until it suddenly struck him that Marmaduke, his precious grass snake, looked depressed. At least he thought he did, so he decided he would give poor, sad Marmaduke a treat by taking him to the wedding. It was only the work of a moment to snatch the little creature up and button him into his shirt – a place to which he was well-accustomed. Then strolling happily, chatting onesidedly to Marmaduke he returned to the nursery and his Pish Pash.

When he had downed two helpings, swallowed a huge glass of water, belched heavily and won another nagging for so doing, he was hauled off to be put into his wedding suit protesting, 'I can do it all myself Nanny when you're so busy. Honestly I can. Just let me show you. I'm a big boy now.'

Nanny weakened. She was longing for her rocking chair and just one quiet cup of tea before it all began. 'Well,' she wavered, 'if you promise Nanny just for once to do nothing naughty and to come straight back to the nursery when you're dressed . . . go along then.'

He went, and thus was able to transfer Marmaduke into the blouse of his white satin suit. Then he returned and was praised by a thoroughly grateful Nanny. Little did she know.

Thereafter, what with the girls to dress, a fit of the shakes to sublimate in Lucien, Stephanie's stricken face as she muttered, 'I cannot remember either a word or a note . . .' there was no more time. Chivvied by Nanny they all clattered down the great stairs just in time to see Sawby throw open the doors of the Great Hall as everyone began streaming in from the dining room and the hall became a milling chaos. This sorted itself at length as the guest-members of the Family who were not to go with the bride or groom began their stroll towards the Chapel.

The route was thickly packed on either side with villagers and estate folk. In front of them all the way from the porch to the steps of the Castle stood two rows of little girls in white. Each held in one hand their end of the rose garlands which linked them all together, and in each remaining hand clutched a pawful of Plum's rose petals. Behind them stood their parents holding the pillowslips and ready to supply more petals for them to strew before the bride.

The last to leave of the main contingent were Gyles and Christine with John de Lorme escorting Petula's Aunt Eustasia.

Then the bridesmaids formed into pairs, Stephanie with her cousin Rosalind, Christabel, Petula's school friend a tiny, very pretty blonde pairing with Lucy; the two little bridesmaids Daphne, Petula's seven-year-old cousin and Priscilla-Claire, also aged seven, bringing up the rear.

At this moment, brushing past the pages came Henry and Charles thundering down the great stairs, dashing across the hall, slowing to a more decorous walk and grinning to familiar faces as they hurried along the route.

Then there was a pause in which the pages were sorted; eight-year-old Gilbert, young Peter and Lucien, who was to slip straight up to the organ loft after helping to carry the bride's train and lastly Richard with his invisible companion Marmaduke who still slept peacefully.

The sun shone, an excited babble broke out among the villagers. In the entrances to the marquee clusters of hired staff gathered to watch. Then the Danement car swept up the drive and Sawby came down the steps to assist the bride.

Her great embroidered train was lifted out and the tasselled ends and centre entrusted to the little boys. The bridesmaids fell in behind in rehearsed order, and finally Petula turned and faced the Chapel her veil falling about her face, a gleaming coronet of pearls catching the sunlight as she stood. She took her father's arm.

'All right?' said Sir Charles, smiling down at her.

'Quite all right,' she affirmed so they began to move. As she went the children cheered and threw their rose petals in her path. Monsieur Paquin was waiting for her at the porch. He took one glance over the dress he had designed for her, then bowed over her hand. '*Exquis mademoiselle, je me suis flatté,*' he said gently. Then he withdrew and a panting Lucien reached the organ loft.

He slipped into the seat Mr Prewitt vacated for him. He settled himself. The tightly packed congregation heard the first notes of the Trumpet Voluntary played by a boy of twelve.

'*C'est incroyable!*' whispered Marguerite to the Dowager. Lucien played on – all nervousness forgotten – a very happy little boy. Among the congregation his father and mother listened with a mixture of pride and bewilderment. As Lucien came to the end of his performance to a hushed assembly, Mr Prewitt, peering frenziedly over the organ loft rail saw the signal – a flash of white from the back of the Chapel. Henry standing rigidly with Charles beside him steeled himself not to look round – everyone else did, as 'Here Comes the Bride' swelled out over those turning heads . . .

Henry turned too. He saw the lovely young thing whom he had loved for what seemed to him like centuries, holding her father's arm, her face partially hidden by the veil, her right hand holding the shower bouquet of white orchids which she and Henry had chosen together. As she drew level with him his rapture was manifest.

Bishop Alaric, assisted by the Vicar, was at his best and simplest. He spoke to them briefly and lovingly. By his words, clearly so deeply thought upon, he drew them together and joined them as man and wife with bonds which he was at gentle pains to remind them were linked with all those other vows taken by Lorme men and women in this little place of worship.

Suddenly it was over. Henry Gyles Justin had taken Petula Alexandra Margaret to be his lawful wedded wife and they were kneeling in prayer.

It was then that Marmaduke escaped. He shot from between two buttons of Richard's blouse. Richard, fidgeting upon his knees and abysmally bored, made a frantic grab, missed, and kneeling still, saw his pet squirming resolutely under the stalls, heading towards the row in front. He clapped his hands to his face and murmured, 'Please God bring him back' – but God was otherwise engaged. The grass snake squirmed on unnoticed, until he came to the large ruched tulle, wholly unsuitable muff which the very large Duchess of Barton and Sale had laid down beside her footstool as she lumbered to her fat knees. Marmaduke found the stone of the Chapel floor cold and unyielding. He investigated the muff. After a moment's indecision he wriggled inside, and there curled up again and sank into a profound slumber. By this time Richard was flat on his tummy peering anxiously about. Nanny spotted him. She leaned down, she caught him by the straps of his satin breeches and hauled him on to the stall beside her. 'Sit still,' she hissed, 'or you will live to regret this day you bad, naughty, wicked boy.'

A few heads turned, but their owners merely saw a small boy being 'dealt with' by his highly respectable Nanny. Then their attention was wrenched away as from the organ loft came some notes on the organ and over their heads rose the clear, sweet young voice of Stephanie singing 'Ave Maria'.

As the last notes died away there was a moment's silence during which Mr Prewitt replaced the small accompanist at the organ.

The bride and groom were returning. Exactly as they appeared from the tiny vestry so Mr Prewitt launched himself and the newly-weds with Mendelssohn's 'Wedding March'. Sawby, barely able to move at the back of the Chapel, unfastened the heavy old door. He folded it back. The sun poured in; Henry, hand-fasted with his Petula – as nearly a thousand years ago the first Lorme bridegroom to be wed on English soil had led his bride Thyra from the little Saxon church in which they had been married – led her slowly through the smiling Family.

Lucien, panting slightly, slipped up the narrow aisle, grasped his tassel on Petula's train and Stephanie slipped into her place beside Rosemary. The procession formed, moved slowly towards the sunlight and, 'At last . . . at last!' exulted Henry as he looked down at his wife's radiant little face.

Smiling brilliantly Petula said an inward prayer, 'Let me be worthy . . . oh let me be worthy!'

As they reached the porch, the cheers rolled towards them. The air was filled with fluttering rose petals as they went slowly, very slowly between the ancient and modern tombstones.

Here they halted, waving . . . waving . . .

Inside the Chapel, the Duchess of Barton and Sale, one of Petula's godparents, grasped her muff as if it were a paper bag and edged her bulk out into the aisle.

At the foot of the Castle steps two rows of chairs had been arranged. The rest of the Family would gather on the steps behind for the photographist who, even now, tripod erected, was dodging in and out from under his black cloth getting himself and his camera in readiness for the first photographs.

Down the drive where the new road forked towards the completed Museum, Sawbridge and Tomkins were already directing the first of the guests' cars and carriages to the Museum Parking from whence everyone would make their way on foot towards the marquee, after the photographs had been taken.

As soon as the group ones were completed the extra hired footmen would whip away the chairs, M. Paquin's assistant would rearrange Petula's train, and the pictures of bride and groom would be taken.

It was just as the Duchess of Barton and Sale had lowered herself into a creaking chair panting, after her walk from the Chapel in the hot sun that Marmaduke awoke. He peered out. He squirmed free of the enfolding tulle and shooting downwards landed upon the Duchess's sturdy ankle. At the chilly touch she glanced down, saw the little snake, let out one unearthly shriek, and toppled over. She then fainted.

Richard darted forward, train forgotten, everything forgotten as cries of, 'Smelling salts, fetch some smelling salts – and move back everyone please, give her Grace some air . . . it's the heat y'know,' and suchlike clamour rose in a confused babble. Only Richard knew what had really happened and now his one frantic thought was to rescue his Marmaduke from the legs and arms and tumbled chairs.

Like a small white snake himself he burrowed and thrust. Gyles, perceiving him, bent down and lifted him by the seat of his satin pants.

'What the devil!' he exclaimed angrily. 'Richard what do you think you are doing?' Richard was beyond awe of his Papa now, his one thought for his pet.

'It's Marmaduke Papa,' he was almost sobbing, 'he'll get hurt Papa. Oh, there he is!' The child broke free, made a great dart forward and by some miracle grasped the terrified snake and had him inside his blouse before Gyles could even move.

In a tangle of legs and chairs the boy crooned to his pet and the Duchess, sprawled upon the gravel, smelling salts to her nose, and fully restored to consciousness eyed him with a gleam in her eyes.

'Damme,' she swore, 'that boy put a snake in my muff!' She sat bolt upright, swoon forgotten as the press around her cleared. Not for nothing was the old girl as tough as her husband. Not for nothing had she spent thirty-five years bedded to the most foul-mouthed man on the hunting field. As she spotted Richard and bade him, 'Come here this instant boy!' sitting with great plumed hat tipped disreputably over one eye, gravel on her gloves and a rent in her voluminous skirts, so she loosed such a flood of invective as caused Richard to gaze at her admiringly. Then the fulness of her character was made manifest. She stopped swearing, while all about her the Family watched, totally spellbound.

'Just you come here boy,' she commanded, struggling to rise to her feet.

Willing hands supported her. Willing hands attempted to dust her down, to such mingled phrases as, 'Mabel are you all right?' 'I am so sorry', 'Take it easy your Grace, here's a chair'.

She shook them off impatiently.

'Come here,' she commanded again, standing upright once more. 'No leave the boy to me,' as someone attempted to interfere. Richard came very slowly towards her until she was able to lay a fat hand upon his shoulder.

'Did you put that snake in my muff?' she demanded awfully and both Gyles and Christine were content to let her hold the floor. They just watched fascinated.

'No,' said Richard stoutly. 'I didn't, honestly I didn't. I had him in my shirt because I thought he looked lonely. He wriggled out . . . while I was praying . . . I tried to catch him . . . then I saw him get into your muff. I watched it. It didn't move so I knew he'd gone to sleep again . . . then I had to take Pet's train. Nanny was very cross with me so I couldn't tell you . . . I tried to . . . honestly I did.'

The Duchess listened. She straightened her hat. She sat down upon the proffered chair and then she began to laugh.

She clapped her hands to her great sides and she rocked with laughter.

'Ho, ho, ho, . . . damme that's capital . . . just like a boy . . . ha, ha, ha! Gyles,' turning to the flabbergasted parent, 'that's a chip off the old block, a true Lorme if I ever saw one! Don't punish the boy. Just let me go inside and be tidied up, you can come with me boy . . . at least . . .' she eyed him dubiously '. . . hadn't you better return that pox-stricken thing to its cage first? Then you can join me and have your picture taken like a Christian.'

Christine caught Gyles's eye. Cars and carriages were already waiting in a long line to enter the Museum Parking. Gyles nodded, perilously close to laughter himself.

'So be it Mabel,' he said, stepping forward and offering his arm. Then he turned and addressed Richard. In a thunderous voice, he said, 'Go, boy, and return immediately. I will see you later.'

Richard fled. His lordship armed her Grace to the Hall where she was engulfed by maids.

Then predictably Gyles came out again into the sunlight and atop the steps dissolved into helpless laughter. This was speedily infectious. As the servants straightened chairs, picked up the muff and bore it inside, restored all to order, the whole Family began to laugh too until the air was rent by their mirth and the atmosphere restored to all its temporarily abandoned calm.

Henry was mopping his face.

'The little sod,' he confided leaning against Charles' shoulder, 'it dam nearly went up her skirts.'

All the Duke contributed, having been a silent watcher throughout the fracas, was a *sotto voce* mutter, which Henry swore ever after was quite unmistakable, 'Farther than I've got for years anyway! . . . and more's the pity,' he stated crossly.

They gathered again on those steps two hours later, when Petula and Henry came out and Sawby, Edward and George carried their bags, dressing cases and Petula's jewel box to the waiting vehicle. This, too, was a surprise. Unknown to any of the Family – a secret held between Sawbridge, old Plum and the little Countess, who had worked half the night with the two men – the eighteenth-century Lorme town equipage had been transformed into a bower of roses. Now this landau stood waiting in the drive. Plum was on the box wearing eighteenth-century dress. The two grooms were 'up' behind ready to dismount to set the footstool the moment the young couple appeared. They would return to their positions thereafter while Sawby handed them in.

In the beribboned shafts, beaming and sweating in the hot sun stood fourteen of the estate men ready to draw the carriage to the station. Petula gasped as she came on to the steps. With shining eyes, 'Oh look Henry!' she cried, 'Isn't it pretty!'

The huge array of guests surged round the waiting vehicle. Drawn up behind it, ready to be taken over when the couple reached what they imagined to be their first destination, the station, was a new motor, a shining Bugatti which was the Family's surprise extra wedding present to Henry.

Petula said something to Henry. He nodded. Then dutifully she threw her bouquet, and immediately ran down the steps and went to the leaders of the harnessed men. She said a word or two to every one of them, shook their hands and thanked them. Henry followed suit, then turning he went to his mother and kissed her. As he approached, Gyles murmured to his wife, 'She'll do, bless her, oh how very wise was the old octogenarian!'

Late that night, when Charles Danement had led Christine out on to the ballroom floor for the first waltz of the Bridesmaids' Dance and Gyles had done his duty by Great-Aunt Eustasia, they went out on to the moonlit terrace together.

'Continuity, Gyles,' she said softly, the moonlight shining down upon her.

'We shall be grandparents soon,' Gyles reminded her. 'You know, my love, today has been not only memorable but absolutely devoid of any sense of loss. They will come back here. They will become parents here and God-willing, we can in the years to come relinquish our responsibilities very, very slowly so that they will be well-equipped when our time comes to take the Swan's Path.'

Christine leaned her head against her husband's shoulder.

'It *is* an ending, but a beginning also. For in our love I see theirs reflected. What a wonderful day it has been my darling.' She lifted her face to his, as always feeling her heart quicken as his face bent towards her.

He spoke again with his mouth on hers. 'You look as lovely as the day you married me . . . neither of us are old yet. Oh, my dear, we have so much to which we can look forward; but this is a night on which I wish you to know that like my father to my mother you are the peak of my heart's desire.'

Three months later they were back in mourning, this time for Eustace's brother Timothy who died in his sleep quite suddenly. Gabrielle and Eustace, now Lord Steyne, departed for the obsequies which Gyles and Christine also attended. There followed another lull at Castle Rising.

CHAPTER 14

An Irish Knight

In the past few years a curious bond had been forged between Chef André and the then house parlourmaid Pansy Appelby for whom Pearson had 'spoken' to Christine.[1] As a result, after some small diplomatic finaglings by Christine, Pansy had taken Pearson's place thus releasing her to become personal maid to her new ladyship.

This far-reaching event occurred when Pansy first arrived; experienced, trained in a household of almost equal stature; but very much 'knowing her place' and anxious not to cause offence in any way. Trained as she was to the ways of Servants' Halls she knew that in its own fashion there were almost as many social errors she could commit therein as above stairs in the pattern of the family whom she was to serve.

Sawby had spoken to her on that first night as the senior servants rose from their supper table to take their 'pudding', according to custom, in the privacy of the Steward's Room.

'Perhaps you will be good enough to bring us our pudding, Appelby,' he asked.

When the girl entered with her tray, he addressed her once more. 'When you return with our tea and coffee tray you had better put on a cup for yourself, girl. Then stay in here. We think we should give you a chance to become familiar with the broad outlines of how matters are conducted below stairs in this castle. So you had better bring in an extra chair,' he added, 'just for tonight,' thus disabusing her mind of any idea that such an honour would be conferred upon her more than once.

In the event, this piece of domestic patronage developed into a series of short, sharp interrogations. Mrs Parsons fired

[1] See Book I, *The Lormes of Castle Rising.*

questions at the now slightly flustered Pansy. Sawby conducted some more kindly but none the less penetrating probings. Mrs Peace contributed nothing, for she had interviewed the girl already while Miss Palliser orchestrated the performance with a series of disapproving sniffs.

Thus it came to light that Pansy had always longed to be a cook. She confessed that she had grasped any opportunity to watch 'cook-in-my-last-place' whom she informed them earnestly was 'ever so kind and helpful'.

André was a silent listener to all this, content to sip his brandy-laced coffee, his long nose rising and plunging for all the world like a heron at a water pool. It had always fascinated his colleagues to watch him demonstrate his ability to insert that nose and still manage to keep his stiffly waxed moustache ends clear.

He thought to himself, 'This is a very agreeable young woman.' Now that he examined her more closely, he wondered if she were quite as young as she looked. Then he heard about her marriage and her children and decided, 'A nice, ripe, plump little partridge with some experience . . .'

Aloud he said, 'For my part, Mademoiselle, I shall extend to you the invitation to watch me working whenever your duties permit. And you may ask me questions and take any notes you wish, provided,' he paused dramatically, wagged a finger at her and delivered himself of his proviso, '*I am not making the sauces.* Sauce-making, she is the peak of a *Maître Chef*'s art. While it is nothing to me to 'ave eight or nine dishes in the making at the same time, when I make the sauces, then they and they only 'ave my full concentration. 'Owever,' he gave a Gallic shrug, 'of all this we can speak later, *en principe* I shall be de-lighted to 'elp Mademoiselle Pansy.'

Pansy flushed becomingly. A gleam lit up the butler's eyes and a very sharp one indeed sparked up Mrs Parsons' beady ones.

' 'Ere, 'ere,' she exclaimed, 'we're runnin' orf with ourselves ain't we? Jest you ark ter me. It'll be Appelby above and below stair from now on Mr André, IF you don't mind.' Mrs Parsons was thinking rapidly as she snapped the words out. She was torn between 'givin' 'em both a set-down,' and 'puttin' that

André's long nose out-er-joint.'

Rivalry won. 'I'll tell you wot my girl,' she leaned forward, beady eyes as sharp as needles now, hands spread out upon alpaca-covered knees, teeth slipping slightly as was their wont. 'Wen time allows of course Appelby – oh drat them teeth! . . . I'll learn yer. Never mind about just watchin'. Times I'd be glad of a pair of 'elping 'ands to fall back upon wen me rheumatism is crool. You come ter me and I'll teach yer.'

Thus even greater rivalry was created between Chef and Cook. From it Pansy profited. First one and then the other began passing on their knowledge to her. Then when it became clear that the young woman was a natural cook and like a human blotter in her absorption of knowledge – one moreover who was capable of copying the experts' movements – the rivalry grew more intense, until with Pansy working and Mrs Parsons watching, 'I learned her that!' she would exclaim when Pansy withdrew a perfect batch of sponge fingers or a faultless tray of fairy cakes from her oven.

Then, when she achieved her first classic omelette under Chef's tuition, *'Voilà!'* he exclaimed with pride, 'See what a good teacher can do with the right material . . .'

Pansy merely treated both with the greatest deference, picked their brains and spent hours at night in her little room copying out her notes into exercise books.

After some months and when an entirely different kind of promotion lay in store for her, she confided in Sawby, of whom she had speedily lost all awe, 'I don't think I'll be at all a bad cook by the time I'm wed again.'

Sawby gave her a curious little smile and passed on down the staircase. That night he asked for and obtained permission to see Gyles Aynthorp privately.

Gyles leaned back in his worn office chair looking with some curiosity at his butler. For his part, Sawby presented his usual unruffled, deferential appearance. Inwardly he was quaking with nervousness.

'Well, Sawby, what can I do for you?'

Sawby swallowed. He made a curious croaking sound and then blurted out, 'With your permission my lord I wish to marry.'

Gyles nearly dropped his monocle, 'Married Sawby!' he repeated. 'Good God!' He told Christine later that he felt like a drowning man who is supposed to see his whole life in seconds. The thought struck him with great force that he and the family were about to lose the man who had been their devoted and loyal servant for so long now that they had come to think of him as part of the family.

Sawby was repeating, 'Yes, my lord, married. I know I am no longer a young man, but I trust I have many years before me in which to be a good husband to the woman of my choice, and of course my lord to serve you and the family who will always be my first consideration.'

Gyles shook his head as if to clear it.

'Are you tryin' to tell me that although you intend marryin' you also intend carryin' on as my butler . . .?' his voice trailed off incredulously.

'But of course my lord. Otherwise I could not, no,' he corrected himself, 'I would not contemplate marriage at all.'

'I see,' said Gyles, for once completely thrown, 'I think I could do with a brandy, so would you have the goodness to pour two, then I can wish you well as indeed I do most sincerely.'

Sawby poured two brandies from the tantalus on the sofa table. He put Gyles' upon a salver, proffered it solicitously and murmured reproachfully, 'Did you think, my lord, that I would ever leave you?'

Gyles nodded, 'I tell you frankly I did not know what to think. It struck me we might be losing you . . . look here, sit down there's a good chap and let us talk this out together.'

Sawby stood rigidly. 'No thank you, my lord. I know my place and therefore would prefer to stand.'

'As you wish, but pray tell me who is the lucky young woman?'

'Pansy Appelby, my lord. She took Pearson's place as house parlourmaid some years back in order that Pearson could become her ladyship's personal maid.'

'I see,' Gyles sipped thoughtfully, 'who knows of this Sawby?'

'No one my lord,' Sawby sounded shocked. 'Pansy, that is Appelby and I agreed that nothing must be said to anyone until

I had spoken with your lordship.'

Gyles grinned at his butler, 'It'll put a pretty cat among the pigeons below stairs I'll dare swear.'

'We know that too, my lord. We thought we would look about for a cottage. Then, with your lordship's approval we need only re-adjust one small factor in our daily lives.' Gyles, with relief flooding through him began to enjoy the situation. He waited. After a moment Sawby went on.

'It would merely be a matter of going home after our duties were completed and coming back in the morning instead of just coming downstairs to begin our duties.'

'Oh nonsense!' Gyles exclaimed. 'You must have some life of yer own! Surely we can plan things, get another footman, do something so that the pair of you have at least one clear day every week when you can be at home together? No let me finish,' as Sawby attempted to reply, himself looking completely taken aback by the suggestion. 'I can give you old Crowbrough's cottage now that he's moved in with his daughter. It's bein' done over, some essential repairs, a decent coat of paint outside, yes, that's the answer, you take Crowbrough's cottage and her ladyship and I will help you with the furnishings.'

They talked for a long time and when at last Sawby closed the office door behind him a broad smile spread across his face.

It had been decided that Sawby would announce his engagement to Pansy immediately, since, as Gyles was at some pains to point out, something was bound to leak out eventually. Once having cleared that hurdle matters could then progress with as much speed as possible. Sawby could scarcely credit his good fortune, as he went below to where the various members of the younger staff were sewing, reading or just chatting together.

He announced, 'I have something to tell you all. Please summons anyone who is not present,' and so saying put his foot upon the last tread and went to the Steward's Room.

He came out again, followed by the senior servants. Edward rose, drew up a chair for Mrs Parsons. Palliser and Mrs Peace were likewise seated and the two kitchen maids came clattering down to join the rest. Then Sawby took up his stance at the head of the big table, nodded to Pansy who shot him one questioning glance and said with some superfluity, 'I have an announcement to make.' Then he paused, looked around them and made it.

'I have a forthcoming event to disclose to you all and I hope that you will share my happiness. Pansy has consented to be my wife. His lordship has been most generous and has given us both permission to continue here in our present capacities. In short, Pansy and I are engaged to be married.'

Mrs Parsons gave a little shriek, threw her apron over her head and began to sob.

Pansy hurried to her and put one arm about her shoulder, 'There, there,' she soothed, 'there's no need to take on so, nothing will be changed, it will all go on as before . . .' she broke off as Mrs Parsons, fearful of missing anything, removed the enveloping apron and reappeared looking sadly dishevelled.

'Well I never did!' she exclaimed, teeth slipping alarmingly as she accepted Pansy's proffered handkerchief and mopped her eyes with it. 'I never suspected nothing, that I never did.'

'There, there,' Pansy soothed on, 'we couldn't let on afore Albert had told his lordship could we? It wouldn't 've been right nor proper.'

Mrs Parsons patted the girl's hand. 'You're a good, kind girl and no mistake,' she said, quivering on the brink of a second outburst, 'but after all these years, when I had thort 'im settled to being a single man for all the rest of his days . . .' and down came the tears until she resembled nothing so much as a gargoyle being drenched by a fountain.

Chef André was staring at the bobbles on the tablecloth. He was shocked too by the announcement. Secretly he had half cherished the idea that one day, in his own good time, he might confer the signal honour upon Appelby of informing her that he would be prepared to marry her. Now a mixture of regret and chagrin assailed him as he realised he had left it too late! He shrugged his shoulders, *tant pis*! He had made a monumental mistake. Now he would have to look elsewhere for the woman who would one day run a small French restaurant with him . . . As he rose, so the drawing room bell sounded.

Edward leapt to his feet, 'I'll go,' he said. 'Just you stay here

Mr Sawby, I'll call you if you are needed,' saying which he rushed up the stairs, taking them two at a time while shrugging himself into his coat. He came clattering down again almost immediately. 'His lordship says as how you are to get three bottles of the Krug, he said Krug, special, so that we can all drink to your health and 'appiness.'

Sawby was in the process of having his hand wrung by the two remaining footmen, André and little Boots, who had been a wide-eyed witness to the scene. He now extricated himself, inquired as he reached for the cellar keys, 'Did you remember to thank his lordship properly?'

'Oh yes Mr Sawby,' Edward assured him, 'and everyone was smiling ever so!'

Christine snuggled up against her husband in the big bed that night and murmured against his shoulder, 'Oh, Gyles isn't it nice? Pansy is such a good, sweet girl and we won't lose Sawby. *Gyles what would we have done without him?*' She stiffened suddenly as the thought gripped her, 'Oh Gyles, what on earth would we have done without Sawby!'

This event caused another Family conclave at which it was decided that the Family's main wedding present would be the furnishings for the cottage. Instantly the Countess and the Dowager pounced.

'We will take care of all that', they announced in unison, so Christine willingly agreed to leave it all to them.

She then asked, 'How have we done staff weddings in the past? It is something I have not yet experienced.' So the Dowager agreed to instruct her, fully aware Christine would only be content if she knew that it was all being done according to Hoyle.

It was then decided that a silver tea service and a canteen of cutlery and silver would be the Aynthorp's personal gift, Christine then said that she would be responsible for Pansy's wedding dress. Letters then sped to absentees from their ranks. Henry and Petula cabled from Kashmir, 'Delighted, sending cheque, will bring present home with us', and Bishop Alaric weighed in with a handsome dinner service.

When the time came Gyles dealt very firmly with the bridegroom, after having had a private word with his head footman who, puffed with pride, undertook to bridge the gap made by a one-week honeymoon, by undertaking to perform the functions of temporary butler. After which, Sawby having been told in no uncertain terms that he was going, drove Edward to the brink of lunacy with his warnings, precepts, instructions, counter-instructions and homilies.

Everyone contributed something. Pearson offered to do double duty as house parlourmaid during the honeymoon, André made the wedding cake, while Mrs Parsons, in an aura of astonishing benevolence, helped herself liberally to her employer's ingredients and made jams, jellies, fruit cakes and all manner of preserves, from old English fruit cheeses to pickles and chutnies, she then demanded and obtained the services of a fruit truck and two boys from Sawbridge and thus personally supervised the installation of her goodies on shelves and in cupboards in their new home.

Mr and Mrs Sawby returned in time for the first shooting party. Then the old pattern of entertaining was resumed and thus the autumn of nineteen thirteen gave way to Christmas with all its traditional celebrations, including the presence of a hitherto unknown hunting friend of John de Lorme.

In mid-January nineteen hundred and fourteen the addition to the Museum was completed which ensured a continuity of activity for the Countess and the Dowager. Wisely Christine left it all to them. She was only too well aware that in such matters lay the only hope for two old people for whom the axis of life had been shattered and who, were there no such concerns for them to be occupied by, would wither in their loneliness.

Thus she drew them into every possible ploy which might amuse them. Then with the coming of the first snowdrops she began her plans for the launching of the two girls into society.

Her initial conjectures had not proved completely accurate. Neither Sinclair or Henrietta put up any obstacle when Christine suggested, in her tactful way, that she would undertake to present both girls if this were considered desirable. Henrietta actually pounced upon the idea, thankful as ever when she could delegate responsibility. But, Gabrielle and

Eustace, Lucy's parents declined her offer and declared themselves very willing to endure the rigours of another London
season.

So, with the girls in the last term at finishing school, Christine
began to plan; for the opening up of the house in Rutland Gate;
for the joint coming-out ball for Lucy and for Rosalind; for
their presentation, the transference of certain staff to the town
house – at which point she was considerably startled by the
Dowager's crisp announcement that it was time she made a
personal re-appearance in the great world and would accompany
them to London.

'If you're going I shall too,' said the little Countess promptly.
'There is nothing to stand in my way. For my part I shall enjoy
the renewal of old acquaintances.' She clasped her hands and
twinkled naughtily, 'Think of the scandal Alicia, we shall be
all at sea after so long,' but then, she added contentedly, 'I
expect we shall soon catch up if we put our minds to it.'

In short they were 'off again' scheming and spending,
writing endless letters, nudging with incomparable skill at
doors which had barely remained ajar after such a lapse of time.

Luncheons were enlivened by bulletins concerning their
latest triumphs among the 'fishing fleet', as the Dowagers of
the '*ton*' were known, and endless reports made concerning how
Cissy – a dowager Duchess – was coming up for her granddaughter's send off, and would expect the Lormes to present
themselves the instant they arrived in town.

Lorme characteristics surged into full flowering. At their
height a cable from Henry and Petula sent them all into
transports of delight: '*Ship docks Monday, expect us for dinner,
love from both.*'

The honeymooners had written home with such surprising
frequency they enabled the Family to follow their route
throughout their year and a half of travelling. With two
additions, they took the journey which Henry had promised
Petula when they shared their disappointment at not being to
marry for some time.

They went to Italy and Greece, but first Henry took his
bride to Paris, where his French connections made much of

her. He also bought her scents in the fashionable shops of the *Rue St Honoré*, where she bought him what the elegant young assistant assured her earnestly was the *dernier cri* in gentlemen's sleeping wear, the new-fangled pyjamas.

They lunched together under the trees at restaurants scattered about the *Bois* where they held hands, looked into each other's eyes and ate an inordinate amount of *Fraises des Bois* with thick cream scooped from little brown pots.

They joined the fashionables at chairs set out along the *trottoire* at *Fouquet's* sipping pink champagne and watching the *Parisiennes*, from hurrying *Midinettes* with be-ribboned band-boxes and exotic creatures who strolled along in gorgeous *toilettes* leading minute dogs whose leads and collars were studded with jewels; to bloused, cloaked artists from the *Rive Gauche* and the endless procession of cars and carriages which flowed up and down the *Champs Elysée*.

At night Henry took his wife, *en grand tenue* to Voisin's where they dined off the finest food and wines in Paris.

They paid pilgrimage to the *Louvre* to stand enraptured before *La Victoire de Samothrace*; came out into the Gardens of the *Tuileries* where children bowled hoops and strolled on down to the banks of the *Seine*. Here they spent hours poring over books and prints at the little stalls behind which fishermen dangled their rods in the river in a faith which represented the ultimate triumph over experience.

He drove her to Versailles; hired hacks that they might ride together in the *Bois* and spent a great deal of money on what Henry vulgarly called 'their Parisian loot'. This they left behind in one vast trunk promising themselves a return visit before they went home.

Italy came next. They went to Florence where they leaned over the *Ponte Vecchio* by the statue of *Benvenuto Cellini* and watched the green water flowing beneath them. Henry bought jewelry from some of the little craftsmen in those Lilliputian shops, where they worked away cross-legged as they had done when the great Cellini had swaggered across the bridge at the height of his renown.

Then Rome saw them for a while, not only for sight-seeing and a slight surfeit of picture galleries; but for their privileged audience with the Pope, for which Petula swathed herself from head to foot in black, covered her head with a superb mantilla and wore her finest jewels. They merely flashed through Pisa for, as they made their way dutifully and on foot through the labyrinthine streets towards their objective, their first glimpse of the famous leaning tower shattered them both.

As she saw it, Petula halted and exclaimed in bitter disappointment, 'Oh darling, what a nasty! It looks exactly like a toppling sugar cake, but not nearly so nice as any of the ones André makes for us.'

Henry nodded, 'Well . . . at least it *leans*,' he acknowledged grudgingly . . . So they went on to Venice which they decided was the most beautiful city in the world. They tore themselves away with great reluctance, were rowed out in a gondola which had been laid on by the Gritti Palace management and was complete with serenaders and strings of fairy lights, to climb thence on to the ship which bore them off to Piraeus.

Greece held them for six months, idling among olive groves, gathering flowers on the slopes of Parnassus, climbing towards the Parthenon over stones made slippery by centuries of sandalled feet; riding mules and devouring goat's cheese, black olives and red mullet, grilled for them over charcoal under vine-awnings by fishermen on small islands where foreign visitors were few and far between. This was the period in which they wrote their longest letters home, for the Islands, from the Peloponese to Crete and Rhodes, had them in thrall.

When they at last reached their Mecca – *Sirinaga*, Henry rented a houseboat and the pair ran wild. They went barefoot, dangling their feet in the lakes which fulfilled their dreams. They rose at dawn to find their blue lilies pointing closed faces to the rising sun. As the heat developed, so it drew those petals apart until the lake became hazed by their incomparable blue.

Petula, watching within Henry's encircling arm murmured raptly, 'Like chalices filled with the morning's dew.' The surface of the lake then began to be pierced by leaping fish whose ripples spun themselves out against fat lily-pads. This was when Petula added, 'Oh my darling, it was so very much worth waiting for!' They had no time for writing letters now.

When they returned to 'civilisation' they were royally

received. Petula had just missed the Durbar on her earlier visit to India with her father; but the British Raj was still *'en fête'*. So, as Henry had profited by his Italian experience with Gyles and could show her much more because of it; now she led and he followed while she retraced her steps to the great palaces of her father's friends.

When the time came for them to return they went via Paris, and making their way thence by easy steps to the coast. They travelled through Normandy. After persistent probing, they encountered an old *Curé* who trotted towards them between the worn tombstones of a tiny Norman churchyard. They knew they were by this time 'warm', but how warm neither realised until, after their lengthy explanations the old man clapped on his weatherbeaten *soutane*, climbed in to their hired carriage with them and directed the coachmen through some winding lanes whose gradient taxed the horses. So, with several halts to rest them, they reached the head of the rise where the *Curé* dismounted and led his new acquaintances over two fields, one stile and so to the ruins which had once been the *château* over which the widowed Lady Mathilde held sway.

Henry wandered about the ruins alone. Petula sat on a crumbled wall talking with the old man. While Henry wandered so a curious thought assailed him . . . *that he had come home*, and some day, somehow, through some unforseeable circumstance he would return . . . He banished the thought for it was manifestly false. How could he, the future Lord Aynthorp, who was destined to rule in his father's stead over the Lorme's Essex acres and Castle make any return to the site of his ancestors? It was ridiculous! Still the thought persisted . . . somehow . . . it . . . would happen.

Eventually, as the sun was sinking behind the hill from whence Henri de Lorme had ridden to join his master, Duke William the bastard of Normandy, Henry returned to his companions; but all the way back again to the *Curé*'s tiny house, the instinct clung to him. He shook it off, of course, but time and again throughout his life that thought, instinct', prescience, call it what he might, whatever it was, *it returned* to make sense of itself only when he was a very old man.

* * *

Christine walked about the Castle holding their cable and smiling radiantly. Her mood was reflected in staff and family alike. It was all so very similar to the mood of the last few weeks before Henry's twenty-first birthday ball; but this time everyone's thoughts were upon the heir's homecoming. Thus it passed almost un-noticed that the First Sea Lord, Mr Winston Churchill, had resigned over what he considered the urgent need to expend some fifty-four million pounds on strengthening the British Fleet: 'A matter of life and death to us all' he was to emphasise only a few weeks later in his speech to the House of Commons.

But the Lormes had other fish to fry.

Yet in his father's study the very morning after his return; after the inevitable, elaborate, twelve course celebratory dinner, attended by both Petula's Papa and her depressive Aunt, and enjoyed in an unflawed aura of felicity; Henry broached the subject within minutes of being invited to 'take a pew' and being told 'it's good to have you home again'.

Gyles studied his eldest son, noting the changes which a year and a half of travel had made. Henry had matured. He had acquired an air of authority and with it the ease of confidence. He was sun-tanned, too, on this cold January day when ice hardened the furrows made by autumn ploughing and the tussocks in the grazing which forced the cattle to roam, disconsolate, until the sun's frail winter powers thawed the grass into palatability. Hunting was suspended too.

Henry came straight to the point. 'I wanted to see you alone sir, as soon as possible. Now that we are home again, Petula will be fully occupied for the next few weeks in gettin' our new quarters done up. She is in fact enveloped in an aura of curtaining, patterns, braid samples and such-like. She and Mrs Peace have little use for my presence. So, with a clear conscience I can take up the ropes again if you are willin'.'

Gyles smiled warmly, 'Willin', I'm thankful! Philip's a good chap, but he has neither the grasp nor the authority you possess and we're dashed busy, what with one thing and another.'

Henry nodded. 'That's what I wanted to hear sir. Y'see

goin' round the world has done a little more for me than
broaden my general horizons. I've talked to rather a lot of
people in high places.'

Gyles' eyes narrowed as he listened, but he made no attempt
to interrupt.

'It seems to me,' Henry went on, 'that war is comin' whether
we like it or not.'

'Ah.'

'You think so too, sir?'

'Shall we say I fear and dread it. We are not prepared y'know.
There are too many fellers in office playin' ostrich, refusin' to
face facts. Consider one aspect alone, the thinly veiled dislike
between Kaiser Willy and the late King; the burning jealousy
which has seethed in this little, handicapped creature, the
resentment . . . Then lay alongside it the inescapable fact that
Germany has been layin' her plans for years.'

It was Henry's turn to look startled, but he too remained
silent now. His father continued, almost as if ruminating to
himself, 'I remember when yer Great-Aunt Felicity went to
finish with the Hohenzollern family . . . she came back full of
their martial attitudes, the great Prussian obsession for war . . .
It's always been there. It's only now a matter of decidin' when
the pot will boil over and when that obsession will become
brutal fact.'

His father's words prompted Henry to rush his fences.
'Precisely,' he agreed. 'That is why, sir, I wish to do two
things.'

'Two?'

'Yes sir, take over the reins in so far as possible in case we
may need to dispense with a number of our estate chaps –
joinin' up and all that – and by so doin' put myself in the
position where I can ease the strain on you by passin' on what
I know to some chap who is unable to fight in the event of war.'

The pain in Gyles' eyes was manifest. He remained silent for
a moment or two longer. Then out came the monocle and after
intense polishing it was replaced. 'You are tellin' me that in the
event of war you will go?' he asked tonelessly.

Henry looked astonished. 'But of course, sir, as you went and
left m'grandfather in the Boer War.'

'I see.'

'Not entirely I think, sir. I know where I stand. I know only too well how my bein' killed would break the line. But after all sir, we cannot suppose that Pet will not, er oblige and I am not your only son. If anythin' should happen you've got Ninian and after him there's Andrew and . . .' he hesitated, 'and Richard. How is the young sod sir? I have not yet seen him.'

'Unchanged,' Gyles told him. Their eyes met. The twinkle in Henry's sparked up a glimmer of response.

'I'll never forget that snake,' he grinned, 'but I think the old Duchess was perfectly splendid. God it was funny though!' He had decided to try and make his father laugh, thinking they both stood in need of something to lighten the atmosphere between them. So he recounted the Duke's addenda to the snake episode saying, 'I heard him clearly sir, you recall how he never said a word durin' the uproar, just stood there watchin' – well as they led the old gal away, I heard him mutter quite distinctly, "further than I've got for years anyway! and more's the pity".'

Gyles laughed, 'Bawdy old monster! It would not surprise me if he spoke from the heart!'

'Heart, sir?' Henry raised an eyebrow.

Gyles coughed. 'Well, er, now enough of that I think; could you tell me if you have already decided what regiment you would prefer – always supposin' I can work the oracle for you?'

'I have,' said Henry, 'The Grenadier Guards, but that's not to say it will make a ha'porth of difference to my goin' in if this is not possible.'

Gyles had by now made up his mind. He said abruptly, 'I think perhaps we'd better let the matter lie for a bit while I make some tentative inquiries. Leave it with me for a few days. In any event, I'm goin' to town on Wednesday. I can arrange to see one or two people then. I'll let you know as soon as I have anythin' constructive to pass on, will that do?'

'Of course.'

'Then how about my beginnin' to put you back into the picture?' Gyles drew a sheaf of papers towards him, 'First, there's the matter of the Museum . . .'

They were still deep in estate affairs when the gong sounded for luncheon and when it was over they went off together to ride round the estate.

It had been mutually agreed that Henry and Petula would install themselves in the Cardinal's Suite which was a large enough assembly of rooms to include nursery quarters. It was so called because Cardinal Wolsey had once occupied the rooms and slept in the great fourposter which became thereafter 'the Cardinal's bed'. Before they went on their honeymoon, the pair had asked Christine if they might delay the redecorating and refurbishing until they returned so that Petula could plan it all herself. Now she immersed herself in this ploy, only dragging her mind away from the subject for long enough to agree that she must be re-presented to Their Majesties now that she was a married woman.

She had 'done' her 'season' when she was eighteen. The oncoming one presented no particular pitfalls to her; no agonies of uncertainty such as beset the young and totally untried who were plunged into the maelstrom of 'Society', just three months after leaving finishing school. Even a colt is broken in gradually, trained patiently to the bridle, while a debutante in effect is nothing more than a schoolgirl with an elaborate wardrobe and a number of 'suitable' girl friends. With these scanty assets, plus a few lessons in How to Curtsy to the reigning Monarchs, how to diminish the depth of such a courtsy for Other Royal Persons, down to minor princelings of foreign countries to whom a mere bob sufficed, she was flung into the maelstrom of the sophistication and expected to conduct herself with absolute propriety at all times; to maintain 'suitable' conversation at imposing dinner parties and generally to conduct herself in a manner which would do credit to her family, ensure her the maximum of invitations, and at least one satisfactory proposal from some eligible *partie* in the brief period of the London Season.

Her training for her début consisted solely of a few dinners in her parents' homes, when, laced into fashionable corsets, hair piled in an elaborate coiffure, she would experience for the first time the elaborate rituals of dining, remember to turn from left hand partner to right hand neighbour with the respective courses, all the while maintaining a steady stream of scintillating chatter on strictly limited subjects, none of which could possibly include religion, politics or serious literature – this last being regarded as indicative of 'blue-stocking' tendencies and therefore to be avoided at all costs.

At least Lucy and Rosalind had strong motives for wanting to enter the fashionable world. Lucy's had been instilled in her for years by Lucien who had drummed it into the pretty little thing that she was furthering their cause by immolating herself upon this sacrificial altar. The girls whom she would meet, the houses to which she would be invited, would all – if she were sufficiently astute – provide the nucleus of the clientele which they would draw *together*, to the house of fashion which they would create *together*, once their years of patient waiting were at an end. Lucy therefore looked upon her season as her initiation period, through which she would achieve her only desire: which was to break away and spend the rest of her life in the shadow of her future dress-designer brother.

Her cousin Rosalind was as unlike her in almost every respect, as it was possible for two young girls of related blood and identical circumstances to be. The vital point of difference between them was that while Rosalind too had a fixed objective; she, unlike Lucy, had no one with whom she could share it. She *must* play a lone hand, keep her own counsel, bide her time, watch for her opportunities and force life to yield up to her what she desired above all else, without any member of her family, or any girlish confidante having the slightest suspicion of what she was about.

Had any member of the Family or indoor staff either, entertained the slightest notion of what was going on, it would have caused endless agitation and disputation above stairs while below stairs would have turned, automatically, to the Dowager's Palliser. Her knowledge of Family history took her back to the days of an identical member of the Lorme family. She, like the awful Edward Justin, was never mentioned – above stairs. Born two years after her brother Justin, the late Lord Aynthorp, this girl had persistently, inevitably, as it seemed, fallen passionately in love with a string of rascals of equal birth and position to her own. Victorian society buzzed endlessly with her disastrous love affairs. All of them led to scenes, dramas, wild and wicked expenditures and dolorous recriminations from relations; while she 'the awful Daisy' as she was called by the scandal mongers of her day, emerged like some naughty phoenix from the flames of each romance, looking more beautiful than ever, more serene and yet hell bent in the pursuit of some other wild and faithless young devil upon whom her ever-changing affections would next fix themselves.

Now, like her great-aunt, Rosalind had fallen in love. She knew full well that the object of this devouring, early passion would be absolutely unacceptable to anyone, yet, like her great-aunt she determined, with a completely un-girlish resolution that this would be the man whom she would marry, with or without parental consent and despite any obstacle.

Nanny had called her devious, but even Nanny had failed to estimate the depth of Rosalind's determination. She was prepared now to play the correct young Miss to the top of her bent, to scheme and plan, dissemble and contrive until she achieved her objective. 'Shoals ahead indeed' with this young woman, as Christine Aynthorp had predicted to herself.

The object of her passion was a hunting crony of John and Primrose de Lorme 'the horsey couple'. They had invited 'the Irish divil' as he was known in hunting circles throughout Britain and his native Ireland, to spend Christmas at Castle Rising. They had mounted him for the traditional Invitation Meet on Boxing Day when Rosalind, looking ravishingly pretty in her dark blue voluminously skirted habit, came down the steps, skirts in one hand, crop in the other, to see her father and a tall, curly-haired man with laughing blue eyes standing chatting together. They both held brimming goblets of the famous Lorme Stirrup Cup as she descended and the Knight's eyes met her wide, bemused gaze. John de Lorme made the introduction.

'Rosalind my dear, come and say how-dedo to the Knight of Bourne, this is my niece Rosalind' – their hands touched for an instant and Rosalind quivered at the contact. The Knight lifted his goblet to her, 'You are very beautiful Miss Delahaye,' he said boldly. 'My congratulations, John, but where have you been hiding such loveliness?'

'Oh, Fudge!' said John carelessly, 'she's not even out yet, so of course you have not met.'

And that was that; but she knew, and the 'Irish divil' knew that what flashed between them was instantaneous and mutual. Hastily the girl dropped her eyes, terrified lest her Uncle should perceive anything.

She murmured a few trite phrases. Henry came up, then Petula joined them and finally Rosalind's groom came round the topiary with her mare. The Irish divil mounted her and again at the brief contact the girl quivered . . . and he knew it.

Standing at the mare's head, gentling her ears, he asked her, 'Will you come down to dinner tonight Miss Delahaye?' his eyes making her feel as if she were sitting naked, like Lady Godiva, upon her roan's back.

'Nooo, I do not think so,' she said regretfully, 'although Aunt Christine did say something . . .' her voice trailed away breathlessly.

'Well at least we can ride together . . . are you a good horse-woman?'

Gyles Aynthorp strolled up to them, 'The best in the family, Knight,' he answered for her, smiling up at the girl, 'but by your standards . . . well let's say I have no doubt you will stretch her.'

The 'Irish divil' bent to tighten a girth then swung himself into the saddle as the field began to move off, 'Well, we shall soon see,' he laughed, 'I have a feelin' you'll give me a run for my money Miss Delahaye.' Crop went to topper rim in salute and they wheeled towards the gates.

As they jog-trotted down the drive and out into the lane between the usual press of villagers and general sightseers, Rosalind's heart was hammering. She was praying silently, 'Please God let me put up a good show for him . . . please God.'

Alas! whatever god she invoked permitted her to put up a very good show indeed.

Wandering between dressing room and his wife's boudoir that night Gyles Aynthorp observed, 'Amusin' feller that Irishman, good all-rounder, don't you think my love?'

Christine, seated at her dressing table, selecting from the jewel box which Pearson had opened out for her, replied equally casually, 'I found him charmin'. What's his history Gyles? It's a title I do not know.'[1]

Gyles sketched it in. 'He's a widower,' he enlarged. 'His wife died in the huntin' field, aged about thirty-eight. There's no money, a crumblin' great mansion in north Cork. He's no end of a swell, but without a sou to bless himself with. He is also one of the finest horsemen in Europe with a string of scandals to his name. He's also descended, like we are, from Normans. . .'

Christine looked surprised. 'Oh did they invade Ireland too?' she asked.

Gyles grinned, 'A hundred years later m'love. Oh he's of the blood all right he's, now let me see, one of Ireland's oldest titles, out of a Fitzwilliam girl who was the toast of Europe in her day, a ravin' beauty who was wild as hell; but then the whole line's wild. They have always been huge gamblers. He has the finest string of polo ponies I have ever seen. He also races yachts – other peoples' of course – and is a first class shot.'

Christine, her hands arranging the necklace which Pearson fastened for her commented, 'A useful man at dinners. I must admit he amused me immensely last night.'

Gyles's expression became a trifle wary. 'That's his stock in trade. He sings for his supper all right. He's *persona grata* and all that; but I would say on short acquaintance at any rate that he's got more than a touch of our swashbucklin' runts about him. Chap who needs watchin'. Not you m'dear, but very dangerous material in inexpert hands. He's far too demned good lookin' for a start, with a fiendish capacity to charm.'

Thus, the man to whom Rosalind, the sub-debutante, had wholly lost both head and heart and who therefore constituted *her* motive for counting the hours until she came 'out'; meanwhile nursing her secret with all the intensity of which her

---

[1] There were only three Knights created in Ireland. They were and are The Knight of Glyn, The White Knight and the Knight of Kerry. The Knight of Bourne is completely fictitious and resembles no one either alive or dead. F.C.

devious nature was capable. Before she left the drawing room that night, having been allowed down to dinner, the Knight waved to her from across the room, 'See you in London Miss Delahaye, and good luck for your first season.'

He stood for a long time at the opened windows of this room recalling some of the evening's experiences. Behind him, a generous fire burned in the wide chimney piece for the night was cold and the Lormes insisted upon warmth being maintained at all times. To one such as Gavin Fitzpatrick, accustomed not only to long, hard days in the saddle, but also to the bone-chilling draughts of his crumbling and ill-heated Irish home, it was too warm! Hence the opened windows at which he brooded over what he had seen of Castle Rising. Here, he decided was immense wealth and with it one of the loveliest young women ever to set his blood tingling and his blood, as he acknowledged amusedly was in a more or less constant state of tingling! So much money! Such great possessions! And to top it all this ravishin' girl, Rosalind Delahaye. They were all living under one roof, and therefore were all clearly hallmarked with Family approval and Family support. His mind ran over what he knew of the Delahayes, for he was as familiar with Debrett as he was with his own stud book. Oh yes, he decided, it would do, it would do famously if he could bring it off!

He began playing with the bobbles on the drawn-back curtains, his fingers going down them as if they were a Rosary. But he was no Catholic, so there would be no obstacle in that quarter! It was time he re-married, no, he contradicted himself, it was essential that he did so for he needed a bride on two accounts, setting aside all other considerations. He had no heir. His one child got of his previous marriage had died in his fourth year and thereafter his late wife's health had debarred her breeding. More's the pity! But more even than an heir to an overgrown estate and a crumbling mansion Gavin Fitzpatrick needed money.

'Faith,' he thought, turning away at last. 'It was Providence that brought me to this family and Providence shall help me now.' He went to the mantelshelf and leaned against it, glad

of the warmth suddenly, for the spectre which haunted him
with growing persistence was the thought of what lay ahead
should he grow old alone. His was an ancient title. He would
not be sueing like an adventurer for the girl's hand, for in
terms of tradition and breeding his stock was every whit as
good as theirs! Like the gambler that he was, he set up the
pros and cons. On the credit side then, his title and his blood.
On the debit side . . . ah, but the scales tipped here! He was
twice her age and more; he had been married before. He had
nothing to offer but himself and his neglected acres. Sudden
desire gripped him as he recalled the two aspects of herself
which Rosalind had shown him already. The girl in the hunting
field, as with excellent hands and a splendid seat she put her
roan at the fences. When she narrowly missed a toss at a particularly nasty bullfence she only laughed, recovered herself
and rode on with flushed cheeks, hatless with her hair tumbling
about her shoulders.

'Game as a turkeycock,' he acknowledged. Then when she
had been allowed down to dinner she had entered the White
Drawing Room in a flowing dress which displayed ever better
the graceful lines of her figure. They had put up her hair, and
her slim throat rose above encircling pearls, then indeed she
was a beauty!

He resolved to try for her; for alongside his crude assessment
of the advantages of such a match his desire ran like a flame.

CHAPTER 15

Damnosa Heriditas

Away went Sawby in his black bowler and away went Mrs
Peace in her best bombazine and new bonnet. She took the
place of honour beside 'Plum' on the box as the dray lumbered
off down the drive, stacked with hooded portmanteaux and
leather-strapped wicker baskets containing the linens and
laces and the staff's personal clothing. There were besides,
two huge metal boxes, securely padlocked, as they were filled
with silver and silver-gilt. Chef André had supervised Boots'
packing of his most important kitchen implements into two
more great wooden chests. This had been done with Chef's
usual stream of French invective and, as Mrs Parsons called it
'Blarspheming'.

André in fact was to follow later. This first contingent was
completed by Pansy – now Mrs Sawby but still 'Appelby' in
the Servants' Hall – and her cousin Violet whom Mrs Peace
had been pleased to engage and Christine to confirm in the post
of personal maid to the Misses Rosalind Delahaye and Lucy St
John. Both females sat demurely on a bench at the dray's tail
in respectable black with small, shiny straw hats pinned
securely to their dragged-back hair, cotton gloves neatly
buttoned at the wrists and shiny, black buttoned-boots set
firmly upon the planking.

The advance guard thus embarked for London and the house
in Arlington Street. The next day Sawby and Mrs Peace
installed themselves in one of the two ground floor withdrawing rooms, for the interrogation of and judgement upon
extra footmen, parlourmaids, house and kitchen maids; while
Pansy and Violet withdrew linen dust sheets and bags from the
furniture and chandeliers and then dusted, swept and polished

just 'to keep them out of mischief'.

The second wave of domestics comprised Chef André, his ubiquitous cousin Jean-Paul, whose employment in Paris was rendered a trifle sporadic by the many demands upon his presence in England for Lorme entertainments; and the junior footmen, Richard and George. This would complete the full complement below stairs, save for such 'extras' as would be required for the girls' Coming Out Ball.

Then the Family would arrive, accompanied by their maids and valets who travelled third class clutching their employers' dressing cases and jewel boxes. A private detective made the journey with them.

Only a skeleton staff was left at the Castle under the despotic rule of Mrs Parsons, Edward and the new extra footman, William. Edward had acquitted himself so well during Sawby's honeymoon that he was deemed qualified to remain behind to 'keep a firm hand' upon the rest, which fate thrust him into a fit of sulks and caused Mrs Parsons to inquire of the world in general, ' 'Ooo's got a narsty black dog on 'is back this morning I would like to know?'

No one was unwise enough to tell her. They all knew the signs and portents. These were made even more abundantly clear over the tea table on the afternoon of the great family exodus by that worthy when she banged down her tea cup and declared, *apropos* nothing whatsoever, 'All the world is vipers, wot bites the 'ands wot feeds 'em! I'm orlright wen it comes to cookin' 'ere for the 'ighest in the land, but when it's Lunnon they're off to for their serciety gallivanterings it's stay 'ere Mrs P wile that Frenchie rules the roost along of the Lunnon kitchens. Bah!' she concluded with a long and bitter sniff. After this all below stairs were plunged into Stygian gloom while the speaker turned her attention once again to her slipping teeth.

Above stairs there remained Sinclair and Henrietta, Stephanie and Nanny's brood. Lucien and Mr Sissingham were off to Paris almost immediately and only occasional visits from the Delahayes' intimate friends lightened the gloom. Stephanie, with her now precious parents remaining for her exclusive enjoyment was in fine fettle. She went singing about her Women's Institute affairs. She was currently very busy organizing first aid classes for the village women which she ran under the guidance of Dr Jamieson whom she had grown to both like and trust. Henrietta dutifully rolled bandages, learned how to apply a tourniquet, splint a limb and bandage correctly in between plying the women with tea and little cakes, made grudgingly by Mrs Parsons.

It seemed as if the future horrors which had engulfed Gyles Aynthorp as he strode about his own hills through that long night when he was dogged by a dreadful prescience of impending doom, had now receded, leaving him in a most unusual state of recklessness. He indulged in such a spending spree as had been regarded by his tempestuous father as the mere small coinage of Lorme behaviour; but to Gyles' nature it was completely alien. He grew daily more and more like his late, wildly extravagant parent. Only Christine who knew him as well as she had known and loved his father, understood the motives behind all this spending. Not that she would admit even to herself that her husband was most uncharacteristically abandoning himself to an 'eat, drink and be merry' last stand policy because he had, for some, to her, unfathomable reason come to regard this particular London Season as an excuse for one last, glorious fling before facing a holocaust.

Gyles accompanied Christine to the florists who always supplied the floral decorations for their London entertaining. He encouraged her to spend when she hesitated at some of the more lavish suggestions advanced by the florist. The frock-coated principal produced sketches; proposed transforming the ballroom into an Italian garden for the girls' ball; suggested fountains; twin bowers of white moss roses as receiving arches for the two young debutantes and, warming to his theme, added that all the trees, shrubs and pot plants should be exclusively those which were found in June in an Italian garden. Thus, 'We could arrange cascades of white bougainvillea though of course the white *is* a trifle costly I must confess.'

Gyles poo-poohed the matter of cost and gave the man a completely free hand. He then whisked Christine off to Bradleys in their new sleek, navy-blue Rolls Royce. Christine emerged from this encounter the owner of a floor length cape of white ermine with a border of little ermine tails, as Gyles put it, 'Just to throw over your shoulders on chilly evenin's m'dear.'

He ordered the chauffeur on to Aspreys where he bought her a diamond brooch for securing her aigrettes in position. When the jeweller produced matching bracelets and long ear-rings, Christine could not help exclaiming, 'Oh no, Gyles, I really do not need them!'

Saying loftily, 'Jewellery is not a matter of need but of adornment,' Gyles told the delighted jeweller to 'include them too if you please. M'y wife must be properly turned out,' and then selected a circlet of grey pearls for his mother and a sapphire brooch for the little Countess Marguerite; all very much Justin Aynthorp behaviour.[1]

Within twenty-four hours of the family's arrival the primrose and white awning was up, sun blinds were affixed to the window boxes and filled with yellow and white iris, interspersed with trailing ferns 'quite the prettiest of all our houses', as a caller assured Christine. 'Everyone is remarking how charming it all looks! The dear duchess is positively *acid* with envy!'

Within a week, Sawby and Mrs Peace had, in their parlance 'licked the newcomers into shape', fitted them out with their correct Lorme liveries and uniforms and set all in motion with such expertise that it seemed as though they had all been 'in residence' for years.

Calling cards began to multiply upon the silver salver on the hall console. Invitations poured in. There was a constant pulling up of cars and carriages outside and a constant traffic of other cars which bore the various members of the family off to endless fittings with dressmakers, tailors, bootmakers, milliners and hatters.

Below stairs an unending stream of delivery men and boys arrived with crates of wine, baskets of provender, plus, of course, a daily delivery of fruit, vegetables and flowers from the Castle.

Then the bouquets began to pour in, so much so Sawby was forever opening the big front door with its gleaming brass knocker to receive them, while endless dress and bandboxes

[1] See Book I, *The Lormes of Castle Rising.*

occupied his footmen at the back door.

The first official event of the season, the private view day at the Royal Academy was on May the seventh. The family attended. Led by the Dowager in palest lavender and the little Countess in silver-grey they flowed down the steps. Christine wore pale lemon, her matching hat massed with chiffon flowers; Primrose looked extremely elegant in black and white with large black and white feathers poised against the crown of her big hat. Gabrielle wore blue with a pale pink ruched lining to her blue hat. Then came the girls. Lucy was in the palest pink with a pink affair perched on her curls and tied under her chin with blue streamers which exactly matched her wide blue eyes. These brimmed with excitement.

Rosalind was dressed in *eau-de-nil* from head to toe. A single, matching curled ostrich plume encircled her ruched tulle hat and only a bunch of dark red roses fastened to her tiny waist made a single splash of colour contrast. The older women all wore long feather boas. The Dowager and the Countess also carried tiny, jewelled lorgnettes which they both wielded with what the young ones thought was a quite terrifying effect.

When they arrived the Queen was moving very stately through the rooms, a regal figure in lavender with feathers around her hat. Lucy gazed at her in awe and then saw and indicated to Rosalind excitedly, the young Princess Mary with her hair up for the first time. As if this were not enough, Primrose whispered to her daughter that the still lovely woman in diaphanous black with a knot of pink Malmaisons and violets secured to her corsage with a blazing, diamond brooch was none other than Queen Alexandra.

And now the lorgnettes came into full play as the family moved slowly forward – their objective – a portrait of Christine by Sickert. He had painted the new Lady Aynthorp in a flowing dress of peacock blue with the famous Lorme emeralds around her slender throat. The Lorme contingent was agog to see the finished portrait. Every few feet the older women were halted to greet and be greeted by old friends; then to present the girls and so move a few paces further towards their objective, only to pause once more. The two young debutantes came in for many compliments and faced a continuous battery of lorgnette-scrutinies.

Contrary to her expectations, Lucy was thoroughly enjoying herself. This put an extra sparkle in her big, blue eyes and considerably enhanced her looks. Only Rosalind moved through the fashionable press murmuring appropriate phrases, going through the social motions with a faint dreamy smile on her lips – which likewise very much became her – while her mind was away elsewhere and she was almost oblivious of what was going on.

During the morning yet another peal at the front door bell had sent Richard hurrying up the basement stairs. Sawby was tucked inside the cramped little Steward's Room drinking his morning tea, so it was Richard who opened the big front door to a little bow-legged figure standing on the top step.

This character, whose legs gave evidence of a lifetime in the saddle, touched forelock to the resplendent footman and in a brogue as thick as treacle said, 'Good mornin' young sirr, shure and 'tis a foine mornin' biGod. Oi'm from his Lordship with this.' He held out a seamed hand with a small white package upon it. His other hand was clenched. This he now opened, too, revealing a new golden sovereign. 'And this is for you, young sorr, would you ever give this into the fair hands of Miss Rosalind Delahaye – and may God bless ye – ye may keep the gold.'

He stood with his head tipped to one side like a cocky robin watching Richard intently. The footman grinned. 'I'll do more'n that for a bright gold sovereign,' he said, taking both eagerly.

Then said bandy-legs, smiling back, 'May ye marry and have many childer and come to die in auld Oireland,' after which he about-turned and went rollicking down the carpeted steps like a small, animated barrel.

Richard took the front stairs two at a time, knocked upon Rosalind's door and when Violet opened it said, 'Vi love, be a good girl and ask Miss Lorme to come to the door a moment it's urgent.'

'Who is that?' called Rosalind's voice from within.

The girl turned, explained and Rosalind ran to the door catching her peignoir around her. She almost snatched the little white thing from the footman's hand. With shaking fingers she ripped the outer wrapping away disclosing a further one of cotton wool. The little, inexperienced maid stared, fascinated.

Rosalind read the card, let out a small, excited cry and tucked it down inside her underbodice. Then suddenly remembering the maid she looked up sharply.

'All right Violet you may go. Have your tea and do not come back for ten minutes.'

Only when alone did Rosalind remove the inner wrapping and cradle the object between her hands as if it were a Talisman. 'He's sent me a present,' she exulted. 'It's Fabergé! for *me* from *him*!'

Recovering herself somewhat, she set the delicate thing on a nearby table, dipped into her underbodice and read the card again. In a bold sprawling hand the Knight had written upon the reverse side, 'A small gift to wish you a wonderfully exciting season,' the signature was simply – *Gavin.*

She crooned over it. The gift was most certainly Fabergé – a tiny pot set upon a rectangular plinth and containing a single spray of Lilliputian flowers, so fragile that the slightest movement set them quivering. It was made of gold, white jade and baroque pearls.

When the maid returned, Rosalind swung round from her dressing table to face her. 'Violet,' she commanded, 'please come here.' The wide-eyed girl obeyed. Rosalind took her hands in a firm grasp.

'Now Violet you must listen to me very carefully,' she commanded. 'Not one word must be said, either above or below stairs about my little package. It must remain a secret. You may never breathe a single word concerning it to any living soul. Will you promise?'

The girl was by now rather frightened. 'Oh but yes, Miss,' she breathed, 'word of honour. Pansy, that is Appelby, Miss, told me I must never say anything below stairs of what went on above. She said a lady's affairs must always be private like. She even told me as how my Lady spoke very free before her, knowing that nothink would ever be repeated anywheres. Is that all right Miss?'

Rosalind relaxed. 'Yes, absolutely right,' she said, greatly relieved, 'so long as you remember it! Then I shall be well pleased. But let me warn you just the same. IF ever you *did* speak a word of anything, and of this in particular, then you would have to go – immediately.'

Violet's eyes filled with tears. 'Oh, I do promise, Miss,' she repeated earnestly, 'Cross my heart and hope to die if I don't.'

With this Rosalind was satisfied. So it was this episode which caused her to move through the company at the Private View as in a dream. Her Knight had sent her a present! It was all going to be as she had planned.

When they eventually returned to Arlington Street the women of the family went straightway to the room which had been set aside for their Treasure. This, was a small, unremarkable, somewhat mousy little woman in her mid-fifties who was one of the most experienced of the social secretaries of her day. Marguerite de Lorme had described her best to one of her cronies.

'My dear the woman is a walking Almanach de Gotha, Debrett and Who's Who, all rolled into one. She wields an elegant pen, has a memory like an elephant and is the embodiment of tact and diplomacy. Positively invaluable, and to think we barely snatched her for the season from right under the nose of Belinda!' – another crony, who was also a Dowager Duchess.

This paragon was called Miss Poole, with an 'e' as she was at pains to remind people. As the Lorme ladies swept in in their finery she drew chairs for them, then seated herself, adjusting her paper cuffs and picking up a fresh pen in readiness.

Christine spoke first, popping the fourteen buttons on her day-length white kid gloves and saying resignedly, 'Well, we have this one afternoon and evening and then we have not one single hour again between today and June the fifth when we present the girls.'

The Mouse rose and came round her desk with a sheaf of papers which she handed to Christine. 'These are your first-draft lists of guests to be considered, Lady Aynthorp as potentials for invitations to Miss Delahaye and Miss St John's Coming-Out Ball. This, as I understand it, is to be given on Thursday, June 26th.'

'Just before Henley,' the Dowager remarked. 'Fortuitous!'

'The day after Alexandra Rose Day,' Marguerite reflected, 'both gels must sell roses. At least in the mornin'.'

'And go on for a while to Mrs Van den Bergh's Garden Party. There are two balls on that Wednesday – but nothing we cannot decline for the twenty-sixth,' added Gabrielle.

Christine nodded, 'Then it is agreed?' she glanced around her, 'Thursday June 26th at ten-thirty p.m?'

No one dissented. So Miss Poole made a note and resumed. 'Those lists Lady Aynthorp I have put in alphabetical order. If it pleases you I will read from my copy,' she produced it like a small conjuror producing a white rabbit, 'and then you can confirm or reject any name and also add any which occur to you as we go along. When you have chosen, if you will be good enough to give me the number to be invited from each family – I shall not need the full names, since I am very familiar with Society – the work may be expedited with as much speed as possible.'

The Dowager settled herself with a slight frou-frou of silken skirts in a hard-backed chair. She could never bear to sit other than very straight-backed. She sighed contentedly.

'You are indeed a Treasure, Miss Poole. We may count ourselves extremely fortunate in being able to obtain your services,' she told the secretary graciously. Her words brought a quick flush to the woman's tired cheeks. The rest added their courtesies and then the formidable task began.

When the dressing bell sounded Christine exclaimed, 'Oh dear, and we are barely halfway through I fancy!'

'Not quite I think,' Miss Poole answered glancing at her papers. 'But while you are dining I can check the total so far. Then you may have some idea of how many more can be invited. I would, however, be deeply obliged if you could spare some thought for those so far forgotten names. It would be unthinkable for you to omit anyone of importance.'

The women of the family were silent, thinking very hard then:

'*Belle-Mère?*' Christine turned to her mother-in-law. 'It did occur to me that as one is always so glad of an acceptable spare man for the middle generation, it might be expedient to say the least, if we invited Prim's friend, the Knight of Bourne.'

'Why not indeed! I am only regrettin' that I do not qualify for that fortunate generation. He is certainly most charmin' and amusin'. Rakehell or no he is certainly eligible!' the Dowager positively twinkled.

'Always assuming numbers permit,' interrupted Primrose.

'Pfui to numbers!' exlaimed the Dowager, 'Gyles said "spare no expense and make our ball the most memorable of all".'

'Then please, Miss Poole, add the Knight of Bourne to your lists.'

'Provided,' Petula added her mite, 'we do not stand in danger of losing him to the card tables. The *on dit* is that he is a prodigious gambler.'

'Aren't we all?' asked Gabrielle stifling a tiny yawn.

When Rosalind slipped in the following morning she found Miss Poole and her assistant writing with great zeal.

'May I disturb you?' Rosalind asked very prettily, 'I thought . . . as it is partly my ball . . . that you might permit me to glance at the final list of guests?'

Miss Poole simply handed it over with an answering smile. Rosalind, searching for that one name alone, found it, thanked the women and went away well satisfied.

Miss Poole for her part laid aside her pen and remarked to the assistant, 'Miss Rosalind will in my opinion be one of the leading beauties of the season *if not the greatest beauty of them all.*'

While the adults were compiling the List, Rosalind and Lucy were in the latter's bedroom. Both girls had unpinned their great hats, kicked off their slippers and were flexing their aching toes.

'I declare,' said Lucy bubbling, 'I do not know the names of one half of the young men to whom I have pledged dances at Lady Mond's tomorrow night.'

Rosalind smiled her secret little smile. 'While I promised none,' she said indifferently, 'I simply assured them all that my memory is *fatal*, so told them to save their requests until they could write their names in my programme!'

Lucy sat down at her small writing desk and began writing her daily letter to Lucien. He, as she knew only too well, had already arrived in Paris.

Rosalind lay back, content to dream. As Lucy had become accustomed to this and in her own gentle, unquestioning way, had decided what lay behind it, she was surprised to hear Rosalind ask some moments later, 'Lucy Locket what do you make of this coming out of ours?'

The scene took on the appearance of being played by two people shut into separate rooms. Neither one would run the slightest risk of entrusting their secrets to the other, so both were compelled for entirely different reasons to dissemble to the utmost of their ability.

'I am enjoying it,' Lucy admitted, surprising herself with this safe truth. 'It's all rather exciting don't you think?'

Rosalind hesitated. 'Oh well I suppose so,' she agreed. 'Didn't Queen Alexandra look deevy?'

Lucy had resumed writing, 'Yes deevy,' she said vaguely.

'Lucy to whom are you writing?'

After a long pause, 'Lucien.' She released the name with all the caution of a Victorian spinster about to put one toe into a bathing pool.

Another pause ensued. Then Rosalind, half to herself said something which caused Lucy to drop her pen and make a nasty blot upon the page.

'Lucien's clever. He's escaped!'

Lucy turned round, astonished. 'You say that as if you wanted to escape too!' she sounded puzzled.

'Well, why shouldn't I?'

Lucy thought this over carefully. 'Well,' she said at length with her usual directness, 'your parents are so nice. You are so beautiful and Aunt Christine and Uncle Gyles are both so kind and generous to us both.'

Another pause ensued. Then Rosalind stood up, 'Could be,' she amended picking up her slippers. 'Go on writing your letter in peace, I'm going . . .'

Lucy looked slightly distressed. 'Are you cross? I haven't

said anything to upset you have I?'

'No, Miss Tenderheart,' Rosalind laughed at her, slightly mocking from the doorway, 'see you at dinner,' and then she slammed the door behind her and left Lucy to pour out her innermost thoughts and love to her brother Lucien.

The little performance which the Knight of Bourne and Rosalind put on for onlookers' benefit when he strolled up to the Lorme contingent on the following evening at Lady Mond's ball was exceedingly well done. *He* saw *them* as they were being announced. Rosalind saw him too. He promptly made some easy excuse to the man with whom he was chatting and in a leisurely way, headed towards the ballroom, pausing behind a convenient potted palm until his quarry again came into view. Even then he approached them very slowly and made his addresses to the older women. Punctiliously he asked for and obtained permission to put his name down for a dance on Primrose's programme, then on Christine's and thereafter on both Gabrielle's and Petula's. Only then did he seem to see the girls. 'Why Miss Lucy, Miss Rosalind,' he exclaimed smilingly, 'I declare you must surely be the belles of this ball. Nor dare I suppose that either of you have a dance left for a dull old Irishman?'

Lucy answered him smilingly, 'Indeed I have Knight,' she replied artlessly, holding out her programme.

'Then I count myself fortunate indeed!'

Only after this did he look at Rosalind, 'And you Miss Rosalind, am I to be doubly fortunate?'

'If you regard it as so,' she said dropping her eyes modestly.

He saw to his surprise that there were several gaps in Rosalind's programme; but he was far too old a bird to be snared by that lure. He merely pencilled his name for the 2nd extra, murmured, 'I shall regard my dance with you as a pleasure deferred,' then bowed and moved away. Even the Dowager, all attention to this little ploy, was satisfied that the 'rakehell' was merely being polite to two young things whose parents had entertained him. She murmured as much to Marguerite when they settled among the 'fishing fleet'.

'Evidently our gallant Knight prefers riper fruit, which I

must own is a blessing. I am bound to confess I am thankful. Our two really do look ravishin' y'know.'

Typically Eustace de Lorme commented to his wife, 'Those two fillies look uncommon promisin' Gaby. They really do. I shouldn't be a bit surprised if they led the entire field a little later on. Give 'em a few preliminary canters and they'll have their noses out in front – I'd risk any sum of money on it.'

Even Gabrielle was shocked. 'Really Eustace,' she exclaimed, affronted, 'It is mortifyin' to have my daughter described in terms which are best kept for the stable . . .' Then she saw the Knight's smile as he came up to claim his dance with her and vanished on his arm.

'Demmed strange creatures women,' said the bewildered Eustace in tones of deepest gloom. 'Oh, it's you, Henry. Tell me boy what won the 4.30? That fool man of mine forgot the afternoon papers!'

Henry paused in the entrance to the card room and answered promptly, 'Roman Holiday, by three lengths, sir.' Then he hurried off to dance with his Petula leaving his uncle to digest the satisfying information.

Gyles was heading towards the card room, his duty dances completed when he caught sight of Christine being escorted towards the little group surrounding Royalty. He paused, saw his wife dip in a graceful curtsy and was struck anew by her unchanging beauty. After twenty-seven years of marriage the old magic of her engulfed him in a sudden surge of desire. He remained, watching until the audience was concluded.

Then, 'Are you engaged for this dance Lady Aynthorp?' he asked, by now at her elbow.

She turned, 'Oh, Gyles, how you startled me! No I am not!' She read the message in his eyes and her colour heightened. Gyles put his arm around her waist.

'I do believe you're blushin' my love, after all these years,' he teased her. She caught up her train and he waltzed her off into the throng.

In the grim years ahead Christine often re-lived that night, with the wisdom of as yet unborn experience. It seemed that there was romance in the air. As she reflected, it appeared inevitable really. Everything conspired to engender it: the

scent of massed flowers . . . the music . . . the glittering
jewels . . . the blazing chandeliers . . . the tremendous, seemingly indestructible sense of absolute security. As Gyles
waltzed her round the great ballroom, she and he seemed, to
the eyes of recollection, to be two immeasurably privileged
people with their wealth and social position rising about them
like a high wall shutting out the cries of the unruly.

She recalled, always with a contraction round her heart,
their acceptance of it all as their right and their inheritance.
Thus she re-lived how Gyles had shamelessly made love to her
on that ballroom floor whispering enchantments in her ears,
from which swung his latest gift, those diamond ear-rings.
With a terrible pang, memory reminded her how all was done
so secretly and under cloak of such easy, smiling courtesies that
no one, not a single person in that great room could ever have
had the slightest inkling of those whispered intimacies! How
then could she wonder, she brooded sadly, that other such
intimacies had passed unnoticed? By and large, she reminded
herself wryly, the Lormes were a pretty unfashionable lot since
all their love affairs – with one exception – were only conducted
in public 'under the rose' in consideration for the proprieties –
not because any of them were involved in what were generally
called 'liaisons'.

The exceptions were also dancing together. When the music
stopped, Christine would recall Rosalind, faintly flushed,
standing up with Gavin Fitzpatrick. She would also remember
commenting to Gyles on what a handsome couple they made
and his light 'no more than we love. I think we do pretty well,
all things considered.' Not one ripple had marred the surface
of their pool. In these later, reflective times she found herself
more and more tending to replace 'pool' with 'goldfish bowl',
but none of this marred the perfection of that memorable
night.

As they moved off side by side so she also re-envisaged her
eldest son with his Petula. They too were chatting and laughing
together. How was she to know that Henry was being assailed
more and more by an anxiety which woke him in the night and
plagued him.

But hind-sight permitted Christine to see clearly enough –

for by then she knew of the discussion between her husband and her eldest son concerning what he felt he must do in the event of war.

Always when she failed to banish such 'remembering', thought drove her on to the point where the ballroom in which they all stood *now* became in her tomorrows like an old volcanic crater over which she had once strolled with Gyles in almost unbearable heat when he had first taken her to Pompeii. Their host had taken them on afterwards to see the curiosity which was dormant *Pozzuoli*. As they walked across the crater floor, he had explained how only three centimetres stood between them and the bubbling lava underneath. Indeed, dotted about over that floor were pools where the lava had actually broken through. The party gathered around one to watch the lazy, dark brown bubbles rise to the surface and burst in ceaseless token of a dormant fury, which seethed so very close to the scorched soles of their shoes; but on that May night no inkling of all this disturbed her contentment.

When at length the family left, Christine stood with Gyles, wrapped in her new ermine cloak as their cars drew up. Gyles whispered to her as he handed her in 'soon my love' almost immediately afterwards exchanging 'good nights' with other departing guests. In the car he quizzed the girls delightfully. The Dowager stifled a yawn behind her fan, then summed up for this their first ball.

'You did very well children, and you looked charmin',' she approved. 'How did you do with the young Duke, Rosalind?' Vaguely Rosalind answered in a sleepy voice, 'He made me many compliments and asked if he might call.'

The Dowager chuckled, 'Did he indeed and young Cunningham?'

'He did also,' she murmured indifferently.

Lucy sitting back in her corner gave a naughty little chuckle. 'Great-Aunt,' she asked, 'who was the young man with the blue sash on?'

'Why my dear?' inquired the Dowager, her lips quivering with amusement.

Lucy chuckled again as the car turned into Arlington Street. 'Silly boy,' she said sleepily, 'he said my eyes were like twin stars and told me I looked like a Dresden china shepherdess. Aren't men funny?'

'Not,' said the Dowager a trifle tartly, 'when they are royalty, wearing the Garter ribbon. Your memory, my child, will prove to be your undoing yet!' Having delivered herself of this revelation she stepped out of the new motor.

In the early hours of that morning Christine conceived her sixth and last child, while Rosalind lay awake until dawn recalling every single word that Gavin Fitzpatrick had said to her. Henry, surprisingly wide awake in the aftermath of making love to his Petula, wondered yet again, if *this time* she would conceive at last.

The season had begun.

The first of the two great events which stood high above all the rest for the two girls was their presentation to their Majesties. They were to attend the second of the two June courts, held on the Thursday and Friday evenings, the fourth and fifth of June.

The Lorme motors, preceded and followed by an immense line of carriages and cars, assembled in the centre of the Mall at a little after six p.m. Here they were halted, before making their way, with infinite slowness down towards Buckingham Palace. Both the girls had wailed at the prospect of such a protracted drive in all their finery.

'The doors of the Palace,' Rosalind protested, 'do not open until eight-thirty for us to assemble in the Ballroom before nine-thirty when their Majesties enter!'

The Dowager soon quelled her. 'When I attended a Queen Victoria Drawing Room,' she informed the girl with a distinct edge to her voice, 'I waited four hours in the Mall with the crowds around the car, peering in, remarking on our dress and shouting at us. The press was so great that we had to keep the carriage windows tightly closed. As a result we could scarcely breathe by the time we were admitted.'

'Will there be crowds to stare at us?' asked Lucy, horrified.

'Undoubtedly, while you of course, will continue to converse as if nothing were happening, I hope that is clearly understood?'

'Yes *Grand-mère*,' replied Lucy meekly.

As ever the Dowager spoke with accuracy. Men, women and children seethed about the vehicles, their comments painfully audible. When they pressed close to the car in which Rosalind sat, one cheerful character with a battered bowler tipped over one eye shouted back over his shoulder to the milling crowd, ''Ere's a pretty one Alf! Come and 'ave a dekko,' then squashing his nose against the car window, 'What about a kiss duckie?' he inquired unabashed.

Lucy endeavoured valiantly to maintain the conversation as the Dowager had decreed, while Rosalind surrendered to her dreams as she sat with her aunt and uncle.

Christine was to present her, as had been expected. With them were the little Countess and Petula, whom Christine would also present for the first time since her marriage to Henry.

In the following motor sat Lucy, frankly amused at the turmoil beyond the windows. Typically, she inquired, 'Can I not smile *Grand-mère*?' as a fat old woman in a battered hat peered in crying, 'God bless yer pretty face Miss.'

The Dowager nodded. 'Just a little nod dear and a quick smile and then re-engage yourself in conversation with us,' she advised sketching in both herself as examples. She then watched, well pleased as Lucy copied her. This evoked a further shout of, 'Look at them dimples! 'Oose goin' ter be the lucky man? You're a dainty one and no mistake!'

Lucy was promptly assailed by a fearful attack of giggles. Putting up a tiny handkerchief to conceal her mouth, with her big blue eyes shining above it, she rocked with suppressed amusement. At length even her grandmother found this infectious. Within moments she had them all laughing helplessly.

Recovery, disciplined by a 'look from Grandmama', soon quietened Lucy however and her mien became more decorous. Gabrielle turned her attention to a last, careful scrutiny of her daughter, her gaze travelling from the three nodding 'Prince of Wales' feathers in her shining curls to the toes of her white satin slippers. Both girls wore white of course; Rosalind wore a satin dress, the train embroidered lavishly, while Lucy's dress was a pretty draped affair of chiffon caught up here and there with tiny white rosebuds. Her only jewellery was a single string of faultless pearls which Gabrielle had given her that afternoon. A triple strand of matching pearls formed the bracelet which encircled one slim, gloved wrist. Both, as Gabrielle told the girl were family jewels, gifts from *her* grandmother.

Lucy was moving through what she had grown to anticipate as a sacrificial experience necessary to her eventual escape with Lucien into the world of their own creation, thoroughly enjoying every exciting moment of it. This enjoyment ensured her countless admirers. They sent her an unending stream of bouquets and nosegays with respectfully flattering messages written on the accompanying cards. They followed her when she rode in the Row each morning; they crowded round her as she entered ballrooms and altogether put her in peril of having her head turned had she been any other than the girl she was; but no tremor stirred in her. No quickening heart-beats followed their romantic murmurings. She simply treated her first season as one protracted party which she was fully prepared to enjoy to the uttermost . . . and forget all about the moment it was over. Her spirit was elsewhere, her heart untouched.

Not that the family had the slightest inkling of all this. They merely congratulated themselves and each other on the wisdom of Gyles' counsel. Of course the whole 'Lucien affair', as they identified the Lucy/Lucien relationship, they assured each other was nothing but an unusually close brother and sister affection. As Gabrielle said complacently to Eustace, when he wandered into her boudoir while Pearson was dressing her hair a few nights before, 'Out of sight out of mind, bless dear Gyles for his wisdom and sound common sense.'

It therefore became essential that Lucy now kept two secrets. The first was of course their pact with one another; but equally important was the fact that every night she wrote to her brother in Paris pouring out her thoughts, impressions and experiences in some perfectly hideous green ink upon scented lavender writing paper. This was 'all the rage' among her fellow debutantes. It caused Lucien, on receiving the first of these missives, to sniff disdainfully, ejaculate 'faugh!' and then put down the letter saying aloud, 'She must be told when next we meet! This paper is quite frightful, she must have gone out of her mind!' All these bulky envelopes went into the customary niche-of-the-day, down Lucy's stays via her cleavage. There they remained until her morning rides in Rotton Row. The town house was providentially positioned, backing as it did on to Green Park, with-in a cul-de-sac at the far end, the opposite one flowing into Piccadilly by the side of Monsieur Ritz's successful hotel. The mews was only a stone's throw away and here were the stables from which the family obtained their morning mounts.

For such a short distance even the Dowager raised no complaints at the girls 'stepping across' unchaperoned. Then it was the work of a moment for Lucy, meticulously careful to be always in the van – to slip a coin into the palm of an admiring stable boy and raise those blue eyes to his while asking in melting tones, 'Can you post this for me please Tommy?'

Having prepared for every eventuality she arrived in London well stocked with penny stamps. These too she hid extremely carefully.

She and Lucien had agreed, with much bewailing, that it was impossible for him to write to her until she was safely returned to the Castle. Thus *his* letters went to Plum who played postman. Lucy had long since suborned him too, with malice aforethought; and who was poor unsuspecting Plum to question the right for brother and sister to correspond with one another without having to suffer the indignity of having their letters read first by one or other of their parents?

Lost in a little happy reverie about all this, Lucy lapsed into silence in the waiting car while Rosalind, doing much the same, recalled with exquisite pleasure every whispered blandishment and endearment which her 'Gavin' had bestowed upon her.

Her Aunt's voice recalled her with a slight start. Christine was saying gently 'Rosalind!' and again 'Rosalind my dear'. The girl started, then turned, her eyes still clouded by her reflections.

'Yes Aunt Christine,' she replied obediently.

'Slip one hand beneath your skirts child, just to be sure you are not creasing your gown.'

Rosalind obeyed. The car began to move. Time passed.

'I suddenly feel like a bride,' she said surprisingly. 'What sort of a wedding could this be described as Uncle Gyles?'

'An important and essential union between yourself and the Society in which we move,' Gyles replied almost pompously. 'Oh dammit this does seem endless. I must be gettin' old!'

Rosalind regarded him thoughtfully. 'You're not old,' she said carelessly, 'you're interesting. I think boys are so boring.'

The car then moved once more. This time it continued very slowly until it was out of the Mall and so passed through the huge crowds up to the Palace gates. Then at long last they were actually dismounting with much shaking out of skirts and looping up of trains.

Nervousness engulfed the two girls. Their lips suddenly became dry and, 'I feel sick,' whispered Lucy faintly as she went slowly across the deep carpets.

'I did too,' Gabrielle whispered back, 'it will pass. I promise you.' Once more they moved, a few steps at a time, much as they had done in the cars. Fleetingly, Lucy thought that it was like one of those terrible dream sequences where the journey goes on and on but the objective is never reached.

'It's like a mirage,' said Rosalind very softly to Christine, 'you remember telling me? There was a city, all mosques and domes and palm trees, yet no matter how far you pursued it over the desert it remained just as far away from you.'

'Not any more,' answered Gabrielle, 'not any more darling. Look!' There before them was the ballroom's magnificence under its glorious chandeliers. Already it was thronged with splendid uniforms and jewelled women. The debutantes clustered like flocks of soft white doves, their crests of white plumes nodding and swaying in contrasts to the brilliance of tiaras and the confetti colourings of the gowns worn by the older women.

Lucy's eyes widened. Sickness forgotten, everything else forgotten as she threw straight back to her covenant with Lucien. 'Now,' she thought, all else reduced to total unimportance for her, 'now I must memorize, study, absorb every detail to tell to Lucien in my next letter . . .'

There was much which she sensed instinctively would displease Lucien's fastidious taste, notably, the over-elaboration of the gowns and trains of the Australians; too many flowers, too much jewellery, an over-lavish use of gatherings, pleatings, ruchings, frillings and bows. 'Oh those bows!' thought Lucy regretfully, screwing up her retroussé nose distastefully. She was brought back to reality by a crisp command from Gabrielle. Almost unconsciously, she was aware of being marshalled into position. Then the Royal Family came in and she with all the ladies sank into their curtseys as the Royal party moved towards their places for the last Court of the Season.

The Royal procession had formed in the white drawing room and was thence conducted by State and Household officers through the great range of brilliantly lit State Rooms to the ballroom. As Lucy saw them enter, so the band of the Royal Horse Guards, posted in the quadrangle, struck up the National Anthem and simultaneously the Royal Horse Guards on duty gave the Royal Salute. Then conducted by the Lord Steward, the Lord Chamberlain, and Sir Arthur Walsh, Master of Ceremonies the Royal Party entered, led by King George and Queen Mary. The King wore the uniform of the Colonel in Chief of the Royal Horse Guards. The Queen was a dazzling and majestic figure, as always, tonight in a gown of pale blue and silver satin broché, lavishly embroidered with crystal and silver beads. Blazing from the centre of her diamond crown was the legendary Koh-I-Noor, rivalling the evening star by its brilliance.

Lucy watched with breathless attention as their Majesties moved slowly across the crimson carpet to the Throne End of the dais and there stood centrally, while the other Royalties grouped themselves around, and slightly behind them.

She began to speculate upon the immensity of the gathering and the immensity of the organization behind this remarkable ceremony. There were close upon nine hundred very distinguished guests and oh!, she thought, how Lucien would like to see this! And how greatly he would appreciate the Indian Princes in their splendid oriental dress with their fabulous jewels, worn with natural ease that there seemed in them such an acceptance of their right to look magnificent as bordered upon indifference. Lucy turned her clear blue gaze upon the representatives of their Majesties' Naval and Military guests, so gleaming, so 'grand' and so stiffly formal in their full dress uniforms; then to the Gentlemen at Arms, to the Yeomen of the Guard, all in full dress uniforms and wearing all their orders and decorations; and so to the King's Indian orderlies on whom her gaze lingered reflectively. They were on duty near the dais.

She absorbed as much as she could of the tremendous scene, with all its moving parts, as they separated, came together, changed positions; all working out the great traditional pattern with such smoothness, conviction and orderliness that it even left them sufficiently at ease for them to manifest the emanations of grace.

Their moment had come at last. When Lucy sank down, she achieved a delightful obeisance, 'Such a pretty curtsey dear!' as she was complimented later and her soon-to-be-famous dimples were again well in evidence. She made such a charming picture that the Queen actually gave her a little nod and the King smiled at her.

Gabrielle was in transports. Even Primrose and Eustace, for all their customary reserve, were beaming at the grace with which both girls had executed the difficult manoeuvre. Trains had been kicked back impeccably, little satin slippers had backed to perfection. They were officially 'out' at last! And now all the gaieties of this exceptionally gay season lay before them and there was a whole three weeks before their next major event, their Ball.

Guarding their secrets they metaphorically took deep breaths and then let themselves be caught up in what was after all more strenuous than a marathon race and more exhausting than anything either of them had ever dreamed was possible.

When they left the Palace it was mutually agreed that with such an obvious success behind them the gels must be seen, at least at two of the most important balls that night. So they went on and on again. Lucy eventually managed just three hours' sleep and then with her fat envelope in its usual place, she trotted off across the mews as the clock struck eight.

The following day they were taken to Hurlingham for the polo and Rosalind had a difficult afternoon concealing her excitement when her laughing Irishman scored two goals in the first chukker and was cheered to the echo by the delighted spectators. In the evening, the Dowager took both Lucy and Rosalind to hear Caruso.

On Sunday they all went to Henley and the girls lay about in punts under the shade of wide-brimmed hats while their 'suitable' escorts punted them up river to their picnic luncheon on the bank where Gyles' launch swung on the tide. They were then entertained to a tea party at Cliveden.

By the time the whole round began again on the Monday, Lucy had found her own particular friend. In fact she was immensely popular with the other debutantes which caused her to endure hours of girlish chatter which she thought most tedious, for, as she dutifully reported to Lucien, 'I do not think they have an idea in their pretty, silly heads beyond the next party, getting married, going to Scotland for the shooting, Cowes for the yachting and coming back to London again for what must be very properly named the "Silly Season".'

She said nothing to anyone else, so was pronounced a tremendous success and only caused her aunt displeasure when she refused the third of a trio of very suitable proposals.

'What do you want then?' asked Christine reasonably. 'Young Lansdowne has twenty thousand a year, an excellent town house and in due course will inherit both the title and Shane Court! Besides dear, he is a very charming young man and there's a superb yacht!'

Lucy remained silent.

Christine pressed her almost sharply, 'Have you already lost your heart?'

This brought Lucy's head up quickly. She looked at her aunt steadily, 'No, Aunt Christine, I have not and what is more I do not fancy that I shall either.'

This caused even Christine to pause and stare. As she said to Gyles that night, when they were for once free, as the two girls were being chaperoned by Gabrielle and the little Countess who was having a rare time and revelling in the anticipated spate of gossip.

'I expect she is tired,' Gyles yawned, 'I know I am.'

'Gyles will you please be serious,' Christine sounded un-usually on edge. 'You don't think . . . I mean . . . she can't possibly be . . . er . . .?' her voice trailed off.

'Frettin' for her brother?' Gyles finished for her. 'Oh for goodness sake, dearest, do not give that a thought. The child looks radiant. Every time I see her she is laughin' and chattin', obviously havin' a most delightful time. There's no hurry, anyway, the gel's only eighteen.'

Christine still hesitated, 'There is something,' she said uneasily, 'I cannot put my finger on what it is; but there *is* something. She seems just a perfectly normal charmin' little gel, and then suddenly some kind of blind comes down and I can no longer reach her. She . . . withdraws Gyles. It is as if a door were being slammed in my face. When it happens I know that no matter how hard I try I shall not be able to open it.'

Gyles thought about this, sitting on the edge of their bed, his long fingers turning the tassels of his dressing gown over and over. Eventually, 'Everyone of any stature has their secret places,' he said finally, 'from the snail in his shell, all of us practise some kind of withdrawal when the strain becomes too heavy.'

'Ahhh!' Christine cried out, 'That's exactly it!' She repeated his words, 'when the strain becomes too heavy! What is there about a successful season to engender that in a young girl?'

'Conflictin' impressions,' said Gyles swiftly. 'Put yourself in her place m'y dear. Remember how you were when you came out. Dazzled, possibly a trifle dazed, certainly in no state to think anything through. No time anyway,' he yawned again.

'Maybe you are right,' she conceded, 'maybe it's only me. Just for a few moments I had a dreadfully cold feeling . . .'

Gyles' face closed down at this. He said, rising and beginning to shed his dressing gown, 'I'm sure that's all it is. What do those actor fellers call it? Oh yes, first night nerves!'

Christine made a visible effort. 'I expect so. What a good phrase! "first night nerves". Oh, Gyles, I do hope and pray that it is only that with Lucy.'

On the eve of her Ball, Lucy wrote yet another long letter to Lucien in her round, still-childish hand.

'I am beginning to worry a little about Aunt Christine. I think she is becoming suspicious of me. It is not what she says so much as the way I catch her looking at me sometimes. It could be my imagination. She asked me after Tony Davenant proposed and I said no, if I were in love with someone else. I told her NO. I couldn't very well say that there was no room for marriage in my life. Just us two together doing what we want to do and being ourselves. Oh Lucien sometimes it seems such a long way away.'

She scribbled on, 'There is something else worrying me, too. You know how it is when you have something you have made up your mind to hide from everyone? Well it makes you very open to receiving other people's feelings. I don't like the ones I have. There is something strange about Rosalind. It is no use your asking me what it is, but I know that it is so. She is not the only one. I think there is something worrying Henry. I do not believe that Uncle Gyles is as gay as he would have us all believe either. You described it to me in your first letter, which Plum gave to me when he was sent for to make arrangements for taking our coach to Lords for the Eton and Harrow match. You said you and poor Sissy had a dreadful crossing to France and you were both very sick. You said that the sea was not rough, but that there was something called a ground swell which went on underneath and made lots of people ill. I think this family is having a kind of ground-swell experience. You will understand. Perhaps you will tell me I am being just fanciful. I do hope so because you are so much wiser than I am even if I am grown up and 'out' and all that, and you are four years younger. Oh dear how I wish we were the same age! Then we would both only have three more years to wait.'

She paused, glanced at her little gilt travelling clock and resumed, 'I must end now my darling. It is half past three and I am falling asleep as I write. I must ride in the morning – which is now – so that I can post this. Oh, I nearly forgot, you like to know what I have been doing. Well the nicest of all was hearing Dame Nellie Melba sing Desdemona in *Otello*, and the second nicest is that Uncle Gyles has actually persuaded Mdlle Genée to dance at our ball. There is going to be a special drugget laid over the ballroom floor while we are at supper and then Mademoiselle Genée will dance. Isn't that a most tremendous honour? We were also taken to what they call the

Theatrical Garden Party. I spoke to Miss Marie Tempest and she was perfectly sweet, but her clothes looked rather odd. There was somebody else called Constance Collier who walked about in a long black cloak. Imagine! at a garden party! London needs you, Lucien, to teach them how to dress and London is going to have their first shock tomorrow night! So think of me darling Lucien. Oh, another delightful afternoon we spent at the International Horse Show at Olympia. Queen Alexandra was there, they say she is nearly seventy, but she looks lovely and rather like Aunt Christine. The Empress of Feodorovna was with her and they played the Russian anthem for her. Of course the horses were best.

'We also went to see a play with a Mr Alan Aynesworth in called *An Indian Summer* which is, so Uncle Eustace told me, when it goes on and on into what should be autumn, but why they should call that an Indian summer is still a mystery to me!

'My friend Nada is *the* debutante of the season. She even eclipses Rosalind who is *much admired*. She is always very aloof which I think is popular with the gentlemen. Nada's ball was lovely too. The Music Room where it was held was decorated very simply – why are the simplest things always the best? You must tell me. Just Dorothy Perkins rambler roses and we sat out in the library where Uncle Gyles pointed out to me a Reynolds and a Zucchi, both of which we agreed were very fine.

Then of course there was Ascot. I should have told you all this in previous letters, but I was so busy talking about us! Everyone was positively dragged down with feathers – there was not much sun, but the King and Queen's State Procession right down the course in open carriages was very fine indeed. All the clubs were there with very nice marquees and my dear, silly young men took me to the Marlborough, the Highland Brigade, the Green Jackets, the Guards, the Cavalry and the Bachelors until I was quite sick of the sight of champagne, salmon and strawberries in all of them. But the teas were nice.

And now I really must stop it is now four o'clock and I have to be in the stables by eight if I am to get this posted *unseen*! I am absolutely dropping with sleep do forgive me.'

Still she wrote another page of injunctions, warnings and loving urgings to take care of himself. Finally she scribbled 'Lucy-Lou' across the bottom, folded the pages, stuffed them into their prepared envelope and stumbled into bed.

This extraordinary pair had laid plans for something else, too, and now Lucy was in the most dreadful flutter lest she fail to bring off what Lucien had said was 'the first move in the right direction'.

When she was dressed and ready to go down to the dinner which Gyles and Christine were giving before the ball, she rang for Violet. The girl came after a slight delay, breathless and full of apologies. 'I'm ever so sorry to keep you waiting, but Miss Rosalind was not happy about her hair and I had to take it down again so that the hairdresser could do it all over.'

'That is quite all right,' said Lucy absently, 'Violet can you now do something for me?'

'Oh, of course, Miss, what is it?'

Instead of answering, Lucy marched over to her armoire and from the big drawer beneath she drew out a large cardboard box. This she unfastened, and shook out the contents. 'I want you to iron this for me very, very carefully when everyone is at dinner and there is no one else in the ironing room. Will you do that?'

'Of, course, Miss. Isn't it pretty!'

'Yes,' Lucy agreed, 'but it is most important that no one should see it yet.' When she had laid sufficient emphasis upon this secrecy, and instructed the girl to lay it out for her, with the pearls that she had worn to Court, Lucy trotted contentedly down the staircase and presented herself in the drawing room.

During dinner, she contrived to drop some claret on her ball gown. Murmuring hastily, 'Oh, it is nothing,' she drew her table napkin over the stain and continued as if nothing had happened.

She said nothing either when Christine collected eyes. Again she contrived to so arrange her fan and handkerchief that the stain went undetected. Then when at last Christine rose, made her excuses and shooed the girls off to freshen themselves before joining her to receive the guests, Lucy sped up the stairs, flung herself into the room crying, 'Quick unfasten me Violet, hurry girl, I must change very quickly.'

'Oh, Miss!' exclaimed the appalled Violet, 'you've stained your lovely dress.'

'Yes I know,' said Lucy vainly struggling to unfasten hooks down her back, 'undo me please I am in a great hurry.'

She was sitting at her dressing table for Violet to fasten her pearls when one of the footmen knocked.

'See who it is – don't let them in,' hissed Lucy suddenly terrified. Violet sped to the door. Then she closed it.

'Her Ladyship's compliments, Miss, and will you please go down immediately.'

Now Lucy was shaking. 'Fasten my pearls then, I cannot go down without my pearls.'

Between them they contrived to fasten the pearls at both throat and wrist; Violet held out the posy she was to carry and her fan. With a quick glance at her reflection in the pier glass, Lucy sped from the room.

Christine and Gyles were already standing with Gabrielle and Eustace. Rosalind was in position too under her receiving arch. Then Lucy appeared, hands clasped over her nosegay, looking like a Winterhalter painting come to life.

Christine stared incredulously. 'Where . . .' she began with shaking lips. But it was too late. Lucy's timing had been perfect. Over them rose the first announcement, 'The Lady Victoria and Mr Cavendish . . .' and the Coming-Out Ball to end all Coming-Out Balls had begun.

Upstairs in the ironing room, Mrs Peace and Violet were working on M. Poiret's discarded gown with table salt and a fine cloth.

Lucy bobbed, and rose, shook hands, bobbed again, rose and shook hands until she wondered if there could be any more people in London. The band struck up, the arrivals having thinned down to a mere trickle. Christine turned, her eyes blazing, to demand, *Where did you get that dress Lucy?* then down they both went as the Prince approached them – Christine once more truncated in mid-sentence.

As in a daze she saw her niece led on to the floor by the young Prince and heard only too clearly his comment and Lucy's reply, 'I hope you will permit me to compliment you Miss St John, I do not recall ever having seen a prettier ball gown?'

Lucy dimpled at him, 'Sir I am so glad,' she said, smiling at him bewitchingly, 'I never dared hope – you see my brother made it.'

During the time little Lucy and the Prince were dancing, all the women of the family had observed the girl's change of dress, and when the couple were seen strolling towards a palm-screened 'conversation piece' the general opinion was that as Lucy looked delightful, little harm if any had been done.

'Except,' said Christine drily, 'that I heard her telling his Royal Highness that she was delighted he admired her frock as her brother had made it!'

As they began to dance and after digesting, in so far as he was able, the startling reply Lucy gave him to his compliment, the Prince observed, 'I did not . . . er . . . know your brother was interested in *couture*.'

'He is in Paris, studying music at the Conservatoire,' said Lucy dimpling up at him. 'You see he managed to persuade Mama and Papa to send him, with his tutor, because he had already met Monsieur Paquin who came to the Castle to my cousin Henry's wedding.'

'I see,' said the Prince, by now highly entertained, 'and what particular significance has Monsieur Paquin for your brother? What is his name may I ask?'

'Lucien, Lucien St John.'

The Prince cleared his throat, 'Would you care to sit the rest of this dance out with me so that I can hear more?'

'It would not bore you sir? You are not just being kind?'

'No,' he assured her, stifling a desire to laugh, 'I am extremely interested.'

Facing him over the curved back of a conversation piece, with her wide skirts spread over the red plush, Lucy proceeded to prattle out the whole story. When she had done, ending, as she did to her Lucien, 'It's just that it is such a very long time to wait, with me being eighteen already and Lucien only fourteen.'

'I beg your pardon?' the royal eyebrows went up, 'Well! yes,

I do begin to understand; but, er, you must confess it is all a little bit out of Lorme character, and St John too,' he added hastily.

Lucy looked at this nice boy and forgot his enormous importance. 'Yes,' she agreed, 'that is why we thought that if *I* could prove *his* point we might be able to hurry things up a bit, say from the time he was eighteen, instead of twenty-one.'

A moment's silence hung between them. Then, 'So in a sense I am responsible for your sudden confidence?'

'Yes, sir.'

'And when he is over twenty-one, you intend doing what you have explained?'

She looked down at her hands and spoke almost in a whisper. 'Yes sir.'

He at least could appreciate to the full what a shock such a course would prove to the various lusty and conventional members of her family. He felt his way carefully. Out flashed his already famous smile, 'Since you have given me the honour of your confidence, may I make just one small suggestion?' he asked gently.

'Oh yes sir, please.'

His hand went up, fidgeted with his white tie, then, 'I think you should not tell anyone else at all what you have told me. Society is very odd you know. It might well be that they would think less of your delightful frock IF they knew that your, er, rather young brother had made it. Let them admire it. Accept their compliments with your natural grace,' he smiled reassuringly, 'but do not invite trouble and difficulties for yourself by saying more outside your family circle.'

He saw the tiny mutinous closing of her lips. Bored as he was with the general tenor of his conversations with young debutantes, Lucy's artless revelations caught his interest. They refreshed him, so now he sought a suitable sop to Cerberus. 'How would it be?' he essayed, 'If you gave me your promise and I in turn gave one to you?'

Lucy waited.

'When you have your house and your *couture* salon together – you and your brother – I will bring *my* friends to see you pretty clothes.' Lucy's eyes brimmed at this. 'Oh, sir,' she breathed, 'would you?'

He rose, 'You have my word upon it. Have I yours that you will say no more concerning who made your frock? It shall be a pledge between us which I will undertake to redeem when the time comes.'

She slipped off the padded seating and held out her hand to him, he bowed over it and kissed it, then tucking her hand beneath his arm he said, 'And now before we become conspicuous, permit me to return you to your Mama, Miss Lucy.' The distinct twinkle with which he said this was totally reassuring. Her hand on his arm, she reverted dutifully and at once to the chatter which he had enjoyed so much being without for a few moments.

Gabrielle saw them approaching her. She played her part too – naturally – but the instant the Royal back was turned she so far forgot herself as to catch Lucy's arm. 'What in heaven's name have you said to the Prince, Lucy, are you quite out of your mind?' she whispered furiously.

'I said nothing,' Lucy replied, 'I was listening to his Royal Highness. He advised me, *after* he had complimented me on my dress, which I then told him Lucien had made, not to speak of it to anyone else as this might cause them to think less of it. I think he is right, that is all.' For a moment Gabrielle was speechless. Then, fortunately, Lucy's next partner claimed her and her mother was left alone for a moment to regain her shattered composure.

When supper ended and the illustrious company moved back into the ballroom to take the seats which had been arranged for them in their absence, Gabrielle claimed her daughter again and bade her sit beside her. Two of her new girl friends passed them, their escorts in tow as they also sought for chairs. One paused long enough to say, 'Lucy you look deevy, everyone is green with envy of your dress, tell me who made it for you?'

Lucy by now had herself well in hand. She just laughed. 'Oh no!' she exclaimed, 'I shall be a tease and tell no one; but I am very glad that you admire it.'

Then Mademoiselle Genée took the floor and the great room was silent.

The newspapers gave as their verdict – 'quite the loveliest of all the season's balls'. They were unanimous. Lucy came in for a great deal of praise in the columns, so did the controversial frock which was described in eulogistic detail. The ball *had* been a tremendous success as Gyles intended it should be and, with Lucy, *bouche fermée* by Royal Decree there was very little left for the family to say. Yet needless to say they said it.

After the ball was over, when water carts were out spraying the lightening, heat-dry streets, they gathered in the morning room for the inevitable post-mortem. Gabrielle exploded and eventually cried; Eustace kept up a subterranean rumbling of incoherent mutterings; Gyles thundered; Christine spoke with the still marked, highly unusual undercurrent of anger in her voice; but both the Dowager and the Countess remained silent, content to sit back in their finery, to watch and listen.

Only when Sawby, imperturbably as ever, came in with a tray and on Gyles' dismissal, immediately withdrew, did the rest pause. They watched Gyles open a magnum, one third fill the coupes with crushed ice and orange juice and top them up with champagne. They watched him hold out a glass to his aunt, say, 'This is somethin' new,[1] it's very refreshin' may I persuade you to try?'

He handed round the glasses. They all sipped. Only then did the Dowager pronounce, 'Delicious Gyles, a welcome new-comer. Now . . .' She set down her half-emptied glass. 'May I say something?'

Gyles shot her a scarcely-veiled glance of suspicion. 'Well Mama?'

'And pray do not "well Mama" me. I am a trifle weary as you might imagine! What I have to say is this. I have been very close to both Lucy and Lucien for some years now and since you all claim, as indeed do the servants, that I have a finger in every pie I will confirm that I have *in this instance* and also tell you quite plainly that if, for example, you Gyles

[1] Buck's Fizz – plagiarized by the author because it seemed so suitable!

attempt to dig in your toes with those two – and heaven knows
a mule is capricious in comparison when you are trying – you
will not benefit. There is a strength in those two which is as
great as it is remarkable. Furthermore, have you considered
one factor? No, pray do not interrupt. I will define it. Their
paternal grandmama, the not-so-foolish Letty, left them her
fortune when she died. She decreed it should be divided
equally between them, observing that as they were the youngest
they might need it. They have control of the income from their
eighteenth birthdays – so Lucy already has it while Lucien
must wait four more years. Then, when they come of age the
capital reverts to them also. IF you force their hand too heavily
now, you will merely encourage them to break with us – should
their chosen course be made impossible for them at home.
You may sow a wind, my son, but assuredly you will reap a
whirlwind! Those two think as one! There is no use funking
your fences.'

She suddenly switched direction and levelled her gaze upon
the astonished, enpurpled John. 'It may be of immense displeasure to you that your son is about to be a *couturier*. Yet, do
permit me to remind you that you received a French one at our
wedding where he was made much of both by this family and
by our most distinguished guests. Finally I would point out
what is now as plain as our Norman heritage by our noses –
that pretty child *always will be Lucien's shadow*. You have only
to look back over the past few weeks. None of us are exactly
inexperienced when it comes to summing up gels during their
first season. Lucy has turned down every single offer for her
hand, but NOT because she is still heart free. In my opinion
she is heart-less, when it comes to considering matrimony at
all since this would inevitably separate her from Lucien. I hold
the view that the time has come to accept this fact and make
the best we may of it. In terms of family history, it is such a
very small setback, if we just pause for a moment and reflect
upon some of the other Delahayes – Stephen . . . Stephanie
. . . let alone our past family history.'

On which note she rose, shook out her skirts and concluded,
heading for the door which Henry scurried to open.

'And now I am very fatigued indeed. I will leave you to your reflections. Pray do not disturb me until I ring.' In the doorway she paused once more.

'Forgive me Christine, in the flurry of this little *contretemps* I had almost forgot myself sufficiently to leave without my most sincere compliments upon a magnificent occasion. Your ball was splendidly conceived, faultlessly executed and the best I have ever attended,' saying which she gave a little conclusive nod and disappeared from view.

' "This little *contretemps*!",' echoed honest John sepulchrally. 'OmiGod, Gyles, your mother will be the death of me one day.'

During the Dowager's monologue Gyles had moved to the window and now stood there staring down upon the water-freshened pavements. 'Amen to that,' he almost snapped, 'who else is feelin' as if they were back in the schoolroom?'

In the end the rest of them climbed their weary way to bed. It had been agreed between them that Christine would write a little note to be delivered to the Dowager when she awoke. Gyles now handed it to George for whom he rang. It said, quite simply, 'We will say nothing to Lucy until you have had an opportunity to speak with her. Sleep well Mama and thank you. Christine.'

A few moments later Sawby opened the front door to affix a card above the bell. It stated 'Please do not ring bell'. He also slipped a pad of wadding beneath the knocker, secured it in position and only then felt free to make his way to the servants' quarters to snatch a few hours rest.

CHAPTER 16

Never To Be The Same Again

There was thunder in the air. Callers complained of it, putting white gloved hands to exquisitely coiffeured heads, on which their vast hats perched heavily. They fanned themselves furiously, too, in an effort to conjure some slight breeze from the airless atmosphere. It made them listless, disinclined even for scandal. The Season it seemed was ending on a note of excessive weariness in contrast to the gaiety with which it had begun.

The Dowager was behaving oddly too. She excused herself from almost all the family's social engagements, claiming other more urgent ploys, then went about these with tightened lips and anxious eyes. Abruptly and against all expectations – for she had seemed tireless – she suddenly looked her age.

Simkins could have told of her curious 'social engagements of vital import' since he drove her, not to any fashionable houses, but to the Admiralty and to the War Office. At both these august edifices she stayed for what seemed to the waiting chauffeur to be an unconscionable time. When she eventually reappeared she looked sad but resolute.

Sawby could also have cast some light upon her activities, for it was he who answered the front door to elderly gentlemen of very senior rank whom he then escorted to the Dowager's little private sitting room. These callers, too, stayed overly long. Neither servant spoke of these matters above or below stairs. Generals came and went. Admirals followed suit. Sawby and Simkins merely exchanged knowing glances and by some tacit agreement said precisely nothing though their eyes looked frightened.

All too soon after the girls' ball, came one week of Court

mourning for the murder of Archduke Franz Ferdinand of Austria–Hungary and his Consort at Sarajevo, Bosnia, by Gavrilo Princip, a student from Belgrade who hated all things Austrian.

The atmosphere continued '*excessivement lourde*' as the little Countess Marguerite described it, while sipping incessantly from fragile cups containing her '*tisanes*', and not eating sufficient to maintain vitality in a wren.

Then Gyles began to manifest signs of unprecedented absentmindedness. He fell into deep thought while travelling by car or carriage and when addressed started, made vague replies and lapsed immediately into his own private terrain of spiritual and mental drought.

He also spent increasing hours at his club which, at this season of the year, could be expected to be fairly empty as the great exodus had already begun. Instead, every room was crowded with familiar faces. Gyles even had to wait for a vacant table for luncheon. Gone was the easy, serene atmosphere. The whole club seethed with unrest as men came and went, grave-faced, preoccupied, each man talking only of the imminence of war. When Gyles walked the short distance back to Arlington Street after these sessions his face, too, was grim.

Eventually Christine could endure it no longer. They had success behind them, as she pointed out with some exasperation. Enough was enough. It was time to go home. When she said as much to Gyles he answered a trifle sharply, 'Not just yet my love. Let us stay with the circus until the entertainment is ended.'

He then gathered his wandering thoughts and produced valid reasons for not leaving . . . yet. It seemed to Christine, whose impatience was growing, together with a sense of profound disquiet, that her husband was waiting for some specific sign before he would consent to leave London. She shrugged her shoulders and stared out of the Royce windows with tightened lips.

She then approached the Dowager who reacted similarly, stubbornly refusing to quit Arlington Street – yet. It was as if some blight had fallen upon them, one moreover which was contagious, for now Eustace, too, seemed afflicted by it.

'I declare,' exclaimed Gabrielle at length, 'we might as well be attended by zombies for all the animation our menfolk show and yet they will not cry off. What in the world is the matter with everyone? I do declare it is most vexatious!' No one answered her.

Meanwhile disaster quickened its pace. After Austria–Hungary had declared war on Serbia, Russia began her overt martial preparations. Then Germany declared war upon Russia. The next day she threatened Belgium and on August the second she declared war upon France too.

By this time Christine had returned to Castle Rising alone, declaring herself utterly fatigued and out of sorts. Only Mrs Peace accompanied her. Chef André was to follow by train the next day having left all in readiness for the Air Pageant picnic and for dinner that night at Arlington House. Pansy Appelby, by now accepted as a remarkably gifted cook, would come up to 'do her best to replace Monsieur André' as she described the summons tactfully. The London household disseminated itself gradually.

The reason Henry advanced for lingering in town was the first Air Pageant at Hendon on August the third. In fact he attended the finalizing of his intentions by Gyles and held himself in readiness for a summons, which came late on the afternoon of August the second. In the meantime the girls read of General Joffre's warning, reported in *The Times*. He had told the French government that every delay of twenty-four hours in calling up their reservists and in putting into force the measures preparatory to general mobilization, would mean the loss of territory of from fifteen to twenty kilometres per day, since the French troops would be thus forced to concentrate further and still further back. The girls read, too, how in this instance the French Government elected to listen to the General. A telegram was then dispatched which set his recommendations in motion. This went off at 5 p.m., and at the same hour the French railways were warned to hold themselves in readiness.

Even then the girls did not see beyond the disaster to their beloved France. For this they grieved deeply; but without a thought for England's involvement. They also accepted that there would be an influx of French relatives to Castle Rising as the male relatives decided to send wives and children from the beleaguered country.

Whether or not it was the blindness of inherent wish, or whether they were so thoroughly safeguarded from the truth by the older women of the family and by all the men; the fact remained they were almost completely unprepared for the truth when it finally pierced their defences like a meteor.

The next morning, August the third, Gyles Aynthorp stood at his windows to watch the laughing youngsters as they entered the new Royce which was taking them to Hendon. He saw André and one of the temporary footmen bestow the picnic hamper and drinks' case in the capacious boot and responded to a small flurry of waving hands as they drove away laughing and chattering.

The skies were heavy and overcast. It was as if the elements conspired with men to multiply the portents. When they arrived they found to their dismay that the great event to which they had all looked forward with such eagerness was in fact fraught with disagreeable surprises. The attendance was poor. There were practically no foreign entrants left. Even now the few remaining French competitors were taking the air in steady succession, heading home for war. One by one the fragile craft soared upwards and away leaving only the nucleus of British entries.

Cousin George left them spreading out their picnic and wandered off in search of programmes. He found them, bought half a dozen, tucked five beneath his arm and casually opened the sixth as he strolled back slowly to his party. Suddenly he halted, staring down at the printed page as if it were Medusa's head. For a moment or two the impact made movement impossible. He stared at the words incredulously while people brushed past him on either side, chattering and hurrying. He seemed stunned. At last he moved. He looked around furtively, spotted a litter bin, hurried to it and hastily pulling the programmes from under his arm he thrust them in, all save the one in his hand. This he then folded very carefully, before tucking it into his inside breast pocket. After he had so done he stood for a moment longer rehearsing his intentions. With an effort, he then forced himself to return to the others.

'Sorry,' he called out, as he came up to them, 'all sold out, it's simply not our day, eh what?'

They only glanced up somewhat indifferently when he returned. Then they went on arranging the cloth. After a moment or two George asked very casually, 'Hen can you spare a moment? There's a perfectly splendid motor over there which is new to me, perhaps you may know it, do come and see.'

Henry grinned, scrambling to his feet, 'Must be somethin' very new if you don't recognise it. I'll come, but we mustn't leave the girls for too long,' and on this permitted George to lead him out of earshot.

When they were safely hidden behind some parked vehicles, George withdrew the folded programme, opened it and held it out. 'Sorry to do this to you old chap,' he said miserably, 'but I think you had better read down that list of entries. I have of course chucked away all the rest I bought.'

Henry took it, saw what he was meant to see and then stared much as George had done.

'Phew . . .!' he whistled, 'a pretty kettle of fish!' His consternation was manifest. He held the programme out.

'For God's sake hide that thing, old man.' He paused for a moment's reflection. 'I say, thanks a million for usin' your head so splendidly. Now I believe there is only one thing to do – go back and try to extricate ourselves before the cat gets out of the bag as it is bound to do if we stay here. Every minute counts in my opinion.' He turned as he spoke, 'Who would ever have credited it!'

They returned chatting rather loudly about the high incidence of absentees. 'Rotten show I call it,' Henry pronounced, 'deuced disappointin', not really worth stayin' long.'

The atmosphere about the now laid luncheon cloth was what Henry described later as 'pretty fraught'. The girls were made uneasy by the unexpected diminution of interest. Their chatter became more and more sporadic. Fear had reached out and touched them at long last.

Incredibly, unbelievably it was all happening. Their world was crumbling about them. Fate had decreed it should be so and from youngest debutante to oldest matron the womens

eyes were shadowed by fear and unwilling recognition. Only
the young men remained excited and all their now unhampered
talk was of 'joining up', until suddenly during their picnic
luncheon, little Lucy burst into tears and would not be com-
forted.

'Where has it all gone!' she wailed, choking into Henry's
proffered handkerchief. 'There is no safe feeling left anywhere
and all you can do is talk of war!' She broke off, lifted her
tear-drenched little face and looked around her. 'War,' she
choked, 'which means death and misery for us all. Oh why did
it all have to happen and who is finding out about Lucien?
He will have to come back and he will hate that above all
things . . . Oh, my poor Lucien, all his plans have failed!'

Cousin George put an awkward arm about her shoulders
and tried to comfort her. Petula sat very still as the import of
Lucy's words began to penetrate. George was saying, 'Listen,
love, *we* are the strongest peoples in the world. Look at the
globe and you will see how vast an area is marked in red. That's
us, red's for the British Empire. No power on earth can harm
us because we have the greatest strength.' He spoke with utter
conviction. 'It will all be over by Christmas,' he assured her,
'honestly, it's only a storm in a teacup.'

The storm then proceeded to break out of the teacup with
massive acceleration, although only twenty-four hours earlier
Mr Arnold Bennett had written in his diary, 'It seems monstrous that the glory of Cowes Regatta should be impaired –
by even the fears of war.'

Ninian suddenly spotted a newsboy wandering among the
crowds. He leapt to his feet.

'Now we can learn the latest news!' he exclaimed and rushed
off to buy early editions of the evening papers. When he
returned they clustered round him.

'Cowes Regatta abandoned by special request of the King,'
they read. 'Never before in history has there been such an
appallingly rapid development of an international situation.'
The whole attention of the group was riveted upon the words
save only for Petula. She, white-faced, was absorbing and
assimilating the full impact of what had been read aloud. Then
abruptly she lifted her head. As she did so she saw such an

expression transfigure Rosalind's face that there was no mistaking it. Simultaneously a figure appeared beside them. She heard a soft Irish voice say, 'How delighted I am to see you all,' and the Knight of Bourne was there, smiling down upon them.

'God in heaven!' thought Petula aghast, 'the idiot girl has fallen head over ears in love with that plausible rogue!'

She had never felt at ease with the man. Now, as he disseminated charm and greetings all her antipathy flamed into a powerful dislike. She just watched. She saw Rosalind sublimate that instant flash of joy; saw those white lids come down to mask the terribly revealing expression in her eyes, heard the girl greet him calmly enough but also noticed how her hands were gripped together until the knuckles whitened in the folds of her flowing skirts.

'And now, Miss Rosalind, may I crave your chaperone's permission to take you for a stroll?' said the 'divil' as Petula mentally christened him. 'Who is your chaperone by the way on this auspicious occasion?'

'I am,' said Petula and try as she would she could not keep the chill from her voice.

'The dear Mrs Henry, will you permit me? I have one of the most famous horsemen in all Ireland in my party, and knowing this child's passion for all things equestrian I should be honoured by your permission to present him to her?'

'He knows,' thought Petula furiously. She met his eyes, in which were combined intense amusement and a be-damned-to-you challenge.

'Well,' she said at length, with deep reluctance, 'just for a few moments, I rather think we shall be leaving shortly.'

'Then,' he replied urbanely, 'I shall return Rosalind to you in a very few minutes, come child.' And so saying, he offered Rosalind his arm.

Ralph – who had been skimming the pages avidly paying no heed whatever to this new arrival nor the exchange which followed – suddenly scrambled to his feet, 'I say Pet, I shall have to go,' he flapped the news sheet at her, 'I must report back to m'regiment immediately.' He grinned happily.

'Don't worry about the car, I'll grab a taxi. I left m'uniform at "Alley House" I know,' this last their vulgar name for Gyles Aynthorp's town house. 'Take care of the girls Hen . . . see you . . . I'll wire home as soon as I know what's up.' And so saying he tore off across the grass.

'Alley House!' exclaimed Petula. 'Really!' Then, 'Henry. . .' she began and broke off again as a frightful thought assailed her, 'Henry he won't go . . . anywhere, will he without our seeing him again?'

'Oh no,' Henry replied automatically, but without conviction, 'though the lucky beggar – my *younger* cousin mark you! Will see whatever action there is long before I shall!'

He had dropped his newspaper on to the spread cloth. George picked it up. After a moment he laid it aside abruptly and looking directly at his cousin asked,

'Hen, are you comin'? I'm off to enlist.'

Henry was caught completely off his guard. 'I'm already bespoke m'y boy,' he answered cheerfully, 'I'm only waitin' for the last word from m'father tonight.'

Petula let out one small stifled cry, put a hand across her mouth and over it their eyes met. 'Oh Henry,' she said in a small, lost voice, 'must you, my darling?'

For reply Henry grabbed the newspaper and spread it out. 'Look,' he said pointing to the headline, ' "Your King and country needs you." *What else can I do?*'

Petula regarded him steadily. 'What else could you do,' she agreed forlornly. Then, with twitching lips, ' "and gentlemen in England now abed",' she quoted . . . 'Oh, who would be a woman at a time like this!'

Henry caught her hand and gripped it reassuringly; but it was to George that he addressed himself. Already she could feel him slipping from her. She heard him, as if he were a long way away saying, 'Tell you what old chap, if you'll just lend a hand with packin' up all this gear, I think it's time we pulled out. *The party's over*. Let's take the girls back to Alley House and then if you wish I'll come and hold your hand.' To Petula he added, 'Cheer up, my love. I haven't gone yet, and it may all be over in a few weeks, as George said.'

He dragged the elaborate picnic basket to within reach and began shovelling in the remains of their luncheon pell-mell.

It was only then that Petula realized Rosalind had not returned. She sent the young men to find her. She finished the packing with a little watery aid from Lucy. Then she sat back on her heels; Lucy was staring at her mournfully. Something in her expression told Petula all she needed to know. She asked accusingly, 'Lucy, you knew didn't you?'

Lucy nodded dumbly. 'Please don't ask me,' she pleaded unwisely, adding, 'I just guessed. I have my reasons for sort of knowing instinctively.'

'What reasons, surely you're not unsuitably in love too?'

'No Petula, nothing like that I can promise you; but please, please find it out for yourself and don't bring me into it.' The ready tears were brimming once again, so in a daze Petula nodded, 'Very well but *where are they now?*'

The young men came back to ask the same question.

'She is not here,' Henry announced, 'an' that's flat. We have searched and searched. That Knight is such a conspicuous figure, and anyway I could spot Rosalind's hat at fifty yards I'll swear to it. I expect she has driven back in his party. Never fear we shall find her at Alley House all wide-eyed innocence, the minx. I would like to turn her over and smack her bottom – sorry Pet but honestly that's what that young Miss needs.' Allowing no time for rebukes at his unpardonable vulgarity he added, 'If you girls will come home now and wait for us, we'll drive you to the Palace afterwards, Buck House is the place to be now, not in this fair-ground.'

They scarcely noticed as they walked towards the car; but all around them other parties were gathering up their impedimenta preparatory to leaving. By the time Henry turned the car round he was compelled to join a queue which crawled with nerve-racking slowness which continued all the way to Piccadilly.

The streets were filling, too, with aimless crowds wandering about waving Union Jacks and looking very pleased with themselves thoroughly enjoying their own demonstrations of patriotism and ostrich-like, wallowing in the drama of it all without sparing a thought to what it might signify.

When at last they reached Arlington Street late in the afternoon, immediately Sawby opened the door, 'Is Miss Rosalind here Sawby?' Henry shouted from the car.

'No, Mr Henry,' said Sawby, somewhat taken aback.

'Then that settles it,' Henry said to his wife, 'we'll not go home tonight. I will telephone Mama immediately. I shall tell her that we are going down tomorrow at the latest.' He turned to his cousin, 'Stay the night with us George and we'll take you to the nearest recruiting office in the morning. I wish you would, m'y father may be able to help you too, but I dunno what time he will return and then we have to find this wretched girl.'

Petula fled. She bushed past Sawby, ran up the stairs, rapped on the Dowager's door. She and the little Countess were sitting at the window together like two old sparrows in a downpour.

'Well, my dear?' the Dowager lifted her lorgnettes with a hand which trembled slightly. 'It has come has it not. May we know your plans?'

Their composure quietened the girl. 'Me?' she asked, approaching them. 'I have no plans. No woman has any plans when war comes. War is not women's business. We do what we must as best we may, is that not so?'

'Certainly not,' said little Marguerite, perking up considerably, although she seemed to have become even smaller since Petula last saw her. 'Come and sit down my dear and let us talk. You see we have been making plans for some time. Now they must be put into operation.'

'Is there no hope?' Petula choked.

'None whatsoever,' the calm voice assured her. 'We have seen it coming for a very long time. We decided what we should do. It is for this we stayed in town. Between us your Aunt and I are, as you may know, not exactly without friends in high places. As all our intentions were necessarily based upon the assistance of such men, we have not seen fit to speak of them to anyone until they on the one hand were prepared to assist us and we on the other were perfectly sure beyond all the futility of regrettin' that war was inevitable. Now it is. Are you sufficiently in command of yourself to hear what we have done?'

The implied reproof was all Petula needed. She stiffened in her chair between them. She looked from one old face to the

other. What she saw was resolution, iron will, absolute mastery
of self and, 'Yes,' she murmured humbly, '. . . but I am
ashamed that you had to make me aware of . . . of what I
should have known.'

The Dowager nodded, 'That's a good gel, I knew you would
not fail us.'

Little Marguerite interrupted her, 'Alicia, should we not
speak first to Christine?'

'I think not Marguerite. Petula is family. Petula can
assuredly be relied upon to exert the utmost discretion over
any advance disclosures.' Then laying aside her intimidating
lorgnettes, speaking much more gently the Dowager commenced her story.

'You see my dear we have lived through other wars. We have
been relegated to positions of comparative uselessness by that
outworn shibboleth that women have no place when men fight.
When we read the portents we thought the time had come to set
an example. Nothin' is more unbearable in times of stress than
waitin'. Anythin' is preferable to enduring that again! Therefore, havin' discussed this thoroughly – as you may well
imagine – we decided what we would do and we have been
extremely busy during the past weeks in settin' the necessary
machinery in motion.'

'What?' Petula almost mimed the word.

'Once we have obtained your mother-in-law's permission –
we do not envisage the slightest difficulty in so doin' – we
women will transform Castle Rising, or rather such parts of it
as are deemed most suitable, into a Convalescent Home for
Wounded Officers.'

It was at this point that Petula very nearly disarmed them.
'Of course,' she cried, 'I might have known! If he had been
alive it is what Grumpy would have had you do, is that not so?'
Laughter suddenly fought with tears as in a strangled voice
she added, 'and oh, what fun he would have had lavishing his
best wines on your wounded! Spoiling them, listening to their
experiences, bullying us all, flattering the best-looking nurses
. . .' she broke off. 'Who will be the nurses – the doctors . . .?'

'Those of us who so wish will become members of the
Women's Voluntary Aid Defence – or in plainer words, un-

trained nurses to do the donkey work. Doctor Jamieson will be our resident medical officer, and our matron – she has already graciously consented to accept the post – will be the Lady Constance Comyngs.'

This brought Petula's head up sharply, disbelief engulfing her, she heard herself asking faintly, 'The suffragette?'

'Yes my dear, the *militant* suffragette. The one whom your father-in-law brought secretly to the Castle to nurse poor foolish Stephanie. He thought I did not know.' The ghost of a chuckle escaped this aged indomitable. 'As I reminded my family in another context fairly recently, I really do have a finger in every pie, it's just that the explain'n becomes a little fatigu'n at my age.'

Dimly, in the distance the dressing bell rang through the house. Petula rose and bent over each white head in turn.

'And now I must dress,' she said and even as she spoke the utter triteness of the old familiar phrase sparked off a little strangled laugh which held more than a touch of hysteria in it. 'I shall also need time to assimilate and acclimatize.' She hesitated, wondering if she should tell them about Rosalind, but decided against so doing; instead she merely thanked them for their confidences and ran from the room lest they should see her weeping.

Henry came into their bedroom to find her attempting to dress for dinner. She dismissed her maid and Henry erupted in a fair imitation of his father.

'We'll see this out Pet! Grab that confounded idiot of a girl, give that damned Irishman something to remember and then go home. There will be quite a lot to do I fancy; of all the unscrupulous, outrageous, monstrous men, that Gavin Fitzpatrick is the *ne plus ultra*.'

Petula set aside her hairbrushes. 'You don't know what is behind it,' she said, 'Rosalind is madly in love with your damned Irishman.'

'What!' he stared at her appalled. 'But he's old enough to be her father.'

'When did a little thing like that stop any Delahaye from doing anything idiotic?' she inquired bitterly.

Up went his hand to his hair. Rumpling it distractedly he managed, 'You mean you think she's run away with him?' he demanded incredulously.

'I just don't know,' Petula sounded infinitely weary. 'I shall have to telephone your mother. She must be told and you must tell your father as soon as he comes in.'

They were silent, brooding upon the enormity of the scandal which would ensue if it were really come to such a pass.

Eventually he came over and knelt beside her. 'My poor darling, what a dreadful end to our wonderful season.' He took her in his arms and she put up her hands, endeavouring to smooth his hair. 'It is all right, my love,' she told him gently. 'You have no more need to fear anything from me. I have myself well in hand now.'

He took her hands down and kissed them. 'My darling love, I am so sorry.'

'Because you want to fight?'

'Yes.'

'Even so,' she said calmly, 'you must fight. I have been recalling my marriage vows. I have been putting myself where Grumpy would have put me had he lived to see this disastrous day – which thank God he did not. He would have turned and flayed me, if I said otherwise and if you had done otherwise . . . he would have contemplated putting you down like a mad hound.' She finished her little speech with her head against his shoulder. 'Women all over Britain are making little speeches, like mine. I am only doing what is my simple duty.'

They stayed thus in silence until Henry abruptly gathered her up in his arms, carried her across to the big bed and began to unfasten her tea gown beneath the canopy which had sheltered lovers since the time of the first George.

There, in the aftermath of so much pain for both of them, Henry made love to his wife with such a sudden fury of passion that it left them both panting and breathless. Like two exhausted children they fell asleep holding hands. They were only awakened by the gong sounding for dinner.

No one at Arlington House went to bed that night. Gyles who received the news of Rosalind's disappearance in frigid silence then telephoned his Christine. Late that evening when the Knight's clubs, rooms, even relatives had been visited by him, he had drawn a blank everywhere. In the morning he took Lucy, Petula, the Dowager and little Marguerite back with him in the Royce to Castle Rising. Henry drove down in his own car. Ralph had rejoined his regiment. George stayed on at Arlington House and it was not until late on the evening of the fourth that he drove down to join them.

In the meantime the terrible prelude played out its last pitiful notes.

The British Government's ultimatum to Germany expired in the evening. That night King George wrote in his diary, 'I held a council at ten forty-five this morning to declare war with Germany. It is a terrible catastrophe, but it is not our fault. An enormous crowd collected outside the Palace. We went on to the balcony both before and after dinner. When they heard that war had been declared, the excitement increased and May and I, with David, went again on to the balcony; the cheering was terrific.' Cousin George was among those who cheered. He told the Lormes when he arrived that it might have been a celebration. Indeed in a sense, he said, it was one.

'They waved their straw hats, their caps, their little Union Jacks and were entirely jubilant.' He added, 'I don't know why, but it made me want to weep.'

The Foreign Secretary Sir Edward Grey when he realized that the ultimatum had expired, and seeing the gas lights being dimmed in Whitehall commented, 'The lights are going out all over Europe. We shall not see them lit again in our lifetime.'

Britain was at war with Germany.

CHAPTER 17

Refer to Drawer

Gyles and Christine remained behind closed doors in Gyles' old office from the time he returned to the Castle until the gong sounded for luncheon. Then he pushed aside a small mountain of papers, excavated his pipe and observed drily, 'It appears to me that we have received a stentorian call to arms.'

Christine sighed. 'I wonder,' she mused, looking down at her hands, 'has it ever occurred to you that we may simply have overdrawn our accounts with God?'

He looked at her sharply. 'We collectively, as a nation or just we as a Family?'

'Both, I think. The Empire as a whole and we as a microcosm, an epitome of the Empire if you like. Suddenly God has had enough, enough of people like us. Our lives have been so wonderful and so wonderfully secure. It seems to me now that we have taken it all for granted, accepted that our funds were unlimited, and drawn upon them and now suddenly our cheques are being returned. What is the phrase used when there is no more money in a bank and another cheque is drawn which the bank refuses to honour?'

'Refer to drawer,' said Gyles curtly.

'Exactly. I think you have known for some time. In fact I think I can tell you when you first knew real fear that this is what would happen.' She looked up, saw the unspoken question in his eyes and resumed with an effort, 'It was when you did not come to bed that night just before Henry's wedding. I believe you spent the night thinking about just this. Oh not in specific detail, but I think the fear of it all came upon you that night and you deliberately pushed it away.'

'What else was there to do?' he asked her wearily.

'Nothing,' she agreed, 'nothing at all except what you did, prepare yourself for it as best you could.'

He nodded, and added his rider, 'And determine to fight the onslaught when it came and, if necessary, to go down fighting.'

They were both silent for a while. Then, taking courage from his reaction to what she had said already she added in a whisper, 'It all began when we opened that Box, didn't it?' She rose and crossed to the windows. When she spoke again her eyes were upon the wide and tranquil lake where once again the old black cob was cleaning his ancient feathers.

'The Lady Mathilde knew,' Christine said suddenly. 'We went against her.'

She wheeled and faced her husband again, 'Nothing, Gyles, will ever be the same again and whether or not we believe in the power of that somewhat ludicrous Talisman, we have brought great trouble upon ourselves. Pandora's Box I think old Boney called it.'

'Are you trying to tell me,' the words came out evenly but Gyles' jaw was taut and strained looking, 'that no matter what we do this line is doomed?'

She regarded him steadily. 'Not exactly. What I am saying, is that I do not think we shall ever know the pattern of peace and utter security which we have known until now. I have come to terms with this conviction. Now,' she laid one hand over his, 'now Gyles we fight!'

Still they did not join their relatives at luncheon. George came, wonderingly. They sent him away. At length when it was clear that Christine had no more to say Gyles began to discuss Castle affairs.

'I suppose you know that already twenty of our employees under thirty have asked permission to enlist?'

'As many as that?'

'Yes and they include Philip, so now we have no agent and Henry who is such a tower of strength to me will be gone in a few days. Andrew is only a schoolboy. He knows nothing. Where do we find a replacement either for Henry or for Philip?' Sitting together, with the sunshine flooding the wide windows they began to examine the extent of the drawn cheques which they must now honour.

Nothing had either been seen nor heard of Rosalind and her Knight. When Gyles pressed his wife as to whether anything the girl had ever done had given the slightest clue she shook her head mutely.

'I saw nothing,' she confessed, 'this is not altogether surprising if you think back. You filled my thoughts. You showered me with gifts, made love to me most ardently,' the colour flooded her cheeks. 'You transformed me into a gel again. I have never stopped loving you for one single instant; but your ardour blurred my vision, you poured a heady wine, my love, even for a seasoned old matron like me to drink.'

He came across and took her in his arms. Here she rested quietly for a little with Gyles' lips on her hair. Then she pushed him away. 'And now,' she sounded close to tears but even so completely resolute, 'we see this thing through – together.'

In the upheaval of their sudden departures from Arlington street, Petula had found no opportunity as yet to tell Christine of the curious exchange which she had had with Lucy. Petula felt herself wholly unable so to do until she first resolved the other problem which Lucy had raised. What special reason she wondered, could such a young girl have for speaking like a mature woman and saying that she had reasons of her own for observing what was going on between Rosalind and 'that beastly Irishman'. Her thoughts invariably wandered when she reached this recurring point in her reflections. How could Rosalind lose her head in such a manner over a man old enough to be her father! A rake, already married, albeit now a widower; one without means from all accounts; a gambler, in fact no more than a well-bred member of that band of rogues who lived upon their wits; in his case using the backing of a great and honourable name to further his impecunious but extravagant ends as their own 'runts' had done.

While Gyles and Christine remained in the former's office, Petula sat at table pushing food around on her plate and brooding upon the 'fatal Delahayes' as she now thought of them. She knew little enough of the Stephen episode; but sufficient to see how devious he had been throughout and how adept he showed himself at concealment. Now, whatever the final result, it was plain to see that Rosalind was possibly even worse.

She said as much to Henry who rallied her for being in some cloud-cuckoo land of her own. She let him tuck her hand under his arm and lead her out on to the terrace. Once there they began walking to and fro.

'How did you know Pet?' Henry asked surprised, 'I never said a word. My father and the old octogenarian made me swear; but now we are married it's different.' Automatically he rumpled his hair.

'I was out riding with Grumpy,' Petula recalled, 'when I saw that little copper-headed child at the "Arms". I realized in a flash that he must be Lorme strain, albeit on the wrong side of the blanket.'

'Did Granpapa see?'

'No, I managed to deflect his attention. I dug my heels in and made out that for a moment my mare had gained the upper hand. When I reined in we were out of sight of the Aynthorp Arms and the toddler. Then I came through the opened doors that night just as Uncle Sinclair came down the stairs with the riding whip in his hands. It was easy enough to complete the sum made by those two quick glimpses.'

'I never saw you that night,' Henry said wonderingly.

'You wouldn't my darling. I turned and fled. No one saw me thank heaven and I did not speak of it even to Daddy.'

Henry sighed deeply. 'Then I suppose I had better tell you the rest, for it's very clear to me already that Rosalind is runnin' true to form.' He took a deep breath and began, relating how accidentally his father had seen the little boy and formed the same conclusions as she. How, when faced, Stephen as good as admitted his guilt. He had been sleeping with the barmaid niece of the Aynthorp Arms' landlord since he was about fourteen and had got her with son when he was fifteen.

Then Henry told of how their 'resident poacher' old Tim had been tickling trout one morning very early when Petula's brother Charles appeared. Tim hid himself in the bushes and thus heard Stephen confide in Charles and beg him to help. Tim, naturally elated by this ripe plum of scandal subsequently

got drunk at the Arms and mocked the youngest footman
George with his tale. George of course spread it about below
stairs. Eventually Sawby very reluctantly went to his master.

'There was family conclave of course,' Henry went on, 'the
whole affair was thrashed out. It so happened that the Trusloves were here at the time. M'father and the old octogenarian
drew them in and demanded their help in covering up this
latest scandal as we have been wont to do with all our 'runts'
down the centuries. The Trusloves coped. In the end the girl
was approached and inveigled into joining a reputable theatrical
touring company with her little boy. They went to Australia
and nothing has happened since until quite recently. Of course
we paid. We paid the impresario to give them both parts and
to keep them out of England. Eventually I believe she met
someone in Australia called Hackington. He was reputedly a
wealthy sheep farmer. Anyway he married her and I believe he
adopted the boy as his own.

'Eventually, after Uncle Sinclair had given Stephen the
father and mother of a beating with that horse whip he and
poor old Aunt Hetty took him on a world tour. You remember
they were away for three years and returned without Stephen.
Another fiddle had been worked. Stephen had conned them
again! First into thinking he was a changed character, then
into what we believe now was a purely fictitious interest in
archaeology. Anyway the upshot was that Aunt Hetty and
Uncle Sinclair put up six thousand pounds they could ill
afford and sent him on his way.'

'Is he still er, digging?' Petula sounded incredulous.

'No, of course not. He never turned up to meet the distinguished old boy who had undertaken to keep him under his
wing. He decamped with the money and again, of course, it
was Grandfather who ultimately settled the score.'

'And he has never been heard of since?'

'Never,' said Henry. 'The longer he stays away the better.
It turned out he was a wrong'un from the start, even at
prepper and later at Eton where there were some ugly incidents.
What matters now,' Henry's voice became more forceful, 'is
that he drew the wool over everyone's eyes and it's just exactly
what Rosalind has managed to do over that confounded Irish-

man. From what I hear he's just another out and outer.'

Gyles and Christine had not failed to notice the pair pacing up and down engrossed in conversation. Now as they halted and stared at each other miserably, Gyles leaned through the window and called them in to his office. 'Can you join us we have problems?' he asked.

As they came in, Gyles explained, 'We are reviewin' the situation, yer mother and I and I have to tell you that it is, er, slightly tiresome. Not only are we worried sick about that idiot girl' – he did not trouble to name her – 'but twenty of our staff are goin'; and with you off Henry I have no one to assist me with the runnin' of our depleted estate.'

Henry made chaos of his hair. Christine and Petula exchanged glances. Then Henry spoke.

'I think,' he said slowly, 'I have a solution for that one.' He swung round on his wife, 'Pet, cry me down if I'm speakin' out of turn, but why shouldn't you work with m' father? You know perfectly well you loathe the idea of nursin'.' Petula flashed him a warning glance which Gyles intercepted.

Before Henry could continue . . . 'It would interest me to know who said anythin' about nursin',' he observed quickly. For an instant Petula was nonplussed then she achieved a rather lame, 'Well I mean, isn't that the only thing that is left for women to do in any war?'

'Not it seems this one,' Gyles was frowning as if he held a clue so tenuously that it slipped from his grasp.

Fortuitously George presented himself and standing just inside the doorway said, 'My apologies for interrupting you, my lord, but her ladyship your mother has sent me.'

'Well?' said Gyles uncompromisingly.

'Her ladyship would be deeply obliged if you would come to her boudoir immediately.'

Gyles dismissed the man and rifled through his pile of papers.

'Christine,' he asked a trifle desperately, 'do you think you can cope with these?' He picked out a small sheaf of telegrams, 'I was comin' to them next. The clan is gatherin'. It's all in here and you will need to warn Mrs Peace of an influx of family.'

Christine nodded, 'Gyles dear, do please go to Mama and let Henry's suggestion lie fallow for the moment. I'll cope while you are gone,' she took the telegrams. 'At least let us cross some of our other bridges first.'

For once Gyles ignored her. His eyes were fixed on Petula.

'I think first I will tell you that if what Henry suggests is to your likin' it would also be to mine. M'y father always maintained you had a first rate head on your shoulders. You have also absorbed a considerable amount concernin' estate management from your father. I would rather say please will *you* think about it and I will leave the matter until you are ready to give me your opinion.'

They made to move. But he halted them.

'Just a minute,' he said, and Henry grinned ruefully as he detected the dangerous note in his father's voice.

'What do any of you know about this surprisin' summons from m' mother? She is more aware than anyone else how deep I am in problems which must be resolved quickly.' He looked from one to the other. No one spoke.

'So,' he said, honing the sharp edge of his voice, 'somethin's up again, on that I am prepared to wager. Somethin' that at least one of you knows of already . . . well I'll go and see her; but before I do let me tell you I will not be ridden over rough-shod at a time like this, not even by those two wicked old loves. Every instinct tells me they have been brewin' somethin' between 'em and I'll lay a pony to a pepper-corn I'll find 'em closeted together now.' He still hesitated, then he challenged his wife: 'are you by any chance attemptin' to inveigle me, my love? For I assure you the time is out of season for such capers and I am in no mood for them.'

A faint, uncertain smile touched Christine's lips. All she said was, 'Gyles please, just go and see *Belle Mère*.' So, with a final shrug he complied.

When the door closed behind him, 'Oh lor!' ejaculated Henry forlornly, 'now his pecker's up – and we'd all better 'ware wire. I'm goin' to see Plum, then I know I shall feel better.'

Christine and Petula sat down to read the telegrams. There were three from Mr Sissingham. The first stated: *'Bringing Lucien home immediately. Undertake to safeguard him. Will advise progress. Sissingham.'*

The second came from Calais and read, '*Reached here without incident. Trains slightly difficult due to mobilization. Have found suitable accommodation. Lucien's friend Monsieur Paquin has supplied ample funds. Sissingham.*'

Christine studied this carefully. 'How in the world has Monsieur Paquin entered the lists?' she speculated. 'Pet we must ask Lucy if she can throw any light on this curious circumstance.'

The third telegram from the Touraine was from Rosemary's husband Charles, it ran, '*Recalled. Sending Rosemary, children and nurse to you, Dieu nous garde, Charles.*'

Christine smiled as she went to the bell pull which brought Sawby. When she had given him her message for Mrs Peace she asked, 'Oh, and Sawby, would you please send someone to the stables to request Plumstead to hold a carriage in readiness to meet Miss Rosemary. I am afraid I have no idea when she will arrive.'

'Just so, my Lady,' said Sawby steadily.

Petula held yet another telegram out to her. 'Oh!' Christine exclaimed, 'and we shall need someone to meet Mrs Christian – it seems the Major has already re-joined his regiment.'

Sawby hesitated. 'There is one other matter my lady, can you tell me where I may find his lordship?'

'His lordship is with the Dowager. I suggest it would be prudent if you were to wait until he left her.'

Again Sawby murmured, 'Precisely so my lady.' But he remained standing. 'My lady,' he almost pleaded, 'will you not take something? A cup of soup? Chef has an excellent consommé . . .'

'I'm sorry,' she regretted, 'I am simply not hungry. Petula, would you like some coffee? Yes? Well then please ask one of the footmen to bring us both some Sawby. Will that satisfy you?'

'No, my lady,' Sawby said stubbornly, 'your ladyship will need to conserve your strength; but it shall be so, if that is your last word.'

'Dear Sawby,' said Christine when they were alone again, 'he is a very splendid man, particularly in a crisis. Now, where were we I wonder?'

No sooner had the coffee appeared with a plate of minute sandwiches then a footman was back to announce the arrival of Gabrielle – alone.

They both hurried out, sandwiches and coffee forgotten to find her standing in the hall amid a welter of luggage. 'Christine, is there any news of Rosalind?' she cried out as she saw them. 'Really this is too much! And now Eustace has damaged his shoulder and cannot travel for a few days.'

In to this scene waddled Bishop Alaric, who held out fat hands while booming, 'It is God's will my dears! Console yourselves, He will protect us all.'

This had the effect of so irritating Christine that she bit her lip, swallowed a retort and contented herself with remarking to Petula as they went upstairs together, 'We have no time to console ourselves, nor shall have as far as I can see until this affair is ended.' But whether she referred to Rosalind or the duration of war she did not disclose.

Together they hurried through the Long Gallery, towards the rooms which were already being prepared for Rosemary. Christine glanced up at the portraits and told them.

'We're closing ranks again. The Lormes are coming home. Soon we shall all be here, save only for our young men,' she choked on this a little, Petula gripped her hand, received an answering squeeze and they hurried on past the fixed gaze of a galaxy of Lorme ancestors.

A few moments later the cat was out of the bag. Gyles had entered his mother's boudoir to find, as he had predicted, that the two old gentle-women were sitting together on a window seat like two small sparrows on one of the new-fangled telegraph wires.

'You sent for me, Mama,' Gyles inquired standing stiffly inside the door.

'Yes, it was good of you to come dear,' said the Dowager appreciatively. 'I can imagine how fearfully beset you must be.' She needed only one glance to tell her that her son was holding himself in check; but that even so, one small slip on her part would touch off one of the famous Lorme tantrums. She merely sighed, smoothed her skirts, invited him to be seated and began her difficult narrative.

He listened in stony silence. When she had done, the enormity of their deceit had the reverse effect, seeming to damp down his rising temper. She repeated, in more detail what she had told Petula and in the silence which followed Gyles predictably removed, polished and replaced his monocle, not only playing for time, but seeking control of himself.

'Since when have you elected to nurse militant suffragettes to your respective bosoms?' he then asked icily.

'Never,' the Dowager spoke for them both and, naughtily gave him a piercingly sweet smile.

'Then . . . what the devil do you expect me to say, Mama?'

'Don't swear dear, IF you please. While I am delighted to see you are comin' to resemble your father more and more; nevertheless I can do very well without any tantrums at this juncture.'

'Tantrums! Mama I am not a naughty schoolboy,' Gyles crimsoned with suppressed fury.

'I am aware of that, my son' – with a tiny emphasis upon the last word, 'it is simply that I know something which you do not. IF you will allow me to share my knowledge with you, I believe you may come to see how it casts an entirely different complexion upon our appointing Lady Constance as our Matron. Furthermore . . .' she broke off, for Gyles interrupted her.

'Mama, with the greatest respect, I *am* the head of this house and would at least appreciate being *asked* for my opinion before being presented with a *fait accompli* of this appalling magnitude. Have you thought about doctors, nurses, consultant specialists, ward maids, everything vital to the running of such a Convalescent Home? It may interest you to learn that since this morning twenty of our employees have asked for, and of course obtained, permission to join the colours.'

The Dowager remained unruffled. 'Would you not have despised them if they had done otherwise?'

'Yes,' said Gyles shortly, 'but that is not relevant. What do you propose to do about staffing such an enterprise?'

'I will give you the list dear, no, Marguerite, you have it I believe?'

There was a pregnant silence while the little Countess rummaged in her reticule. Then she produced a scrap of paper, raised her lorgnettes and read from it. Half way through Gyles did explode. 'Flaming hell Mama!' he ejaculated, 'You have worked this thing out in every minute detail! Am I not to be consulted about anything in this Castle? Do you intend to take over the reins completely once again? A finger in every pie is one thing; but this petticoat administration! This plotting under the rose, is more than can be borne. Have you obtained permission from anyone?'

'From all the necessary authorities.' Her composure was driving him distracted, 'I went to Jelly and Johnnie,[1] they gave me all I needed under their blessin' . . .'

Gyles clapped hands to his head, 'Ohmigod!' he exclaimed. 'One would have imagined that a gentlewoman of your years was past suborning old *beaux* in order to obtain her own way in a matter of this kind. Really, Mama, you are incorrigible!'

She lifted her eyes to his. 'Yes,' she agreed. 'Indeed one might say so; but one would be wrong. You must please comprehend that to use your own words "a matter of this kind" is women's work. There is not a woman in this family who will not prefer to be doin' something constructive while this war lasts. The idea of sittin' around waitin' is anathema. We two had more than a sufficiency of it during the Boer War. Now while we still have our health and strength we will at least have a responsible occupation to help keep fear away.'

Gyles flung out his hands in a small gesture of defeat.

'Mama!' he exclaimed exasperated, 'you are indomitable. Your health and strength indeed! What part may I be permitted to inquire do you intend playin' in this new venture?'

A tiny, wicked gleam appeared instantly in two old pairs of eyes. They had won and they both knew it. Now they were in unspoken agreement that the time had come for them to swerve from attack to magnanimity.

'It was proposed by Lady Constance that Marguerite and I should act as her assistants,' the Dowager told him with a scandalous counterfeit of humility. 'We are to handle the distribution of books, play chess with our convalescents, write

[1] Lord Jellicoe and Sir John French

their letters for them. Lady Constance was good enough to say that we should be . . . now what was that new-fangled phrase she employed, Marguerite?'

'An invaluable therapeutic influence upon young men suffering from shock as a result of frightful battle experiences,' Marguerite obliged.

Gyles jumped up and started his usual pacing. A minute wink passed between the conspirators. Then he wheeled round abruptly to ask.

'Pray what is the, er, extenuatin' circumstance which is to make the Lady Constance acceptable to us all?'

Again they exchanged glances. Marguerite after some hesitation gave a nod and the Dowager played her trump card.

'Amnesty dear, for all militant suffragettes. This we have on the very highest authority. Furthermore, the instant the amnesty is granted, Mrs Pankhurst will give the lead for the whole membership of womens' suffrage to relinquish their current activities and turn their whole endeavours to war work upon the home front.' Having delivered herself of this broadside she quickly followed it with a gentle, 'Therefore, my very dear son, may we please have your permission and your blessing on what we so much desire to do?'

That sank him, as was their intention. He looked from one to the other in exasperation. 'Would you, I wonder consider it impertinent,' he asked caustically, 'if I so far forgot myself as to inform you that you are a pair of wicked conniving schemers. Now I know from whence comes the Delahaye deviousness. From the distaff side. From Henrietta via you Mama and since *Tante* Marguerite is your sister-in-law . . . Oh!' he flung out his hands. 'Nor, may I add, do either of you improve with age. First you suborned m'father, a major achievement I might add since a mule was capricious by comparison; and now with malice aforethought you seek to do the same with me. Certainly you have my permission, but only because to withold it at a time like this would be to lose the chance of absorbing you in a ploy so arduous and so damnably important that it might just contain you sufficiently to put a stop to any more hell-brews from seething in the cauldrons you call your minds – at least for the duration of this conflict.' Saying which he kissed both their hands punctiliously and marched from the room.

Left alone together they wiped their eyes in which the tears of combined laughter and emotion were shining. Suddenly Marguerite said, sitting bolt upright, 'Alicia, your son was very rude.'

'He was my dear,' the Dowager agreed with quivering lips, 'but you must admit he was also really rather funny.'

When they had dabbed at their eyes with their lacy handkerchiefs, 'He is very cross,' said Marguerite reflectively. 'Oh yes, but it will pass, indeed I think we did very well, all things considered. Much more important I believe is the fact that, even for us, and takin' all our past dramas into consideration we are in a considerable pickle – as a family.'

Little Marguerite held up one small be-ringed hand, so that she could enumerate the 'considerable pickle' upon her fingers.

'One,' she counted, 'Henrietta is collapsed again, which in itself is no great matter; but it does impose a further strain upon Sinclair besides creating additional demands upon the servants who are hard-pressed already and look to be even more so in the days ahead.'

'Two,' the Dowager took a turn, 'Sinclair is such a wreck over that tedious little wretch that, if I speak frankly I will confess it leaves me extremely anxious both for his health and his sanity.'

'Three,' counted Marguerite, 'our little Lucien is adrift with only Mr Sissingham, and all we know is that he is somewhere in France. Then I have to add number four, of which I suspect you know nothing. Ninian, if you please, is threatening to leave Sandhurst a year before his passing out so that he can join the colours. Five, is equally disturbin' and concerns that young Monster Andrew. He was inquirin' of Sawbridge in the garden just before luncheon if anyone really checked on ages when young men enlisted.'

This startled the Dowager. 'If that child even contemplates doin' anythin' so frightful, at seventeen and still at Harrow, Gyles must be informed immediately,' she exclaimed. 'The idea is absolutely monstrous. What with all the rushin' to and fro and the servants under pressure, that boy cannot be watched every minute of his holidays and he might go off before we could have time to stop him.'

'Precisely.'

'Well we must tell Gyles.'

'That,' said Marguerite in the tone of one being asked to confront a boa constrictor, 'is an experience I can well forego.'

The Dowager rose to her full five feet, 'Then,' she said crossly, 'I shall have to tell him myself. Come Marguerite, at least you can give me a little moral support.'

Marguerite still hesitated. 'I think,' she said slowly, 'I . . . can suggest . . . a better . . . way.'

'What better way pray, than informing that naughty boy's Papa?'

'You,' said Marguerite, 'you, my dear little Dragon. No one knows better than I how intimidating you can be when you so wish. Save Gyles if you can. Send for the boy now. Assume your most terrifying mien. Deal with him as only you can when you so wish. That should postpone the evil day, even if it does nothing more. Anything which eases Gyles should surely be attempted?'

The Dowager pondered, pursing her lips and twitching the lower one between finger and thumb as she considered the proposition.

'Very well,' she said. 'Let us have him up here.'

Andrew came, running in from the stables and being escorted breathlessly by George, who ushered him into the presences. Marguerite sat some distance off in a window embrasure, the gleam in her eyes concealed as she bent over her embroidery.

The Dowager opened the onslaught by commenting,

'Goodness gracious, I had forgotten how tall you were child, it makes things awkward surely, when your appearance suggests you are on the brink of manhood when you are really still very much a schoolboy.'

Andrew opened his mouth to protest, but before he could speak the Dowager, following up her advantage went for him hip and thigh. When she had done and the performance was concluded, for so Marguerite regarded it, a very chastened Andrew was made to swear upon holy oath that he would do 'nothin', absolutely nothin' to add troubles to Papa and Mama until I am eighteen'.

The oath taken Andrew was dismissed on the line, 'and now you may go and reflect upon your scandalous behaviour,' which sent him disconsolately away.

The day wore on. When Gyles quit his mother's boudoir he so far veered from custom that he went straightway to the library, where he mixed himself a stiff brandy and soda. No sooner had he settled thankfully in one of the deep red leather chairs and crossed his legs than the door opened to admit Sawby with the evening papers. Having arranged them, fan-wise and freshly ironed upon the central library table he cleared his throat rather loudly.

Gyles looked up, as he was intended to do. 'Well, Sawby?'

'It's the bonfire my lord,' Sawby told him without preamble, 'the village gathers their branches now.'

Gyles clapped hand to forehead, 'How could I have forgotten!' he exclaimed, 'They will go tonight of course?'

'Yes, my lord. Some having very young children they hoped you might permit them to go just as soon as the menfolk finish work? And I think my lord it may please you to know that except for the very aged and the infirm, every man, woman and child will climb Puck's Hill this evening.'

'And so will we,' Gyles drank his brandy down and rose with new vigour. 'But how about the Castle staff, would it not be more convenient for everyone if they went before the changing bell?'

'That is what we had hoped my lord. All save Chef André and my wife that is.'

Gyles raised an eyebrow, 'And why, pray, should they be excluded?'

Sawby elucidated. 'Chef has prepared a dinner which he considers suitable for the occasion. He requires my wife's assistance. This has the somewhat necessary approval of Mrs Parsons. Therefore with your permission I will carry my wife's brand and Mrs Parsons will take Chef's.'

'How fortuitous,' Gyles twinkled, 'I had always thought those two at daggers drawn!'

Again Sawby explained and when he had done Gyles felt his

spirit lift unaccountably at the small change of this domestic amnesty. He left his butler, undertaking to inform the family. Sawby in his turn promised that Sawbridge would carry a sufficiency of branches to the drive for each member of the family to bear one up the hill.

Earlier in the day Chef had reacted to the news of war with a typically Gallic eruption.

Having predicted nothing but the worst; wept a little for *La Belle Patrie*, and caused Mrs Parsons, who still could not understand a word to clap her hands over her ears at the vituperation which poured from his trembling mouth over that 'deformed shit of a seven months dwarf' by which he was pleased to refer to Kaiser Wilhelm of Germany, he set about the preparations for *'un banquet'*.

Down came the copper pots and pans from their wide shelf above his stoves. Bang! clatter, wallop! went the pans upon the *bain marie*. Muttering like a Lascar sea cook, his moustache quivering, he sent the gaping Boots scurrying for Mr Sawbridge, the head gardener.

'Allez-y,' he commanded, *'aussi vite que possible.'* Then he turned his frenzy upon the kitchen maids and having so done seized a pencil from Mrs Parson's hand and sat down beside her to make a menu. Even she was lenient.

'Ee's all distort,' she observed with remarkable tolerance, 'and oo can wonder, wen I think of that low down cunning . . .' she faltered and chef immediately looked up and supplied the word at which she baulked. *'Bâtard,'* he said coldly, and followed with another stream of invective.

'Bat-'ard,' repeated Mrs Parsons. She reflected – and then made the concession of her life to the enormity of present circumstances. Thereby she evinced what proved to be an unswerving loyalty to her old enemy. This was to last for over four long, bitter years. When hostilities ended, it was the belief of all below stairs that provided they were still alive and together, hostilities between them would be resumed upon the signing of an armistice.

'Bât-'ard,' Mrs Parsons repeated. 'You know, M. André, I'm not at all sure it don't sound even nastier in your lingo,' saying which she gave a small nod of benign approval and screamed for Pansy, newly arrived and still in her bonnet, to ' 'urry up my girl and give me an 'and with them sponge fingers'.

It was a day of broken records at Castle Rising. When Sawby progressed with his usual majestic step down the staircase to the servants' hall, Chef looked up and observed, 'Mistaire Sawbee, I 'ave decide not to burrden Miladi with a menu for tonight. You will therefore please to inform 'er that André will attend to dinner, *n'importe les nombres* – no matter 'oo gets 'ere by then.' The little man, then opened his menu book and inscribed in his flowery copperplate:

Le Diner. Le 5 Août. 1914. Castle Rising

In after years, future Lormes were to read the record of the Family's dinner on the first evening of what came to be called the First World War with some amazement. It read,

Les Blinis de Sarrasin
Les Fonds d'Artichauts à la Victoire

Consommé Alexandre
Velouté Georges V

Suprêmes de Sole au Champagne Marie
Homard à la Crème en Bateaux Normand

Les Pintadons en Soufflé Prince des Galles
Les Croustades des Huîtres de Poularde General Joffre

Le Foie Gras aux raisins Entente Cordiale

Bombe de la Victoire

Les Friandises sous L'Arc de Triomphe

When André had completed his last entry, he murmured, '*Alors! Ça suffit, c'est léger mais c'est pas mal du tout.*'

In the light of what followed this proved to be André's greatest masterpiece – if not of the culinary art – then undoubtedly of understatement.

* * *

Sawby saw to it that each new arrival was reminded of the custom which dated back to the Napoleonic wars and was informed that it was being revived. He then returned below stairs to explain it all to his wife. Pansy, round eyed and enthralled, listened to the story Sawby told, beginning with how the then Lord Aynthorp had ordered a great bonfire to be laid upon the brow of Puck's Hill, 'An eminence which is held in great superstition among the village folk. When the news was bad, during that Napoleonic conflict the villagers made pilgrimage to the unlit fire, carrying more branches to lay upon the stack, in token of their unswerving confidence that on one not too far distant day peace would reign once more and then the fire would crackle merrily. This custom has been observed ever since,' he concluded. 'So now tonight it all begins again.'

'Very right and proper too,' supplemented Mrs Parsons from her rocking chair.

'Why is it called Puck's Hill?' Pansy inquired.

'Because,' replied Sawby tolerantly, 'the villagers claim that Puck lives under it, in caverns down in the womb of Mother Earth. They swear that he comes out on All Hallows' Eve and plays tricks upon them still. And now my dear you must go back to Chef and tell him if you please that his lordship would be deeply obliged if the hour of dining were advanced by one half hour in order to give our household time to dress.'

Pansy grimaced, but obeyed, pausing only to bring a large hazel twig and set it beside her husband's chair.

'Mr Sawbridge gave me this for you to lay for me. He says it should be hazel because such a branch in the right hands, *which is us* can divine water, and will be a token of our wish that every flood and pestilence are visited upon our wicked enemies.' And so saying she braced herself for yet another Gallic eruption from Chef. Instead, he set aside the ladle from which he was tasting, indicated his own hazel branch and asked her if she would give it to Mrs Parsons adding, 'Eet is better, I 'ave much to do still upon my *Arc de Triomphe*.' Flustered, Pansy reminded herself that nothing was running true to form on this dreadful first day of war.

✳ ✳ ✳

As the shadows began to lengthen a thin, straggling line developed across Lorme land to the summit of Puck's Hill as master and man, mistress and maid made their way towards it. It heartened them. They felt sustained by it, not only because of the simple pagan ritual; but because the presence of 'the Family' intermingling with the procession gave them a sense of security.

On the way back Gyles held Christine's hand down the long slope. 'Do you remember Gyles,' she asked, 'how we leaned from our bedroom window on that wonderful Christmas Eve in nineteen hundred and ten?'

'I do,' Gyles recalled, 'you said, with your head against my shoulder, "As it is now . . ." and I added, as I do again now, "if I have my way . . . as it ever shall be". But this time I must append my rider, if it is God's will it should be so.'

The Family went in to dinner because this was their custom and it gave them some solace though, as Marguerite confided in the Dowager as they came down the staircase together, 'I feel much as I imagine our ancestors must have done when they dressed in their finery, and went by tumbrel to the guillotine.'

'One must preserve one's dignity,' retorted her sister-in-law sweeping in with rustling skirts, and standing behind her chair while Alaric said grace.

The news was scarcely encouraging. There was little pleasure among the Cabinet at the forthcoming clash of arms. Only Winston Churchill seemed in high spirits. For the rest, Lord Morley had resigned and the overall tenor was of intense anxiety, while their leader, knowing little or nothing of military strategy, showed himself very willing to let the generals and admirals conduct the war. The general consensus was that the government would endeavour to carry on much as usual. Britain's strategy was plain. The Royal Navy would engage the German High Seas fleet and – naturally – destroy it. A British Expeditionary Force would be sent to France to plug a few gaps while the French in the west and the Russians in the east speedily employed their twin strengths to crush both the German and Austrian armies into submission.

These matters were discussed while André's dishes came

and went. No one did justice to the little chef's endeavours. Christine did manage by superhuman effort to simulate both astonishment and admiration at chef's sugar *Arc de Triomphe.*

'Ask Monsieur André,' she requested Sawby, 'to put it away very carefully so that it may be used again when we have won this war.' Thus feeling that she had done the best she could in the circumstances she gave a small sigh of relief as the doors closed behind their butler. They had scarcely done so when John and Primrose came in saying they had already dined. They took their places, however, and Andrew as youngest present, rose. At a nod from his father he gave them the loyal toast.

Gradually, the Family events were then told to the new arrivals. The sound of distant thunder rolled in through the open windows like a giant's stentorian breathing. The night was hot and the atmosphere oppressive. They fell silent again. Gyles, his face in shadow, leaned back in his chair, one hand toying with the stem of his port glass.

Like families throughout England and France they were gathered together for comfort, yet their fears denied them any such solace. They seemed to be listening with reluctance for what they did not wish to hear, some atavistic instinct working in them as though to reduce them to mere animals whose bodies were poised for instant flight. Ears pricked, nostrils twitching, they were dreadfully aware of some impending danger whose scent had so far eluded them.

'Impala!' said Henry into the silence.

' 'Eh? What?' the bishop looked up startled.

'I said sir, that we are like Impala.'

'Oh yes.'

Then Sinclair spoke, 'Guns in the distance sound like thunder,' he muttered.

'Yes, yes dear boy,' John de Lorme frowned at his dessert plate.

'I suppose,' from Sinclair again, 'if the Hun gets near enough to the French coast we shall hear the guns as we are hearing thunder now.'

Petula shivered. Stephanie stared at him with eyes like a frightened hare. 'Oh daddy!' she exclaimed reproachfully.

Sinclair peered at his daughter seeming to find it hard to see her, 'I have the most curious feeling, I think that if or when that does happen I shall not hear it. Now how I wonder, could that be so?'

'Idle fancies born of stress, dear Sinclair.' Christine sounded nervous. 'We are all given to such misleading thoughts when we are bayed.'

Their heads came up again, just as Henry had said like Impala, as familiar, cheerful voices behind the closed doors were heard. Then Ninian and James walked in looking both fit and cheerful. Ninian kissed his mother, then went round paying his respects while James greeted his Papa, inquired after his Mama and dutifully executed his round. The pair then inserted themselves at the table, shot their long legs underneath and Ninian, eyeing his father exclaimed, 'I say, sir, the port's with you, can a chap have a drink?'

Gyles smiled. He immediately re-circulated the decanter, his eyes upon the pair of them. 'The outbreak of war does not seem to have disturbed either of you unduly,' he observed drily.

In chorus as usual they exclaimed, 'Isn't it what we've been waiting for sir?' Ninian added, 'We're tickled pink, in fact we've cut our shootin' to come home to ask if we can skip our last year at Sandhurst. We can't go loafin' on there while the country's at war. Thousands of the chaps are cuttin' loose y'know.'

Gyles who was nearing exhaustion rallied himself. 'I'm sure they are,' he agreed, 'and if I were your age I should be askin' my father exactly what you have asked me.'

Ninian took a swig of his port.

'Told you it would be all right,' he said derisively to James, then, to his father, 'It's all right then sir, you'll give permission?'

'I can't speak for James,' he hedged, 'that is at your Aunt Gabrielle and Uncle Eustace's disposal. I said if, you recall, that *you* are both reactin' precisely as I would have done at your age.'

'Yes sir, we heard you.'

'But I fancy that I have not yet said what my father would have replied.'

Their faces fell. 'Oh no!' Ninian exclaimed, 'You mean you won't let us?'

'Look at it my way for a moment.' Gyles' eyes were wary. 'Put yourself in my place. If you had a son, as one day God willing you will, would you let him endanger his prospects, throw away years of preparation, run the risk of bein' killed before it was right and proper for him so to do?'

'I told you so,' said James resignedly.

'But sir!'

'But nothing,' Gyles still spoke kindly, but there was a hint of danger in his voice. 'You will not provide cannon fodder one instant before you are of age. You are on your way to becoming a professional soldier. If this war ends, there will be others. So, when you have passed out of Sandhurst next year and joined your regiment then you will be your own man and can make all your own decisions – you will then both be over twenty-one' – he underlined his refusal.

During this exchange, two guilty pairs of eyes met across the table as the Dowager and the little Countess exchanged glances. Andrew intercepted the look and glanced down hurriedly, knowing full well after what he had just heard that his father would have no hesitation in going to the authorities if he attempted to cut and run, as his Grandmother had warned him.

The gloom spread. Christine made no attempt to collect eyes. It seemed that she too, was waiting for something which exerted its influence so powerfully that she could not give her signal.

The opened windows were eloquent of nightfall now, starlit, impenetrable as their future destinies. Unbidden, swiftly rejected, came the thought to Henry, 'Where shall we be a year from now?' While Christine stared from one to the other at the untouched faces of their young and asked herself the agonizing question, 'Which will be the first to go of the children who are hankering for war?'

It was then that disaster struck again. Sawby came in with a telegram. He lowered his tray in front of Rosalind's father.

'A telegram for you, sir.'

'For me!' Sinclair looked with repugnance at the yellow envelope. 'Never did care for telegrams,' he muttered, nerving himself to take this one. His hand reached out to it reluctantly, then closed over it. Sawby drew back the empty tray.

'The boy bicycled up with it sir,' he explained, 'he is in the servants' hall being given some refreshment. Should you wish to send a reply you have only to pull the bell.'

Sinclair remained slumped in his chair. Eventually, with a deep sigh he murmured, 'Excuse me, everyone,' then taking up his unused dessert knife he inserted it in the flap of that hated yellow envelope.

The Dowager made a valiant effort to raise small talk. In a measure she succeeded. The family rallied to her. Even so, they could not fail to hear the strangling sound which emerged from Sinclair's throat nor how one hand flew to it as he scanned the brief message.

The chatter dropped half an octave, became so muted that they could all hear the crackle as Sinclair screwed up the piece of paper, then tossed it across to his brother-in-law.

'Read that, all of you,' he said chokingly, adding, 'pray excuse me.' Somehow, lurching like a crippled drunkard he stumbled to the doors wrenched them open and pulled them back behind him.

Gyles spread out the crumpled thing. Then, 'I think I had better read this to you,' he said slowly. 'It runs, *Married quietly in Bourne Abbey this morning. Deliriously happy. Please give us your blessing.*' After a slight pause he added, 'As you probably realize it is signed *Rosalind and Gavin.*'

The crash which followed brought them to their feet on the instant. Ninian rushed to the doors and wrenched them open. The Family flooded through.

Sinclair was spread-eagled across the last two treads of the staircase. Dreadful bubbling, gasping sounds came through his opened mouth. Stephanie rushed forwards screaming, 'Daddy, oh my darling Daddy, oh whatever has happened to you!' Gyles took one look at the stricken man then went straightway to the telephone to summons Dr Jamieson. They all heard his voice saying, 'Is that you Jamieson? So sorry to trouble you, but could you please come up to the Castle immediately. I think my brother-in-law, Sinclair Delahaye, has just had a stroke.'

CHAPTER 18

Some Measure of Freedom

Rosemary arrived the next morning with her son Charles-Louis, now nearly four; and Charles-Louis's '*Nou-nou*' who was destined to cause havoc in the nursery wing, besides confounding the Castle staff with her complaints . . . '*pas un bidet au Château, c'est incompréhensible! . . . où sont les salades?*' . . . and '*qu'est que c'est cette Marmelade, c'est terriblement acerbe!*'

Sinclair lay helpless, unable to make any intelligible sounds. Stephanie tended him ceaselessly. After standing back to watch the ministrations of the village nurse she rushed to her Grandmama with tears cascading down her cheeks and implored her to send for Lady Constance.

To her and everyone else's astonishment, the Dowager did so. She sat down at her escritoire, wrote out a telegram, read it to the distracted girl adding, 'As you will appreciate, I have signed myself in such a manner as to dispel any possible unease for Lady Constance.'

Stephanie took the paper and endeavoured to read through her veil of tears.

'There, there,' soothed her Grandmama. 'Pray do not blot that paper with your tears! I have put "warmest regards Alicia Aynthorp" so that she may know she is indeed welcome.'

After the girl had rushed away the Dowager sighed heavily and went in search of Gabrielle.

It was already afternoon. Anxiety was running high concerning the whereabouts of Lucien and Mr Sissingham. In desperation, Gabrielle set out for the village on foot intending to interrogate the postmaster. The family let her go, thinking it better for her than pacing the Castle rooms and corridors. Gyles Aynthorp then made a number of abortive telephone calls to men in high places. All the information he could obtain was that all cross-channel vessels were under escort, mine-sweepers were very active and the ports of embarkation from France were thronged with British nationals which at least made the delay seem understandable.

Henrietta lay in bed, heavily sedated by Doctor Jamieson, watched over by Nanny who only forsook her post when the news filtered through to her that her Charles-Louis had returned to her. Then she scuttled away, sending for her old ally Mrs Plumstead to take her place beside the prostrate woman.

By this time a number of decisions had been made. The Museum had been closed 'for the duration' as the local news-paper announcements proclaimed. An elderly caretaker and a nightwatchman were engaged to tend the stove-heating, keep the place aired and patrol the area at night. The architect who had so ably designed and supervised the erection of the Museum premises was summonsed to work with the Lady Constance and her 'assistant matrons' on reconstructions to the wing which was to become their convalescent home. Even now, with Rosemary in attendance as note-taker the old pair prowled the Castle in search of a suitable area.

Their perambulations took them through a great many rooms which had not been in use for years. Here they debated amid swathed furniture, bagged chandeliers and sheeted looking-glasses while little Marguerite surrendered to nostalgia and regaled her companions with reminiscences.

'Now let me see,' she paused, looking round thoughtfully at one large room covered with Royal Stuart tartan. 'Ugh! those fearful antlers!' she eyed with distaste the horns of various beasts which protruded weirdly through yellowing dust sheets. Then, 'Of course!' she exclaimed. 'This was the principal sitting room of the old Queen's Suite! I remember being shown it when I was a little gel. I must have been about seven, yes that would be right, I was born in 'forty two, so it must have been somewhere between 'forty nine and 'fifty that this entire wing was re-decorated for her visit. Such execrable taste! But there it was, the Queen positively doted on what I remember my mother always called '*le plaid*', a barbarous fashion, but she adored it poor soul.'

'So she had been married some years already to Prince Albert?' queried Rosemary.

'Exactly so, and I can even remember a curious conversation, just before the Royal party was due. Mama, your Great, Great Aunt, Rosemary was discussin' a dinner service, Leeds I think, which was bein' "struck" for the visit. Mama saw that I was confused. She then explained that new dinner services were always "struck" in honour of Royal visits.' Marguerite chuckled, 'Mama was most emphatic, she said, "Never forget, child, that one either inherits such things or 'strikes' them for such occasions, *one never purchases them*." I was puzzled at the time because she made such emphasis upon it. Later I understood. You see my poor Papa had what Mama thought to be a Terrible Flaw in his character. He actually collected fine china! He went to people like Spink and to auction rooms like Sothebys and he purchased pieces which appealed to him. Mama was horrified. On one frightful occasion during a luncheon party, Papa picked up his dessert plate, turned it over and began recounting to a very distinguished guest how he had "picked up the entire service for a song" at some sale-room or other. I was a young gel when it happened, not yet out, but just down to luncheons occasionally. When this happened I saw Mama was absolutely seethin' with anger. Thinkin' to save Papa a terrible wiggin' afterwards, I flung myself into the breach. And do you know what I said dear?'

'No-oo,' admitted Rosemary, enthralled.

'Well, somethin' had to be done – but oh! When I think of it now! I cried out, "Oh pray do not worry Lady Manville, if Papa thought that you were valuable he would turn you up to see if you were marked." '

As they laughed, so, abruptly her mood changed. 'Such nonsense!' she exclaimed a trifle crossly. 'The time is sadly out of season for it. What do you think Alicia, could not this room be incorporated?'

The Dowager hesitated. 'I like the entire area so far,' she admitted, 'it has the virtue of bein' far removed from all the occupied part of the Castle. Yet, my dear, those stairs! Stairways and convalescents do not do well together!' She paused to marshal her thoughts, 'Of course,' she added, 'IF Gyles could be persuaded to install one of those lift affairs, then it would be ideal!'

If any further sobering were needed this suggestion provided it. The prospect of asking the head of the family for any more concessions lowered the temperature drastically.

'Oh dear!' said Marguerite.

'Oh no!' exclaimed Rosemary.

'Let us go on,' contributed the Dowager. So on they went, through what had been ante-chambers, bed-chambers, dressing-rooms where they encountered such distractions as old wig-tables in little powder-rooms where eighteenth-century Lormes had submitted to the re-powdering of the enormous wigs in which they even slept! More reminiscence. Eventually, descending the unsuitable staircase and finding themselves looking through the French doors which led to the Urn Garden, with beyond it one of the outstanding beauties of the grounds, the Woodland Garden which had been Marguerite's Grandfather's obsession, they surrendered to the inevitable.

'Imagine,' exclaimed Marguerite, 'those poor boys takin' their first walks along those paths between the trees, when the azaleas are in bloom . . .'

'Or the lilies,' supplemented the Dowager, 'or in spring when the bulbs are flowerin', or later on the rhododendrons . . . there is no doubt Marguerite, this is where our convalescent home must be. We shall just have to leave it to Providence to show us the way to get round Gyles. Now we must hurry back and make ourselves presentable for tea.'

Providence obliged. A telegram awaited the Dowager. As she read it she gave a sigh of relief. 'Thank goodness,' she exclaimed passing it to her sister-in-law, 'Please pass that to Christine when you have read it.'

The message was simple in the extreme. It read: '*Arriving Lower Aynthorp Station 12.45 p.m., tomorrow.*' It was signed: '*Respectfully Nurse Cummins.*'

On the following morning Rosemary received word from her

Charles. This came by French courier, one who was a friend of both families. It transpired he had visited the *Neuilly château* of some French Lormes, the *d'Hautvilles*, while Lucien and his tutor were spending a Friday to Tuesday with them. Rosemary read out the relevant part of the courier friend's message to them during breakfast. First she unwrapped it from a second envelope which she laid aside. '*Please excuse this hasty scrawl. I saw and recognised your young cousin Lucien and his tutor waiting on the quai at Calais. They told me they had been there for some time. Indeed there is terrible chaos; but I managed to put in a word with the right quarter just before I sailed. Both are well and in good spirits. They will come over on the "Maid of Kent" tomorrow; but embarkation time is quite unpredictable. Lucien seemed to be enjoying himself immensely. I left him persuading his tutor (what a charmer that boy is!) to accompany him on a tour the Harbour Master had suggested, to see something of the coastal defences. I think this fellow has taken the pair of them under his wing. You may confidently expect them both some time on the day after tomorrow.*' Rosemary looked up with shining eyes, 'Oh Gabrielle,' she exclaimed, 'I am so thankful for you!'

Then she picked up the inner envelope. It contained a letter from her Charles. Excusing herself, she read the scribbled pages eagerly, murmuring as she read, 'he's all right . . .' and 'fancy so' . . . until, retaining only the last half sheet, she passed it round the family.

'How fortuitous,' said Marguerite thankfully, her mind still upon Lucien.

'Fiddle!' Gyles looked up from the letter, 'was it not you Mama who said that when put to it Lucien possessed hidden resources? I think that young monkey is well able to take care of himself and a downright little schemer to boot.' After which he resumed his reading. The letter was headed '*Somewhere in France.*' Charles wrote: '*I was ordered to Grand Quartier Général on the 5th. We all got into a huge racing machine whose owner had been mobilized as chauffeur. We went off to cheers from hundreds of orderlies and clerks who had just been marched back from "La Soupe".*[1] *We had a young British officer with us so the*

[1] Their dinner. Service slang.

driver stopped at the first bazaar and bought two Red Ensigns
which he fixed to the windscreen as a sign that the British were
really in this with us now! The roads were quite deserted. This was
fortunate for our pace was furious. We only pulled up at posts
manned by elderly men in plain clothes who were guarding level
crossings and bridges with shotguns. They were all members of the
gardes des voies et communications.

'We reached our destination towards evening, stopped in the
large place at General H.Q., and saw General Joffre pacing up
and down deep in conversation with his aide. I was taken to him,
he spoke to me briefly and kindly, then resumed his pacing, so I had
plenty of time to study him. He wore the general's gold and red
cap, a black tunic which from about the third button sloped gently
outwards and red breeches which fitted him ill and sagged badly
. . . He looked impenetrably calm.

'A billet was found for me in the house of some rather dazed
people who told me they were in terror of the Gardes Forestiers –
game keepers extraordinary and smuggler-catchers in peace time.
Woe betide any unfortunate who fails to give both sign and
countersign by night when challenged by these stealthy patrols. I
learned that the Russian Military Attaché was nearly done in one
night. The password was "Austerlitz" which incensed him. So,
when challenged he advanced pouring out invective while bolts
clicked back ominously. At this perilous moment the R.M.A.,
concluded his abuses in the nick of time shouting "Austerlitz!"
Austerlitz! What a word to inflict upon a Russian!

'We are Deuxième Bureau,[2] I have a desk and my chief is
Colonel Dupont. I will keep you posted as to my movements, but
not alas their locations.' Rosemary looked up.

On the morning of August the eighth Lucien arrived distastefully grubby, tousel-headed, but quite unruffled. Mr Sissingham, in sadly rumpled clothes, expressed his relief at arriving
home safely in a completely unintelligible bout of stuttering.
He was only saved from apoplexy by George's appearance to
inform him that baths had been drawn, hot towels were waiting
and his lordship's man, Groom, was on hand to assist.

Lucien, after a quick glance around him demanded anxiously,

[2] Intelligence.

'Where's Lucy?' at which Nanny appeared exclaiming in horror at his appearance. She answered tartly, 'Upstairs and you'll see her *after* your bath young man, I declare you look like a chimney sweep.' She then chivvied him up the stairs towards the nursery wing.

'If you'll be a good boy and let us make you presentable once again, you can go into the schoolroom and see Miss Lucy just as soon as you're fit to be seen again.' She added more gently, 'She's waiting, love.'

Henry and Petula slipped away. He was due to leave before luncheon to report for training. The Royce would take him to the station where Simkins would collect 'Nurse Cummins'.

Hand in hand the pair made for the stables where Plum presented such a dolorous face that as their mounts were led out to them, Petula exclaimed, 'Dear Plum, pray do not look so glum. Mr Henry is not going to France!'

'Nor I shouldn't imagin',' Plum retorted, 'a green'orn like 'im! But howsome ever, I never thort ter see this day when you two was wed.' He turned a severe countenance towards his future master, 'I'll tell yer this Mr 'Enery, for someone must, your Pa bein' all at sixes and sevens an' no wonder. Jest you listen ter a word of advice . . .'

Henry smiled down at the old man affectionately. 'What is it Plum?'

' 'Ot 'ead yer are, like all the Lormes,' Plum began; but broke off as a glimpse of grubby white shirt proclaimed the presence of Richard in the harness room. 'Nah, jest you come along er me,' he shouted, 'where I kin keep me eye on yer, and not bring none them pesky hanimals along of yer neither!'

This flushed the boy out. He came running, to stand legs straddled, staring up at his eldest brother. ' 'Ere,' he inquired interestedly, 'are you goin' to kill some of them pesky Huns?'

Petula choked, 'Oh Plum!' she reproached, 'that's you talking.'

'Wot ken I do?' Plum retorted defensively, ' 'Ees a born mimick – 'ow many times 'ave I tole yer?' he eyed Richard balefully, 'yer not ter talk common like me or yer Pa'll 'ave you away from me in two shakes of a bloomin' duck's tail.'

'Can I see one please?'

'One wot?' Plum scratched his head.

'Duck making two shakes of his tail.'

'Don't be higgerant,' Plum snapped, 'ducks is 'ers not 'ees yer silly ha'porth.'

They plunged into argument. Henry winked at his wife and the pair moved off quietly. Henry called back over his shoulder, 'See you when we get back Plum, then you can lecture me,' and so saying they cantered off across the paddock into the home park beyond.

They were making for the saddle-back, their perennial refuge in times of stress, though Petula had herself well in hand on this occasion. She determined that there should be no acceptance of any break in the continuity of their lives together. Her attitude, staunchly maintained, was simply that her husband was going away for a while and would be back, not only soon, but frequently. Therefore she could hold fear at bay for some time yet.

Henry took his cue from her. They talked, primarily of estate matters. In the two hours left to them he gave her as comprehensive a briefing as possible on what her envisaged duties would be. He told her frankly, 'I think you will find it fascinatin'. It will give you more insight into family history in a few weeks than you could otherwise learn in years. What's more you can always turn to yer father as well as mine for advice and counsel.'

Petula said, 'Yes – poor Daddy?' which puzzled him. 'Why poor, my love?'

She hesitated, but at length told him that Charles Danement was in somewhat of a predicament for his sister Eustacia had announced her intention to leave him.

'Goin' for good?' exclaimed Henry.

'Oh yes. She told him last night. It seems we are losing staff too and Aunt does not feel, in her state of health that she can possibly go on running the Manor with inadequate support as she puts it. She has been asked to stay with an ancient school chum who has recently been widowed. As far as I can gather there is plenty of money. As all the servants are old and have been there all their lives, so there will be no staff problems unless they all die which is unlikely.'

'So your father is to be left all alone in that great place. Does mine know?'

'Not yet,' Petula admitted, 'but he told me he was going over this morning so I expect Daddy will tell him then.'

Henry reined in. 'I'll tell you what,' he said suddenly, 'the best possible thing that could happen is for him to move in with us for the duration. He'll be more than welcome. He will be on the spot to advise you, that in itself will give him an added interest; then he can close up the Manor and yet be near enough to keep an eye on things just as much as if he were in residence.'

Petula thought this an excellent suggestion, said so and Henry reverted to 'his' estate.

'I suppose you know,' he inquired, 'that father has already decided all the men who enlist will have their pay just as if they were here? No? Well you will be responsible for handin' over the married mens' monies to their wives. I can tell you the drill. You fill in a cheque for the old man each Thursday, get him to sign and open it, send someone to the bank and lay in orders that the wives come up each Friday so that they have their money in time for Saturday market day.'

All too soon they turned back. As they cantered down the slope Petula asked, 'Will you be back again before the shooting? I shall need briefing on the handling of game for the London hotels. It was your job wasn't it?'

Henry nodded, 'It was and I shall be back well before. Besides from what I can learn you'll be surrounded by Lady Constance's female hearties. They will execute orders for you. Remember you just have to give 'em their instructions and see that the work is carried out. It's the chasin' that does it. Now as to money . . .'

Plum and Richard came out to meet them, 'Us wants ter see yer in uniform!' Plum announced as they dismounted.

'Then I shall have to look slippy,' Henry grinned. He glanced at the very new watch which was strapped to his wrist. 'Look Plum, come round to the drive. Bring the youngster with you as soon as the Royce leaves here, then I can wave you goodbye.' He moved off, but Richard halted him again, 'Hi! does your regiment have a Mascot?'

'Mascot?' – up went one hand to his head, 'Lor, I don't
know.'

'Well find out,' said Richard, 'and tell your Colonel that if he
hasn't I'll give him my Mr Gooseyplum – my beautiful
Aylesbury duck.'

Henry held out his hand, 'I'm sure,' he said, with admirable
control, 'm'y Colonel will be honoured.' His eyes were very
warm. They shook hands solemnly. Then Richard delivered
his Parthian shot. 'Keep yer legs crorsed, and mind yer Ps and
Qs sojer,' he said outrageously, saw Plum's face, turned and
fled incontinent.

It sent the couple back to the Castle on a wave of laughter.
'An Aylesbury duck!' quavered Petula, 'can you imagine . . .
waddling out on parade leading a battalion of Grenadier
Guards . . .'

'It's not so much that,' agreed Henry weakly, 'but the
spectacle of me offerin' the bloody bird to m'General! Sorry
Pet!'

The Family gathered on the steps to see him off. Henry ran
down, threw an uncertain salute in Plum and Richard's
direction, nodded to the footmen, shook hands with Sawby and
climbed in beside Simpkins, saying very quietly, 'Don't drag it
out, Simpkins, give her her head there's a good chap.' Then he
swivelled round and waved to them all. They waved back.
Everyone diligently emulating Mr Dickens' Lady Deadlock to
ensure there was not the slightest display of emotion from any
one of them. Thus Gyles Aynthorp's eldest son set out upon
the first lap of a journey which would eventually lead him to
the futile battlefields of France.

As soon as luncheon was over Petula went to her own rooms to
curl up on the window seat of their sitting room. From her
eyrie she could see over the apricot brickwork to the stove-
houses in the kitchen gardens. Everything shimmered in the
full heat of August sunshine. Sawbridge was pottering in and
out of the stove-houses with fruits for delivery to the kitchens.
She watched him pause to draw a huge bandanna handkerchief
from the front pocket of his green apron and then mop both

face and neck. Beyond him three men bent as they moved between the serried rows of vegetables. To her right a group of women were busy gleaning, thrusting their armfuls into sacks which they dragged along beside them. There was no breeze. Sound carried far, bringing to her the complaint of a dray's creaking wheels, grinding along the laneway to the home farm; the lowing of cattle being driven milk-heavy to the milking sheds; the whining of a saw as it bit into timber. From the distant river she heard the faint tap-tapping of a woodpecker while from between the great trees wood-pigeon cooed. Nearer to her rose the slow clop-clop of hooves on cobbles which told of horses being led to their stalls. It was all ordered, regulated, immeasurably sweet and sweetly familiar. Henry should be here with her to make all complete! Not speeding away from her towards his mission of destruction. Yet it was all happening, though the scene she looked out upon, the sounds she heard defied such reality. Nothing could surely happen to destroy this now doubly precious heritage.

With agonizing timing a new sound reached her. Someone was playing in the music room. It must be Lucien. He must have opened the windows wide before settling on the music stool for his playing was very clear. He had chosen what she thought must be the saddest of all sad songs, Tchaikovsky's 'None But the Lonely Heart'. This was too much. She lifted shaking hands to her face and wept as the music broke over her.

She wept for the menace to all which had seemed so indestructable, not just for the separation from her love. She wept, too, for all the men who were about to die as much as for the ones from Castle Rising who would not come back. She wept, too, for all those other sons and lovers and for their womenfolk who would soon be left to live out their tally of years alone. Above all she wept because she was dreadfully aware that they had drawn these forces of evil upon themselves, because they had all taken the wrong way and now were to be punished for it.

There was no gainsaying that Lady Constance possessed a disconcerting capacity for cutting the ground from beneath his lordship's feet. She had done it before and now as she walked briskly into the library in her nurse's uniform she demonstrated her ability to do so again.

Gyles was perched upon the top rung of a pair of library steps. As he reached up for a book which was only just within his grasp, 'Nurse Cummins, My Lord,' announced Sawby from the doorway.

Gyles dismounted hastily dusting his hands together.

'Good afternoon, Lord Aynthorp,' Nurse went straight to the point, 'please do not mis-interpret my dress. I merely considered it more discrete to remain so until the amnesty is publicly announced.'

'Quite so,' Gyles said weakly, unused to such tactics and somewhat taken aback. 'It was indeed kind of you to come so speedily,' he then observed, drawing her a chair. He stood while she sat down and then drew one for himself.

She folded her hands over her starched apron and continued, 'I gather that something in the nature of an emergency prompted your mother to telegraph.' She permitted a faint smile to touch the corners of her mouth and her eyes were kindly. 'Please may I know the nature of it? I have as yet seen no one else.'

'Quite so,' Gyles hesitated, then reluctantly provided the salient points of the sorry story.

Within the hour Lady Constance had taken charge. She obtained an interview with Dr Jamieson. She installed herself in a room adjacent to Sinclair's. She sent Stephanie to bed – for the girl was verging on collapse. She arranged with the Dowager that all meals should be sent to her there and when George brought in the first tray apologized so charmingly for the extra work thus involved, that by nightfall she had won approval of all below stairs.

After dinner the Dowager announced *her* intention. So far, as she was at pains to emphasize, she had only exchanged a few brief words with 'Nurse'. So now she would go to her. On this occasion it was she who took the lead from the onset and actually managed to retain it.

When she was settled in a straight-backed chair before a cheerful fire and Lady Constance had opened the connecting door so that she could watch for any sign of movement in her patient, she came back to the little table on which George had set their coffee tray, poured for them both and eventually sat down facing the Dowager, who said as she took her cup and saucer, 'I would like to thank you my dear for your delicacy in electing to remain, er, incognito until your suffrage amnesty is declared. It was well thought and we all appreciate it. Yet, as we have so much to do, and there is so much which must be discussed immediately I felt it would not be advisable for us to postpone our initial chat a moment longer.'

The grey eyes watched her steadily. The head inclined slightly.

'Dear me, she is a beauty!' thought the Dowager. Aloud she said, 'What I wish to make perfectly clear to you now is this. You are to be our Matron by my direct request and of your own consent. You will be in complete charge of our convalescent home. Therefore, until your approval has been obtained as to the matters which we are hoping to set in train immediately, we cannot do anythin'.'

From then they had no difficulties with one another. For her part the Dowager felt an immediate renewal of the liking she had formed for this courageous woman when they had first met in London; while for her part Lady Constance, who could pay no higher compliment, considered the formidable little figure which confronted her would have made a magnificent suffragette. Here, she realized full well was an indomitable spirit. It evoked both admiration and respect in her. Besides she sensed that warmth which transcended her formality.

Late that night, when the conference was extended to include the little Countess, the trio completed their plans.

Then on the evening of the tenth Lady Constance received a message. She passed it on to her host who straightway rang for Sawby whom he directed to order a dozen or so copies of the *Daily Herald* for delivery to the Castle with the usual morning newspapers. This brought the occupants of the Stewards Room, heads together like hens at a trough of grain as they pecked away at such a remarkable development.

'The *Herald*, is not among the newspapers which are ever read either above or below stairs in this establishment,' as Sawby announced portentously.

But in the morning they were all able to read the words which gave women their first emancipation. It ran, '*The remission of sentences on the suffrage prisoners was a natural step: for people have not been slow, at the very outset of this war, to turn to the women for aid. Let us note above all that it has not been aid to the task of destruction. To ask the aid of women at a period of national crisis involves two things. It means in the first place that we recognize them as part of the nation. It means in the second place that their help is a thing worth having. The first point is the recognition of their citizenship and of this the vote is the one adequate symbol. The second point is the recognition of our stupidity in so long delaying what we now acclaim as a thing of value.*'

Mrs Pankhurst immediately suspended all militancy, calling upon her followers to assist in the defence of their country unasked. That night Lady Constance dined with the Family.

After dinner she bearded Nanny, whom she privately considered was her strongest opponent. She did the one thing which just might win the old dragon round. Like an Aynthorp in the hunting field, she went hell for leather, not giving Nanny time to interject more than an occasional grunt. She revealed herself as the 'nurse' who had brought Stephanie out of her slough of despond, and herself as the erstwhile suffragette. Throughout, she managed to imply that she was talking to an equal, this worked the oracle.

Nanny, who above all respected 'the quality', saw at a single glance from those beady, penetrating eyes that Lady Constance was just that; and immediately perceived the immense advantages implicit in this *tête à tête* which would give her such status in the servants' hall as even she had never aspired to before.

For her part, as she unbent, rocking gently – but with none of that furious see-sawing which Rose dreaded, as it invariably denoted that the old woman was in a fury over something, Nanny began telling her now highly amused caller that she had 'seen it all in the tea cups!' by which she meant the disasters which had befallen both Stephanie and Rosalind; though how, as Constance Comyns marvelled, as she traversed the long corridors afterwards, Nanny had found out that

Rosalind had run away with her Irish Knight she could scarcely hope to discover.

'No money!' Nanny wailed, accelerating her rocking temporarily, 'not even a proper God-fearing title like you my lady and my family's ladies; not even an "honourable" just fancy! To be called Madam which is nothing more than an address given by servants to female employers without title.'

'As to that Nanny,' said Lady Constance soothingly, 'while I deeply sympathize with your views, Madam Fitzpatrick is a very old and distinguished title. There are so very few Irish Knights and only their wives can command this address which so displeases you.'

Nanny shrugged. 'And wot about that crumbling old place in that outlandishly named Cork!' she demanded, 'they say he lives on his wits too gambling and horsecoping.'

Gently Constance laid a hand upon her arm. 'Remember Nanny, I was a convicted criminal until yesterday.'

'Yes,' the old turncoat riposted, 'and then the Government came to its senses and recognized the lot of you for the 'eroines you are!' This coming from Nanny, who had consistently inveighed against all members of womens' suffrage was the final accolade.

'You mark my words my lady,' she diminished rocking-speed and wagged a prophetic finger, 'the nex' thing will be honours from his Majesty for what you have suffered. So please do not underestimate your own bravery!' With a brief pause, she was off again. 'I saw this coming with Rosalind when she was in the nursery. Rose!' she raised her voice to a hoarse shriek which brought the nursemaid running.

'Yes Nanny?' she replied. Then she saw Constance, dropped a curtsy and stood waiting deferentially.

'Tell 'er ladyship whether or not I told you time and time again Miss Rosalind would come to no good. Do you remember?'

Rose nodded mutely.

'Well, what did I say?'

Reluctantly Rose stammered, 'That she was like one of her aunts wot you said was nicknamed The Bolter when you was, were a nursery maid, and that there was shoals ahead for 'er and later on for Miss Anne.'

'Right!' Nanny was triumphant, 'that's all, now you may go.'
She added when they were alone again, 'She'll not stay with
'im, she'll bolt, as more than likely with another Johnnie-go-
likely.'

Once again her listener steered her towards the salient point.
'Have you always known Nanny?' she asked, with something
more than curiosity in her voice.

'Mostly,' said Nanny. 'Mostly. That Gilbert now, Mrs
Henrietta's youngest. I called him little Mr Moneybags afore
he was out of petticoats. One day, wen he's grown up he'll be
a fin-an-seer. You'll see. Then there's Mr Ninian and Mr
James, cousins, but always together like Miss Lucy and Master
Lucien. Them two boys was different though! Steady, 'ealthy,
all they arst out of life, then, now and always, was horses, stud
books, games and soldiering. As for Miss Lucy and Master
Lucien well, there's something odd about the pair of them;
she's his shadder. Always wos. Now look how it's worked out;
they separated them; they sent him to France to study music;
they gave her a London season. Proper triumph she was too,
turned the men's heads proper by all accounts. She had no end
of suitable proposals. Would she have any of 'em? I could have
told them NO! Them two is deep as a well and you can't
separate 'em. They just bide their time and then come together
again. What's the good of hitting your head against a brick
wall. What is to be will be, is what I always say.'

All in all Lady Constance had been given much food for
thought by Nanny, she decided, as she returned along the many
corridors to Sinclair.

Gabrielle, the Dowager, the Countess, Christine, Primrose, the
Bishop, John and Gyles were gathered around the big library
table.

The immensity of the traffic throughout the day and the vast
diversity of matters requiring immediate rearrangement made
it impossible for them to thrash out the problem of Rosalind
any earlier. Now, they were, as Gyles reminded them, compelled to take action without further delay.

Gyles presented the facts briefly. Henrietta was in a state of total collapse, and Dr Jamieson had expressed grave anxiety concerning her, so much so that even now she knew nothing of Sinclair's stroke beyond complaining querulously that Sinclair was absenting himself from her bedside deliberately.

The family was only too well aware that as matters stood it was they and not Rosalind's parents who must decide what to reply to that telegram. Sinclair's last gesture before stumbling from the room had been to toss the crumpled paper to Gyles with a muttered, 'You had all better read that.'

Now they must decide how Sinclair would have acted had he been able and then do likewise themselves.

Gyles posed the vital question. 'Mama, would Sinclair have sent his blessing?'

'Never,' exclaimed the Dowager.

'Then what must we do?' Gyles looked at his relatives.

'What can we do?' asked Christine wearily.

'And anyway,' – from Honest John, 'how can we pass unbiassed judgement on the affair?'

'We can try,' said Primrose.

'As I see it,' from the Dowager again, 'there are only two alternatives open to us; we ignore the telegram or we tell them of their parents' condition due to their deceit and recklessness.'

'And have them come pelting back here at a time like this?' Gyles worked away at his monocle furiously.

'Is there not something called a caveat?' Petula intervened, 'I seem to remember when that scandal blew up over the Southwell gel that her father issued one forbidding the marriage . . .' She saw the expression in their eyes and her words died on her lips.

'Out,' Gyles told her, 'kindly meant my dear; but envisage the consequences! Saving your presence and becoming indelicate, Rosalind has, er, been deflowered already. She is now married. To do such a thing would be to ruin her more effectively than she has done for herself already.'

'Precisely,' Alaric rumbled, 'Of age . . . under age . . . it is of no importance now since their union was solemnized in the house of God.' He yawned cavernously. 'Whom God hath joined together let no man put asunder, let us keep that in the forefront of our minds.'

'Charmin',' Gyles grunted.

'But nevertheless His law.' Having thus unburdened himself and being over-full of food and wine as usual the Bishop promptly dropped off in his chair. The remainder of the debate was punctuated by his snores.

Gyles' temper was fraying rapidly. 'Aunt Marguerite?' he then appealed, 'What do you say?'

Marguerite started. 'Oh dear, I am sorry Gyles, my thoughts were strayin''; it struck me suddenly how very much our behaviour over the past few days resembled us when we prepare for a ball or some such happy event – disputin' points, rushin' in all directions – thousands of details to be settled – and how such activities have always been the breath of life to us all. Now they have become utterly distasteful with all zest gone from them because we are at war.'

Eustace elected to ignore this *non sequitur*. Newly returned, his arm in a sling he hammered away at 'the Rosalind affair' with his usual one-track mindedness.

'We have two courses open to us as has already been said,' he announced. 'I merely see them differently. Until both Henrietta and Sinclair are recovered, we either ignore that telegram or we write an explicit letter detailing the results of their monstrous behaviour and stating that they will not be received here in any circumstances. Then we can let matters rest until Sinclair and Henrietta can make their own decisions.'

'Harsh Victorian parental stuff eh? never darken these doors . . . and so on.'

'Possibly,' Eustace sounded stubborn, 'IF they are permitted to come here it will certainly infer, at least by implication, that you are condoning what they have done.'

'I just wish,' Gyles was working himself up now, 'that you would not all persist in allocating equal blame to the pair of them. On the one hand we have a man of the world who is already advanced in years . . .'

Across the table Petula raised a questioning eyebrow at John who mouthed back, 'Thirty-eight'.

Gyles was still in full spate, continuing, 'On the other we have a silly, feather-brained young gel, dazzled by her first season and that absurd obsession which assails so many young gels, the glamourizing of a man old enough to be their father. As I see it, had Fitzpatrick not schemed to suborn Rosalind none of this could possibly have happened. The weight of blame must be seen to rest squarely upon his shoulders! Therefore I do not accept your two suggestions. I . . . reject . . . them.'

'Then what the devil do we do?' Eustace asked gloomily, 'And can't someone wake the Bishop, really this bubblin' and gruntin' is too tryin'.'

Marguerite obliging, gave her brother a great nudge, which made no difference whatsoever.

'I must admit,' Eustace continued, 'we do seem to be tryin' to equate the powers of a day old chick and a golden eagle!'

'Ah-hem,' the Bishop awoke with a start, 'that's more to the point.' Adding hastily, 'The Christian point of course.' After which he went back to sleep.

'Tcha,' said the Dowager.

'Mother?' queried Gyles.

'My dear, whatever you say at this juncture will only stiffen Rosalind's resolve to stay with that man. You are thinkin' logically, but do you imagine that logic plays any part in her reasonin' when she is hock deep in her first great love affair; or so I am assured she sees it, if we do not – anyway no female is capable of pure logic! None of this fashionable prattlin' about equality of the sexes takes into account the fundamentals; by which I mean the diametrically opposing physical conformations and reactions of the male *vis à vis* the female.'

Gyles eyebrows went up. 'Pray do not act the prim with me dear, it is another sleeveless errand I can assure you.' Gyles looked resignedly at Christine.

'I do rather incline towards the same view,' she acknowledged.

Looking around with an expression of extreme distaste, Gyles inquired, 'And to whom goes the delightful task of writin' these letters might I inquire?'

Again the Bishop opened his eyes. 'No one would do so well as you dear boy,' he said benignly.

At which Gyles so far forgot himself as to exclaim, 'Faugh!'

At length they reached agreement. Two letters would be

despatched. In the one to the Knight, Gyles would give full rein
to Family opinion on his scandalous and underhand conduct
and would also make it abundantly plain that he could never
again be received at Castle Rising. He would write more gently
to the girl. He would advise her to stay away at present,
explain what had happened to her parents, without ascribing ·
the blame to her for the events and would then wish her well.
At the same time he would stress that while she could never
expect any of the Family to accept her husband, the Castle doors
would always remain open to her. He was to make this quite
clear; tell her they all expected the marriage to fail which they
well knew would be dismissed scornfully. Indeed he should say
that, too; going on to assure her that should she ever regret the
step which she had taken, she could always return home
confident that she would be welcomed.

'The main thing is,' as the Dowager defined for them all,
'that this marriage must eventually end in disaster. When that
happens she must be made to feel she can come home.'

After a brief pause, Gabrielle hesitantly raised the vexed
question once again as to her son Lucien's future.

The subject of this, their second agenda item, was in fact the
only contented member of the family at this time. He was
enjoying himself immensely. Since his return, Mr Sissingham
had caught a severe cold so was confined to his room to keep
his infectious germs to himself. Lucy, due to the general
disturbances, was also left to her own devices. As a result –
being extremely careful to put in punctilious appearances for
meals – the pair spent a delightful interim period, mostly in
their old bolt-hole, that ear-wiggy summer house. Turn and
turn about they told each other every detail of their separate
experiences. Only when these subjects had been wrung dry did
Lucy reveal to him the news which she had been cherishing as
a *bonne-bouche*. She explained what she had only so recently
learned herself; that they both were possessed of very adequate
private fortunes. Afterwards, and when the first transports of
delight had been diminished, she calmly announced *her* plans.

'When this horrid war is over and I am twenty-one,' she
told him, 'which is only three years from now my darling, I
will find and buy a London house for us. You shall tell me
exactly what you want and then I will do the rest. In the

holidays from wherever you have to go, we will get it all ready together, we can contrive a way to do so secretly. Then no time will be wasted and you can start just as soon as you are twenty-one.'

'Mayfair,' said Lucien promptly, his eyes brilliant with excitement. 'It must be somewhere *very* fashionable. Somewhere near that hotel where Papa and Mama took me to luncheon on my way to Paris with old Siss,' he groped for the name . . . 'I think it was called Claridge.'

'Oh, Claridges!' exclaimed Lucy, 'I know that. My friend Nada had her coming out ball done by Claridges and she also took me there to luncheon with her parents. Then Great Aunt Marguerite told me the story of how it all began.'

'Tell me,' Lucien invited.

'Well now, let me see, it all began because Mr Claridge was a butler who had saved quite a lot of money during his years in private service. As soon as he had saved enough he gave notice and with his wife opened a very exclusive sort of boarding house in Brook Street. The people whom he had waited on and his 'family' came to stay with him and liked it all very much indeed. After that it just grew and grew . . .'

'Just as we shall do,' said Lucien nodding. 'You look around Brook Street, and that nice chic square? What's it called?'

'Grosvenor?'

'Yes, but there's another better one.'

'Berkeley?'

'That's it,' he confirmed, 'there are lots and lots of little side streets there with suitable houses. You will need to have several floors you know.'

They made their plans, blissfully indifferent to that 'horrid war'. At length Lucien said surprisingly, 'I have made up my mind that as this beastly war has messed up everything I shall go to Cambridge. I shall make them send me there. I am quite willing to study really hard if they will do that. Anyway it will be far better for us than my going to Harrow. I think I can do one without the other. They have acting at Cambridge too, I heard our *D'Hauteville* cousins talking about it, when I was staying at *Neuilly*. They called it something funny I can't remember; but if there is acting and I can get into it, a sort of club as far as I could understand, someone has to make acting clothes and that will get me started long before I can come to you.' He paused. 'Won't you need something dreary like a chap, chap . . .'

'Chaperone.'

'That's it. Some stuffy old thing like Pet's Aunt Eustasia to keep the Family from fussing?'

'You get on with your arrangings and leave all that to me,' said Lucy confidently, 'Nada, my special friend will help. Oh, there goes the changing gong! Let's be angels of good behaviour. Just imagine what would happen if they had heard what we are planning!'

They ran towards the house laughing. Lucy wore a white muslin dress with a blue sash tied around her small waist. She looked extremely pretty. Lucien was in white too, long duck trousers and a sailor blouse with a blue handkerchief knotted in front. The sun glinted on their fair curls, as they ran together across the lawn.

From the windows above, Lady Constance saw them and thought how charming they looked together. Then, as they vanished on to the terrace she turned away frowning. They reminded her of something . . . what could it be? She stood staring at the carpet. Ah! She had it! It was a painting she had seen somewhere; but of whom, and where, try as she did she could not recollect.

Throughout the afternoon, drawing room tea, when returning up the wide staircase to visit her patients, even when changing for dinner with Mrs Peace rustling in to fasten her gown, the elusive painting evaded identification.

It was only when she sat at dinner with the family that memory returned. The painting she had been reminded of so vividly after watching the two fair-haired young things running over the grass together, laughing happily, had been of the young Byron and his half-sister. It had been painted long before the latter became Mrs Leigh. Suddenly it all became very clear to her. She realized who those pretty things were – the Lucy and Lucien of whom Nanny had spoken with such curious vehemence.

CHAPTER 19

The Exodus

It had been Henry's declared intention to tell his father the whole story concerning his and his cousin George's startling experience at and after the Hendon Air Festival.

Initially both had agreed to shelve it because of Rosalind's disappearance. Then father and son separated, Gyles drove off to Castle Rising from Arlington Street, Henry perforce stayed behind. His General sent for him. He drove round to the General's club feeling as if he were being summonsed to the Head Beak's study all over again; but, waved into a shabby, old leather chair and facing the distinguished, bristling-moustached soldier under whom he was destined to serve, he swiftly re-gained his composure. In place of the grilling he had anticipated, Henry found himself thoroughly enjoying what turned out to be no more than a friendly talk over several 'pink gins' – a restorative hitherto unknown to him. The General never mentioned war, nor even touched on Henry's future under his command. Instead they talked of the School, mutual acquaintances, hunting, deer-stalking in Scotland, salmon fishing on the Wye and Usk; until the General unbent so completely as to open the gun case at his side to show Henry his latest acquisitions from Purdy's, adding regretfully, 'I had thought to try 'em on the Twelfth.'

It was only when Henry let his Bugatti out on the open road, heading home at last, that he began to realize how the 'old man' had turned him inside out 'while chattin' in such a deuced relaxed manner!' Then he reflected on how, once again, his way had been made easy for him through the power of his family and his illustrious Papa in particular. To the soft-throated roar of acceleration, he at length began to plan that 'quiet chat' with Gyles, but this was not to be.

Matters were worse when Henry reached the Castle. No opportunity arose to talk to Gyles. First there was Sinclair's stroke following on top of that disastrous telegram. Then the subsequent comings and goings, the frantic arrangings and orderings engulfed everyone. No sooner had some of the first frenzy subsided than Henry's telegram arrived with orders for him to report immediately.

At length, when he did at last manage a quiet word or two with his father, Gyles took the initiative. Henry, always a human seismograph to parental moods, sensed that it would be for him 'the other side of hellish to start up another hare,' so he said nothing; but when he stood in the Great Hall with Ninian and on the point of leaving he said abruptly,

'Look here Number Two, I hate to do this, but you'll have to take over for me. I haven't had a single chance to talk to father. You'll have to do it. Sit tight, watch for the right moment and then take it, there's a good feller.'

Ninian glowered. 'Thanks a million, you ruddy stinker,' he said crossly. 'If I've got to do it you'll let me tell James of course?'

Henry hesitated, then shrugged his shoulders, 'Oh you two!' he said helplessly.

Ninian sounded relieved. 'Thanks, thanks a lot old boy, after all, two heads are always better'n one I always say and anyway,' he added artlessly, 'I always tell James everythin'.'

'And James always tells you!' Henry supplemented, grinning as he said it. He glanced at his reflection in the great looking-glass over the mantel, exclaimed 'Gosh what a mess!' smoothed his hair, adjusted his very new, white-banded cap and turning to his brother asked, as a Parthian shot, 'as a matter of interest, you two chaps don't by any chance still pot each other do you?' then, ducking as Ninian moved, he ran down the steps to the waiting car.

When Henry had gone, Ninian caught James' eye as he came up the steps. Then murmuring to his parents, 'Shan't be long,' he pulled at his cousin's arm and they moved off together. Gyles, standing in the entrance with Christine watched them. They were heading towards the lake, deep in conversation.

'Inseparables is the right name for those two,' Gyles commented. 'They're good chaps though – very steady. We can do with a bit of that kind of steadiness in this family.'

The Inseparables produced some bread from their pockets and threw it to the swans while they made their plans. When they returned they found more new arrivals at the Castle. The first was Cousin George, already an enlisted private, who had returned to spend his forty-eight hours prior to being drafted to the training battalion of the Sixtieth Rifles.

Then Christian came. He was inspected critically and though inwardly admired by his juniors he came in for his fair share of 'ragging'. He was their only 'reg'lar'; already a Major and now second in command of the third Brigade, Royal Horse Artillery. Hot on his heels came Ralph. As soon as he appeared Ninian, George and James pounced on him and dragged him, protesting, into the gun room. James had tentatively suggested co-opting Christian. The rest cried him down. Not surprisingly they fought shy, because, after all, Christian was 'no end of a swell' and besides, as Ninian was at pains to point out, he was also seventeen years older than any of them.

Thus the four held council, perching on tables and sprawling in shabby old chairs in the assured privacy of the gun room. Ninian dispensed King's Pegs deeming the occasion called for 'somethin' special'. When some of this potent beverage had been ingested, George took the floor with an unusual air of authority. He began,

'Now just let me get my lines cleared and then I will explain.' He turned to the Inseparables. 'You say Hen told you he couldn't get a word in edgeways while he was here and left you two the unenviable job of tellin' Uncle Gyles?'

They both nodded portentously. Ralph sat crossing and uncrossing his long legs irritably.

'Look here George,' he cut in, 'can someone kindly tell me what all this pother is about? James here pounces on me. I get hauled in here and not a word said except it's some family drama! Well for Pete's sake I ask you, when ain't there dramas in this family? There's enough goin' on already without you lot adding more. Of course I'm deuced sorry for everyone concerned; but *I am on embarkation leave.* I want to have some fun before I go. For all you bastards know, I may get killed!'

'Pooh,' scoffed James unfeelingly, '*you* won't get killed. You were always the crafty one! Managed to wriggle out of every blasted scrape. We were the chaps that went down like ninepins. You just stepped clean over us! Lay any odds you like, I'll still wager you'll come clean out of all this you lucky bastard!'

Ralph was forced to smile. He began to unbend a little, 'Yes aren't I,' he agreed more cheerfully. 'But come on now – give. What's this all about?'

George had subsided, deeming it prudent to let the rest 'barney about a bit' as he described this heartless exchange. Now, however, he intervened.

'Pack it up,' he said, rather loudly, 'anyone 'ud think there wasn't a single one of you born on the right side of the blanket from the way yer carryin' on. Quieten down now, this is a bloody serious matter.'

James went so far as to say, 'Sorry George'; so then, of course, Ninian had to do the same. George looked at them slightly ruefully but he pressed on.

'As you know I have just come from London. Now *you have not.* So I'm in this particular picture in a way you cannot possibly be. After I had done my stuff and got myself into the ruddy army, I began prowlin' around a bit and I managed to find out a whole lot more than Nin can possibly have told you.'

This provoked an aggrieved chorus, 'Nin hasn't said a word.'

'All right,' George agreed. 'I'll give you the whole story from the very beginning.'

The Inseparables were staring at each other over their King's Pegs in obvious consternation. Neither were noticeably quick off the mark and it had taken a moment or two for the import behind George's opening remark to develop its full significance.

'Do you mean,' demanded Ninian, 'you have actually seen him?'

'Oh for God's sake shut up,' George's patience was cracking. 'Of course I've seen him and talked to him too. I can tell you here and now that despite – er – everything that has happened I was rather impressed!'

This silenced them effectively and into that silence George injected his story at last.

When at length, they streamed into the library, they found that the atmosphere was as thick as a London pea-souper. It shocked them. There stood Gabrielle newly changed and in deep mourning. At her side her husband, also in conventional black was endeavouring to combine some measure of grief with a certain suppressed excitement; while Gyles and Christine, who stood with Sawby between them, were searching through time tables.

The startled young men heard Gyles saying as they entered, 'You can make it all right provided you get on the three fifteen train. It stops at Lower Aynthorp does it not Sawby?'

'Oh yes my lord, and I have taken the liberty of ordering the car already,' Sawby replied promptly.

Beyond the opened doors footmen were hurrying down with valises and dressing cases.

'Then,' said Gyles, still reading, 'you will have a bit of time in hand before you catch the night train to York. We can telephone for one of your cars to meet you there, which will be around six o'clock tomorrow mornin' – provided of course the train is runnin' to time.' He looked up, saw the young men and turned expectantly to Eustace with a slight lift of his eyebrows.

Into the ensuing silence Ralph and James in particular were startled to hear their father saying heavily, 'Your grandfather died a few moments ago boys. They telephoned the news from "Steynings". Your mother and I are leavin' almost immediately.'

Ralph was the first to assimilate the full import of his father's words. 'I'm very sorry sir,' he said rather stiffly. Then after a momentary pause he asked, 'You would, of course, wish me to come with you?'

Before Eustace could reply:

'No!' exclaimed Gabrielle sharply, 'No Eustace, please. Ralph is on embarkation leave remember.'

'That is not the question, Mama,' said Ralph steadily.

Eustace looked hesitant. 'It is really only right and proper that you should be present at the interment of your grandfather,' he said a trifle pompously.

'But that he cannot do Eustace,' Gabrielle protested, 'in another forty hours Ralph will be compelled to rejoin his regiment *which is going to France*. I imagine you do not wish to involve him in desertion, which is what overstaying his leave would mean at such a time as this! Eustace pray reflect, *we are at war you know*!'

The room emptied rapidly. Christine hurried away to make certain the 'tiffin' basket was ready. The rest stood about the hall talking quietly.

'Set-back six-thousand,' grumbled Ninian, 'God how frustratin'! But what a thing eh?'

The Dowager had seated herself and was now wielding her fan vigorously for the day was oppressively hot. James asked her, 'Does that mean, *Belle-mère*, that Uncle Eustace is now the Earl?'

'Of course, my dear.'

'Gosh!' exclaimed Ninian, 'Then old Ralph will be his flamin' lordship! I can see we shall have to take *him* down a peg or two.' Then, catching his Grandmother's eye, he added hastily, 'When things have subsided a bit of course.' This did not deter Gyles from expressing himself strongly concerning untimely vulgarity, monstrous ill-breeding, etc, and the atmosphere was leavened for a while by the somewhat forceful expressions of displeasure which Ninian drew down upon his luckless copper head.

Ralph did not accompany his parents. He went to the station with them, received a number of instructions, shook hands formally with his father, who wished him luck and slipped an impressive cheque into his hand. Then Gabrielle held him in her arms for a moment and wept a little. The guard blew his whistle, Ralph sood back, the door slammed and he was left standing bewildered upon the platform.

When he returned, Sawby admitted him. 'I trust everything went all right my lord?' he said thus underlining as nothing else could have done, Ralph's so recent elevation to the peerage.

The new Lord Steyne wandered off in search of 'the chaps', convinced without their confirmation that once again they could do nothing which could increase the problems with which Gyles was beset.

Instead, Ralph spent his leave riding, rough-shooting and dancing at impromptu 'hops' as they were now called. Young men were hurrying to their homes all over the country to bid good-bye to anxious parents and round up their girl friends for whom they rolled back carpets, played the gramophone and then danced the new tangos with them on their parents' parquet.

Christine and Gyles, feeling guilty at not accompanying Gabrielle and Eustace, returned to their multitudinous tasks while Alicia Aynthorp, with Marguerite and Lady Constance completed their plans for the convalescent home.

There was no change in Sinclair's condition. When the young men had all gone, Gyles and Christine sat up late into the night compiling the two letters which it had been agreed should be sent to Rosalind and her husband.

Even as George and the rest had sought and failed to find a sufficient break in the avalanche of troubles which beset them all; so Christine nursed a secret of her own which she knew very well could not be withheld from Gyles for much longer; but this latest bereavement, together with the steady departure of their staff, merely increased the pressure upon those who remained behind.

No sooner had the Castle emptied than it filled again with Lady Constance's erstwhile fellow suffragettes whom she had summoned before leaving London. Under Mrs Pankhurst's direction she had asked for and obtained their pledges of further allegiance to the cause of war. Indeed there was no lack of volunteers. The women and girls were ready and willing to replace the men. Overnight there came into being Land Girls, Lady Gardeners, Kennelmaids, Poultrymaids, Chauffeuses, even Stable girls.

Within a matter of days, the vacated posts at the Castle were filled with suitable applicants. Sawby, with tightened lips, accepted that he must train and direct Footwomen to replace Edward, Richard and George, all of whom had asked permission to absent themselves 'for the duration'.

Petula, having met Lady Randolph as she was still called

among certain of the cognoscenti, recalled for her in-laws what this remarkable woman had planned for her 'footwomen'; how she intended to dress such persons, 'should necessity arise' and Petula proposed that they do likewise at the Castle.

'Soft black boots,' Petula enumerated, 'neat white caps with black velvet streamers, plain skirts, long – but not too long, hence the boots – and white jackets to be cut like mess jackets and worn with severely tailored white blouses finished at the neck with small black bows.'

After a spasm of mirth in which hysteria was not a million miles away, Christine undertook to thus inform Mrs Peace who, equally tight-lipped, took the chosen girls' 'measures' and then set out for London to make the necessary purchases.

Plum put up the toughest resistance of them all. 'I'll be danged,' he swore when he first heard what was to be given to him, 'ef I'll have a passel of silly females muckin' abart with my 'osses,' a reaction which the chief kennelman endorsed most earnestly in the matter of hounds.

The gamekeepers were not exactly enthusiastic either. 'Blunderin' about,' grumbled Twitch, 'upsettin' the young pheasants ... more likely killin' each other than any vermin!'

Sawbridge, who like the rest of the remaining staff was profoundly shaken, then proceeded to cause havoc in both the Servants' Hall and Stewards' Room by extending the olive branch to Mrs Parsons.

Having so done, with the utmost magnanimity and having been met and handwrung – 'more'n 'arf way' – as Plum said approvingly; Sawbridge consented to take his tea in the servants' hall! He opened the proceedings by praising Mrs Parsons' Pound Cake. This set the kitchen maids choking into their teacups. Sawbridge then expressed his opinion, with all the bitterness he had hitherto reserved for Mrs Parsons, 'Won't know a dandelion from a *dendrobium* I'll wager. I know wot it will be. Ef one or t'other of them lassies can so much as stop a tomato my name is not wot it is. And as fer pollenatin' melons or graftin' stock ...'

'Oh you pore sole,' exclaimed Mrs Parsons, oozing new-found sympathy, ' 'ere, 'and me yer cup and I'll fill it for yer. Jest you try a nice piece of this Lardy Cake what young Pansy made for us special.'

They were, for the most part, agreeably surprised. In the first place, the cause of Womens' Suffrage had been pursued by a cross-section of women and girls from every walk of life; nor did they exclude from their ranks those curiously masculine women who spent their lives running kennels, breeding horses, gardening, farming or pursuing the more unusual forms of sport, like javelin-throwing and playing lacrosse. These women generally moved in pairs; one tweedy and inclined to stride, the other smaller, usually slightly faded, evincing remnants of what might have been a fluffy prettiness in youth; but they were all excellent workers, extremely efficient and clearly anxious to acquit themselves well.

It was not, of course, from any of these groups that the Footwomen were selected. They came from a less privileged class of erstwhile suffragette. The three who were finally singled out by Lady Constance for interviews were, after an extensive interrogation, engaged by Mrs Peace. All three had spent years in private service. They had all lost their employment to the 'Cause' and during the interim had endured many privations. Moreover each had been a parlour maid in a large household where work had been done under experienced and – as Mrs Peace deduced from what she heard – somewhat over-strict disciplinarians. She further guessed that this as much as anything was what turned them towards Women's Suffrage in the first place.

Sawbridge, who insisted on seeing his potential lady-gardeners singly, found himself in each case beginning with some small measure of pontification, and ending, after a lengthy perambulation along the paths of the kitchen garden and through the many stove houses, by chatting companionably and comparing experiences.

'They'm not bad,' he was forced to admit grudgingly. 'More like a passel of young men in skirts than females; but they know what they're about. I shall mannidge – some 'ow.'

Thus it went, until the vacant places were filled and extra rooms taken over in the Castle as dormitories for Outside

Staff who had never before aspired to admission inside the Castle walls.

Meanwhile Sawby and his new footwomen began by putting the White Drawing Room, the Ballroom and the Chinese Room into dust bags and sheets, thus investing each with a ghostly appearance. Despite spotless cleanliness, there was more than a touch of Miss Haversham about them when they had done.

In the meantime the British Expeditionary Force with Ralph among them, marched through London singing 'It's a Long Way to Tipperary'. They embarked for France on August the sixteenth and by August the twenty-first had made their first contact with the enemy.

CHAPTER 20

The Last Encounter

Christian wrote again to his wife Claire telling her, 'the British Army will have to hurry up if they are going to share in the fun'. By the time his letter containing this somewhat abortive prophesy was on its way to England he had had his first glimpse of them moving up towards that 'fun'.

He stood outside the *estaminet* in which he was billeted, watching a small detachment of the Irish Guards as they clattered over the *pavé* between the long lines of poplars along the *chaussée*. The British Expeditionary Force was moving up to the front line at last. They were to level with the French Fifth Army. The remainder pressed on behind them.

Already General Joffre had informed the British Commander-In-Chief, Sir John French, that his army was ready to cross the *Sambre*, leaving one army corps on the *Meuse* to guard its flank.

By August twenty-third, the B.E.F., was concentrating along the line *Le Cateau–Avesne–Mauberge* and it was here that Christian encountered the first refugees of the war.

He had turned into the one big room which did duty as a bistro in an *estaminet* further up the line, only to find it was already crammed with people. They were lying all over the floor and under the tables. Some lay about in the sleep of total exhaustion; others sat propped with their backs against the walls, staring hopelessly at the opposing ones. Men, women and children alike were smothered with the white dust of the dry, August roads. It clung to their hair, it rimmed their eyes – already reddened with fatigue, and the women's with weeping, too. This dust clung to their clothes making them look like a huddle of corpses. Christian realized with a quick stab of shock that they were the vanguard of the terrified, uprooted population, who had run until they could run no further from the terror which had swept down upon them, killing . . . destroying . . . raping . . . burning everything which they encountered.

A brother officer picked his way across to Christian at the same moment as a quiet voice at his shoulder bade him, 'Good mornin', sir.' Christian swung round, his expression changing as he saw who addressed him.

Ralph flung him a punctilious salute and then said smiling, 'Good mornin' Uncle Christian.'

'My dear Ralph,' Christian gripped his hand then effected introductions, 'M'nephew Ralph St John, Captain Henderson.'

Shyly Ralph corrected him, 'I'm er, not a St John anymore sir, but a Steyne, m'y Grandfather's dead.'

'Good heavens!' Christian stared, 'I beg your pardon, "Lord Steyne".' Henderson and the cousins laughed, a trifle embarrassed.

Almost immediately they were interrupted again, this time by a runner with a message for Christian. He unfolded it, chortled, gave his reply and the man about turned and ran off.

'Typical!' Christian commented with a wry grin, 'This is a fair example of the British doin' their level best to maintain the *status quo* – even under duress. The Captain in charge of a small detachment is askin' permission to loophole the walls of the farmhouse they are occupyin'.'

'*Mon dieu, les Anglais!*' Ralph then added quizzically, '*C'est magnifique, mais ce n'est pas la Guerre!*'

'Precisely.'

The word '*Anglais*' had roused an old man who was sprawled out asleep beside them.

'*Les Anglais,*' the Belgian sat up, '*alors nous sommes sauvés, C'est vrai M'sieur? . . .*' then as he recognized their uniforms, '*Oui c'est vrai, les Anglais sont arrivés*', and he began to weep, the tears making furrows down his dust-caked cheeks.

Others awoke and took up the cry so the trio bolted outside. They stood awhile on the cobbles and then they went their separate ways. It was the last time they would meet for four bitter years.

As Ralph walked slowly along the *trottoir* he revised what he knew of the present situation. He had been told by his Colonel that General Henry Wilson had become convinced that the right policy was to attack. The General had managed to persuade the Commander-in-Chief that this was so. As a result, a letter of the same date was sent by Colonel Huget to the G.O.C., Fifth Army at Le Cateau stating, 'I have the honour to inform you that I have communicated to Marshal French the information brought to me by Captain Loiseau. Sir John French asks me to say that it is difficult for him to engage his forces fully without knowing what is in front of him. He will therefore continue to send out aerial reconnaissances. They will begin again at dawn today, flying north, north-west to Mons to determine the enemy forces in the neighbourhood of Ath, Soignes and Nivelle.'

Ralph knew, too, that as far back as August the sixteenth, Numbers Two, Three and Four Squadrons of the Royal Flying Corps., and Headquarters had left Amiens for Mauberge in preparation for the vital part they were to play in frustrating the German plan. This as conceived by Von Schlieffen was known too. The Huns were to throw all their troops against the French in a huge, encircling movement, marching first through Belgium then turning their left flank in a furious onslaught which they predicted would finish the war in one tremendous thrust, by their capturing Paris.

Ralph was well aware that even from August the nineteenth, the Second, Third and Fourth R.F.C. Squadrons had been flying on reconnaissance up and down, searching out enemy movements and also locating enemy batteries. Their trail had been blazed for them by Captain P. B. Joubert de la Ferté of Number Three Squadron, flying a *Blériot* and this was the only type of machine to carry armament, though pilots and observers did carry revolvers, *carbines* and occasionally shot-guns. In the absence of any bombing gear, pilots also filled their pockets with hand-grenades and slung or tied a few large bombs around themselves. Of such great matters were lesser ones compounded.

On the same evening, Ralph and some brother officers turned into the *estaminet* where Ralph had encountered

Christian. They hurried in calling for beers. Their throats were dry and rasped by the dust which now rose in clouds as the unending stream of refugees stumbled past. They had not long been seated when a party of R.F.C. pilots came through the doorway laughing and talking together. Ralph glanced at them and was about to glance away when one laughing face among them brought him to his feet abruptly. He stared disbelievingly as the owner came threading through between the tables.

'Hellow, old sport,' said Stephen Delahaye. 'How are you? I never thought to run across you again so soon, especially in this neck of the woods.'

'Nor I you,' replied Ralph quietly.

Stephen glanced around, saw a chair and with his hand on it asked with consummate ease, 'May I sit down?'

Ralph nodded. With a struggle he pulled himself together and made the necessary introduction with only a slight hesitation when it came to saying, 'M'cousin.'

'Need a gasper,' said Stephen delving in his tunic pocket. 'Expect you chaps could do with one too.' Out came a slim gold case with the familiar Asprey slide-opening. He proffered it all round, took one himself; only Ralph refused, 'I'm afraid I do not smoke, thank you.'

By this time the atmosphere was so charged that Ralph's companions could not fail to sense it. They moved off with a few murmured excuses and crossed to the bar to pay their reckoning, leaving Stephen and Ralph alone at the table eyeing each other warily.

'Well Stephen,' said Ralph not making any attempt to keep the chill from his voice.

'Never better,' Stephen replied confidently, underlining his ease by putting his immaculate boots up on another chair and lounging back on his own. 'Having the whale of a time, actually. We're on reconnaissance. It's a great game. Gettin' up the bloody Boche's shirt and droppin' an occasional egg.'

'Quite so,' Ralph was studying him. He was unchanged. He was exactly the same Stephen as heretofore, charming, plausible, totally indifferent to his cousin's chilly responses. Un-capped and with the family hair glinting in the rather dim lamplight he was also infuriatingly good-looking.

Ralph heard him say, across the welter of his own thoughts, 'I say, this calls for a celebration, Mademoiselle, *Chérie*!' A pale girl hurried to his side, stood there, her tired eyes suddenly bright with admiration.

'*Oui M'sieu?*'

'*Vous avez du champagne?*' Stephen smiled, which lit two tiny fires in those attentive eyes. Watching, Ralph thought she resembled a hungry little mongrel, hoping for this lordly one to toss her a bone to gnaw. Stephen slipped an easy arm about her waist, '*Alors ma belle, allez cherchez, dépêchez-vous je vous en prie, et n'oubliez pas, la meilleur marque, est en magnum s'il vous plaît.*' The hand was sliding gently over her small buttocks.

'*D'accord M'sieu,*' she moved reluctantly calling to the old man behind the zinc-topped bar . . .

They fell silent. The girl hurried back, presented the magnum, bending down so that one small breast brushed Stephen's tunic. Stephen nodded carelessly.

'*C'est bien frais m'sieu,*' she assured him. They watched in silence as she set out the glasses, whipped a soiled cloth from her waistband and with great care, turning the bottle, removed it from the cork with silent expertise.

'Took old Sawby ages to learn that trick,' Stephen commented reminiscently, 'of course, it's second nature to these people.'

Staring down at the winking bubbles in the glass, raising it, saying 'Chin-chin', he asked casually, 'when did you leave Sandhurst, old boy?'

'Last year.' Ralph picked up the glass reluctantly. 'Good luck,' he said, as if the words stuck in his throat.

They drank.

'Any of the rest of the Family out here yet?' Stephen then inquired. 'Nice bottle this ain't it?'

'Excellent, thank you. Christian is here. He's a Major now, second in command of his brigade, no end of a swell' – he unconsciously repeated what his younger brother had called him. 'So is Charles de la Coutray, who married Rosemary in nineteen eleven, he is *Deuxième Bureau* I believe – Intelligence and all that.'

'Sooooo,' Stephen drained his glass, reached for the bottle.

'Fill you up?'

'Thanks.'

'And the rest?'

'The boys you mean?'

'Yes.'

'Ninian and James have another year to do at Sandhurst, they're as thick as mud. Henry's under trainin'. He's goin' on the Staff, so he won't be out here yet awhile.' He added, 'He and Petula have been married for two years now.'

'Any sign of an heir?'

'Not so far as I know.'

'Well, well, that won't please Uncle Gyles!' Stephen raised his glass again. 'I'll give you a toast,' he said abruptly. 'Here's to us, damnation to our enemies and safe return to every member of the Family.'

Ralph unbent so far as to smile at this. 'I'll drink to that,' he agreed. They drank. The constraint between them hardened. The silence was punctuated by small bursts of gunfire which rattled the doors and windows.

'Noisy sods,' said Stephen.

In a far corner a clutch of subalterns was teaching the waitress to sing 'Pack up your troubles in your old kit bag . . .'

Despite himself, Ralph then asked, 'May one ask how you got here? We saw your name on the programme at Hendon as I told you.'

Stephen smiled reminiscently, 'I saw you too,' he acknowledged, 'and the gels. Rosalind's turned into a beauty hasn't she? But I didn't much care for the chap she was trotting around with, he looked like a high-born horse-coper to me.'

'You can say that again,' said Ralph bitterly.

'Oh well,' Stephen shrugged, reverting to the earlier question. 'Mine,' he said crossing his ankles and moving their supporting chair a fraction, 'is a long, long story, d'you want it from the beginning – from the moment I made my unlovely exit from parental bondage?'

Ralph's temper flared. 'I don't want it at all!' he exclaimed, suddenly livid, 'But I believe it is my duty to ask you and to listen carefully if you decide to tell me. There are others involved.' Their eyes met and Ralph's anger increased. He was shocked to see Stephen was enjoying himself, all too clearly entertained by having drawn blood at last.

Stephen again withdrew his gold cigarette case, opened it, extended it, withdrew it again as Ralph shook his head, 'I don't,' he said curtly, 'remember?'

'You soon will.' Stephen took one. 'It calms the nerves.' He brought out a small gold match case, struck a match, inhaled, then blew three perfect smoke rings. Then he stabbed his cigarette through them, one, two, three and began talking.

'After a series of unimportant adventures, I succeeded in gettin' out of Africa. Then by a somewhat devious route I made for Canada and eventually crossed into America from the lake-side house of some perfectly charmin' Canadians with whom I had stayed for a considerable time. By then, in spite of some pretty lavish hospitality, funds were gettin' a bit low so I headed for Dallas in Texas, where I had been offered a job.

'I took my time. I stayed a while in South Dakota, where I had other contacts. Then the chance came up to get lifted to Kansas in a chap's motor so I took it. This chap invited me to stay with his people, too, so altogether it was over three years from the time I went to ground in Africa before I made my objective.'

'Since when?' Ralph inquired, while Stephen paused to replenish their glasses once again, 'Have you been workin'?' Try as he did he could not exclude a tinge of disbelief from his voice.

'Oh yes old boy, but never fear there were Ulterior Motives.'

Like his Uncle Gyles, when taut with suppressed anger and contempt, Ralph limited himself to the comment, 'Quite so.'

'You see,' this time Stephen lit a fresh cigarette from the stub of the old one, dropped it to the floor and ground his heel on it, 'There was a girl involved. Pretty as a picture, gay as a linnet; and of course her father, who offered me the job was by way of bein' a millionaire.'

'Your main objective of course bein' to marry money?'

'Of course,' said Stephen quite unruffled. 'Now comes the twist to my story. That old boy's no fool. He's as shrewd as they come in fact. He saw clearly enough which way the wind blew with Sue-Ellen, so he propositioned me. Either he'd make it worth my while to clear out or I could work for him. If I proved satifactory – he knew who I was of course – Sue-Ellen and I could be married with his blessing and I would automatically become his heir. You see he had lost his only son years before in a shootin' accident.'

So far, as Ralph realized, Stephen's story tallied exactly with the one which George had found out in London when they had both seen him, which he later retailed to them in the gun room.

'So,' Stephen was saying, 'I stayed. The old boy had a bee in his bonnet about mastery in the air. He lived, thought, breathed aircraft. As you know I have always been pretty keen myself so I had it made. Then just over a year ago he announced he was building his own aircraft factory. We already had a private air strip and I had flown a number of machines for him – he bought them like other chaps buy cigars! – then one day he called me into his office and said he wanted me to gain experience in the handling of European aircraft. He produced some English paper which said that the Royal Flying Corps. was willin' to give commissions to suitable applicants who were already experienced pilots. I jumped at it. Tell the truth I was gettin' a bit weary of bein' in one place all the time. The old boy offered to finance me then and there if I would volunteer for the R.F.C. After all there was no war on, and no likelihood of any war that either he or I could actually pin-point. He used to go on a bit from time to time at his pet theme; that war would come and then when it did the U.S.A. would be drawn into it and would need all the aircraft they could get.

'Finally, when I made out I was still undecided he dangled the final carrot. Sue-Ellen and I could become officially engaged and when I returned we could be married. He had of course swallowed my original story hook, line and sinker. I fed him the line that I had left m'family because I could not stand the oppression of the path prescribed for me. I presented myself as the young pioneer, blazin' m'own trail, and as he had done just that thing himself he was most sympathetic. He said some worryin' things about wantin' to bring about a reconciliation after we were married. I think he rather fancied havin' a 'Lord' as he called it, in the family. Anyway, you know my motto, never cross bridges before you come to them. I applied for entry, was told to send in my credentials and what with our engagement party – which was simply colossal – and Sue-Ellen pleading with me afterwards to stay until after her greatest friend's wedding – and that was another all-out shindig I can promise you – it was May before I reported for duty.

'No sooner had I been gazetted than the war rumours grew to alarmin' proportions. I and a couple of the chaps in my squadron entered for the Henley Air Pageant . . .'

'And the rest,' Ralph interrupted, 'I already know.'

Indeed, it all tallied in every detail. This time, unpalatable though it all was, Stephen was clearly telling the truth.

The champagne bottle was empty by now. 'Let's have some brandy,' Stephen said abruptly.

'No thanks, I must go.' Ralph rose, then stood looking down at Stephen, but made no attempt to move. 'Have you any message for your people?' he asked with some difficulty. 'I might just get home for some leave later on.'

Stephen shook his head. 'What's done is done, old boy. Best let sleepin' dogs lie; it's no use rakin' over the coals at this late stage.'

Ralph nodded. He pushed from his mind the thought of Sinclair, Henrietta, Rosalind. He had listened with the utmost attention. Nowhere in Stephen's story had he shown the faintest indication that he was even interested in what had happened to his family, let alone regretful for what he had done to them.

All Ralph said, as he picked up his cap and cane was, 'Well then, I must push off. Thanks for the champers, oh, and er, Good Luck.'

Stephen did not reply. At the door Ralph turned and looked back. Stephen had his arm around the waitress's waist and once again was laughing.

Stephen Delahaye strolled across the improvised runway from the barn where his Commanding Officer had briefed his pilots on the morning of August the twenty-fourth. He fastened the straps of his leather helmet as he went and slipped his long leather coat over tunic and breeches. It would be cold at this hour in the open cockpit of his *Blériot* as he well knew. Drawing on his gloves he climbed into the aircraft tossing a few cheerful words to the two mechanics. Then with some care he bestowed his 'bantam's eggs' in his pockets and with even greater caution tucked the two 'larger eggs' down at his offside. Thus armed with five hand grenades and two bombs he made ready for take-off.

He gave the thumbs up sign, the mechanics swung the propeller and a moment later Stephen was bouncing along the uneven surface preparatory to take-off. Behind him, a second *Blériot*, piloted by a brother officer, Second Lieutenant Malcolm F. G. Mac Neill of the Argyll and Sutherland Highlanders taxied into position at his rear. The two had gravitated to each other automatically. It was not for nothing that the baby-faced Scot was nick-named 'Randy' Mac Neill. Their brother officers spent a large proportion of their free time in hauling one or other of them out of female involvements. These appendages they acquired wherever they went and, as one young peace-time ornithologist put it aptly, they behaved as if they were male oak-egger moths, who will fly up to three hundred miles in pursuit of a female of their species.

Their craft became airborne. They circled the site, took off once more to seek out enemy movements and locate enemy batteries, these latter, usually camouflaged and situated on the edge of small woods or spinneys.

The wind hummed through the frail structures. Stephen began to sing a version of 'Mademoiselle from Armentières' which was quite certainly not the original;

> *Mademoiselle from Armentières,*
> *Parlez-vous,*
> *Hasn't been humped for forty years,*
> *Inky-Pinky Parlez vous . . .*

At first they could see little activity below them as they crossed over enemy lines. Stephen stopped singing in order to yawn. Sleeping as they had done in a barn, fully clothed, burrowed down for warmth into enormous heaps of straw was not conducive to dawn-freshness, moreover he itched, but due to his clothing, and the proximity of his 'eggs' he felt it unwise to scratch. As the air cleansed his lungs so he began to feel better. He leaned out and down; below him a huge and heavy movement of enemy troops with cavalry, guns and transport was advancing upon the forest of Mormal.

'Gawd!' ejaculated Stephen, 'Only that ruddy forest between them and our G.H.Q.!'

He signalled to 'Randy' and having safely indicated his intention, made a wide turn and came back along the line Charleroi, Maubene, Landrecies, dutifully followed by his Sancho Panza. They touched down and taxied in a short distance from G.H.Q.

Spotting a pair of motorcycles drawn up close at hand they leaped on and raced towards G.H.Q. Here they made their report.

At 3.35 p.m., they were sent once again to reconnoitre and report. By this time the B.E.F. was falling back along the line Landrecies, Rainsars, Macquenoise; but G.H.Q. was still at Le Cateau. As the two pilots became airborne and although the order to retreat had been given, only now were they beginning to move.

Stephen, once more in the van, turned eastwards and again worked back towards Mormal Forest. Randy was flying too close to him so he signalled back for him to drop further behind.

In response Randy pulled back his joy-stick and began to climb.

Shouting joyously above the din of wind and engine, Stephen dropped down deliberately. Then he levelled off, flying so low on the Landrecies side of the forest that he could not only see the enemy's van advancing through the trees and the heavy transport lumbering along on either side of them, but before he pulled back his stick and gained height once more, he was able to confirm what he had suspected.

Working frenziedly, like ants about an overturned heap, the crews of a battery of six field guns had wheeled into position and were even now un-limbering. For an instant Stephen saw their astonished faces lifted to him as he roared over their heads. Then back went the joy-stick again and up and round went the *Blériot* skimming over the treetops as it gained height, turned and came in for the final run.

Shouting abuse he fumbled for his bombs and this time, flying so low that he had a final glimpse of the terrified uplifted faces he dropped his first and then a second.

'Take that you bastards!' he shouted, still laughing. Even as he pulled back the stick for the third and last time the shoosh and thud confirmed he had hit his target. But the second bomb fell wide thudding plumb on to the stacked ammunition. There was a second and a third explosion. Stephen failed to hear these last. He heard the whoosh, heard the explosion as men, limbs and bursting shells erupted like the vomit from some devil's cauldron; but all he knew of the other crack was a dull thud against the right side of his head.

He slumped forward in the cockpit. His aircraft, out of control, spun down turned over and crashed. As it threw up earth with the force of impact so it burst into flames.

CHAPTER 21

The Echo in the Cup

There were more changes made at Castle Rising in the first few weeks of war than had been done in centuries.

Men with scaffolding pinned back ceilings, supported uncovered beams and unearthed small treasures as they heaved and shovelled, preparing the cavity which would contain the lift which Gyles had sanctioned without protest when Lady Constance asked for it. They were all local men who had worked on the Museum so they knew to whom they should take the little things which they had unearthed from the rubble of centuries.

The little Countess cleaned them – where such was permissible, wrote little cards for them and set them on a *papier mâché* tray which had slid down disconsolately from behind an old mantelshelf. She laid them all out and carried them into the small Blue Drawing Room where they all spent their few moments of leisure. It amused them and took their minds away from the war news for a short while. There was a crown, in seemingly mint condition still, though it bore the head of the first George. Three groats were set down beside it. There were too a little garnet pin; a pair of sadly tarnished silver cuffs which had once been worn by some forgotten Cavalier; a minute gold thimble; an exquisite necklace of French paste inset with small diamonds; a baby's rattle carved in ivory; and a faded invitation to the wedding of King William IV and Queen Adelaide. With these things, Marguerite halted the incoming tide of war talk for a little while.

There was nearly as much dust everywhere as on the roads of Belgium and northern France. It made the occupants cough as they hurried through rooms and corridors.

In the emptied rooms of what was now called the 'Convalescents' Wing', the painters were busy with their pots while paperhangers slapped away on trestle tables as they set about hanging fresh wallpapers.

In the carpenter's workshop men sawed, planed and hammered; putting together bed-screens, ingenious bed tables which Lady Constance had designed and notice boards. In a remote corner old Mr Pennyroyal worked ceaselessly, restoring furniture, while from time to time he absented himself, trotting off to the special room set aside for his French polishing.

Vans and drays plied steadily between Little Aynthorp station and the Castle, bringing bedding, blankets, nurses' uniforms, linen, coverlets and stationery. Carter Paterson's men were constantly drawing up to unload medical supplies which came direct from Messrs. John Bell and Croyden of Wigmore Street, London.

Nor was this all, for in the rooms set aside for the separate feeding of both patients and staff, barrows of concrete were being trundled in to the men who worked on the foundations for the very latest gas stoves, sinks and warm closets.

Meanwhile in the main wings, pictures were coming down. Special packers were at work crating up some of the more priceless treasures, all to be stored in the Museum . . . 'for the duration'.

Everyone had far too much to do and far too little time in which to do it, for they all knew that hospital trains were already bringing wounded back to England. Thus they set themselves a deadline.

It was better so. It gave them less time in which to reflect upon what was inescapable fact – that this was the end of an era and with it the end of Castle life as they had always known it.

The wheel had come perilously close to full circle. As their Norman ancestors had done when they hacked down their virgin forests where wild boar ran in order to build their first wooden Castle upon English soil, so they were aware of unseen dangers now. *Then* they had erected palisades inside which every worker, vendor, owner, man, woman, child and domestic animal must be contained by nightfall; so now all thoughts of pleasure banished, these current Lormes were preparing in a different way for yet another enemy.

Gyles Aynthorp, in his old office, laid aside his pen and stared across the room at the plans which covered the walls. He had at long last completed the final copies of the letters which would go off that night to the Knight's crumbling mansion in county Cork.

He picked up his pen again tiredly, signed his name and began folding the sheets when he noticed that he had omitted the date. He glanced at his calender which proclaimed August the twenty fourth, so he filled this in, sealed both envelopes and left them on his tray for the servants to collect on their next rounds.

He then left the room to walk along the corridors, standing back for men who came towards him carrying those crates of fragile treasures. He made way for them saying, 'Come through please,' and flattening his lean body against the wall each time to let them go by. All the while, like this remarkable new invention – the cinematograph – processions moved across the backcloth of his mind: his mother and father receiving, as guests streamed in to one of their Christmas balls; his own wife coming in on her father's arm for their engagement celebration; himself as a small boy, rushing breathlessly along and only slowing to a more decorous pace as he arrived within sight of the ballroom where Justin, his father, in one of his many lavish-spending moods had decided that his six-year-old-son and heir must have 'a birthday party to be remembered'.

Now the beautiful things which had been silent witnesses to so much gaiety and laughter were vanished into packing cases and Gyles no longer dared speculate as to when they would be brought out again.

Nothing of this showed on his face, long schooled, during his father's tempestuous reign, to impassivity. He nodded to a passing Footwoman and went on up the staircase to his objective – nursery tea.

Suddenly he halted. The Footwoman was sorting the afternoon post on the great hall table. She saw him lean over the banisters to look at the sunburst clock whose hands stood at precisely three minutes to four o'clock. She saw him dip into his waistcoat pocket, bring out his half-hunter and check. Then she returned to her sorting.

Gyles stood still, his figure stiffening abruptly. Somewhere, surely, in the distance he could hear a great hound baying! He shook his head as if to dismiss such an absurdity; but the baying came again, faintly but unmistakably. Once before that same sound had chilled his bones. Then, he had stood over the body of his father with the hunt all grouped around him and hounds whimpering.

Despite himself, he stood listening; but the sound had gone, so at length he went on up and waited for a moment or two with his hand on the doorknob of the schoolroom. Then, reminding himself angrily 'the wish is father to the thought,' he opened the door.

Without intent, his hand had turned the knob very slowly and without sound. Thus he saw the room before anyone was aware of his presence; the cheerful fire, the high guard set before it, the big schoolroom table set for tea with the white cloth and the china decorated with immortals – Mrs Tiggy Winkle, Squirrel Nutkin, Jeremy Fisher, Asia, Australia and Jemima Puddleduck. His face softened perceptibly. Here was their only remaining security dressed in goffered pinafores and wearing bibs, with high-chairs and straight-backed ones drawn up around the table – Christine presiding and Nanny facing her with Rosemary's baby Dominique on her knee. Nanny was testing the heat of a mug of milk by holding it against her chin.

As he warmed inward coldness with the simple scene, so he heard Christine say to Nanny with a tender little smile playing round her lips, 'I am so sorry Nanny dear. I wonder can you really cope with another baby? Although I am personally delighted, I feel very guilty . . . at my age.'

Gyles halted. The children and Rose looked across but he laid a finger on his lips so they were silent.

Nanny, giving little Dominique the milk, replied, 'Such nonsense my lady! Nothing could be more wonderful and his lordship will be ever so pleased I'm sure.' She added, wiping Dominique's milk encircled mouth, 'after all my lady, babies is the very breath of life to me.'

Gyles moved. Nanny turned with the rest, she lifted her head. 'Oh my lord,' she struggled to rise and Gyles said quickly, 'Please don't move Nanny.'

Nanny obeyed, glanced around the table, 'Andrew, draw up a chair for your father,' she ordered, 'quickly now; Richard, wipe your hands immediately if you please and leave those cakes alone. Really there never was such a naughty boy!'

Richard, halted with jammy paw outstretched towards Mrs Parson's plate of 'fancies', withdrew it reluctantly. 'I don't want any more mouldy bread and butter; why can't I have cake?'

Nanny snapped back, 'Because I say so, young man.'

Ignoring this small change of nursery life, Gyles said, 'Hello everyone,' bent over Christine, kissed her cheek, murmured, 'So that is why you have lost so much weight my dearest! But what joyous news, now you really will have to take care of yourself.'

Christine looked up, suddenly radiant, 'You don't mind?' she asked nervously.

'Mind!' Gyles laughed, 'I'm delighted, as you might know I should be – just so long as you do not give me another Richard . . .' he added pinching his son's cheek teasingly as he sat down.

'How can you have another me, Daddy?' demanded Richard suddenly bored with Nanny and all her nagging. Then, 'Are you going to have another baby Mother?' he demanded.

Before she could answer, 'I say what a lark,' exclaimed Andrew. 'Congratulations, and all that. I, for one, could do with another brother to bully now that Richard's growing up.'

Anne had slipped down from her chair. Ignoring Nanny's protest she ran round to her mother's chair, laid her cheek against Christine and murmured, 'Dearest Mummy, what a lovely happening, shall it be a little girl do you think?'

Gyles was assiduously polishing and repolishing his monocle.

'That will depend, my love,' Christine's hand came up to stroke her daughter's curls, 'on what your Papa has arranged.'

Richard, staring bright-eyed at his father, his mother, Nanny and then back again now demanded, 'How are babies born Father, I want to know how they come?'

There was a startled silence. Nanny broke it, 'The stork

brings 'em when everything is ready,' she snapped, 'everyone knows that.'

'What stork?' Richard persisted.

'The chosen one. Now you can have a cake as you have finished your bread and butter.'

This diverted him; but not for long. Reverting to the fascinating matter of Nanny's storks, he took a huge bite out of his cake and with his mouth full mumbled, 'I don't believe a word of that stork bit. Anyway it's not how animals are born; not calves, nor pigs, nor rabbits . . . I think you're just having me on so there! You've just made up your mind you won't tell. I don't care, I'll ask Plum and I bet he'll tell me.'

Nanny's little beady eyes flashed fire. If she could have conjured up some brimstone to go with it she would undoubtedly have done so. There was a short stricken silence while she rose; inserted Dominique into her high-chair like a cork into a bottle, turned, and gave judgement. 'How . . . dare . . . you!' she said furiously, 'now get down from that chair.'

Richard hesitated, then slid to his feet.

'And,' Nanny continued, 'go . . . to . . . your . . . room . . . at once . . .!'

Richard looked around for aid . . . at his father, who was studying the tablecloth intently . . . at his mother, who sat, cheek on hand, her face in the shadow.

'And,' finished Nanny, 'shut the door quietly as you go out – NOW.'

As the door closed behind the culprit, 'I really am sorry my lady,' she apologized. 'What a thing to say!'

Christine could contain herself no longer. Her shoulders had begun to shake as her small offspring dragged his feet towards the door. Now she took down her hand so that Nanny, astonished, could see that she was laughing weakly.

'It's all right Nanny,' Christine assured her, 'but really he is incorrigible. Gyles we must send him to school as soon as possible. He should have gone more than two years ago!'

The rest of the children, fascinated by these grown-up exchanges sat like mice. Gyles turned to Nanny. 'Has he not been better under Mr Plumstead's influence?' he inquired.

Nanny sniffed. 'Better possibly,' she admitted, 'just so long as he is kept occupied with them animals my life is just worth living my lord, but when there's no animals –' she broke off and for once looked appealingly at her employers, 'it's more than flesh and blood can stand. The only way it can be done is to let him bring ferrets and rats and nasty squirmy snakes in here. Or else it's little boxes with spiders, beetles and other creepy-crawlies. Why I took up a match box only the other day and a 'uge spider scrambled out. That, er, new Footwoman, was coming in with a tray of cakes and bread and butter. She screamed. She dropped the lot. It was pan-dee-monium! Through it all that young limb of Satan was crawling around like a Dervish screaming, "Don't tread on Bishop Alaric" – he was a mighty fat spider you see my lady and Master Richard said it was the best name for him the Bishop being as it were so fat himself!'

Even Gyles laughed, but presently, reinforced with some excellent coffee he sobered enough to inquire, 'What does my son respect, if anything, Nanny, can you tell me?'

'Plum,' she said sepulchrally, 'and sometimes, when I'm proper mad with him like jest now ME; but whatever he does it's all forgotten in a moment and he's off on some other wickedness.'

Gyles returned to his study of the tablecloth. The children were still silent. Christine became aware that this was not being a very happy tea party for them so intervened. 'Gyles,' she suggested, 'should we not discuss this later? Yes? Well perhaps Nanny you would spare a few moments for us in my sitting room before the dressing bell? Then we could discuss the problem undisturbed and not spoil our tea with our discussions.' She then spoke to the table at large, 'Well what have you all been doin' today?'

Andrew was lounging back in his chair, hands thrust in pockets, bored stiff with all this 'kid's stuff'. He was now seventeen, more than sufficiently endowed with the family's good looks; a blood at Harrow, about to enter upon his last year. He was also, as had been said of his cousin Ralph in a somewhat different context, 'no end of a swell' both in his own and in junior Harrovians' opinions.

He looked across at his father now. 'I was hopin',' he ventured, 'to have a word with you myself sir?' he now began, showing some nervousness none the less, which evinced itself in his fidgeting.

'Oh, what about?' Gyles asked uninterestedly, breaking off to say, 'Nanny, could you cut me a piece of that Sand cake? I have a weakness for Sand cake, especially when it is made by Mrs Parsons.'

'A chap at School sir,' said Andrew.

'Oh yes, what about him?' Gyles showed no conspicuous rapture at the subject matter. His mind was still on other things. He was only just recovering from the surprise of discovering that his wife was once again pregnant. He had managed to mouth across to her the one word '*When?*', and when Christine mouthed back, '*February*', he did some rapid calculations.

Quite forgetting his question to his son he suddenly said, 'The Mond Ball!' and was rewarded by a ring of surprised faces. Only Christine smiled in a very particular kind of way. 'Yes – The Mond Ball,' she confirmed. Then she attempted to placate the frustrated Andrew, saying brightly, 'Aren't parents tiresome? I expect you have discovered already your father and I do tend to go off at tangents sometimes?'

'Yes mother,' answered Andrew gloomily.

'Well now, darling, you have our full attention. Who is the "chap" and what is it all about?'

Andrew picked up a teaspoon and began playing with it. 'It's quite a long story,' he warned.

'So, we shall just sit here and listen, won't we Anne?' Anne at her shoulder merely nodded. 'Just pass my cup for me darling and ask Nanny if I may have some coffee, no sugar thank you Nanny, and only a little milk and then Andrew can tell us from the beginning to the end.'

Little Dominique had fallen asleep in her high-chair. Nanny said benevolently, 'Before you begin, Andrew, let us ask Mummy if Gilbert can run and play?' Gilbert looked up hopefully, then slid from his chair, went off to the window seat, picked up a copy of the *Financial Times* dated August 24th and began reading absorbedly.

Peace reigned for a few moments. Priscilla Claire, Christian and Clare's youngest, on a nod from Nanny, likewise went off to put her dolls' house occupants to bed.

Only Lucien, Peter Christian and Anne remained with Andrew and the grown-ups at the table.

Andrew began to speak. 'Well it all began when I was crossing Bill Yard. I saw a little chap going along ahead of me. Actually it was his hair I noticed, because it was the same colour as ours which was odd. At first I thought I must be mistaken, so I put on a bit of speed and as I got closer I saw it was actually identical. So, thinkin' it might be young Paul, you know sir – m'cousin, who had just started at School, I yelled out "Beltinge", but he didn't turn. By now I was dead curious, so I trotted after him. Then I shouted just behind him, "Hi Beltinge, didn't you hear me call?" He turned and bless me if it wasn't a face I'd ever seen before in my life!'

Gyles nodded, 'I've done this too!' he acknowledged. 'We're such a self-centred lot we seem to forget there are other families whose chaps have hair like ours.'

'That's right, sir. Well anyway, this one had been at school a year as I learned later that day when he fell into step beside me and we got chattin'. It was all very brief, but somehow, havin' remembered to ask what house he was in, I made some inquiries. I found out he was puttin' up a good show for a young 'un.'

At this point it was Gyles's turn to lean back and drop his face on one hand, elbow resting on the arm of his chair, for even he dared not, even now, put an elbow on to a table in Nanny's presence. As much as anything, Gyles did this to conceal his amusement. It made him chuckle inwardly to hear his seventeen-year-old son talking about 'A young 'un'.

Andrew was still in full spate. He said, 'It came to light the boy was shapin' up very promisingly; in fact he looked like developin' in to a good all rounder. He was already in Remove 1 A, had been picked for the Fifth Form Game, and the term before it seems he had shown some rather outstandin' form at Soccer – can't stand the game myself! never.'

'Where'd he play?' asked Gyles interestedly.

'Inside Right, sir. Over the months I also found out he had

fagged for a man called Allinson. He was the Head of his Landing, so I kept an eye on the feller, discreetly, for you appreciate sir that in my position I could not afford to be seen hob-nobbin' too often with first year fellers.'

'Quite so,' said Gyles by now highly entertained. 'Did you see anythin' of him at all?'

'Yes, that's what I'm comin' to, in a bit of a round about fashion I'm afraid. Just before the end of term it was, I saw that head, I yelled to him and asked him how he was gettin' on. He said, "Splendid, thanks awfully, but it will be pretty dull here when you all go off for the hols." That was how I learned that the poor little devil spent his hols at School. You see his parents live abroad.'

'Hard luck for the youngster,' Gyles agreed.

'Yes, you see he can't even see them. He did say he was hopin' they would come over for a trip next year; but now the war'll 've put the stopper on that I must suppose.'

'Where are his parents, India?'

'No sir, his mother is English, his father, Australian. At least I believe it's his step-father – his mother's been married before – they live in Australia. He's, er, he's not by our standards out of the absolutely top drawer, I gather. You know how much less, er, demandin' Harrow is becomin' these days.'

Gyles merely grunted.

'I think his father is a wealthy sheep farmer. The word is that he owns thousands of acres in what the little chap told me was called the "outback". He's Australian you understand, his mother was, I gather, once an actress.'

Suddenly it seemed to Gyles and Christine that the room had become intensely chilly. Christine looked up with a sudden expression of horror. Gyles' hands clenched involuntarily so he thrust them deep into his pockets. Still Andrew ran on . . .

'What I am tellin' you all this for is simply that he really is such a nice little chap. I have taken quite a shine to him and, by the way, his manners are top-hole. So, I was wonderin' whether you would let me ask him back here for next hols so that he wouldn't have to maunder about the School?'

Andrew added hurriedly, 'I needn't have him in my pocket all the time, he'd be great sport for young Richard. It wouldn't surprise me if he brought the little devil to heel quite a bit. Well, now I've told you all about him, what do you say sir? Can I invite him?'

Gyles wondered for a fleeting moment whether he had inadvertently administered himself a dose of hemlock! Then with an almost superhuman effort, he forced himself to speak with even some semblance of normality.

'You missed one small point,' he said.

'Oh did I, what was that, sir?'

'I do not think you ever told us the boy's name and it might be as well to know it.'

'Oh, of course, sir, what an idiot, it's Hackington ... hang on a sec., yes, Stephen Hackington from Wackaroo in Australia.'